"A thousand-mile-an-hour thriller in which you're never sure who's predator or prey. It left my head spinning. Immensely enjoyable!"
—Stuart Turton, bestselling author of
The 7½ Deaths of Evelyn Hardcastle and
The Last Murder at the End of the World

"Brilliant…absolutely enthralling."
—John Marrs, author of
The One and *Keep It in the Family*

"It's Knox at his mesmerizing best."
—*Financial Times*

"A dark and riveting thriller that plunges readers into the chaos of its characters. Knox's sharp prose and gritty atmosphere create a hauntingly atmospheric tale where nothing is as it seems."
—*Glamour*

"Truly immersive: complex, disturbing, unexpectedly funny, and very smart."
—*The Guardian*

"Fierce, funny, and flint sharp."
—Cara Hunter, author of
Murder in the Family

ALSO BY JOSEPH KNOX

True Crime Story

IMPOSTER SYNDROME

JOSEPH KNOX

sourcebooks
landmark

For Iris

Published by Sourcebooks Landmark, an imprint of Sourcebooks
P.O. Box 4410, Naperville, Illinois 60567-4410
(630) 961-3900
sourcebooks.com

Originally published as *Imposter Syndrome* in 2024 in the United Kingdom
by Doubleday, an imprint of Penguin Random House UK. This edition
issued based on the hardcover edition published in 2024 in the United
Kingdom by Doubleday, an imprint of Penguin Random House UK.

Cataloging-in-Publication Data is on file with the Library of Congress.

Printed and bound in the United States of America.
PAH 10 9 8 7 6 5 4 3 2

"We are what we pretend to be, so we must be careful about what we pretend to be."

KURT VONNEGUT — *MOTHER NIGHT*

1.

When you're living a lie, you find it's best to avoid close attachments entirely. Other people might see you for what you really are, and that might mean anything. From a beating to a jail sentence to never being seen again. Walk into someone's life with the right energy, a convincing enough smile, and you might leave with something. But if you want to get away with it, you'll be on your own. In the end, you're supposed to be.

If you steal from people, you spend your whole life watching them, looking for patterns and missteps. You can get so hung up on their failures that you don't even notice yours. I think that's what I like about it. That's why Clare had to go. She saw things she shouldn't have. And things in me I didn't see in myself. Clare thought there was hope for everyone. She thought I could still change.

—

I buy a drab, secondhand suit on my way to the station, trying to look like somebody I'm not. At Gare du Nord, I stand in line and pay in cash. Then I clear security and catch the first train off the continent. I never got around to packing that bag, and I spent the last of my euros on the ticket. After the way things had completely unraveled with Clare, it seemed only right to leave empty-handed. When I start to see the smoke rolling through London, it feels more like a mistake. I'm blowing Paris with a cheap mismatching suit, a dead iPhone, and my pride. Climbing off the train at St. Pancras, it doesn't feel like enough.

I grab an apple from the food court and slide a Coke into my pocket from the fridge in a Starbucks. There's an unattended phone charger I've got my eye on, but then I'm hovering over a handbag, left out on the same table, and I have to walk myself to the door.

I need to slow everything down somehow. Even if I'm not quite ready to stop. I need somewhere safe where I can close my eyes and unclench for a few seconds. So I take an escalator underground, pick my moment, and hurdle the barrier. I walk through a long, winding tunnel, then take the first train I see, ride it for a while, and change. I change again and again, until it feels right.

And at some point, I must finally let my guard down and nod off, because when the train jolts, I snap back, with the sensation that I'm being watched. I hold my eyes shut for a few seconds, giving no outward hint that I'm awake. Then I open them wide, taking everything in. It's just disinterested commuters and warning signs.

Looking up and down the carriage, I can see I'm the only person on here without any luggage and that even though the train's full, the seats on either side of me are both empty. I see I'm sending out all the wrong signals and try to smarten myself up.

When the train terminates a minute later, we come to an abrupt stop. The lights flicker, then fade out. I don't move for a few seconds, listening to the hum of the engine powering down. The doors slide open, and the other passengers grab their stuff, groping their way out of the dark carriage. I start to follow them, but then the light comes back, and I'm surprised by my reflection in the window. No cash, no case, no traveling companion. I'm the only person here who's going nowhere.

———

Out on the platform, a sign confirms what I thought the driver had just said. Heathrow, Terminal 5. It's the last stop on the Piccadilly Line. And with no cash, that might be a problem. For starters, I haven't gotten a ticket to get off the platform and into the airport with. And there's a security goon, standing on the barrier. I'm stuck for a second until I spot an older woman on the platform, wrestling with too much luggage. I take a deep breath, smooth back my hair, and approach her with a smile.

"Excuse me," I say, neutralizing my accent. "I couldn't help but notice…"

I insist on carrying all three of her cases at once, then make a big thing about it at the barriers. Like I'm struggling with the weight and can't spare a hand to find my ticket or phone. The guard looks past me at the people waiting, then opens the gate and lets us both through. I take the old girl's cases as far as the lift for her on the other side; I even give her a little salute like a bellboy.

"What a nice young man," she says with one of those blue-veined hands on her heart.

"Safe trip," I say with a smile.

Once I'm inside the terminal, my lack of luggage won't even look strange. Right now, I know it marks me out. After buying my discount suit this morning, I'd found a quiet alley, off the boulevard, then dowsed the clothes that Clare bought me with lighter fluid and burned them.

—

There's a woman standing in front of me on the escalator, holding her little girl's hand. They're on their way up to departures, and the woman's wearing a backpack that she hasn't closed since showing her ticket.

I can see her purse, just hanging out.

My stomach growls so loudly that the little girl turns to look, catching me staring at her mother's purse. I dig out my stolen apple and take a bite.

When I glance down, the girl's still staring.

"Excuse me," I say to her mother. She turns with a blank expression. "I can see your purse."

"Oh." She zips the bag shut, looking relieved. "That's really kind of you, thanks."

"Can't be too careful," I say, smiling and looking down to include the kid. As I do, we get the top of the escalator, and I widen my smile for the three cops I see standing there, all holding semiautomatics. I become suddenly uncomfortably aware of the object in my jacket pocket. Then I walk in pace with the mother and daughter, my shoulders slumped, looking like a family man to the casual observer. Once I'm safe, when we've passed through the entrance into a neon-lit walkway, I straighten up and let them drift on ahead. I can only seem to manage these short-term relationships lately anyway.

Once I'm inside the terminal, I go to the elevators, avoiding my face in the reflective steel. The doors open, and I see the old girl whose bags I just carried through the barrier. Meekly, I take her purse from my jacket pocket.

"I think this must have fallen out of your case," I say, handing it back to her, unopened.

She smiles and puts her hand on her heart again. "Oh," she says. "What a nice young—"

———

If taking the purse was stupid, then giving it back was even worse. And I know now I can't trust my instincts until I've had some real sleep. I've got to at least try and find a room for the night. Somewhere I can shut down and reset. But with no bank card and no one to call, the only way I can imagine making that happen is by meeting someone at a hotel bar, convincing a stranger to let me crash.

Somehow, I don't like my chances.

It's not just that I can't afford the price of a drink. I look all wrong for it too. If charming people was about being a good guy, I'd be fine. If that's all it came down to, I could lie. But this new suit feels like a lot to overcome. I'd pieced it together from one of the sad, street-side vendors on my slow approach into Gare du Nord this morning, haggling the mournful French salesman down to almost nothing. In the hazy predawn light, the material had seemed dark enough. Under the industrial neons at Heathrow, the suit looks cheap and dishonest. So shiny you can almost see your face in it.

So when I get to the Sofitel, a luxury chain attached to the terminal, I'm smiling for my life. Because all these loose threads and wrinkles are dropping dark hints about the kind of man I might be, and some of them are too close for comfort. I stand in the doorway, watching the careless, first-class people passing through the lobby. The lipstick widows and sloppy drunks, the single travelers and smashed execs. Sizing them up, seeing dollar signs…

But for some reason, I can't make myself go through with it. For some reason, I start thinking about Clare. I stare into the lobby another second, then shake my head, trying to rid myself of her. I'm turning to leave, just wanting to disappear, when I collide with a haunted-looking woman who's standing right behind me. I'm not a big guy, and it feels like I barely touch her, but she lands hard and skids back across the floor.

"What the *actual* fuck?" she shouts out.

Everyone in the lobby looks over.

They see a young woman, wearing all black and a large pair of sunglasses, collapsed on the floor. Then they see the burnout in a secondhand suit standing over her, trying to keep his face turned away from them.

"Christ," I say, taking a step forward, holding out a hand. "I'm sorry. I didn't—"

That's when she looks up at me properly for the first time and shrinks back, surprised by something.

"Are you OK?" I ask, but it's like she can't talk, and a concerned member of staff starts drifting over.

"*Heydon?*" she gasps finally. "Aitch, is that you?"

2.

Heydon's not a name I've ever used before. The girl's confusing me with someone else. If she didn't look so torn up about it, I might even play along.

She so badly wants me to be him.

"It's me," she says, getting up off the floor. "It's Bobbie. You remember." Bobbie's wearing black clothes, black shades, black everything. We've never met before. I'd remember Bobbie. I look back at her for a moment, still tempted to tell her what she wants to hear.

"No," I say instead. "I'm sorry. I don't think so."

"How about now?" she says, sliding the shades down so I can see her face. They're covering a swollen-shut black eye, and the gathering members of staff start mumbling. One of the guys even looks like he's about to take a step toward me, like I had something to do with it.

I turn and walk in the other direction, the same way I came in. I hear the girl call after me, but I'm already gone, pushing through people, not needing the attention. I'm fifty feet away before I look back, and when I do, she's following me into the terminal.

She holds up a hand.

"Wait, please..."

"No, thank you."

"Listen," she says, drawing level with me. "I know. I get it. I'm a mess. Can you just slow down?"

I stop walking and stare into her shades.

"Look, Bobbie, I'm sorry about your eye. But I'm not who you think I am, OK?"

She takes a step back, then just stands there, looking lost for a few seconds, and for the first time, I see how much her friend, this Heydon guy, must mean to her.

"I know that," she says quietly, but it doesn't look like she was really sure until now. "I just wanted to speak with you." From her accent, she sounds like serious money, and close-up, she looks pretty smart too. Her black boots, jeans, jacket, and bag all look designer, and she keeps on blinding me with the stone on her ring. "If you've got a moment, perhaps I can explain things," she says. "What do you say, join me for a drink?"

The words sound forced, but I guess she's nervous, just trying to style out her mistake. A free drink feels like winning the lottery right now anyway. So I say, "Sure," and follow her back inside.

——

We take a table in the cocktail bar, sitting opposite each other. Bobbie leaves her shades on, and I'm glad. They give me some protection from the black eye and some protection from Bobbie herself. Outside, she'd seemed nervous, but I see now that was just to get me into the room. When the waiter arrives, she interrogates him about his mixing technique, then asks for a martini, her teeth glowing white against the dark lipstick.

I tell the waiter I want the same thing, then we sit in near silence for a few minutes—listening to the occasional robotic "*Ground Floor*" announcement from the nearby lift bank—until our drinks arrive.

"So who's Heydon?" I ask the second we've been served, much sooner than I'd meant to. Bobbie pauses, her glass not quite to her lips, then she takes a quick sip and puts it down. "Is he the guy who did that to you?"

"Did what?" she asks. Then she remembers her eye. "Oh, sorry. I'm so doped up, I keep forgetting it's there. I suppose you could say I got it from him though. Like a delayed inheritance."

"I don't get it," I say.

"Heydon's my big brother. Or, I mean, he *was*. He went missing five years ago."

I look up. "I'm sorry," I say. "So wait a minute. You thought I—"

"Pretty much."

Bobbie's got a croaky, vocal-fry thing going on. She makes it sound like she's taking me into her confidence, making me lean in.

"Can I ask what happened?"

"We don't know," she says. "No one does."

"He just walked out one day…"

"How else do you think they do it?"

"I just mean, there was no special reason?"

"He had plenty of special reasons."

I frown.

"Heydon was diagnosed bipolar," she says.

"Like, sometimes happy, sometimes sad?"

Bobbie stares at me for a moment.

"*Ground Floor*," says the robotic voice of the lift.

"What I'm saying is Heydon wasn't always himself."

"Who was he when he walked out?" I ask.

"When he walked out, he was someone else entirely." I raise my eyebrows, but she quickly goes on. "The police found his car parked illegally on Albert Bridge at four in the morning. The driver's side door was wide open."

"I'm sorry. Albert Bridge is…"

"The one beside Battersea Park," she says. "Overlooking the Thames."

"Did they find anything in the water?"

Bobbie smiles sadly.

"Most of the time, they don't," she says. "You need to get lucky with tides and times and river traffic and stuff. Anyway…" She sounds like she's trying to draw a line under it all. "I just wanted to explain what that was back there. Convince myself I'm not going crazy."

It's the perfect chance to smile or say something nice, but I don't trust my motives, and in the time it takes to second-guess them, the moment passes.

"Are you flying in or out?" I ask instead.

"Out," she says, recalibrating. "Or that was the idea. My flight got canceled at the last minute. Some union thing with the crew. Now I'm on the eight fifteen to LA tomorrow morning. What about you? Are you staying at the hotel?"

"Sounds like a long day," I say, dodging the question.

"Oh, I don't know. So far, it's been fine. At least BA comped the room. Truth be told, I'm sort of dreading LA."

"Why? What's so bad about LA?"

"Oh, it's kind of a family thing."

"Are you guys traveling together?"

"No," she says. "I'm on my own tonight."

I see myself reflected in her shades.

"You don't get along?" I ask.

"We're volatile."

"Since your brother, or—"

"Since always. I mean, don't get me wrong. I'm really fortunate and stuff. But in my family, nothing you do matters if you step even slightly out of line…"

"Have you stepped out of line?" I ask.

"I was talking about my brother," she says coolly.

"Did you really think I was him?"

Bobbie looks away, then back at me.

"Why not? You look like you've been out of the country for a while. And I don't think he killed himself."

"Right," I say. "Yeah."

"That's not based on nothing," she says, responding to some skepticism in my voice. "You don't know what Heydon was really like. You don't know about his heart."

"His heart," I say slowly.

"Heydon got a tattoo on his face a short while before he walked out." She touches her shades to show me where it would have been on his cheek. "A tiny heart, like a teardrop at the corner of his eye." Bobbie smiles. "That's one of the reasons I don't think he hurt himself," she says. "Why go to the trouble of doing it, then…" She trails off. "Daddy went ballistic. Miranda couldn't speak."

"Miranda?" I say, shaking my head.

"We're one of those annoying families who calls their mother by her first name."

"Right," I say. "So in a sense, you deserve all this."

Bobbie smiles, then fishes the lemon rind out of her drink and throws it at me.

"Can I see a picture of your brother?" I ask, wiping it out of my eyes.

"Sure," she says, vaguely amused.

It feels like the fastest way out of here, and I'm not even thinking while she goes through her bag, because I know I'll just say, *Wow, you're right. I can really see it.*

Then she hands me her phone, and my face goes hot. I look at Bobbie, then back at the screen.

Heydon's got the same lapsed swimmer's build as me. The same brow and jaw. It's not exactly like looking into a mirror. His eyes are green, and mine are blue. But it's more than just a passing resemblance. It looks like he's stayed awake all the same nights I have. There's still some puppy fat left in Heydon's cheeks, but if anything, that helps the comparison. When this picture was taken, you wouldn't have confused us so easily. My cheeks had gone hollow when I was a boy. I'd been more wiry and sharp-eyed than this. But now my face feels like one route that his might have taken in the time since, especially if he'd kept up with the late nights.

"Right?" says Bobbie.

"Right," I say, shaking my head at the likeness. "How old would he have been here?"

"This was the week before he left," she says. "So twenty-nine." She leans over and swipes to the next shot.

There's a dazzling blond girl sitting on Heydon's lap. She's wearing a bright summer dress and laughing about something, completely unaware of the camera. And suddenly, it's like I've got martini for blood. It feels like I was born into the wrong life.

"Who's that?" I ask.

"Ha," says Bobbie.

I look up, and a second later, I see it.

"I mean," I start. "Your hair's just so different now."

The woman sitting opposite me looks transformed from the carefree girl in the picture. She's thinner than that, paler too. Her hair's dyed dark as it can go, and she's wearing sunglasses indoors to cover a black eye.

"I just fancied a change," she says.

Heydon's smiling in the picture as well, but it's pained, like he's faking it for his sister's benefit. I feel bad for the guy, but somehow it makes his disappearance seem less surprising. Like he's the kind of person who might cut and run on you, or worse. Bobbie must see this thought occur to me, because she starts drawing my attention to Heydon's tattoo, trying to prove how invested he still was in life.

"See here?" she says.

In the picture, the tattoo on Heydon's left cheek looks like a teardrop. When she taps the screen to zoom in, I see it's actually the outline of a broken heart, as she'd said. It's upside down, a crack running down the center.

"Yeah," I say. "It's great."

Y'know. It's fine. The tattoo's tough and gooey at the same time; you could take it either way. But when Bobbie zooms out, I see Heydon's face again, that troubled smile, and the ink says something different to me. Heydon's not thinking about the future. He can't even see himself there.

"I did it myself," says Bobbie.

"Did what yourself?" I ask, looking up.

"The tattoo. I did it, *prison-style*." She knows it sounds funny through her cut-glass accent, and we grin. "Heated ink, a needle, an electric toothbrush motor…"

"Wow," I say. "Well done."

"Do you have any?" she asks. I shake my head. "I could do you one, if you wanted?"

"Yeah, sure," I say. "Tattoo my face."

She smiles. "Anything in particular?"

"Nah, I'll just take a Heydon."

"Cool. I'm in a heartbreaking kind of mood."

"Yeah?" I say carefully. "Why's that?"

"Don't I look inspired to you?"

Bobbie's talking about the black eye, and I see now that everything's been leading us here. Either I can ask about the bruise and go deeper, or I can let it go and say good night. I'm still not sure what I'm doing when I lean in again, lowering my voice.

"You said it felt like an inheritance."

Bobbie reaches for her drink, finds an empty glass, and starts looking for the waiter. Then her phone goes off on the table, and she freezes. It's an incoming call from a withheld number. The ringtone's "Bad Guy" by Billie Eilish.

Bobbie doesn't move.

"Should you get that?" I ask.

She reaches over and sends the call to voicemail, then turns her phone face down on the table, trying to stay calm. She goes through her bag with shaking hands and produces a scuffed pack of cigarettes. They're designer, Yves Saint Laurent.

"Some fresh air?" she says.

———

We're the only people in the terminal smoking section outside. From here, it's just multistory car parks, going on forever. Bobbie gets the cigarette in her mouth, and she's about to light it when she stops, looks at me, and says, "Sometimes, I think I've fucked everything up."

"Like what?" I say, rubbing my eyes.

She lights the cigarette and takes a drag.

"Like my whole life," she says, then exhales. "I think I've pretty much fucked it all."

"I'm sure that's not true."

"You asked about this," she says, waving smoke in front of her face, her shades, the bruised eye. "It was handed down to me."

She doesn't offer me one of her designer cigarettes but holds up hers for a drag. There's dark lipstick on the end, but I take it anyway.

"I don't understand," I say, inhaling, handing it back.

"I'm not going to LA for family stuff," she says. "They're not even speaking to me right now."

"Why not?"

Bobbie takes a deep drag and lets it out.

"Because I'm on my way to MBR." She drops the name like I should know it, but I shake my head. "Malibu Beach Recovery. Rehab."

She takes another drag, then exhales.

"You're on your way to rehab?" I say.

"Surprise."

"Should you be smoking and drinking?"

"Should anyone?"

"Just seems weird that they sent you out on your own," I say, still trying to get a grip on her situation.

"Oh. It's one of Miranda's developmental tests. If I can make it to the Pacific coast and do my ninety days in the hole, then she won't cut me off. Otherwise…"

"Rehab it is," I say, wondering what she's on.

"But that's what I'm saying. Rehab's not the problem. Rehab makes sense."

The opening notes of "Bad Guy" start playing again. She pulls her phone out from her bag and cancels the call.

I can't decide if Bobbie's in trouble or just coming down from something. But I'm not sure if it's such a good idea for her to be talking to someone like me.

"Look, Bobbie, what's going on here?"

She closes her eyes for a moment. "When my flight got canceled tonight, I called my dealer."

"To an airport? The night before rehab?" I can feel the last forty-eight hours finally catching up with me. "For what?"

"Nothing crazy, like, a couple of grams."

"And now this guy's pulling up…"

She's still watching me, deciding something.

"He'll share location when he gets here," she says. "Park nearby, just down the road."

I take the cigarette, take a drag, and hand it back.

"And what are you going to do?"

"I don't know," she says. "Go and meet him?"

Just the hint of a question mark in her voice.

Making me decide if it's an invitation or not.

"You know you could just tell him you've changed your mind," I say.

"But, sweetie, that's just the problem." She takes a final drag on the cigarette, then exhales out the side of her mouth. "I don't think I have changed my mind."

———

We follow the map on Bobbie's phone to a multistory short-stay car park on terminal grounds. She leads us up to the third level and starts to look around when the driver of a black SUV flashes his brights from a parking bay.

"Stay," says Bobbie, going on ahead.

I'd been hoping to get hold of the coke before she could, to try and keep her sober somehow. But Bobbie strides over to the SUV, getting in on the passenger side. As soon as the door shuts, the car starts up and screeches out of the bay, passing me by, taking a ramp up to the next level. At first, I think Bobbie's gone, that it's all been some weird game. In a sense, I'm almost relieved. Then the black truck reappears, pulling up at the far end of the floor, catching me in the headlights. Bobbie gets out and starts walking toward me. She's still wearing her shades, but as she comes closer, I see that her dark lipstick's smudged, and she's uncertain on her feet.

Bobbie's already high.

"White privilege," she slurs, walking right past.

I take one last look at the SUV, but all I can make out's a smashed wing mirror on the passenger side. A moment passes, and I get the same weird sensation of being watched that had woken me on the underground. Then I turn and follow Bobbie back toward the terminal.

3.

Bobbie pops the bottle and pours us both a glass. I'm not even tempted by the coke. Besides anything else, I've been awake for so long, I think one more night might finish me off. I have a drink and make a dent in the room-service pizza instead.

Once I feel up to it and once I'm sure that Bobbie's settled in her bath, I flip slowly through the free news channels, watching for any mention of Paris or France, listening for certain trigger words. But somehow, they just never come up. There's no description of any perpetrator being circulated. No apartment block, no body. There's no named suspect, and most importantly, there's no red notice issued by Interpol. It turns out that the queen's passed away, aged ninety-six, and luckily for me, it's the only thing that anyone on any channel's talking about.

—

I realize it's been a minute since I've heard Bobbie in the bathroom. When I knock on the door, she doesn't answer. I push it open, bracing myself for some kind of scene, but find her OK, sitting in the tub, still wearing her underwear, drinking champagne out of the bottle.

"Come in," she says half-heartedly.

"What's up?" I ask, standing in the doorway.

"Hashtag selfcare," she says, not looking at me.

With her shades off, I can see the black eye.

"What happened there?" I ask. "Really?"

She touches her face but still doesn't look over.

"Why? What would you do about it?"

"I could listen," I say.

Bobbie thinks for a moment.

"What's the worst mistake you ever made?" she asks.

I see myself in the café off Rue Bobillot last week, when Clare was trying to talk to me. I see myself walking away. I can't answer, and Bobbie glances up.

"I'm sorry," she says. "That's a personal question."

"Just too many to choose from," I say, trying to sidestep it. "What about you?"

"I think I trusted the wrong person," she says, almost to herself. Then she remembers me and smiles. "Like, no offense, but I always seem to trust the wrong people. I always seem to do the wrong thing."

"You know, you're saving my life tonight, Bobbie."

"What do you mean by that?" she asks, looking at me properly for the first time since I've opened the door.

"I've got nowhere else to go," I say. "I'm broke."

"What?"

"I moved to London today, sort of by accident."

"Like, for work?" she says, reaching out a hand.

I cross the room and help her out of the tub.

"More like getting away from it all," I say.

Bobbie stands there, looking at me for a few seconds. There's just the sound of the water dripping off her. For some reason, I feel like the half-naked one.

"But enough about me—" I start to say.

"Does your skin always look that way, or is it a tan?"

"It's a tan," I say. "I've been traveling, on business."

"What is it that you do?" she asks, not letting me change the subject this time.

"Well, right now, I guess I'm between jobs."

"You guess?"

"I sort of walked out on the last one," I say.

"With just the clothes on your back?" She looks at the shining suit. "Must be a pretty cutthroat industry."

"Yeah." I try a smile. "And what is it that you—"

"What *is* the business?" Bobbie asks, her head tilting.

I see myself standing outside the hotel, sizing people up. "Acquisitions," I say after a moment.

"Acquisitions? And what don't you like about it?"

"It's all take, take, take," I say.

Bobbie's smile looks mildly disappointed. "I believe you, but at the same time, I don't. If that makes sense?"

"Yeah, that definitely makes sense. Look, I realize this is weird. If you'd rather I left…"

"No," she says. "Whatever it is you don't do for a living, I think everyone deserves a second chance."

She says it like something she needs to hear.

"Yeah," I say, taking the opportunity to hand her a towel and walk out. "I think so too."

When I get to the door, Bobbie calls after me.

"What if I told you I could solve all our problems?"

I turn to her. "How's that?"

"By the power vested in me."

She smiles, and I close the door.

———

I go back into the bedroom and finish my drink, flicking through news channels until I find the Russian-Ukrainian war. The shower runs for twenty-five or thirty minutes, and when I put my ear to the wall, I'm fairly certain I can hear Bobbie murmuring.

Talking to someone quietly on the phone.

When she's finished, she comes through in a robe.

Her hair's wet, and her makeup's gone. She lies down on the bed next to me, and I feel myself sinking into the sheets. When I close my eyes, I see thousands of intersecting lines, pouring into the darkness over my head. Like all the unwanted messages and warning signs and bad static that's flying over me, all the dark energy that's leaving me alone, because it doesn't know I'm down here, hiding in the black with Bobbie. Then she's astride me, and I feel the wet tips of her hair, tickling my face. When I look up, she's holding a pen, concentrating. I guess drawing the broken heart where her brother's was.

She finishes, then sits back.

"Where on *earth* did you find this suit?" she asks.

"I imported it myself."

"From, like, the past?"

We both laugh and go quiet again, then Bobbie squints at me and looks closer. "You *know*," she says, "you've got red on you."

She's got one hand flat on my chest, and I let my eyes fall shut. I've got a low resting heart rate, fifty beats per minute, and I try to focus to keep it from creeping up. Bobbie licks a thumb and rubs at the red stain on my neck that somehow I must have missed this morning.

"I think I cut myself shaving," I say.

Bobbie fingers my stubble, forward in a way that Clare never was, and I feel myself clenching up.

"But you haven't shaved."

"Then I don't know what to tell you." I open one eye and watch her, studying the red-stained thumb.

"Looks like you trusted the wrong person too." It sounds like she's only half joking. I open both eyes and look up at her, anxious to change the subject. Luckily, Bobbie does it for me. "Gosh," she says. "Sometimes, it's just scary how much you look like him."

"Bobbie, I'm not—"

"I know that," she says. Then her tone changes. "But let's just say you really were stuck for cash. You could easily go to Daddy and Miranda…"

"Ha," I say. "Right."

"I'm serious," she says. "You'd walk in and out."

My eyes are closing again, so she climbs off me and lies by my side.

"You could just show up at their place while they're out and tell the help that you're Heydon. They haven't changed the locks or codes since he left."

"And then what?" I ask after a moment.

"Well, then there's my father's collection. Then there's the safe in Miranda's study. I could get you the key. I could give you the combination." I roll over, grumbling. "I can turn everything into cash," she insists. "All you'd need to do is get inside that house."

I can't tell if she's fooling around or if it's just coke-talk. Then a warm, unfamiliar feeling washes over me, and for some reason, I feel like it's all going to be OK. If she says anything else about Daddy, Miranda, or her dead brother, then I don't hear it. I just plunge down into an effortless deep sleep.

4.

I can sense the warming sun without opening my eyes. It's hard to remember the last time I felt so chilled out. I'm comfortable, lying across a king-size bed alone. I'd been half-conscious of some movement a few hours ago. The sound of the alarm and the shifting bedsheets. The shower, the hair dryer, the click of the door.

Bobbie had been gentle when she got up for her flight. She hadn't woken me to say goodbye. I'd tried opening my eyes for her, but they'd been so glued together I'd gone back to sleep. It wasn't the kind of night where you wake up in the morning wanting to compare notes anyway. Christ knows what I'd said to her, and she'd said some shit herself. No regrets though. All told, it was one of the better nights of my life lately.

I jolt upright to the sound of a vacuum cleaner in an adjacent room, then I rub my eyelids apart and roll out of bed, still wearing my shining suit. I make a crack in the curtains so I can see the damage, then pull them closed again, groaning. The desk's caked with empty miniatures from the minibar as well as the pizza crusts that Bobbie wouldn't eat. I fold one of them into my mouth before taking another look at the room. The TV's still going from last night, playing the news on mute. Both chairs have been turned over. The lampshades have been torn apart. Bedclothes are strewn across the floor, and there's stubbed-out cigarettes everywhere you look.

What the fuck did I just sleep through?

I search for the TV remote, but when I find it, it won't work, and I see that the battery's missing. I push some buttons on the side of the set, and a message flashes up on the screen before fading to black.

Goodbye, Doc. Renee Yiph.

Renee Yiph? What? Is this even Bobbie's room?

I go to the bathroom and throw water in my face. That wakes me up, because my left cheek starts stinging, like it's been burned by something. I glance at the mirror and see the biro sketch of a broken heart that Bobbie drew on my face has turned red. When I lean in to look closer, I have to grip the sink, because it feels like the floor's falling away from me. I stagger back into the bedroom, tearing through the wreckage on the desk. Underneath it all, I find a gutted biro that's been turned into a makeshift tattoo gun using the motor from an electric toothbrush, a melted and bent-double manual toothbrush, and the room sewing kit. It's got the battery from the TV remote still plugged into it. Bobbie tattooed my face while I was asleep.

She did it *prison-style*.

I take a few seconds to process this, then check the time: 12:15 p.m., probably long past checkout. I take one last look at the wreckage, the gutted minibar, and decide it's time to leave.

In the few seconds I take to smarten myself up and search the room, I find Bobbie's bag of coke, seemingly untouched, alongside a rolled-up £10 note. I'm about to flush the coke down the toilet when there's a knock at the door—"*Housekeeping*"—and I force it into my jacket pocket with the cash instead.

———

When I get to the front desk, there's sweat running into my eyes, but I ask for a bandage, and they give me one. It's bright white, one square inch of gauze.

"I think my friend's already checked out," I say, backing off from the counter.

"What's the room number, please?"

"Erm…" I say, shaking my head. "Two-two-nine?"

The woman on the desk frowns briefly, looking down at her screen. "No?" she says. "That's all fine."

I'm not exactly sure what that means, but I smile and walk away, not wanting to get stuck with the bill if there's some kind of problem. Then I put the bandage on in the lobby gents, even though it makes me look weirder.

In the terminal, I'm so heated I don't know where I'm going or what I'll do when I get there. I charge past a pack of happy families and loved-up couples, then skid to a stop at a phone charge point, digging out my iPhone and plugging it in. Once there's enough power and once I've fought my way onto the free Wi-Fi, I google *Bobbie Pierce*. The first result takes me to her Instagram account. Her last post shows a boarding pass and a bottle of water. The caption's *#SELFCARE*.

———

I create a new account under the name @Heydon2 so I can be sure that she won't miss it. Then I hammer Bobbie with messages. After a few minutes, when none of them have been read, I start commenting underneath her posts, saying I need to talk to her urgently. The other people at the charge point stand as far away from me as possible, either because of the bandage on my face or because I'm mouthing obscenities at the phone.

Finally, I get a notification from Instagram:

Ahaha. Hey! Its great to hear from you!

You made the flight?

Watching west side story at 50,000 feet.
Thx for last night, I rly needed that x

You're in the air?

Wi-Fi baby! What's up with you? What
are your plans for today?

Well, Bobz, I was gonna try and lie
low, but that won't fly now.

???

YOU TATTOOED MY FUCKING FACE.

There are just three dots for a minute, meaning she's writing something, but they disappear entirely a few times when she stops.

I guess these are moments where more exciting things are going
on in *West Side Story*.

Finally, she says:

YOU ASKED ME TO!

WTF??? No.

U SAID 'SURE TATTOO MY FACE'

I WAS BEING FUNNY

Three dots again, then:

How was I supposed to know that?!

Nice

I don't get the big deal, it's tiny and it looks cool
AF, if anything you should be thanking me! Do
yuop kno how big a compliment that waS?

Did you not think that it might be inconvenient
for me to have a tattoo on my face, Bobbie?

Oh? And why's that then?

The question just hangs there for a minute.

Or are you still too much of a
man of mystery to say??

> **People tend to remember men
> with face tattoos, Bobbie.**

Well, isn't that a good thing?

> **Not for me.**

When I see it written down like that, my response feels like it gives too much away. It sounds like I've got something to hide, and I think of Bobbie last night, examining her red-stained thumb. Then I see she's typing again.

Why don't you just do what we talked about?

> **What?**

Show up at my parents' place and say ur Heydon(!)

I look up at the terminal whirling around me. With the tattoo, it would be more simple to sell the idea that I was Heydon Pierce. At least for a short time. Maybe suffering from some kind of memory loss, unable to explain his whereabouts. If the parents were both blind, I might get lunch out of them. It even sounds like the kind of haywire soap opera lark I might have gone on in Europe.

But in Parc Güell, Barcelona, or in Saint Charles in Marseille, I'd been exotic. When I was talking my way onto the yachts in Corsica or into the convention center in Cannes—and yes, even when I first met Clare in Naples—it had been so much easier to fool people into thinking I was someone else. Probably because it had been so much easier to fool myself. But after Paris, I'm not quite so convinced by my performance. And the less said about my motivation, the better.

When I glance down, the screen on my phone's turned black, and for a second, I see myself clearly. The bandage on my cheek looks cynical, like part of a costume, and I can't help but think of all the other ones I've worn. The flash suits and silly watches, the false aliases and phony docs. As well as the countless, nameless characters I've played, just to get me from A to B. They were never about getting off the grid or getting even. And they weren't about getting away with murder either. You only churn through identities like that when you can't stand the kinds of people you keep turning into.

So I light up my phone to decline Bobbie's offer. Then I remember what she'd said last night, about her mother's safe, her father's "collection"—how I'd walk in and out—and I find myself scrolling back through her messages. I'm about to swipe Instagram shut, to get rid of the temptation, when she sends me an address in Chelsea, followed by two four-digit numbers.

WTF is this?

My parents' place. 1st is pin for dropbox on the door
w/ the spare key. 2nd is the code for the alarm.

Delete this Bobbie, Jesus Christ.

Look. Everyone's out paying their respects to
her maj and Anya wont start supper util 6. Your
giving me the fear and making me feel bad
WHILE FLYING THROUGH THE AIR. Go and get

something to eat, grab some cash out of my old room. It's the one on the right, on the second floor. There's at least a couple of hundred quid lying around. The place is empty for the next six hours at least. If you feel like stealing some of Miranda's hideous artwork, then be my guest.

I stare down at the phone for a few seconds.

5.

I've got no intention of going along with Bobbie's *plan*, if you can even call it that. But I'm not sure what I will do if I find her parents' place empty. I buy an Oyster card with Bobbie's tenner, and the train rattles back into London. The address she'd given me was for a house on Tregunter Road in Chelsea, somewhere I've never really been before. I walk slowly, soaking up the morning sun, my crumpled suit jacket slung over my shoulder.

The streets are wide and tree-lined, and the people seem used to the light, with tanned skin and lean, beach-ready bodies. I see sports cars and kids in private school uniforms, and when the glowing rich girls in their summer clothes go striding by, it's like I don't even exist. When I turn onto Tregunter, I stop. The traffic sounds of the main road fall away, and even the sunlight looks like it's in HD.

The houses are cream-colored and three-tiered, looking like oversize wedding cakes. It's not the kind of street you live on if you've hit it lucky once or twice. Not even if you've come from good stock and swung *the* job. This is wealth, handed down in wodges, kept in the family at all costs. Places worth tens of millions of pounds. And it gives me the same feeling that the smiling blond Bobbie in the picture did. It makes me wish I'd been born him.

I walk, dimly aware of a car starting up, creeping slowly down the quiet street behind me. When I glance over my shoulder, I see it's a black SUV, and I flash back to the one Bobbie got into at the airport. I even stop and stare at it for a stupid second. It's a tank-size truck with tinted windows, but I can't tell if it's the same one I saw last night. I never got the plate, make, or model, and the light had been too bad to see any real body detail. The one thing I did catch, that smashed wing mirror, was on the passenger side, currently obscured to me. The SUV crawls by, and I let my eyes go dead, then look casually away. The driver puts their foot down, and they tear off to the end of the street. The tires *skrrt* when they take the corner.

From here, Bobbie's house looks like it's set over three stories, like the rest of them. But once I'm through the wrought iron gate and standing on the empty driveway, I count five. There's a lower ground level with some steps leading down to it, and craning my neck, I see what look like windows from a converted loft.

There's no way around the camera over the door, so I stare straight forward when I ring the bell, listening close for sounds of life. When I don't hear anything, I open the panel for the dropbox and input the code that Bobbie gave me. I feel a spark of something when the hatch pops open, because I almost can't believe there's a key inside. I take a step back, looking up at the house again for any kind of clue why she hates them so much she's sent me here. When I put the key in the door and turn it, I know Bobbie must have some kind of ulterior motive, but I can't help myself; I do it anyway.

It opens onto a light hallway with a bouquet of flowers in a vase at the foot of a grand staircase straight ahead. The alarm starts beeping, and I input the second code, switching it off. When I kick the door closed behind me, there's a sudden golden hush, and my eyes go to the family pictures on the wall.

Bobbie looks like an outsider next to her much straighter older sister and next to her mother, the actorly, dramatic-seeming Miranda. Miranda's a severe, beautiful woman who I think I half recognize from a film or two here and there. The dad looks like some cocksure city boy, now in his midsixties. There aren't any pictures of Heydon at all. Or so I think, until I see that smiling baby boy...

I run my hand across the oak banister at the bottom of the stairs, then turn left into what I guess is the living room. Or would they say lounge? A six-person corner sofa and a coffee table take up most of the space, with floor-to-ceiling windows looking out onto the street, letting the light in. I glance outside for the SUV, but happily, it's not there. The room leads into an open-plan reading space with french windows. A fully furnished wooden deck and a leafy back garden beyond.

I retrace my steps through the lounge to the staircase, erasing my fingerprints from the banister, walking past it into a study. It looks out onto the back garden as well, with a large bay window making an alcove in one corner, one big enough for a round, six-person meeting table. I wonder if this is the study that Bobbie mentioned, but I don't start feeling behind paintings for a safe. I'm not playing Bobbie's game. I just want to soak it all up, breathe the still mansion air. If I only get a few minutes here, then walking around's more valuable to me than any loose change down the back of the sofa.

Backing out of the study, I see I'd missed another staircase leading down, and I take it to the lower ground level, coming to a second lounge that feels like a replica of the one upstairs, only more private, with no street view. Past that, I come to a showstopping kitchen. The fixtures are stainless steel, set into the walls, and there's a cream-colored marble island running ten feet down the center. I follow it through into a dining room with a round wooden table set for eight.

There's another staircase down from here, a basement, so *six* floors, not five. It leads to a wine cellar on the left and a private cinema on the right. And there's so much pleasure flowing through me it should be illegal. Doubling back on myself, I find more rooms underneath the stairs, coming to a mirror-lined gym—two treadmills, two cross-trainers, two weight benches, etc.

Then I walk through into the subterranean swimming pool, hearing myself breathing hard. It's something like twenty meters from end to end and softly lit by hidden floor lights. It's dark, warm, secret, and safe, and when I crouch down to hold my hand under the water, I close my eyes, listening, willing the moment on.

Then a man standing behind me clears his throat.

"Can I help you, friend?"

———

I don't move for a second, trying to work out how to play it. The guy's got a broad London accent. He sounds more like the hired help than a family member. But if he's on his own, I can probably push past him to the stairs. I take my hand from the water, then rise, slowly. When he arms the Taser, it goes off like a rattlesnake.

I stop with my back still to him.

"There we go," he says. "Good lad. Now, for a gold star, I need both hands on top of your head. Then you can turn around. Nice and slow."

I turn without putting my hands up.

He's a bland white guy in his late thirties. My height but heavier. He's got a square head, with neat dark hair jutting out into a widow's peak. From the dark suit and the Bluetooth earpiece, from the ugly, functional shoes, he looks like private security. He raises the Taser, but his eyes go wide when he sees my face, and he lowers it again, trying to speak.

"I was just leaving," I say, making to pass him.

"Nah," he says bluntly, moving to block the way. He shakes his head, and his mouth twists into a smile. "I mean, I can't allow that just at present, sir." He must get the sense I'm about to walk right through him, because he steps back, blocking the door. "Now, now," he says, still smiling with just the bottom half of his face. "I don't want my *colleagues* to get excited when they see you coming up the stairs."

"All right," I say.

"Can I ask how you got inside, sir?"

"I used the key from the dropbox."

"May I ask how you got the code for the box, sir?"

"Honestly?" I look at him. He's dropped the attitude and started calling me "sir" since seeing my face. If I was a betting man, I'd say this guy's never met Heydon before. He's seen pictures though. He's spotted the bandage. And he thinks there's a chance I might be him. "Honestly, I don't recall," I say, shifting my accent out of neutral, matching it more closely to my memory of Bobbie's.

"Sir?" he says.

"Can I trust you?" I ask after a moment.

The smile again. "Of course you can."

"Can I ask who you are? Do you live in this house?"

The man doesn't take his eyes off mine but reaches into his

jacket pocket, handing me a business card. His name's Mike
Arnold, and he's an agent for something called the Rayner Group.
When I glance up, he's watching closely, staring at the bandage on
my cheek.

"What don't you recall?" he asks.

I look back at him for a moment, then decide to just make
life easy for myself. At least until I can talk my way out of this
basement.

"Yeah," I say, going up a few classes, committing to my best guess
of Heydon Pierce. "That's the thing. Like, I don't remember who
I am or how I came to be in London. I woke up on a train with no
ID, coming into town, a couple of days ago. When I looked in the
mirror, I didn't recognize myself. There was this strange mark on
my face." I touch the bandage. "I can't see any further back than
that."

"You must remember how you got here though."

Mike's accent shifts, more closely matching mine.

"I swear down," I say, shaking my head, staring at the floor. "I
just had those codes in my mind. This house, more than anything.
Somehow, it felt like the one thing in this world I could be sure of."

When Mike scrunches his eyes shut, then opens them again, I
feel like Marlon Brando. Then he turns to a gasp from the doorway, and I see a pale-faced woman standing there, aghast. She's
smartly dressed in a gray knee-length skirt and matching jacket,
and—oh fuck—it's Bobbie's older sister. My face seems to hit her
hard. I start to say something, trying to explain. She puts a hand
to her mouth; she shakes her head. I take a step forward, but she
backs out of the room.

——

"Best we give everyone some space," Mike says, leading me back up the stairs. He seems to have taken the reaction of Bobbie's sister as a positive ID. I'd agreed to follow him up so I could find her and explain myself. But when we reach the ground floor and pass the study, I can hear her taking a phone call. With the door closed, the conversation's too muffled to make out, but it sounds intense.

As soon as we're outside, two more Bluetoothed men in black join us. I stop walking and look at Mike.

"How did you know I was in there?" I ask.

He turns and takes a step forward, boxing me in.

"Camera on the door, sir," he says, nodding back at the house. I don't believe him, because he'd been surprised by my face. Besides, as we get closer to the car, I see it's the same black SUV that followed me down the street a few minutes ago. Mike and the gang had been sitting outside, waiting for something to happen.

He opens the car door, still being my friend but not exactly giving me a choice. There's a flicker of doubt in his face that I might do something crazy though. So I smile to put his mind at rest, then climb inside.

The SUV's dark and spacious, with what looks like a bulletproof screen dividing front from back. There are six seats in the rear. Chilled water too. But it's still just a soundproofed cage, disguised as a hundred-thousand-pound truck. A portable jail cell. Whatever the Rayner Group does, they definitely mean business.

So I'm expecting Mike to climb in after me. I'm expecting some kind of Q and A. But he slams the door and has a clipped conversation with his colleagues instead. They come to some kind of decision, then he walks toward the house with what looks like a clear sense of purpose, probably to console Bobbie's sister. One of the guys puts a hand to his earpiece and speaks quietly for a moment while his colleague keeps guard. Then they just stand there, their backs to the car. I think about banging on the window and making something happen, but right now, I'm happy to watch.

I take Bobbie's bag of powder from my pocket, open it, and have a sniff, just out of curiosity. For a second, I think it's designer, like her cigarettes. I think they've got flavored coke here, along with everything else.

Then I realize I'm huffing castor sugar.

The bag's a fake, a prop, a piece of set dressing.

So those missed calls, the multistory car park, Bobbie's drug deal, and the black SUV. None of it had been quite what it seemed.

So what the fuck was it?

Twenty minutes go by, and I'm peeling off the bandage, trying to see the state of my new tattoo in the rearview mirror, when another car pulls up at the gate. It's a cream-colored Rolls-Royce Phantom, with an illuminated pearlescent grill and shimmering twenty-two-inch platinum alloys. A driver gets out to hold open the rear door, and a long, thin woman emerges, wearing a charcoal herringbone suit. When I see her in side profile, just for a second, she looks like a wisp of smoke. She reaches her full height, then starts for the house, walking with the aid of a cane.

Another ten minutes go by, then Mike comes down the driveway, says a couple of words to his colleagues, and opens the door. His eyes snag on the tattoo.

"Looks sore," he says, brought up short.

"I didn't realize it was permanent when I saw it in the mirror at St. Pancras," I tell him. "I rubbed it red raw."

"Huh," he says, seeming to accept this off-the-cuff explanation, looking preoccupied with something else. "Look." His mouth makes a dry, clicking sound when he talks, like the sight of all this money's making him thirsty. "There's someone inside I'd like you to meet."

I consider telling the poor bastard the truth. Then I remember the way his attitude had changed when he thought I was someone with money. How his accent had shifted with mine to mirror Bobbie's. Either he's so checked out that he can't see the tattoo for what it is, or worse, so set on getting a result that he's willing to believe anything. Either way, that's his problem.

"Thank you, Mr. Arnold," I say, climbing out of the car. "Please, lead the way."

6.

Mike leads us through the lounge to the french window, past a billowing, cream-colored curtain, out into the blinding light of the back garden. I shield my eyes, seeing for the first time how large it is, enclosed on three sides by a thick canvas of evergreen trees. The grass has been left long, with poppies and bluebells swaying against the light. It looks like someone paused a meadow, then transplanted it to a central London garden.

We cut through the wildflowers to a summer house at the rear. The older woman I'd seen unfurling from the car sits at a table on the veranda, looking like a breeze might blow her away. Bobbie's sister's sitting beside her, now wearing a pair of gold-rimmed glasses on a chain. When she sees me looking at her, she puts them on almost protectively.

Mike stops just short of the porch, and I'm left standing in direct sunlight. Then he strides onto the creaking deck, making introductions while I squint back.

"Miranda Pierce," he says, nodding at the implacable gray woman, the undisputed center of gravity in this garden. The

Miranda I'd seen in family pictures a few minutes ago had been dark and elegant. She'd had dramatic, plaited black hair, a sensuous face. But now it looks like she's been cut down by some kind of serious illness. You can still see why Bobbie calls her by her first name. There's something definitive about Miranda. She's the very first and last of her kind, and as if to prove it, she doesn't move or acknowledge me in any way.

Mike motions to the woman sitting beside her.

"And, of course, her daughter," he says deferentially, "Ms. Reagan Pierce." Reagan doesn't look up while we're being introduced. "And *this* gentleman—" Mike says finally.

Miranda breaks in, impatient.

"Well, are you him or aren't you?" she demands.

Her voice is rigid, and she's sitting with one white hand on the table, clenched into a fist. And I can't help but think about Bobbie's plan, the house, the safe, her father's collection, when I clear my throat to answer.

"No," I say. "I'm sorry, Mrs. Pierce, but I'm not."

Miranda's eyes seem to catch the light for a second, then she blinks it away. Mike's staring with contempt now, but Reagan's completely unmoved. She's waiting to find out what her mother thinks.

Miranda fixes me with a stare. "That's just what I was hoping you'd say."

———

"Perhaps you could tell us how you arrived here? How you came to have that ghastly thing on your face."

"Well," I say, looking between them. "It's sensitive." Miranda blinks. "I don't mean for me, Mrs. Pierce."

"I'm not accustomed to being protected from the truth," she

says, suppressing a cough. "Besides which, as you can no doubt hear, I no longer have the luxury of time. I asked you a straight question. Please don't force me to repeat myself."

"I met Bobbie last night, out at the airport."

"Of course you did," she says, stiffening, looking past me into the garden. "And how did you find her?"

"She seemed well," I say. "She thought I looked a lot like her brother though. I guess she got carried away…"

"So I see," Miranda says, her gaze flicking from the garden back to the tattoo. "And what?" she says, her eyes meeting mine. "She sent you here as some kind of cruel joke? You've really come for what little I have left?"

I see for the first time how strained things must be with Bobbie, and I feel the sun bearing down on me.

"Nothing like that," I say, holding eye contact. "The tattoo was a kind of miscommunication. Bobbie thought you might help me get it removed."

"The shakedown," Mike says. "So finally, we get to it. Well, let me explain something, pal. Mrs. Pierce doesn't owe you squat. And by the way, twa—"

"Enough, Mr. Arnold," Reagan says.

When Mike breaks off, he's out of breath. There's sweat in his eyes.

"How did you come to meet my sister?" Reagan asks.

Her voice stays carefully neutral, but from the way her eyes fall on me, I'm glad of an innocent explanation.

"By chance," I say. "We bumped into each other."

"Really." There's no question mark. "And she was able to deface you without your knowledge because…"

"I've come a long way," I tell her. "Until last night, I hadn't slept in three days."

I don't mention how I'm becoming increasingly convinced that her sister dosed me with something last night. There'd been that warm, unfamiliar sensation right before I fell asleep, and I can still just about feel its afterglow. Bobbie could have gotten something from the guy in the car; she could have easily slipped it into my drink.

"A long way," Mike says bluntly. "From where?"

"From kind of all over the place," I tell him.

Mike blinks furiously.

"Look," I say. "I'm not trying to shake anyone down here. I just want what's fair."

He snorts. "Was it fair to break into the house? Was it fair to impersonate Mr. Pierce?"

"First, I didn't break in. Bobbie gave me the codes. Second, I just went along with what you wanted to hear." I glance at Reagan. "I will say that Ms. Pierce walked in at a bad moment though. I'm sorry about that. It just seemed clear to me that the only way I was getting out of that basement without unpleasantness—"

"Unpleasantness?" Mike says.

"—was by letting Arnie think he was right about something. I went along with him, and I shouldn't have. You had every right to be shocked."

Reagan's face doesn't change.

"Well," Miranda says, watching me carefully. "Of course, if your story's true, then one reserves judgment. My daughter's a troubled young woman. When you met her, she was on her way to a rehabilitation facility."

"I was surprised no one went with her."

"We didn't part on the best of terms," Reagan says, speaking for her mother.

"You weren't worried she might use again?" I ask.

"We knew she'd do it anyway," she says easily.

"So did she make it out there, to the Pacific coast?"

Reagan winces slightly at the detail, then flashes a quick smile. "She checked into MBR this afternoon. How *kind* of you to ask. I don't think we got your name, Mr....?"

I glance over my shoulder at the two guys guarding the patio, both of them staring at us through aviator sunglasses.

"Lynch," I tell her after a moment.

"ID," Mike says, still scowling. "Now."

I reach into my jacket pocket, and he braces like I might have a grenade in there. Slowly, I withdraw the black passport and hand it to him. It's the genuine article, issued by an official at Ireland's Department of Foreign Affairs who'd been in hock to the O'Sullivan syndicate. Clare knew their youngest girl, and we'd run a *Spanish Prisoner*–style con in Greece, selling futures that didn't exist to a cohort of American tech bros. We'd gladly accepted new passports as payment. And since Ireland was still a part of the European Union, it meant that we could move freely through twenty-six other countries. We could settle, buy property, work, study, retire. Or that was the idea. The passport got me on the Eurostar this morning, so I'm 95 percent sure it's still solid. But when Mike backs off with a finger to his earpiece, reading the details to a colleague, I'm watching closely.

"So what now?" I ask.

"Now we'll be speaking to the relevant authorities," Reagan says. "Yes, Mr. Lynch, that's right. I'm afraid—"

Miranda silences her with a raised hand, then regards me for a moment. At length, she turns and nods at her daughter, who seems surprised—almost affronted—and it takes her a second to compose herself.

"On second thought," Reagan says, "we'd be only too happy to make the arrangements." She flashes a loveless professional smile. "I'm sure we can scare up a suitable laser surgeon in town. If you provide us with your schedule, we'll find the first available consultation."

"And you'll take care of the bill?" I ask, looking between her and Miranda.

"Of course," Reagan says, pleased to conclude our business. "The consultation and all subsequent sessions."

"Well, my schedule's wide open, but I was just passing through town. I don't have anywhere to stay."

Reagan stiffens. "Perhaps we can arrange something with a local hostel," she says. "If you're amenable."

"A hostel," I say. "Out of interest, how much is Bobbie's trip to LA setting you back?"

I feel Miranda's eyes move on to mine.

Several seconds pass, then she turns to Reagan, saying something quietly into her ear.

"The family is also prepared to make a donation of five thousand pounds sterling to a charity of your choice for the inconvenience," Reagan says. "Of course, we'd transfer those funds to you personally to disperse as you saw fit."

"I'm sort of unbanked at the moment."

There's a black leather binder on the table, and Reagan opens it, removing some paperwork.

"I'm sure we can work something out," she says. "We'll need your signature for the nondisclosure agreement. Not today, just—"

"Bullshit," says Mike, looking up as someone relays the results of my background search to him. He looks at the passport again, then turns it over, shaking his head, not liking what he's hearing.

"No criminal record," he says at length.

Reagan looks at Mike impatiently. She doesn't care who I am. She just wants me gone. "We can't very well hold that against him, now can we?" she says.

"No social media," Mike goes on, reeling off the list like a death sentence. "No tax payments, no bank accounts. No driving tickets, no addresses." He throws the passport at me, and it bounces off my forehead. "No nothing."

"Well," I say, bending to collect it. "I guess that means there's nothing to find."

"Where were you flying in from?" he demands.

"Nowhere," I tell him. "I took the train."

"The train from where?"

"St. Pancras," I say.

"You—" He blinks. "That tan didn't come from St. Pancras, did it? How did you get there?"

"I already told you. I don't remember."

Mike takes a deep breath.

"I'm sorry to have wasted your time with this, Mrs. Pierce," he says, still staring at me. "I'll be only too happy to take this gentleman off your hands."

"Catch up," I say. "They're not paying me off for the tattoo. They're paying me because I know where Bobbie went. And by the way—" I look at Miranda. "Your man's illegally detained me once already today. If he does it again, it's because he's charging you by the hour."

She doesn't respond.

"Why should we be concerned about you knowing my sister's whereabouts?" Reagan asks.

"That's what you've got me asking myself." I look between

them. "I got bored in the car. I opened the bag of powder that Bobbie left in her hotel room."

"Excuse me?" Reagan says with a frown.

I take the bag from my jacket pocket and drop it on the table. "It's Tate and Lyle. So unless Malibu Beach Recovery is treating sugar fiends, you're sending her there for some reason other than her being a junkie."

No one says anything for a moment.

Mike looks genuinely confused, Reagan blushes, but Miranda's got a thin, slow-spreading smile on her face.

"You're quite welcome to accept my daughter's proposal," she says. "It seems like a fair price, given the circumstances. But I think I'd like to make a counteroffer."

"Mrs. Pierce," Mike says, rubbing the bridge of his nose. "This guy's a chiseler. He's a gouger. He's—"

"A con artist," Miranda says. "At best. Yes, I see that. You don't have to try and fool me though, Mr. Lynch," she says, pausing to strain at her throat. "I'll lay my cards on the table. I'm running out of time, and there are certain things I need to know very badly. All conventional means at my disposal have brought me bitter disappointment. You might be the one person in this world who can help."

She says this with dignity while looking me in the eye, but it's clear how much it costs her to ask. That, more than anything else, convinces me that this really is some kind of last resort.

"Miranda," Reagan says, turning to her mother and talking quietly. "Perhaps we should discuss this."

"This is a bad guy, with a capital *buh*," Mike goes on, becoming exasperated. "In the cold light of day—"

Miranda snaps. "I've come to the conclusion that the kinds of people we're dealing with aren't afraid of the daylight, Mr. Arnold. If they were, then perhaps you'd have had some success."

Mike's face turns gray with the strain of not saying anything, but he just about swallows his pride.

"Perhaps it's simply the late shadows drawing in," Miranda says. "But what I want right now is someone who can see in the dark."

Mike closes his eyes, and Reagan looks down at the deck, both of them sensing where she's going next.

"How dark are we talking?" I ask.

Miranda considers me for a moment.

"Bobbie must have told you about my son."

"That he had his troubles, that he walked out."

"But not the circumstances?" she asks.

"I'm afraid not."

"At the time of his disappearance, Heydon had come to believe that he was being followed."

"What could have given him that idea?" I ask, looking between them. Miranda's eyes move on to Mike.

"Well, there were certainly some nuisance calls," he starts. "Some suspicious online activity in the weeks and months leading up to the disappearance. Hacked accounts, phishing scams, things of that nature. Before my time, of course," he says, seemingly at pains to distance himself from an unsatisfactory investigation. "But the group was unable to verify Mr. Pierce's more extreme claims."

"Extreme?" I ask.

Mike looks uncomfortably to Reagan, who speaks quickly.

"Heydon said that strangers had begun to film his movements, in the street, around town."

"Filming him why?"

I'm asking Reagan, and although she starts to answer, Miranda speaks over her. "At the time, we thought he was delusional," she says.

"But not anymore?" No one answers. "So what happened on the night he walked out?" I try.

Reagan glances at Miranda, then rolls her eyes. "On the night of my brother's disappearance, he arrived home in something of a state," she says briskly. "He claimed to have been run off the road."

"Run off the road by who?"

"He couldn't say."

"Was his car damaged?"

Reagan nods. "And he was extremely anxious that my parents give him a large sum of money—fifty thousand pounds. He said he had to have it that night. He claimed that someone's life was at stake. He wouldn't say whose."

When I look at Miranda, she's completely still. "What did you tell him?" I ask.

"My mother was working late," Reagan says, sensing that Miranda might not want to field this one herself. "Reshoots. It was my father who dealt with Heydon that night. When my brother became agitated and began breaking furniture, he was forced to call Mr. Rayner."

Reagan looks at Mike, pleased to hand off the story.

"Well," he says, picking it up reluctantly. "The Rayner Group dispatched a crash team to the house, and they were able to calm Mr. Pierce down. He voluntarily took a sedative, and all parties agreed to talk it out the next day. Except Mr. Pierce stole out in the early hours of that morning."

"Did he go straight to the bridge?" I ask.

"Did he go straight to the bridge?" Miranda repeats. "What an interesting question, Mr. Lynch." Her eyes glow coldly on Mike for a moment. "If only the professionals had thought to find out."

She nods at Reagan, who doesn't say anything.

Miranda snaps her fingers at her in exasperation.

"We recently learned that my brother took out a substantial loan," Reagan says. "In the early hours of the same morning he left, before his car was discovered."

"A black-market loan?" I ask. "With whom?"

"The gentleman's name was Mr. Badwan," she says, the thin gold rims of her glasses catching the light. "The terms were extortionate, but Heydon could be rather free with his signature."

"These terms..." I say gently.

"Yes," Reagan says. "Heydon left some...personal items with Mr. Badwan as collateral."

"And now this Badwan wants?"

"Low seven figures," Mike says after a moment.

I look between them. "Then it's extortion. Go to the Met. You'll have to explain it to them slowly, but—"

"That was our first instinct," Reagan says.

She straightens the papers on the table, and I see that her hands are shaking.

"But?"

"But perhaps when you 'bumped' into my sister, you saw that she'd been the victim of a physical assault?"

"Now that you mention it. She wouldn't say why."

"Two days ago, it appears that Bobbie decided to visit this Mr. Badwan, to prevail upon his better nature."

"But Badwan hasn't got one," I say. I glance at Mike. "Where was Arnie in all this?"

"We found out after the fact," he says. "And why don't you try and keep my name out of your mouth?"

"Yeah," I say, only half listening. "So why's Badwan only coming out of the woodwork now? And why would Bobbie go there by herself?"

Reagan goes on without looking up. "To secure the loan, it seems that Heydon handed over certain *personal* items belonging to Bobbie," she says. "My sister met with Mr. Badwan socially earlier this week for the first time. He brought the matter to her attention."

"How so?"

"He said he'd come into possession of certain collectors' items related to my family. He was offering my sister the opportunity of buying them back."

"What were these collectors' items?"

"I haven't the faintest idea," she says.

I let out a long breath. "OK, why now?"

"One assumes that the interest on my brother's loan finally started to make Mr. Badwan's eyes water."

"So Heydon went to him and borrowed…"

"Sixty-seven thousand pounds," Reagan says.

"Your brother didn't just have that lying around?"

"No," Reagan says flatly.

"Is the figure significant?"

"Just in so much that it seems to cover the original sum he asked my father for, with seventeen thousand pounds left over."

"Do you think he used it to run away?" I ask.

Reagan stares at me for a moment.

"I think that my brother's dead, Mr. Lynch. Do you have any further questions for me?"

"Well," I say, glancing away. "Just so I've got this straight. Badwan wanted collateral for the loan, so Heydon gave him some kind of dirt on his little sister."

"Yes," Reagan says. "I think you've got it straight."

"But we don't know what that dirt was."

"No, Mr. Lynch, we do not," Reagan says. "And believe me, with Bobbie, that's the best way."

"What's Badwan saying?"

"He wants payment in full by the end of the week."

"Or else?"

"Or else he'll destroy the items in his possession. The same goes should the authorities become involved."

"Maybe I'm being slow, but wouldn't Badwan destroying this stuff solve all your sister's problems?"

"Perhaps," Reagan says. "But there are Heydon's belongings to consider too. Badwan claims he left a locked suitcase there. Who knows what might be inside?"

I shrug. "Then pay him."

"Yes," Reagan says. "Thank you for your advice, Mr. Lynch. As far as I was aware, that was what we'd decided." This last is aimed at Miranda in an attempt to pry at her mother's motives for keeping me around. Miranda makes a face but deigns to say her piece anyway.

"Mr. Lynch, I'm prepared to offer you ten thousand pounds to assume my son's identity for one night."

Mike looks between Miranda and me.

Reagan's mouth opens, but no words come.

"It's very kind," I start to say. "But I can't give you—"

"Not for me," Miranda says. "No, no, Mr. Lynch, I'm afraid that while you seem to have *taken* Mr. Arnold and even caught poor Reagan by surprise, your performance doesn't quite fool me."

She pauses for a moment, massaging her throat.

"Though perhaps I'd have let you pretend," she says. "My thinking is that you might well fool this Badwan character. As far as Mr.

Arnold can tell, he wasn't someone my son was well acquainted with. There's a chance they only ever met this one time, some years ago."

"As far as Mr. Arnold can tell," I say. Mike starts blinking again. "How would you want me to fool him?"

"It's simple," Miranda says. "My son met with this man in the early hours of the same morning he vanished. I want to know what the circumstances were, and I know that Badwan won't be forthcoming. But if you were to go there and present yourself as Heydon…" She leans forward. "If you were to speak with this man personally, then we might learn one thing at least."

"And what's that?"

"How he reacts when he sees a dead man walking."

I've been squinting into the light for so long that the frown on my face feels permanent.

"You think he had something to do with your son's disappearance?" I ask.

Miranda inclines her head ever so slightly, and a sudden breeze chills the sweat on my skin.

"Well, I can think of one way he might react."

"That's right," she says breathlessly. "If Badwan thinks you're the real thing, then I suppose he's innocent. But if he knows you for a charlatan, then there's a chance it's because he killed my son. Either way, should something happen to you after making contact, you're quite right," she goes on, her voice fading. "We'd know with some certainty that Heydon was murdered."

When I glance at Reagan, she looks away.

"Yes," Miranda says after an extended pause, like she's seeing it my way for the first time. "You're quite right. It's a bigger job than I'd thought. Shall we say twenty-five?"

"Whoa there," Mike interrupts. "Mrs. Pierce, I need to take all of this back to base. But if you're set on this course, then we'll need to start assembling the team now," he says, trying to regain some control. "There's not just his safety to consider." He side-eyes me. "There's your liability too. And if you're considering putting cash into his hands, then—"

"I've got one condition," I say, interrupting him.

"Go on," says Miranda.

I nod at Mike. "I never deal with this guy again."

Reagan takes off her glasses. "Mr. Arnold has been working with us for three years—"

"On Heydon?" I ask. "Where's that gotten you so far?"

Mike takes a step forward. "You piece of—"

"In any event," Reagan says, sensing her mother's impatience and trying to use its momentum to close the subject. "Mr. Arnold's quite right. This would have to be a Rayner-led operation. That's nonnegotiable, I'm afraid. Hiring you directly would be unacceptable exposure for my mother."

"Cool. But you're saying Arnie's in charge, and I'm telling you my life means more to me than that."

"Mr. Arnold's a trained professional," Reagan starts.

"Mr. Arnold thought I was your brother."

Mike snorts. "I had your number from the word go."

"You're still counting on your fingers, pal."

"Mr. Lynch," Miranda says, interrupting. "You know how I feel about people wasting my time. You've heard my terms. Kindly take them or leave them."

"There's another way," I say, nodding at Reagan. "She could hire me."

Reagan puts a hand slowly to her mouth.

"OK," I say, backing off. "Then it's not for me."

Miranda glares. "You can't be serious."

"I hope it works out for you, Mrs. Pierce. I'd be happy to accept your original offer."

Miranda looks irritably to Reagan, but her daughter glances away, not wanting to help. "We must be able to come to some kind of an arrangement," she says.

"Yeah," I tell her. "I think we can. Twenty-five thousand, and I'll go all the way for you. I'll look this Badwan in the eye, and I'll tell you if I think he's lying." I glance at Mike. "But I can't be explaining every little thing. And if it hits the fan in there—which sounds likely—I want someone rock-solid outside."

Mike laughs and shakes his head.

"Gentlemen," Miranda says. "If you'd be so kind as to give us a moment."

I exchange a look with Mike, then we stomp across the garden back to the house while Miranda and Reagan talk. Mike goes straight inside, not wanting to breathe the same air as me. I ask one of the two goons for some gum, since he's making such a meal of his. He ignores me, and I lean into the wall, soaking up the sunlight. When I open my eyes a minute later, Reagan's walking through the grass in my direction. The light hitting her lenses means I can't see her eyes until she's standing right in front of me.

"Deal," she says, holding out her hand, not looking especially pleased. I'm wondering if I should even take it when Mike reappears.

"This isn't happening," he says. "Do you read me, *pal*? Mr. Rayner's involved in this personally. Him and Ronnie Pierce go back."

"Sounds like you've got some important calls to make," I say, giving him a big thumbs-up. Mike takes a step toward me, and for a second, I think I've done it.

"Mr. Arnold," Reagan says.

He stops, still staring.

"You're not gonna be in my life long enough to care," he says. Mike glances back at Miranda on the far side of the garden, spits on the path, turns, and walks. He's closely followed by the two stooges. One of them clips my shoulder on his way out.

Reagan puts a hand to her mouth again and watches them go. "I hope you know what you're doing," she says.

7.

Reagan leads us into the study, asking me to take a seat. It's clear that she's trying to regain her composure, but at the same time, she's uncomfortable with Miranda's proposal. She gives me a smile that looks like a wince of pain and sits opposite me, opening a MacBook, hesitating for a second, then working efficiently, making arrangements of some kind. She takes two calls, speaking so softly I can only guess she's giving verbal consent or authorization.

"Very well," she says, looking up at me finally. "Dr. Oberg can see you this afternoon on Harley Street. She estimates the initial work should take somewhere between four and six sessions, no more than a couple of weeks. As I said, the family is only too happy to cover your costs. And you'll be pleased to hear we've made arrangements for you to stay at a hotel near to the clinic for the duration. The Mandarin Oriental. It's rather splendid." She gives me her professional smile again. "We'll cover your expenses. Meals, spa treatments, and so forth. And I'll ensure that the donation my mother authorized is delivered there as well. Of course, we will need that signature."

"Of course," I say, mildly confused.

"Please accept my apologies on Bobbie's behalf. A car should be here to collect you any moment."

She smiles and motions to the door. When I don't move, she stands awkwardly, then goes over and holds it open. I look back at her for a moment.

"Reagan, what are you talking about?"

She lets the door fall shut.

"Setting my mother's mental state to one side for a moment, you heard Mr. Arnold yourself. He means to make sure that you can't go ahead—"

"And? Who's he to someone like Miranda?"

She gives up on me going to the door and walks back into the room, pacing slowly behind her desk. "It's not him. It's his employer," she says. "It's Mr. Rayner. He's a well-connected man, used to getting his own way."

"So this should keep him on his toes," I say. "Anyway, I thought he was supposed to be working for Miranda, not the other way round."

"Up to a point," she says. "But as Mr. Arnold alluded to, my father and the Rayner organization go back."

"Is your dad a problem?"

"Aren't they all?"

"Where is he in this?"

"Business," she says. "Back Monday."

"Oh," I say, shrugging. "Monday, fine."

"Excuse me?"

"You said the deadline Badwan set was the end of the week. It's Friday now. We'll be going our separate ways by Monday. Anyway, Miranda doesn't seem like the sort who lets her husband do the thinking for her."

"Well, Miranda's not what she was," Reagan says. "I'm sure she didn't understand what she was asking you."

"She knew exactly what she was asking me," I say. "I think I agree with her as well. When this guy sees my face, he's going to react a certain way. Everyone else has."

"And what?" Reagan says. "You think you can just sense what we're all thinking?"

"Well, my sense is Bobbie wanted me to be him."

"Ooh," she says. "Do another."

"You wanted to get as far away from me as possible."

"And what about my mother?" she says, deflecting. "What did you sense from her?"

"She's different. I didn't fool her for a second."

"Shouldn't that make you reconsider pulling the same stunt on someone who's so much more dangerous?"

"What I'm saying is I could tell I didn't fool her. Before she said anything."

Reagan looks at me as if in a new light.

"That's why you admitted you weren't Heydon."

"All I'm saying is Miranda's right. Catching a similar response from Badwan could tell us something."

"I suppose that's what con artists do, isn't it?" she says with distaste. "Watch people for signs of weakness."

When she looks at me, her own words seem to reach her ears, and suddenly she's self-conscious about my eyes on her.

"That's right," I say. "If you're asking whether I've got the skill set..."

"It's not that," she says, taking off her glasses. "If anything, you seem overqualified."

"Cool," I say. "So how do we contact Mr. Badwan?"

Reagan opens a desk drawer, then unfolds an actual receipt, looking like something printed from a cash register. She hands it over to me.

"Badwan gave this to your sister?" I ask.

Reagan nods.

There's no business name at the top, just the time and date of issue: 15 January 2017. 1:45 a.m.

"This was the morning your brother walked out?"

Reagan nods again, not looking at me.

Below the time and date, the receipt shows a "storage fee" of £67,000 as well as the itemized bill of interest and service charges that had allowed the original debt to mature into a total of £2.2 million. Fuck me. The fact that Miranda's prepared to pay says a lot about the questions hanging over Heydon's disappearance, but it's still crazy money. And the fact that Badwan's prepared to ask for it tells me he might have a screw loose too. At the bottom, in small print, there's contact details.

Need to talk, face-to-face? Just drop us a text and share location 🙂

The number's printed right next to it.

"And the money?" I say.

"Try not to concern yourself with the money, Mr. Lynch. Miranda's made up her mind to clear the debt and get the case back, so that's that."

"I'm just wondering why Bobbie's got a black eye," I say. "I mean, if Miranda was prepared to pay?"

"My sister tried to handle things herself. She stole some priceless items of Miranda's jewelry."

That explains the warm welcome from Miranda when I mentioned Bobbie's name.

"So what happened?"

"Badwan collected Bobbie. Then she says they just drove. Through town, at night. He was in the car with her. She said he wouldn't accept the stones."

If Badwan liked to keep things moving, then it complicated any potential surveillance operation. And the close confines of a car wouldn't leave me much room for maneuver either.

"How did she get the black eye?" I ask.

"She claims that once Badwan froze her out, she tried to score drugs and got mugged."

"You don't believe her?"

"Would you?"

"So you're saying there's more to it."

Reagan smiles tightly. "If there was, then she certainly wouldn't tell me. The first I knew of the whole thing, she was walking in late, wearing sunglasses. I asked where she'd been, what was wrong. She took off her shades, like, *happy now?*"

"What did you say?"

Reagan turns away, not wanting to tell me.

"I was shocked. But she showed me Badwan's receipt, and we took it to Miranda. Things are tense between my parents. But my father proposed that we employ the Rayner Group to make the payment, and for once, my mother agreed."

"Was Bobbie around for that conversation?"

I'm wondering how Bobbie might have reacted to the Rayner Group making the pickup. It seems like she'd risked an awful lot to try and get this stuff back quietly.

"No," Reagan says. "My sister wasn't present."

"What do you think she's hiding?"

Reagan doesn't answer, and it's clear that she won't speculate on what Bobbie's personal items are. But from the way Bobbie had gone behind her family's back and from the way she'd been dispatched to rehab right after, it's got to be something compromising.

"Well, you know what your mother wants," I say. "But I guess the choice is yours. With Rayner, you pay the money and get the case back. With me, you get the case and maybe something more."

Reagan watches me, weighing options. She can see I'm more of something all right.

"How come there aren't any pictures of Heydon here?" I ask, going for broke. Reagan looks at me. "The family snaps when you first walk in," I say. "It seems pointed to only have baby pictures."

"Mr. Lynch." Reagan frowns. "What could possibly be pointed about baby pictures?"

"I don't know," I say. "It feels like you're pinpointing the last moment he was still lovable."

"What a strange life you must lead," Reagan says after a moment. "I'm sorry to shoot down your theory, but the baby pictures aren't of Heydon at all," she says.

I'm not sure I believe her, just because of the way those pictures had been positioned, but I can't imagine why she'd lie.

"Miranda likes to be in control of when she sees Heydon," she goes on. "You can understand that, surely?"

"Of course," I say. "I'm just wondering if it's because they were close or…"

"Or what, Mr. Lynch?"

"Or if their relationship was more complicated."

I'm wondering if there was any significance in Heydon going to his father for money instead of Miranda. She's a forceful personality. I'd seen firsthand how she handled Reagan. Bobbie had preferred to steal from her than ask for help. And after that slipup, she'd been sent abroad.

Reagan's about to say something, but then there's a knock at the door. "There *are* pictures of my brother here," she says. "My parents had his room converted into a memorial. You'll excuse me?"

She goes to the door, where she has a brief, murmured conversation with the maid.

"I'm afraid my mother's exhausted from our meeting," Reagan says. "There are some things I'd like to discuss with her before she retires."

"Of course," I say.

"Perhaps you'd like something to eat or drink?"

"Sounds good."

"I'll ask Anya to call up from the kitchen."

She closes the door behind her, and I flip casually through some of the highlighted screenplays piled high on the desk. Then I take a seat, contemplating the middle distance while Miranda, Reagan, and Anya make their way back across the garden, none of them talking, all three looking up at the house. They enter through the lounge, and I wait until they're on their way up the stairs, then walk out of the study, listening close.

When she'd urged me to come here and rip off her parents, Bobbie had told me that her room was on the second floor. I walk quietly up the stairs. There's only one door leading off from the first floor. I can hear Miranda behind it. I go on, up to the second landing, past Bobbie's door to the next one, guessing it might be Heydon's.

I turn the handle and walk inside.

The room's been renovated from whatever it looked like before into a kind of memorial to him, as Reagan had said. It feels like something between a museum piece and an art installation. There are professionally framed pictures on the walls, glass cabinets containing personal items, and, in one corner, a messy desk, carefully designed to look like its owner just walked out.

The lamp's on, like he'll be back any minute. There's a large movie poster on the wall above it for a film I've never heard of called *Irma Vep*. It shows an iconic-looking woman wearing a black catsuit, standing against a dramatic cityscape, and it stands out as one of the few genuinely personal touches I can see.

The framed pictures chart Heydon's progress from child to adult, then right up until the week before he went missing. And I see that Reagan was telling me the truth. He's not the baby boy on the wall downstairs.

The photo of Bobbie sitting on his lap's the last one here, and I catch Heydon's troubled smile again. He'd looked like a pretty normal guy up until his late twenties. That's when the worry seemed to set in. Maybe six months to a year before Bobbie gave him the tattoo. Somehow, it's distinct from the physical strain he's under. You can see the effects of late nights and bad living, but there's something else. Four or five pictures from the end, in the months leading up to his disappearance, something just seemed to change in Heydon.

Suddenly, the light shifts, and I'm startled by my reflection in the glass.

"Did you find what you were looking for?"

I turn to the door and see Reagan standing there.

"Not exactly," I say. I can see that she's annoyed with me for walking off, for snooping around, so I go quickly on. "I mean, I'm not even sure what I am looking for. I just know it's not here."

"I don't understand," she says.

I motion at the room. The framed pictures, the gleaming display cases, the art installation desk.

"None of this stuff's real," I say.

Reagan frowns. "Of course it's real."

"It's stage-managed. It's a film set. Everything's been cleaned up and made nice."

"Well, what do you expect?"

"We were talking about their relationship before you were called away."

"Were we?" Reagan asks, her guard going back up.

The fact that she'd hesitated the first time makes me feel sure there's something there. "I think so," I say. "I asked if it was complicated."

"Between Miranda and Heydon? Of course. My brother could be difficult."

"Because these are the kinds of details that might inform my performance."

"Well, I don't deem them necessary," she says. "Heydon was taciturn in day-to-day life. He spoke as little as possible. I'll show you. He wasn't shy. He could even be rather intense. But mostly, he just watched people. Yes, he had some blowouts with my parents, but—"

"Blowouts about what?"

"I'm afraid you'd have to speak with them about that." Her eyes go to the pictures on the wall. "Tell me what you're thinking," she says, taking a step forward, staring at them as if for the first time in years.

"It's this one," I say, flicking a picture at random. Heydon on Carnaby Street, holding two shopping bags.

"What about it?" Reagan asks.

"Well, two questions first," I say, looking for a way to put her more at ease. I nod at the movie poster, and she turns to it. "What's that?"

"*Irma Vep?*" she says, looking even more vexed. "It's a cult film from the nineties, my brother's favorite."

"Weird title."

"It's an anagram of 'vampire,'" she says.

"Huh," I say, staring at it.

"You said you had two questions."

"Oh," I say. "Yeah, I was mainly wondering what Miranda said about me just now."

Reagan looks at me flatly.

"Come on, man. You must have talked about it. If we need this thing done by Sunday, then you need a new security team."

"I know that," she says. "And don't call me *man*."

I'm not wild about working with a security outfit, but they'll be handling the logistics of our surveillance operation, which could be considerable. Especially if Badwan insists on driving the entire time. If the team is good, then all I've got to think about is being Heydon Pierce. If they're rubbish, I'm on my own.

"It's a big job," I say.

Reagan looks at me.

"You've done this kind of thing before?"

It takes a moment to reach for the right answer.

"We're passing me off as your missing brother to try and coerce a murder confession," I say. "From what I can tell, no one's done this kind of thing before." I see this doesn't inspire much confidence, so I go on. "I've impersonated people," I tell her. "And I've worked surveillance. Solo and as part of a team."

"Stealing from people," she says.

"Well, only when they asked me nicely. And I'm no Rayner guy, but my guess is we're talking six cars and a couple of bikes. Air support if you're serious. Maybe a close protection team or two, depending on how much you like me."

She looks away.

"I'm saying it takes a lot of bad breath to do these things right. Especially with a moving target."

Reagan looks back at me for a moment.

"Miranda's speaking to a firm in Mayfair," she says. "She asked me to give you this." She passes me a card. "It's Miranda's cell. Her direct line. I'll need yours too." She hands me her phone, and I type it in. "So there you are. You're on. Now, what's Carnaby Street got to do with it?"

"Well," I say, going to the mirror, reexamining my shining suit. "I was just thinking that if I'm going to convince anyone, we might need to go shopping."

Reagan knows I'm not telling the truth, but her mouth sets into a firm straight line, and she calls my bluff.

"I'll fetch my things," she says.

8.

The car drops us on Piccadilly Circus, beneath the IMAX-size screen you see in the pictures. When we get out, there's a tribute to the queen filling the frame. Then an ad for classic Coke surges across it. Reagan leads us off the main drag into Soho, past family theaters and adult massage parlors as well as smut shops, gay bars, and jazz clubs. The people we pass on the street all look like the lead characters of their own TV shows.

On the ride over, Reagan had shown me some videos of Heydon from her phone. They were interesting for a sense of the way he moved, and I was pleased to hear that my strategy of imitating Bobbie's speech patterns had served me well with his voice. Although Heydon was quieter than that. *Quite intense*, as Reagan had said. I still can't connect with him though.

She takes us to the place where Heydon got his hair cut, a Turkish barber on Berwick Street. I'd taken pictures of the framed photographs from Heydon's wall before we left, and I show them to the barber. She agrees to cut my hair as close to the pictures as possible, slightly lengthening and updating Heydon's buzz cut style. I glance up and catch Reagan in the mirror, staring at the pictures as I scroll through them.

She looks quickly away.

It's only later, when I'm walking up and down in the sun-dappled showroom of a Savile Row tailor, demoing suits, that I feel Reagan looking at me. There's something weirdly personal about trying on clothes for someone you hardly know in an otherwise empty room. The tailor caters to an exclusive clientele, and the place has got the relaxed air of a gentleman's club.

Or so I imagine.

Reagan sits in one of the red leather armchairs, her legs crossed, watching, while the cutter explains how he needs to see me move to capture the full dynamic range of the suit, to make it feel like a second skin. I've never been professionally dressed before, and at first, I feel myself balking at the attention.

The tailor had kept Heydon's preferred styles and measurements on file, and it saves me a lot of questions I can't answer, about custom fabrics, pockets, pleats, and lapels. In the end, I'm wearing a slim, darker-than-navy-blue, single-breasted suit. When I show Reagan, she smiles, but my sense is she can't quite see it. She pays and arranges for the finished article to be sent to my hotel.

Later, once we've found some green contact lenses and moved on to the small, showroom-like stores where Heydon bought his day-to-day clothes, she broaches the subject with me.

"What were you really looking at?" she asks.

We're standing in line, waiting to pay for a couple of pairs of trousers, some shirts, T-shirts, and underwear.

"I'm sorry?"

"When I walked in on you in Heydon's room, staring at those

pictures on the wall. You asked me what changed in him before he walked out. What did you mean by that?"

We get to the front of the line and pay. Then we exit the shop with our bags, moving slowly down the street.

"Can I ask you one more question first?"

"Go on," she says shortly.

"If Bobbie wasn't mugged, then what happened to the jewels?"

"I assume that she used them to buy drugs."

Bobbie hadn't looked like she was coming off the kind of bender that priceless jewelry could buy. The bag of sugar says different too. But it feels like as much as I'm getting.

"Is your mother plotting some kind of comeback?" I ask, trying to find my way to something lighter.

"What makes you say that?"

"I thought I saw some scripts in the study."

Reagan bristles. "Do you make a habit of going through other peoples' things?"

"Well, kind of."

"Why shouldn't those screenplays belong to me?"

"Oh." I glance at her. "I'm sorry. I didn't realize you were an actress."

"Actor," she says. "You and the rest of the world."

"Tough gig?"

She blinks quickly, really not wanting to talk about it with me. "I've been afforded certain privileges in life, of course. But my mother casts a long shadow, especially on the stage." She flashes me a look. "I know what you're thinking. *Boo-hoo*, sad story."

"Not at all. I think—"

"My brother," she says, putting the walls back up. "You said one question, then you'd tell me what you saw inside his room."

I take out my phone. "It's no revelation," I say. "It just looks like something was happening in that last year. I don't know if it was in his head, if it was to do with these paranoid feelings, or what."

Reagan steps closer, and I scroll.

In the first of the pictures, he's sitting at some kind of family meal, glowing with money and boyish health but looking preoccupied with something, some problem that takes up his entire brain. In the next shot, standing in the garden with Bobbie, Heydon's straining to appear normal but looks scared of something. Not something right there and then. Something worse. He looks like he's stuck with some terrible secret, like he's being eaten alive by it. In the third, Heydon's visibly aged, permanently losing that sheen of youth, with broken veins around his nose, gray smudges underneath his eyes, and worry lines in his face. It looks like he's found out all his worst fears are true.

"Yes," Reagan says, seeing the same look I had.

"Bobbie told me he was bipolar," I say.

"He struggled for a time as a younger man," Reagan says, scratching her neck uncomfortably. "But I think that's quite normal while they're calibrating the dosage. As far as I knew, he lived a full, normal life until—"

"Who's the baby boy on the wall?" I ask.

Reagan stops walking, and I turn to her.

"What does that to do with..." She trails off and shakes her head. "Very well," she says. "Those pictures are of my baby brother, Theo. He drowned in a swimming accident when we were small."

"Right," I say. "I'm sorry, Reagan. That's awful."

"It was worse for Heydon," she says at length.

"Worse how?"

———

We find a café with street-side seating and order two coffees. Reagan stirs a succession of sugars and sweeteners into hers but doesn't drink it.

"My mother left them by the pool while she went upstairs to take a work call. A problem on set. She thought she'd be a minute at most. Heydon was ten. Theo was two. Heydon was supposed to be watching him."

"What happened?"

"Heydon was on a lounger, on his Game Boy, with his earphones in. He didn't realize Theo was in the water until it was too late."

"Then what?"

"Then a lifetime of recrimination," she says. "Heydon felt that the family blamed him, of course. At different times, I'm sure we all did. He certainly blamed himself. And after that, to some degree or another, he was out of control for the rest of his life."

"Out of control?" I ask.

"A tailspin of drink and drugs," she says. "Brushes with the law, bad debts, bad company, you get the picture. Miranda blamed my father for not being around, and he blamed her for the same thing."

"What about you?" I ask.

"What about me?" Reagan says, still stirring sugar into her cup.

With some sense of what Heydon was dealing with, I'll feel more comfortable slipping into his skin. In my mind, there's no way I could pass myself off as him without knowing something like that. But I can see why Reagan might feel differently.

"I know it can't be easy to talk about," I say. "But if we're serious about doing this, then I need your help."

She blinks. "What next?"

"That camera above the door at your folks' place…"

"What about it?"

"Was it there when he walked out? Have you still got the footage?"

"I mean, I suppose," she says. She tucks a strand of hair behind her ear. "I could probably dig it out."

At first, I think it's going to be like this all the way, that I'll have to fight her on everything, but then I see.

"If you don't feel comfortable watching—" I start.

"No," she says. "That's the point. I think I have to."

"OK," I say, glancing over her shoulder into the street. "I can…" I trail off, and she turns, following my gaze, then she looks back at me, frowning.

"What is it? You look like you've seen a ghost."

"No," I say. "But if you think you can find that footage, we should probably get on."

"OK," Reagan says, confused by my change of tone.

Her car service comes to collect us, and we head back to Tregunter Road with the shopping bags. I'd seen a black SUV. But it wasn't the one belonging to the Rayner Group. The car I'd seen had a different body shape altogether. It was right in front of me, sideways on, crawling past us on a parallel street. It had dark windows and a smashed wing mirror on the passenger side. Just like the one I'd seen Bobbie get into at the airport last night.

9.

When we get back to the house, Reagan sets about finding the CCTV footage from the night of Heydon's disappearance from the camera above the front door. She explains that the tape's been professionally archived as part of an appeal for information, then she turns the MacBook so it's facing me.

The footage is black and white, but the night-vision filter casts everything with a certain glow. It shows the doorstep as well as the driveway, and the time stamp says 1:05 a.m. Heydon bursts out of the house, wearing just his pajama bottoms and a T-shirt. He's not even wearing shoes. He freezes on the doorstep, seemingly afraid to go any farther, then he twists around, looking over his shoulder into the house. He's breathing hard, and he screws his eyes shut before turning back to the drive. Slowly, like he's forcing himself to take each individual step, he walks toward the two-seater sports car in front of the house, climbs inside, starts up, and leaves.

"What happened?" I ask.

"We don't know," she says. "He was in bed, asleep. As far as they knew, he was out cold from the sedative."

"Miranda was back by this time?"

Reagan nods. "I suppose my brother's tolerance for that kind of thing was higher than they thought." She slides the MacBook closer to me so I can start and stop the footage myself. I scroll back and go again. "It's a smart house," she says. "That means we'd usually know more. What time he turned his light on, if the fridge door was opened, etc. But there was some kind of power outage on the fifteenth. No data collected between midnight and 1:04 a.m."

I look at the time stamp on the screen again.

"He ran out of the house at five past one," I say.

"That's right."

"So what happened in that hour?"

"As far as my parents knew, nothing."

"They were the only ones around?"

"Bobbie was still in film school, and I was doing a show in town, on set the whole week."

"On set," I say, looking back at the screen. Even though there was footage of him leaving the house at 1:05 a.m., the power cut meant that Heydon could have easily taken things out to the car first, then staged his exit. "And as far as you know, he took nothing with him?" I ask.

"No clothes or bag. His laptop and phone were still plugged in."

I start the footage from the beginning and let it play through again.

"What are you looking for?" Reagan asks.

I pause it on Heydon, looking back at the house, frozen rigid with fear.

"I don't know," I say. "If it's there, I'm missing it."

"The look?" Reagan asks.

"No." I shake my head. "It's something else." I close the laptop. "We need a bigger screen."

———

Projected onto the private viewing screen in the basement, the footage loses some clarity. Not because the picture suffers but because the big screen makes the images look cinematic and unreal. The moment Heydon freezes and stares back at the house in particular looks like the jump scare from a horror film. Reagan shows me how to control the screen from her MacBook, and after watching the footage through a few times, I start pausing it, second by second, watching in freeze-frames. It's slow, absorbing work, and for a few minutes, the only sound in the room is the rhythmic tapping of my finger on the laptop, starting and stopping the footage. When we reach the moment where Heydon looks back at the house again, I pause it. The tendons in his neck are pulled so tight that they're visible on the screen. But it's lower down, on his pajama bottoms, where something becomes clear.

"There," I say, getting up and walking over. I point at his pocket. Reagan gets up and joins me. "You said his phone was still plugged in at home, so what's that?"

She's looking at me, half-lit by the projector, and she opens her mouth to say something when we both turn to a sound from the door. The shape of a large man. He walks slowly into the room, not looking at either one of us, just staring into the screen.

"Papa," Reagan says, stepping away from me. "We weren't expecting you until next week."

Ronnie Pierce is wearing a long greatcoat and matching scarf. He stops in front of the still image of a terrified, wide-eyed Heydon. When Ronnie raises a hand, reaching out to his son, I see he's still wearing driving gloves. He turns slowly from the screen and looks at Reagan.

"What is this?" he demands.

"Research," she tells him after a moment.

Ronnie walks right up to me, staring closely at my face in the half-light. The green contact lenses. "Hm," he says, walking away. He paces in front of the screen with both hands in his pockets. "And I suppose this research is to better inform Mr...."

"Lynch," I say.

"I suppose this research is to better inform Mr. Lynch's grotesque impersonation of my deceased son." He turns on me. "No answer to that?"

"I didn't hear the question," I say.

"Are you planning to impersonate Heydon?"

"That was the idea."

"Yes," says Ronnie. "Well, I'm afraid you'll just have to think again. Reagan, sweetheart." He never takes his eyes off me. "I think you're about finished for the day."

"I—" she starts, glancing at me.

"*Now!*" he bellows, turning to her.

Reagan hesitates for a second, then walks out.

Once she does, Ronnie turns to me, watching for a long moment. At first, I think he won't say anything, but he seems to sense something that needs to be handled.

"Five years ago, my son took his own life," he says. "It's not a fact I'm proud of, simply one I've come to accept. I thought that my wife had come to accept it as well. Perhaps at one time, she had. But an unexpected side effect of Miranda's failing health is that she's found herself questioning things she used to believe in." He runs a hand through his hair. "No doubt she mentioned me."

"Not really," I say.

He goes on as if I haven't spoken. "She's questioning me, questioning her daughters, even questioning Heydon. She's losing her grip."

"I'm sorry if that's the case, Mr. Pierce, but it's not the situation here—"

"Some blackmailer appears out of nowhere, with new evidence, after all this time?" He shakes his head. "Why, even six months ago, she'd have seen through it. But then I'm afraid that's the way with his kind," he says, glaring. "They all turn up at once, sniffing blood."

"He's not exactly a blackmailer," I say, ignoring the part about me. "He's a kind of loan shark. From what I hear about Heydon, it sounds like that's in line with his behavior. Then there's Bobbie's involvement too."

"Yes," Ronnie says. "How was Bobbie? No doubt she really had some things to say about me."

I haven't got the heart to break it to him.

"I think you know that this is for real, Mr. Pierce. So why are you pretending otherwise?"

Ronnie looks sharply up, then he catches himself and smiles. He watches me closely as he takes off his gloves. "Don't read too much into the symbolism of this gesture," he says, smiling, but I can see that he's frustrated with me. I'm supposed to take what he says as fact. "I won't deny you have a certain…*street* likeness to my son," he says at length. "It's one of the things I find objectionable about you. In any event, I've already paid Mr. Rayner's retainer. His boys can deal with Badwan. I'd suggest that you collaborate, but I'm told that his organization intimidates you."

"It's the Bluetooth earpieces," I say just as Mike appears in the doorway. "I keep thinking they're about to break into song."

"How amusing," Ronnie says, turning and walking out. "Perhaps you should make it a duet? Needless to say, we shan't be requiring your services. Good day, Mr. Lynch."

———

Mike marches us up the stairs, me in front, him behind. I know as soon as we're outside we'll be joined by his colleagues, but there's not much I can do about that right now. When we get to ground, almost all the lights are out, and I guess that Anya's left for the day. Reagan too. Miranda must have retired for the night.

Mike takes us to the front door and opens it.

"Don't move," he says, looking at me seriously.

I nod, and he steps through to confer with his colleagues, waiting on the driveway, drawing the door to behind him. I immediately turn and walk into the lounge, then through it to the french window, then out into the black back garden.

I move through the long grass to the wall, then climb over into the next garden, working my way around the motion sensor lights. The garden after that's in total darkness, in the middle of some major redevelopment works. I edge around the crater where the new hot tub's going, then climb on top of a pallet filled with building supplies, go over the wall, and get off Tregunter altogether, cutting through a garden square to the underground. It's dark, gone ten, and the streetlights are throwing wild shadows off the trees. I make the eleven-minute walk in five, hyperaware that Mike must be looking for me by now.

Turning into Earl's Court, I dig out my Oyster card. Then I hear tires screech outside and lower my head, pushing through people to the barrier. There's a guard there, but when I glance over my shoulder, I see two guys in suits scanning the crowd, then

Mike, standing in the doorway. I roll over the barrier, hearing the guard shout after me, then throw myself down the escalator, into the station, shouting at the people in front to move.

I split up a kissing couple at the bottom and break left onto the first platform I see. A train just arrived, and luckily for me, it's busy. The train's past capacity, and most people can't get on. I push through them, head low, glancing back and seeing Mike stagger onto the platform, red-faced. We lock eyes, and he starts pushing through the crowd toward me. I force my way onto the packed train, feeling sweaty hands pressing into my skin, taking a lot of hostility, turning just in time to see the doors slide shut in Mike's face. I'm packed in too tight to give him the finger, so he gets a nice smile instead.

When we start moving, I breathe a hot sigh of relief, feeling the crazy sweat coursing down my back. I change at the next station, then change again.

I go aboveground into a dark, station-adjacent boozer, sitting by someone's half-finished drink. I need to get off the street somehow, but even though Reagan's booked me a hotel room, I know it's the first place they'll look. I could try and get in touch with her, but she might want to talk me out of what I'm about to do.

Nine times out of ten, when they try and scare you off, it means you're onto something. I just can't say what. If Heydon really did need that money to save someone's life, then whose? And what were these "personal items" he'd handed over as collateral? Why did Bobbie try and get them back on her own? And how did she end up with a black eye? Most of all, I'm wondering what Mr. Badwan can tell me about Heydon's disappearance.

I take out my phone and input the number I'd seen for Badwan. I've got a pretty good memory, but in this case, I've made it infallible by stealing the receipt that Reagan showed me. I send him a WhatsApp message, saying my name's Heydon Pierce, that I'd like to meet him as soon as possible. I feel a reinvigorating jolt of fear, then share location. I get an almost immediate response.

20 minutes, it says.

10.

The engine's so quiet that the only sound comes from the tires, turning slowly on wet tarmac. It's an electric black cab. The *Taxi* light on the roof glows yellow, even though I can make out two figures sitting in the back. I can feel them watching me as I cross the street, but I don't break stride. I just walk, with all my senses turned right up to ten. I take hold of the handle and open the door.

The guy's a bearish European, wearing a dark, nondescript suit and an omnipotent, all-knowing look. He's somewhere in his midfifties, and he watches me with hooded black eyes. The woman looks shocked silent by something he's said, and she's so lost in thought that she doesn't look up when I open the door. I'd received a WhatsApp message, sharing location. A back alley, five streets over. Just three words. *Come out now.*

I'm not sure what to expect from Badwan, and maybe that's why I can't remember the walk over here. Most likely, the last time they'd met, Heydon had been wearing pajamas. He'd been running from something or maybe toward it—apparently trying to save someone's life. The full details of their arrangement aren't clear, but Heydon had handed over personal items belonging to both him and Bobbie and received a loan of £67,000. Whether they'd had any other dealings remains to be seen.

For all I know, Badwan had Heydon killed.

I just grip the door handle and stare into the cab.

It feels like I'm interrupting, and for a second, I think I've gotten the wrong car. Neither the man nor the woman says anything though, so I climb inside, taking a seat with my back to the driver, facing them. When I close the door, the man's in total darkness, but I can feel his eyes on me. The woman grips her seat belt tightly. The car starts up, and we drive. When the doors lock automatically, it hits me for the first time that no one knows I'm here.

━━━

We drive in silence for a few minutes, taking narrow backstreets, a route likely calculated to keep the car out of sight and to keep me disoriented. When lights from outside sweep across the man's face, I see he's looking absently out the window, making it clear he's not ready for me yet. At length, we pull into a large, unusually quiet city square, and I wonder if we're in the City itself, the financial district. Ronnie Pierce country. A postcode so hot, not even Londoners can afford to live here. It's long after hours, and all the grand streets have emptied out.

The driver parks in one of several vacant spaces in the shadow of a great, white-stoned church or cathedral at the center of the square. It's enormous, several stories high, but this close, with no streetlights, it just means we're sitting in a solid black shadow. A few minutes pass, then I see the headlights from a second cab, drifting toward us out of the dark. It parks up in the next bay. The man leans across the woman and opens her door.

She closes her eyes.

"I'm afraid our time's up," he growls.

I'm not sure which one of us he's talking to, but the woman reluctantly unclicks her seat belt and climbs out. When the door opens, the light comes on, and she looks back for a second, speechless with fear.

"*Good night*," the man says, pulling the door shut. After that, she's in the dark. She gets into the other cab, then they start up and drive. And now I can feel the full focus of the man turning on me. A peal of bells rings out from the church, echoing through the otherwise silent square. I wait a minute, letting them play out.

"Shall we get this show on the road?" I ask.

———

My Heydon Pierce is malnourished and lockjawed. He's squinting and frazzled. Some of those decisions have been made for me; I'm working with what I've got. But there's something about Heydon's character I'm leaning into as well. I'm wearing my short hair mussed up, my Heydon street clothes wrinkled. The top two buttons are missing from my shirt. It feels like about the right balance. Badwan doesn't say anything until his driver's started up again, until we've pulled out and started winding through the backstreets.

The doors lock automatically.

"How can I help?" he asks.

There's so much gravel in his voice that I have to fight the urge to clear my own throat. There's no clue in his form of address whether he's prepared to accept me as Heydon Pierce or not and no introduction at all. But I feel safe in the assumption that this is Mr. Badwan. And safe in the assumption that that's probably not his real name.

"I think we both know why I'm here," I say, tight and controlled with just a hint of suppressed arrogance.

"No," Badwan says, laughing sportingly. "Truly not." But those closed-circuit television eyes never switch off.

"I'm here to close my account," I say. "What else?"

"May I see your receipt?"

"What if I haven't got it?"

Badwan tuts at me.

"Then I'm afraid that I cannot help," he says. "I need the unique transaction code to cross-reference your case with my own personal records. I'm sure you understand."

"So if I had it, we'd be cool?" I say. Badwan inclines his head ever so slightly. "Oh." I put my hand in my pocket. "You mean this."

When I hand it over, Badwan smiles, just for a second. Then his gaze turns inward, reviewing his records. "The Pierce account," he says. "We've opened that file once already this week."

"So I saw," I say.

Badwan waits for me to go on.

"My sister's black eye," I say. "She had it when she came back from seeing you."

I'd been testing the water, wanting to see how he'd react to me calling Bobbie my sister, but he skips that part.

"Did she now?" he says, more interested in the fact that I seem to hold him responsible. "Tell me, is this why you came here? Because you believe—"

"I just want my stuff back," I say.

When the light crosses Badwan's face again, I see that he's smiling. "*Your* stuff?" he says.

It's not clear if he's calling me a fake or just saying that Heydon's case is his property until the debt's paid.

One reason I'd decided to take a chance on this was because I hadn't totally agreed with Miranda's thinking. From the moment I'd first seen a picture of Heydon, I'd been struck by the weight of whatever burden it was he'd been carrying, and it went some way toward convincing me that he had taken his own life. Everything I'd seen since just reinforced it. His mental health problems, the paranoia he'd been wrestling with, the fact of his car on that bridge. Even the tattoo seemed to suggest he hadn't been thinking long-term in those last months.

But the real reason I'd taken a chance on Badwan was because loan sharks aren't usually killers. As a rule, they prefer to advertise, turning bad clients into walking public service announcements. Or limping ones. Murder's bad for business, and the sharks I'd known lived for cash.

But Badwan seems like a totally different breed. I can tell that he enjoys sliding through the night like this, moving from one cab to another, dealing secrets and lies. He's not quite as fascinated by money as the rest of them though. Badwan's all about owning people.

"Some kind of problem?" I ask.

"The main one is that you don't seem to have two point two million pounds on your person," he says.

"Got a phone?"

Badwan reaches inside his jacket pocket and hands me one. I dial the number that Reagan had given me for Miranda. It rings for one minute. Then two.

I glance at Badwan, then put it on speakerphone, holding the handset between us obnoxiously, daring him to tell me that my time's up.

The call goes to voicemail.

Badwan releases a long breath through his nose.

I share a look with him and redial. It rings for one minute, then two. The call goes to voicemail for a second time. I disconnect immediately, just smiling down at the phone now. I shake my head, wait a second, and redial.

"Hello?" Miranda says hazily.

"Yeah, Miranda," I say, careful to make sure that my accent stays inside the pocket of hers.

"Who is this?"

"Who do you think?" I roll my eyes at Badwan. "You made such a big deal about Bobbie getting a black eye that I thought I'd better come and sort it myself. Happy now?"

Badwan's watching me closely.

"Earth to Miranda," I say. "I'm sitting here with a scary guy on a dark street who's not letting me go until we pay up." I wink at Badwan. "You've got the cash, so why are you being such a fucking bitch?"

Miranda doesn't say anything.

"Fine," I say. "But something tells me I'll be gone a lot longer than five years this time."

Badwan glances out the window.

"I won't pay anything so absurd as two point two," Miranda says briskly. "You might be a fool, Heydon, but I'm not."

"Miranda," I say quickly. "This isn't the time to—"

"And I take it that your sister's things are included?"

I glance up at Badwan. He shakes his head.

Then he leans in and whispers it to me.

"Badwan says Bobbie got her stuff back already," I say, trying not to show my surprise.

There's a brief silence while Miranda computes it.

"All the more reason he should do something on the price," she says finally. "I'll stretch to one and no further."

Badwan doesn't move. There's just the low hum of the car, moving through the backstreets.

"I don't think you're getting this—" I start.

"No, Heydon, it's you who's misunderstood," Miranda says, sounding like she's talking to her real son instead of me. "You've depreciated in value." I let out an involuntary, hollow laugh. "*Badwan*," Miranda says, raising her voice. "You've heard the terms of my counteroffer. Kindly take them or leave them."

Badwan smirks blackly for a moment, then nods.

"You're on," I say, not breaking eye contact with him.

"Send Reagan the details," Miranda says.

——

We drive in silence for a few minutes until Badwan gets some kind of invisible signal that the transfer's been successful. Then he leans forward, talking to the driver.

"Next exit," he says.

The driver speeds up, moving with precision. He pulls into the courtyard of some kind of office building. There's another black cab there, idling in a parking bay. We pull alongside it, and Badwan opens the door.

"You'll find your key inside the car," he says.

"My key for what?"

Badwan watches me, then glances at the clock.

"You may want to hurry," he says. "Your collection window closes at midnight."

"What happens then?"

"The case is simply returned to deep storage." He smiles.

"However, another window might not open for days or weeks. I have no tolerance for the prospect of my archives being exposed. In these circumstances, of course, there would be an additional storage fee."

"Say no more."

I climb out of his cab and cross the courtyard to the next one. When I open the door, a silver key catches the light on the back seat. I look back at Badwan, but his car's already starting up and pulling out. I hesitate for a second, then climb into mine.

———

I ask where we're going, but the guy up front doesn't answer; he just starts the engine and drives. The doors lock automatically, and we head out of the city, getting on the motorway, going in the opposite direction of town. The road signs I see suggest we're on our way out to Heathrow, but mainly I'm watching the clock. Badwan said I had until midnight, and it's 11:51 p.m. now. I'm about to say something when the driver takes an exit, coming off the motorway, pulling onto an industrial estate, past the forecourt of a monolithic multistory cube with neon yellow detailing on the exterior. A self-storage facility but clearly locked down, long out of hours. The driver cuts the engine, and we sit in silence for a moment.

"What now?" I ask.

He doesn't say anything.

I look at the clock, see I've only got four minutes left, then swipe the key off the back seat and climb out. As soon as I shut the door behind me, the cab starts up and drives away.

I'm standing beside the staff entrance to the perimeter wall of the self-storage site. When I push against the door, it swings open.

There's a short, floodlit path leading to a fire exit at the rear of the facility. I go along it, glancing up at a wall of unlit windows. When I reach the exit, I can see a crack of light running down the far side of the door, and when I get closer, I see it's been propped open with an empty pack of cigarettes. There's no time to think, so I push it and step into a garishly lit concrete corridor, back of house, following it to another door at the far end, through into the commercial space. I'm standing in a long, double-wide corridor with corrugated steel walls and numbered bright yellow doors lining both sides.

I can feel the seconds counting down, and I look at the key ring, seeing it's for door 117. I'm standing right by room 101, and I start walking fast. When I come to the door, I put the key into the padlock and pull it apart. The room's no larger than a wardrobe, and the only thing inside's a black flight case with wheels on the bottom.

I go to lift it and almost throw out my back.

I roll the case out of the room, close the door, relock it, and walk. Then I hear someone whistling, coming down the corridor behind me. I heave the case up under my arm so it won't make a sound, then retrace my steps as quietly as I can, half running until I'm around the corner. I find my way back to the fire exit, walk out, kick the cig packet away, and let the door fall shut behind me. Then I go down the path, through the staff entrance, out of the perimeter gate, and on to the road, where I slam the case down heavily, getting my breath back.

When I walk back up to the motorway, I can see waves of head-lights coursing out of the blackness. I watch them for a minute, flowing past, flying on into the dark. Then I turn and start walk-ing back toward the city, dragging Heydon's flight case behind me.

11.

The waitress sets a stainless-steel coffee pot down on the table, then asks if there's anything else that I need. I'd arrived at the hotel in the early hours of the morning after thumbing a ride back into town with the case. I'd been walking for a while when someone finally took mercy on me and pulled over, a young couple in a rented white van. There was no room up front, but they'd offered me the three square feet of space in the back, between all their boxed-up stuff, and I'd gladly accepted.

The Mandarin's a five-star hotel in Knightsbridge, with views over Hyde Park. Six stories of Edwardian red brick. A lot more legroom than I'd had in the van. A short flight of white stone steps led up to a grand entranceway where a top-hatted doorman had welcomed me warmly. *Rather splendid*, as Reagan had said.

I'd been expecting some ice when I walked through the door, but the night manager had found my reservation and handed over the key to 401 without incident. Then he'd pressed the bell on the counter, and a flat-nosed porter with cauliflower ears had appeared out of nowhere.

"My *colleague* can assist you with your luggage," the manager had said, not quite meeting my eye.

"I'm traveling light," I'd told him. "Thanks anyway."

The manager had glanced over my shoulder at the porter with something like fear in his eyes. For some reason, they must have been expecting me to walk in with a case. I'd crossed the lobby and pressed for the lift. When the doors opened, the mirror lining the back wall showed the night manager and the porter, staring at me. I'd turned, smiled back, and pressed for the fourth floor. The room was a beautiful executive suite with an adjoining lounge. I'd called down to the front desk, asking for a phone charger from the lost property, and a bellboy had brought one up. After that, I'd dragged the heaviest pieces of furniture in front of the two entrances, taken out my contact lenses, and gone to bed.

They'd knocked on the door at eight a.m. with the new suit. It had been meant for my meeting with Badwan, but I'd put it on and gone down for breakfast. Scrambled eggs, bacon, toast. Two pots of coffee and a pile of newspapers. I'd turned past the queen, through the energy crisis, to the Ukrainian counteroffensive, occasionally looking up at the immaculately suited traveling businessmen. The five-star families with fat kids in designer clothes, traveling with au pairs and live-in nannies, the mums and dads, scrolling through Instagram on blinged-out gold iPhones, bored out of their minds. When the waitress seats a smartly dressed man at the next table, I can tell from his tight smile that he's seen the tattoo, that he doesn't think I belong here, but I go back to my coffee, back to my news.

It's a little after nine a.m. when Ronnie walks in. He stands in the doorway for a moment, scanning the room, then he locks eyes with me and walks over. The girl on the front desk says something to him, smiling politely, but the girl on the front desk might as well be dead.

"May I?" he asks, gesturing to the free seat opposite.

"Please."

He plucks each finger of his calfskin driving gloves off, then drops them on the table, sitting heavily, his coat still on. "This won't take long," he says. "We got off on the wrong foot last night. I didn't take you seriously. I see now that I should have."

It's probably as close as someone like him can come to an apology, so I don't force it.

"No harm done," I say.

He watches me shrewdly, and I get another glimpse at the operator in Ronnie Pierce.

He lets out a heavy sigh and gets frank.

"As I alluded to last night, the last five years have been the most sustained period of anguish imaginable for me. Although perhaps I should have elaborated. A missing person isn't like any other kind of loss," he says. "Quite simply, it never ends. You can see why we're so haunted."

I look at him for a second, then nod.

"Naturally, if I could have borne their pain for them, I would," he continues. "But the final indignity of Heydon's disappearance has been watching my family tear itself apart. Bobbie, in and out of treatment facilities, in and out of bad relationships." He pauses, then goes on gravely. "In and out of her mind. Reagan frozen to the spot by it all. Unable to step out from her mother's shadow. And then there's Miranda," he says, looking at me. "Diminished. Worn down. Less of her with each passing day."

"Then there's you," I say.

Ronnie twitches like I'm talking out of turn, then he catches himself, looking thoughtful.

"True enough. I'm not what I was either."

"Ronnie, if you're here to pull the thorn out of my side, then I'm the one who's sorry. I've got a thick skin."

"You certainly keep a cool head," Ronnie says with a smile. "I can see why my wife—"

"But if this is about the case, then you can't have it."

The smile freezes. "Where is it?" he demands. When I just sit there, looking back at him, he goes on. "My wife placed a great deal of trust in you."

"Which is why I'm not handing that case over to anyone but her."

"Tell me where it is," he says, leaning forward, waving my objections out of the air. "Tell me where it is right now, and there's a chance this won't have to hurt."

"I honestly don't know."

"Excuse me?"

"Well, I knew I couldn't bring it back here," I say. "Not with the smooth operators you've got on the payroll. So I left it with some friends."

Ronnie smiles down at the table.

"My smooth operators were given to understand that you were new in town."

"Some Polish kids picked me up last night."

Ronnie squints. "I don't follow."

"I left the case in the back of their van. Buried in all their stuff. They didn't even know it was there."

I glance over his shoulder and see the flat-nosed porter from last night, lingering in the doorway.

"Where did you find a uniform that big so late in the day?" I ask, nodding over Ronnie's shoulder at the guy. He turns stiffly and looks at the man. "Does he still get to keep it if I walk out of here?"

"I don't know what you're talking about," Ronnie says, turning back to me.

"Yeah, me neither. I wouldn't go too crazy trying to find those Poles, by the way. Now I think of it, they might have been Albanian."

Ronnie smiles with absolutely no pleasure.

"Your agreement with my wife," he says.

"Twenty-five," I tell him.

"And these Good Samaritans of yours?"

"I got their phone number so I could thank them."

Ronnie nods with comprehension, then takes out a beige-brown checkbook from Coutts Bank as well as a silver ballpoint pen.

"So how about I give you my number," he says, making a check out for fifty thousand pounds, signing it with a flourish. "And you give me yours."

He holds out the pen.

I look back at him for a few seconds, then take it, writing the number down on a napkin and sliding it across the table. Ronnie takes out his phone and dials, watching me while he holds the handset to his ear.

Then he frowns.

"It's disconnected."

"Shit. I really should have written it down."

"You fool," he growls. "You've fu—"

"Those are the right numbers," I tell him. "They must just be in the wrong order."

He makes a sound almost like laughter, but when I look up, it seems more like Ronnie's struggling to breathe.

"I'm sorry for your loss," I say. "If I can help in any way, I will. But Miranda hired me to get that case and take it back to her."

"That doesn't work for me," Ronnie grumbles.

"Well, that's how it is," I say, making to stand.

Ronnie bangs a fist on the table, turning heads. "What makes you think you're going anywhere, *Lynch*?"

We stare at each other for a few seconds.

"OK," I say. "Sound. The guy you've got on the next table's sitting too close." I nod at the man who'd given me the tight smile on his way in, showing Ronnie the steak knife in my hand. "So he just lost the sight in his right eye."

The man pretends not to hear me, but I see him stiffen and sit a little straighter. Then I lift the lid on the coffee pot, letting some steam out.

"How do you take it, Ronnie? Because, right now, I'm thinking directly to the face."

Ronnie sits back, watching queasily.

"Then it's just me and the big guy," I say, nodding at the far door, twenty feet away, where, for some reason, that porter's still hovering. Only now, he's not even pretending. He's just looking me dead in the eyes.

"And what about the ones in the lobby?" Ronnie says, folding his arms. "What about the ones on the door?"

"Well, that's where it gets interesting. The problem you've got is I'd cut up a family of five to walk out of here." I wait until his eyes meet mine. "Touch me, and I'll paint the fucking room red, Ronnie. That goes double for the guys on the door."

When the words leave my mouth, I really mean them. I know that's the only way they'll work. Ronnie's friends are here to try and press me into a room or a car, some corner where they can finesse the case out of me. They're prepared for some strong-arm stuff to get me there, of course. But the rules of their stupid game say that no one makes a scene, and I'm not playing.

"You're bluffing," Ronnie says, smiling rigidly.

"Only one way to find out," I say, getting up before he can react. Ronnie calls after me, but I walk through the room without looking back, my heart beating double-time. I'm still holding that steak knife, and I give the porter a really good look at it on my way past him. I walk into the hallway and through the lobby, grinning at the manager I'd seen last night, watching the blood drain from his face. Then I walk out of the building, down the white stone steps, and onto the busy street. The guys on the door don't do shit.

12.

The Athenaeum's a symmetrical white-brick building, a monster, taking up an entire city block just off St. James's Park on Pall Mall, the road that leads to Piccadilly Circus. The fact that you could place Miranda's private members' club on a Monopoly board says something about how long it's been here. There's a pillared entranceway as well as a life-size golden statue of a woman with a spear standing on top of it. Athena, at a guess. A suited doorman bounds down the steps, offering to carry the case for me.

"I've got it," I tell him a little too forcefully.

"Very well, sir," the man says, taken aback.

Inside, the club looks like a palace, with gleaming stone floors and walls. Marble columns with gold-leaf detailing line the way to a grand staircase, one you could probably drive a tank down.

I give my name at the front desk, telling them that Miranda Pierce is expecting me. Everyone stands up a little straighter, and I'm led to the grand staircase, which I see branches off both left and right. There's a marble statue at the top of the first flight, a guy wearing a gold leaf over his junk, pointing left. We follow the statue's lead up another flight, while the man from the front desk fills me in on the club's history. He says it was founded in 18-something by two men whose names I'm supposed to know, that more than fifty members have won a Nobel Prize. I'm just watching where I'm going. I'm just thinking about the case.

The drawing room's so much like the ones I've seen on prestige TV shows that I guess a few of them must have been filmed here. We walk under glowing chandeliers, past dark-wood bookcases crammed with weighty, leather tomes, through tables and chairs filled with well-dressed men and women, some reading newspapers, some making conversation. I'm taken to a private room where I find Miranda, Reagan, and another woman, all waiting for me. Reagan starts when I walk through the door.

Both Reagan and Miranda look pale and thin—even more so than usual—like they haven't eaten or slept since we last spoke. The third woman, the one I haven't met before, looks Southeast Asian. Formally dressed, not personally involved, clearly some kind of professional.

"You're late," Reagan says.

I look at the clock on the wall. It's a little after two.

"I had to make sure I wasn't being followed."

Reagan frowns. "Followed? Followed by who?"

"Ronnie came to see me this morning," I say.

Reagan's eyes go to the door. "My father?"

"There was a guy from the Rayner Group waiting for me when I got back to the hotel last night. Your dad turned up with a few more of them this morning."

"But," Reagan starts, shaking her head. "Then…"

"I never took the case back to the hotel with me," I say. "I knew it wouldn't have been safe there."

"And my father just let you leave?"

"We talked it out," I say.

She stares at me for a moment.

"You're certain that you weren't followed?"

"Ms. Pierce—" I start.

"It's Reagan."

"Reagan," I say. "Well, from the chat I had with your old man this morning, it sounds like he's highly motivated to get this case." I glance at Miranda, who still hasn't said anything. "If he knew where I was, he wouldn't have let me walk into the building."

"No," Reagan says, nodding to herself. "I suppose not." Her eyes go to the case. "Have you opened it?"

"Course not," I say, setting the heavy case down on its wheels and giving it a little push toward them. The woman I haven't met before puts on a pair of latex gloves, then takes the case and quietly leaves the room through a second door. I take her for some kind of private-hire security or forensics expert. Once the door closes, Reagan lets me have it.

"What you did last night was incredibly reckless," she starts. "Not at all in the spirit of our agreement. If something had happened to you—"

"If something had happened to me, you'd hire the next guy and pretend we'd never met," I say. She looks shocked. "Reagan, that's what I'm here for."

I turn my head to the muffled banging sounds coming from next door. No one else acknowledges them.

"We are grateful," Miranda says, speaking finally. When she does, it almost feels like I've never heard her voice before. Either her health's deteriorated even further in the night, or sending me to Badwan took more out of her than she'd like to admit. "My husband had no right to send you away last night."

The banging sounds break off, and so does she.

"When I called, I wondered if he might have talked you out of it," I say.

"You certainly like to take chances, Mr. Lynch."

"I thought that's what I was being paid for."

"Well, you're safe on those terms at least," Miranda says. "My husband and I haven't exchanged so much as a word since Heydon left."

"You haven't spoken in five years?"

"That's correct."

"You live together," I say slowly.

She doesn't respond, but when I glance at Reagan and see the exhaustion in her face, I know that Miranda's telling me the truth.

"Well," I say. "Either way. Thanks for coming through for me. I wasn't sure you'd even pick up. The haggling was a nice touch too."

"You're not the only one with ice in your veins, Mr. Lynch," Miranda says. "I don't share my daughter's dismay at your intervention. You're still satisfied with the terms of our agreement?"

"Of course," I say.

She nods at Reagan, who gets up and hands me a sealed envelope. I can feel a bank card inside it.

"It's one of the household accounts," Reagan says, not looking at me. "You'll find the code in there. As well as instructions on how to transfer the cash to an account of your choosing, once you're... able to do so. Your fee has been paid in full."

I can see that Reagan's uncomfortable with this transaction, but I can't tell if it's personal or if she just feels morally compromised by it on some level. I'm about to thank her when there's a knock at the door. The woman from before opens it, nodding at Reagan.

"You'll excuse me," she says, looking glad to go. When she walks out of the room, it's just me and Miranda.

"Mr. Badwan," Miranda says significantly.

I take the seat opposite her.

"He kept his cards pretty close to his chest," I say. "When we met, he was careful not to call me by name. And when I pressed him on Bobbie's black eye—"

"You pressed him?" Miranda says.

"Just gently. I referred to Bobbie as my sister, and he didn't correct me."

"And then?"

"I don't know," I say, going over it again in my head. "He barely moved until he heard us on the phone."

"Then what did he do?" Miranda asks.

"When I told you I'd be gone a lot longer than five years this time, he glanced out at the street." Miranda watches me, weighing my words for value. "I wouldn't read so much into it, except it was more or less the only time he moved in our entire conversation."

"So you think he was involved."

"I don't know," I say. "He didn't seem any more psychotic than your average thriving businessman." I wait until I'm sure it's landed. "It doesn't necessarily follow that he's involved in Heydon's murder. The case felt like another asset to him. He's one of those walking spreadsheet kind of guys. Everything gets compartmentalized and put in boxes. Even people."

"You couldn't…see through him?" she asks.

"Honestly, what I saw was the kind of person who'd let things play out either way."

Miranda looks hollowed out by my lack of any real answer, and she stares into nothing for a moment, like she's counting the seconds she's got left.

"Was there anything else?" she asks absently.

The last stand-out memory was my impression that Badwan was surprised to hear that I held him responsible for Bobbie's black eye. In the moment, it had been more important to maintain my cover by acting flip, to change the subject like I couldn't care less. But something about it makes me uncomfortable now, and I realize I'm carrying the detail around with me like a stone in my shoe. I don't know what it means though, so I shake my head.

"That's all I can think of," I say.

Miranda's watching me, about to say something more, when the second door bursts open and Reagan walks through. She doesn't stop, just goes straight for the exit, then out, like she's about to be sick.

The woman I'd taken for some kind of private-hire security expert appears.

"We're in," she says.

"I could have stamped on that case for you five minutes ago," I say.

"Not the case." She looks at Miranda. "Mrs. Pierce, you might want to see this."

———

Miranda tries to stand, and I help her to her feet. It's not entirely charitable. Technically, my job's done here. She'd hired me to assume her son's identity for one night, to approach Mr. Badwan and bring back the case, alongside any impressions he'd made on me. That's what I'd done. And I'd been well paid for it too. But after seeing Reagan's reaction, I need to know what's inside that case. If that means I'm in the room as a crutch, then that's fine by me.

The windowless office next door's been set up like a lab. The case is on a metallic work surface that looks alien against the oak-paneled walls. Two guys wearing white Tyvek suits, overshoes, and gloves are cataloging its contents, talking softly into a tape recorder. I can't see what they've found, but there's dust and gravel from a broken concrete block on the floor.

Like something had been set inside it.

The woman leads us to a desk, then looks between Miranda and me, hesitating. Her eyes go to the tattoo.

Miranda shakes her head. "It's quite all right, Miss…"

"*Lao*," the woman says, not for the first time today.

"Yes, of course. Well, it's quite all right, Miss Lao. Mr. Lynch has been assisting the family."

"Very well. My colleagues are still processing the case, but I thought you'd want to know about the phone."

"You've found it?" I ask, surprised.

"Inside a Faraday cage," she says, lifting the broken remains of a metallic black box from her desk. She looks at Miranda and me, sensing that she needs to elaborate. "It prevents electronic signals from getting in or out. Then it was encased in a block of cement for good measure."

"Can you get the phone working?" I ask.

"We've broken the passcode," Miss Lao says easily.

I feel Miranda's grip tightening on my arm.

"So what's on there?" I ask.

——

We sit at the table, and I see what I take to be Heydon's second phone—the one he'd had in his pocket when he left the house— plugged into some kind of console, attached to Miss Lao's computer. There's a screen set up to show Miranda and me what she's doing. It shows a blown-up version of the default home page for an iPhone. Miss Lao opens the gallery app, displaying one saved video. The still image shows Heydon, looking dangerously thin, with what appear to be permanent black marks underneath his eyes from lack of sleep. It's four minutes, twenty-seven seconds long, and it was recorded on 14 January 2017.

The day before he went missing.

"You've watched it?" I ask.

"Most," Miss Lao says. "I'm afraid that Ms. Pierce found it distressing. If you feel—"

"Play it," Miranda says.

Miss Lao selects the video and presses play. Heydon's staring into the phone's camera. He places the handset on a raised surface, facing himself, and I see that he's sitting in the lower ground-level lounge at his parents' house. It's dark out, and the room's lit by a single lamp. Once he's happy with the phone's position, he sits back.

"My name is Heydon Pierce, and I'm making this recording on the fourteenth of January, 2017." Heydon looks over his shoulder, around the room, like he's caught a glimpse of something. Then he remembers himself and turns back to the camera. "I'm of sound mind. Though by no definition other than my own. And I'm making this recording because tomorrow's the most exciting day of my life."

He breaks into an exhausted smile, and I see the shadow of all those haunted photographs in his face.

"I think I can bring us back together," he says. "I think I can fix everything. But I suppose you could call this tape a kind of dead man's switch. In the event I don't make it back to clear my debt with Mr. Badwan, it continues to accrue. Until one day, he'll come knocking on your door with it, Miranda." Heydon glares into the camera. "When my crippling interest becomes yours."

"Pause it a sec?" I say.

Miss Lao hits a key.

"Miranda, are you sure you want to watch this?"

"You think he took his own life," she says.

For some reason, it takes me a moment.

"I think he was going through a hard time," I say.

"He certainly had before." Her eyes return to the screen. "Now, I wonder…" She nods. "Play the video."

——

"We've never talked about it before, but we're going to now," Heydon says. "The magpie. You remember."

He stares into the camera for a few seconds, but Miranda doesn't move.

"Bobbie and me were being shits at the breakfast table. Ray was getting up my nose, as per. So I was taking spoonfuls of Weetabix from her bowl. She turned on the waterworks, we all started fighting, and you barked at us to cut it out. I can't remember where my father was at the time, but because Theo was so small, and because it was the holidays, and because the weather was so shit that Eva was running late, and because you were due on set two hours ago, it all felt kind of crazy. And suddenly we were all screaming. At each other's throats. Then there was a thud at the window."

There's a digital crackle as Heydon exhales.

"When I went outside, I saw a magpie, just lying there. I brought it indoors and asked if there was anything we could do. The girls didn't like to see it. They walked out. But you sat me down at the table, put the dead bird under a napkin, and placed it in front of me. You said of course there was something we could do."

He pauses, still interpreting the moment.

"You told me that if I focused, if I filled my heart with goodness, and if I wanted it badly enough, I could bring that bird back."

When I glance at Miranda, she's completely still. "I was nine. Old enough to know that dead meant dead by then, but you were so compassionate. So persuasive. You really would have been wasted on set that day, Miranda. Then you took Theo and left me there. I must have spent an hour or more, staring at that napkin, growing increasingly desperate, feeling like it was my fault. But of course, nothing happened. When Eva finally arrived, you glanced in. You swept the bird off the table into the dustbin, then started to leave. I caught your eye. I told you I'd tried."

Heydon sits there for a moment, staring past the camera into the memory.

"You stopped in the doorway and said, '*You didn't try hard enough.*'"

When I glance at Miss Lao, she looks away.

"There was nothing explicitly cruel in it for you," Heydon goes on. "You were going through your crystal phase after all. You probably thought I could do it. You'd never had any kind of problem turning your own dreams into reality. Perhaps you thought we were all so fortunate?" He takes another shaky breath. "Ultimately, I know you just needed a moment's peace. And of course, I know that you deserved it. But I think it's fair to say that moment's gone on to have an outsize impact on my life."

There's a pink shoebox on the table in front of Heydon, and he stares at it for a moment.

"It wouldn't have gone on to mean so much if not for Theo," he says. "He drowned later that same summer. I know that you blamed me. And I know how hard you worked not to show it." Heydon smiles. "It's the role that you were born for. But of course, the damage was done." Heydon pinches his eyes shut for a second. "And besides, I lied to you about what happened that day."

Miranda leans forward, staring into the screen.

"I lied to the police and to you and to my father, and I lied in my sessions with Dr. Carr. I'm even lying now with Dr. Matten. Until just lately, I've been too ashamed to even admit it to myself." He looks up. "When you found me, I told you it just happened, but minutes had gone by. When I pulled Theo out, I could see he wasn't breathing. I knew I could run and get help or stay with him. And I couldn't leave him alone," he says. "I don't know why the idea even came to me, except that the magpie was the only dead thing I'd ever seen. So I laid him down. I filled my heart. I really focused." He screws his eyes shut, reliving it. "But of course, nothing happened. And when I heard you scream a few minutes later, I knew it hadn't worked." He opens his eyes. "I knew that I hadn't tried hard enough." Heydon lifts a glass of wine from the desk and takes a shaky drink. "I'm not saying any of this to try and make you feel bad, Miranda. You suffered more than anyone else. I'm so sorry. I simply wanted you to know that just once, I really did try."

The house phone starts ringing behind him. It's an old-school rotary dial with a long cord, fixed to the wall. Heydon closes his eyes for a few seconds, and I see that he's trying hard to control his breathing.

"I'm not answering that for a particular reason," he says, opening his eyes, sitting rigid, refusing to even turn to look at the phone.

Finally, it stops ringing.

"I'm not sure how I became a targeted individual," he says. "I'm not sure when they first started watching me. It felt like they made a sort of game of it in the beginning."

The phone starts ringing again, and he winces.

"At first, it was just a weird echo on my calls," he says, raising his voice to compete with the ringing. "There were messages marked as read on my phone or in my Gmail that I'd never seen before. I was getting all these emails from companies I had accounts with, failed log-in attempts, links to change my passwords, message after message, saying, *Is this you?*"

The phone stops ringing, and he lowers his voice.

"Well, sometimes I had to wonder. Friends would make reference to conversations I couldn't recall having. Then I'd scroll back through our message logs and see them sitting there. Messages sent from my accounts in the early hours of the morning. Always some time I wasn't conscious. There was something tantalizing about that at first. Like I had a kind of shadow. The messages from my end always started the same way, saying I needed to talk, some emotional plea, inviting response. Then it was a verbatim retelling of the magpie story. My great tragedy. And of course, people were forced to respond. I'd get all these calls and messages the following day. I'd be walking along, not thinking about it, then *boom*. Right back there. Paralyzed by that broken bird I couldn't save." Heydon rubs his face. "But in the end, I beat them at their own game," he says. "In the end, I blocked everyone who called."

He lays a protective hand on the shoebox.

"Then, on Theo's birthday last year, the start of May, I was working down here by the window when I heard a thud. I went outside, and of course, there was a magpie, lying at my feet. Theo's *birthday*," he repeats, staring into the camera. "I couldn't pick it up. I couldn't even look at it. Somehow, I'd never had that happen to me again, across all these years. Would you believe it's happened three times since?"

Heydon takes the shoebox and holds it on his lap.

"But now, I think I'm beginning to understand. The harassment, the hacked accounts, the canceled cards, the people in the street, the calls, the texts, the subliminal messages..." He opens the shoebox, revealing an injured magpie, lying prone but alert. "Vincent thinks it means that they're afraid of us," he says. "It means they're not sure what we're capable of." Heydon takes the bird from the box and holds it in his hands, looking down with awe. He refocuses. "And underneath it all, Miranda, this could be the most unexpected, the most wonderful surprise. You'll think I sound crazy. I didn't believe it myself at first. But I've seen things that suggest the impossible." When Heydon looks at the camera, his pupils are like pinpricks. "*Theo,*" he clarifies. "Somehow, I really did bring him back. They took him from us because they couldn't understand. But I think I've found him. I think I can bring him home finally."

Heydon sounds like he's trying to convince himself, and for the first time since he's started talking, the mania seems to fall away. Underneath it all, he looks worn out, confused, and afraid.

"I just wish I felt more certain about some of the people I'm mixed up with," he says. "I'm afraid that if you're watching this, then it means I failed. Once again. There'll be no family reunion, no forgiveness, no miracle. And I won't be coming back either." He stares into the camera. "It's my hope that you never have to see this recording. But if you do, then I'm afraid it's goodbye." Heydon takes one last shaky breath. "I'm not lost, Miranda," he says finally. "For me, it was worse, being here like this."

He reaches a faltering hand out to the camera in an affecting, fearful gesture for his mother, looking as lost as a person could possibly be.

Miranda puts a hand to her chest.

The screen cuts to black.

——

Miranda doesn't say anything, and neither do I. Miss Lao continues to work quietly at her computer. The tape was heavy, but at least Heydon had dropped some hints. For one thing, it didn't sound like Badwan was involved past lending him the £67,000. And storing the case, of course. Although Heydon had liked the idea of sticking Miranda with the bill, it sounded like there was something much darker than black cash at the root of all this.

The magpie story seems like the kind of thing he might have been able to shrug off or forget about if it hadn't been for Theo's accident so soon after. But the way those two events had become intertwined meant that Heydon couldn't have one without the other. If someone worked that out, they'd have a powerful hold over him. Clearly, he hadn't succeeded in bringing his brother back from the dead. But until now, I'd felt more or less convinced that his delusions were self-generated. I don't like the mention of this other guy. *Vincent.* To my ears, it sounds like he was taking Heydon for a ride, playing off his paranoia and mental health problems. Somehow convincing him that his dead brother was still alive. But why? The fifty grand that Heydon had tried to demand from his parents?

It doesn't seem like enough.

I'm trying to work out what to say or do or think when Reagan walks back into the room, carrying a glass of water. It looks like some of her color's returned.

"You've seen it then," she says, looking between her mother and me.

I nod. "It doesn't necessarily mean that he—"

"I'd rather not discuss it with strangers," she says.

"Of course."

Neither Miranda nor Reagan will even look at me, so I keep my mouth shut. For a moment, it feels like the tension might never break, then Miss Lao speaks up.

"There's something else," she says. "Some text messages between Heydon and another person."

"Who?" Miranda asks.

"It's a mobile number," Miss Lao says. "Saved in Heydon's address book as CTRL. Unfortunately, it seems that their earlier conversation took place on a different device. What we've got here seems like the last—" She stops. "I mean. That is to say…"

She trails off, realizing how it might sound.

"They were sent the same day he went missing?" I say.

She looks between us, then nods. She clicks something, and the messages appear on-screen.

It's H

New phone?

Burner

Yes bro! You got it?

50 man. Where are you? You OK?

Soon.

They're all over me bro…

There's a dead gray box, showing that Heydon had sent some kind of media, most likely a photograph or video, illustrating who he was referring to. Miss Lao tries to open the file, but it must have been deleted from the phone after sending. The only clue to its content is CTRL's reaction. *Jesus fuck. Is that now?*

And that was that. The last messages he'd ever received. They'd been sent in the early hours of 15 January, between 1:46 and 1:55 in the morning, giving us some idea of Heydon's last movements. The surveillance footage from the house showed him leaving at 1:05 a.m., and by 1:45, he'd concluded his deal with Badwan, according to the receipt. From the time stamps on the texts, he'd started messaging CTRL almost immediately after. A fast back-and-forth, most likely because he'd been about to seal the phone in cement, then hand it over to Badwan for deep storage. Then, finally, his car had been found on Albert Bridge at gone four in the morning.

And then? And then nothing.

"And that's it?" I say to Miss Lao.

"That's it," she says.

"They don't say where they're meeting or when."

"There was a call from an unknown number a few minutes later. It lasted six seconds."

So CTRL had come through with the location.

"We might learn more from the phone data," Miss Lao continues, "but right now, that's what we've got." She opens the maps app, and the phone prompts her to set it up, suggesting it's never been used before. There's no previous searches and no further messages or saved files.

"Is CTRL's number registered?" I ask. "Do we know the owner's name?"

"Pay-as-you-go," she says, looking up at me significantly. "The number was never used again."

So the phone's in a landfill somewhere by now.

"That name he mentioned in the tape," I say. "*Vincent.* Does that mean anything to anyone?"

Miranda and Reagan think about it, then look to each other and confer, but both of them draw a blank.

"And Heydon's comment about his brother," Miranda starts. She's waiting for someone else to say something, but no one wants to touch it. There's a long silence. "Of course, it's quite impossible," she says finally, sounding dazed. "So my son went to meet this man and…"

"The phone can only tell us so much," Miss Lao says. "Wherever he went next, he didn't take it with him."

But it doesn't sound good. Someone had done a number on Heydon, somehow manipulating him into believing that his dead brother was still alive. Extorting him for fifty grand in the process. If you're willing to go that far, then murder's not a stretch. It might even make you feel better about yourself.

It feels like the right moment to make my pitch. That we find this Vincent guy, then I go and meet him, dressed up as Heydon Pierce. We find out how he reacts when he sees a dead man walking. My stock seems to have plummeted with Miranda, but I think I can still win her around. Then I look up, seeing that she's exhausted.

I catch Reagan's eye instead.

"Maybe we should take a break?"

———

Miranda, Reagan, Miss Lao, and I return to the private room, leaving the men in white suits to study Heydon's case. Miss Lao offers to accompany Miranda to the drawing room. Reagan eyes me until they're gone. The click of the door hasn't fully rung out before she says, "What do you want?"

She's standing as far away from me as the room can allow, her back against the far wall.

"She's slowing us down," I say.

Reagan's mouth falls open.

"Excuse me?"

"Your mother's sick. It's a fact. We can honor what she wants and find out what happened to Heydon, or we can sit around wondering about Theo."

"Mr. Lynch," she says, more shocked than I'd actually been banking on. "You couldn't be in possession of a more appropriate name if you'd chosen it yourself."

"What are you really saying?"

She looks annoyed with me for wanting to know.

"I'm saying I don't know what you're doing here." She tugs uncomfortably at the collar of her dress. "You feel like a rope around my neck."

"You're wishing me all the best."

She closes her eyes.

"I didn't mean it to come out that way," she says. "I am grateful, of course. I'm also tired and overwhelmed. I'm also afraid."

"I know that," I say. "I think I can—"

"You're what scares me," she says.

When I look at Reagan, I see she's telling the truth.

"And to your credit," she goes on, aiming for something lighter, "your work here *is* done. You did everything we asked of you and more. Now I think we'd feel much more comfortable talking to the professionals."

"The professionals who thought I was your brother," I say, but she goes on, sweetening the deal.

"We'll add a further ten thousand to the account today. Something to cover medical costs and additional expenses. And of course, the room at the Mandarin's all yours until the end of the month."

She's plainly afraid of something, and I don't doubt it's me causing it. I'm just not sure why.

"Fair enough," I say. When she doesn't look back, I collect the envelope from the table, waving it in thanks. "If you ever need someone to talk to, you know where I am." She looks at me then. "At least until the end of the month."

Reagan doesn't say anything, and I walk out. Back through the ITV-drama drawing room, past the well-read men and women in leather seats, down the grand staircase, and through the pillared entranceway.

Kicked out of the club entirely.

I'd taken her to one side hoping to streamline things, and in a way, I'd got what I wanted. Her reaction wasn't entirely unexpected or entirely unfair. And on one level, I'm glad to be getting out of that room, away from the emotional trauma and indecision. Getting sacked doesn't alter my next move much anyway. I need some fresh air.

13.

It feels good to walk after so much time cooped up with the Pierces, and I head north, away from the crowds of mourners gathering for the queen, in the direction of Piccadilly Circus. With the haircut and the healing tattoo, with the close attention I'm paying to the way I walk as well as the new suit—my second skin—I get a glimpse of what it felt like to move through this world as Heydon Pierce, some idea of what it felt like to be him.

Tearful blond girls glance up at my broken heart, then quickly away from it, their doughy small-town boyfriends cutting cynical looks in my direction, like it's the oldest trick in the book. At first, the tattoo strikes me as a weird choice for someone who felt paranoid about being watched. The girls aren't interested in me. They're just glancing at the tattoo on instinct, because it's there.

Heydon had felt eyes on him everywhere he went. He was paranoid, possibly under the influence from what I'd seen, convinced he was at the center of some dark conspiracy.

Could the tattoo have helped to offset some of that?

Had it allowed Heydon to tell himself that people were just

looking at him reflexively, with no forethought or malice? They weren't plotting his downfall or wondering if he could bring people back from the dead. They were just looking at his little broken heart.

Either way, after a few minutes, it feels like I've gotten all the insight I need, and I decide it's time to get off the street and test-drive my new bank card. I turn to cross, then lock eyes with Mike Arnold. He's leering at me from the other side. I shake my head and turn but bump into the two goons in aviators. They just stand there, smacking gum at me for a few seconds, while we wait for Mike to join us. It's the first time I've seen him since those doors slid shut in his face.

"Please," he says, reaching my side of the road, motioning me to walk on. "Pretend we're not here."

I look between them for a moment, then walk.

Mike falls in beside me, the two goons behind.

"When I tell someone not to move," Mike starts gruffly. "I want them to be there when I get back. If they're not, I look bad. I have to take it out on someone else."

I start to laugh.

"Something funny?" Mike asks.

"Why don't we just talk about what you're really doing here, man?" Mike starts to speak, but I go on. "You came for that case, but you were late, like always, and now you're trying to save face by threatening me. I get where it's coming from. I just want you to know that it's pathetic."

A slow smirk leaks out onto Mike's face.

"Y'know," he says, "I could see arguments on both sides for why she picked you."

"Pros and cons," I say, motioning between us.

"Pros and cons," Mike says, sounding impressed. "Yeah. Not bad."

"So come on then. Hit me."

"With pleasure," he says, counting them off on his fingers. "Well, you're not an investigator, you're not trained, and you've got no experience. Then there's your attitude." Mike's voice darkens. "Which I'm sure you yourself would agree isn't suited to serious work."

I stop walking and look at him.

"So what are the cons?"

Mike doesn't smile. "So far as I can see, the one thing in your favor's your face," he says.

A few seconds pass, then we start walking again.

"Sounds like you've given it a lot of thought," I say. "Listen, Mike, if you're looking for a man on the inside, then you're too late." He looks at me. "I know, it's the story of your life. But my work here's done. I've been paid and everything. I'm out, baby."

"Is that right?" Mike says, smiling, blinking rapidly. "OK then. Even better. If you're not involved anymore, then there's no conflict of interest."

"Between?"

"You and me," he says.

I stop, looking between him and the two goons.

"Well, listen, I'm flattered, but I think I see you more as a friend."

"You stupid fucking prick," he says, meaning it.

"*Sound.* Is that it?"

"That's it," Mike says. "For now."

"OK," I say, looking at the two goons. "So who's following me today?" They just stand there, smiling. "Well, I'll make it easy. I'm going this way for some lunch. I'll get us a table for three."

I turn to leave, but Mike grips my arm, hard.

"Ah," he says, like he's just remembered something. "I think I owe you an apology."

I look down at his hand until he removes it.

"Y'know. Just don't let it happen again."

"*Heh*," he says, shaking his head. "One day, someone's gonna wipe the smile off that face. And when they do, there'll be nothing left."

I don't say anything.

"I didn't believe you about taking the train from St. Pancras. But you'll be pleased to hear that we've been tracing your movements, Mr. Lynch. That's why I wanted to apologize. You were telling the truth. Very careful with those cameras on arrival, but we found you, coming in on the Eurostar from Paris. Course their end's a bit trickier, but I think we've got the picture. Economy ticket, purchased with cash, on day of travel. No baggage," he says. "All seems a bit desperate."

I start to walk, and Mike follows me, still talking.

"So we got to thinking. Why would someone need to leave the city of love in such a hurry?"

I don't answer. I don't look back.

"Do you know Quartier Asiatique?" Mike calls after me. "Chinatown," he goes on. "Nice place. Only if you're thinking of seeing it, I'd go soon. Colleague of mine spoke to one landlord who found bloodstains in a room he was renting out. And scant hours after you left town. I'm talking to him this afternoon. Yeah, I'd keep walking too if I were you, Lynch."

14.

I cross Piccadilly without looking back, taking a foot passage through a pedestrianized area, then a right into the first restaurant that catches my eye. The doorman lets me in, and I glide through a chic café on the ground level, down a mirrored staircase, into a grand, subterranean lobby with a chandelier and tiled floors. I can see the restaurant through an archway, straight ahead. It's enormous, like a food court in a mall, except there's a guy on a raised platform, playing a piano, and the patrons are all formally dressed. An entrance on the right leads through to a darkened bar lounge with a glowing red sign above the door that says *Bar Américain*.

The host smiles and leads me inside, seating me at a corner table with a view of the jazz-age cocktail bar at the far end of the room as well as the exit. I hadn't been especially shaken by my confrontation with Mike at first. The public setting had decided our ground rules after all—they weren't about to grab me or rough me up in broad daylight. But the threat had certainly been there, and I sense that without Miranda, things might be very different. I wait a minute, but neither Mike nor the two goons so much as sticks a head through the door. Either keeping a safe distance or just giving me the rope to hang myself with.

I order a big gin, then take out my phone. There's no signal down here, but I get on the Wi-Fi, even though it keeps cutting out. First, I go to my contacts, scrolling to Clare's name in the address book. She's the only person I want to talk to right now. I close my eyes for a second, then delete her number instead. I don't google the room in Paris but work my way through some French news sites likely to cover it, finding nothing.

Not that there's much of a story there anyway.

Just a bloodstain so small I hadn't even noticed it. No body, no victim, no crime. No one had seen me on my way out, and the room hadn't been in my name. I stare at my phone for a few seconds, then swipe the news sites away, feeling the weight of Reagan's card in my pocket. There's enough cash on there to walk out and disappear.

I could start all over again. Again.

But somehow, I keep circling back to Heydon's harassment. Assuming that's what it had been. If he was telling the truth in that video, if it wasn't him sending those messages, then Heydon's shadow, whoever it was, had done a beautiful job.

They'd turned his contact list against him, using Heydon's friends and acquaintances to hound him with the one subject he didn't want to talk about. The emotional plea in Heydon's outgoing messages meant that people felt forced to respond, and the subject matter meant they were always talking about the magpie, unknowingly invoking Theo's death. When Heydon started to block his friends, he'd thought he was protecting himself, but I wonder if that's what his shadow had wanted all along. By the time he went missing, he was isolated, open to suggestion. Ready to believe even the most hopeless of dreams.

I just can't work out why. There are easier ways of extorting a rich kid. And besides, for someone like Heydon Pierce, fifty thousand feels like small change. From the contents of his second phone, it seems clear that Heydon was targeted for something more than money. I decide that I need to know what. I need to know who put this together. They sound like my kind of people after all. I need to look them in the eye and see what's there.

——

The first result I get when I search for *Heydon Pierce* is Miranda. I guess that's the long shadow that Reagan had been talking about. In a world obsessed with success, none of them would ever match their mother. She wasn't just a one-of-a-kind talent; she'd come of age in a glittering empire of celebrity, becoming a chic icon along the way. Now that I see pictures of Miranda as a younger woman, it all starts to click. I even remember sitting upright when she'd walked on-screen as the fallen society girl in *Every Man for Himself*, a sleazy European potboiler I must have caught, channel surfing in some black hole, at some three in the morning, somewhere.

Scrolling Miranda's Wikipedia page, I see that her mother died when she was small and that her father was an oil man who'd pulled hundreds of millions of pounds out of the North Sea. There's an entire subheading on his Wikipedia page marked *Alcoholism*, and I get the sense that things were difficult. Maybe that's why she's been teetotal since the 1980s. Maybe that's why she'd become an anti-fossil-fuels campaigner. She'd lent her voice and image to various green campaigns, and she'd even spoken at the UN. Go, Miranda.

She'd continued lobbying the government on clean energy right up until Heydon's disappearance, when she'd retired from public life. After Theo's drowning in 1997, it seemed that Miranda had rallied creatively. She'd done award-winning work through the noughties, winning roles of greater depth as her profile increased. She'd never had any kind of trouble turning her own dreams into reality. Or so Heydon had thought. But after he went missing, I see that she'd never issued another statement, interview, or performance. Miranda had never worked again.

—

When I scroll past Miranda to a story about Heydon's disappearance, there's not much there for me, and the facts of the case don't alter. Heydon Pierce, a twenty-nine-year-old trust funder, had walked out of his family home in the early hours of 15 January 2017. His car had been found on Albert Bridge, overlooking the Thames, but nothing had really floated to the surface at the time of writing. And not in the five years since either.

Once I've gotten a grip on the official narrative, I start searching for cracks. Corners of the internet where people might say what they're really thinking. I want rumors, theories, gossip—anything—but find surprisingly little and no trace at all of Heydon's online presence from before he went missing. Somehow, that feels wrong to me, not lining up with his preoccupations. There's no old pictures or videos, no dead social media accounts. I get the sense that his predisappearance data must have been scrubbed. I google his name and scroll down.

A message at the bottom of the screen reads:

Some of the results on this page may have been removed under data protection law in Europe.

No shit. I stare at it for a moment, then think back to the video and type in the term that Heydon used: "*targeted individual.*" Wikipedia redirects me to a page called *Gang stalking*.

Gang stalking or group-stalking is a set of persecutory beliefs in which those affected believe they are being followed, stalked, and harassed by a large number of people. The term is associated with the targeted individual virtual community formed by like-minded individuals who claim their lives are disrupted from being stalked by organized groups intent on causing them harm.

Generally, stalking has a single perpetrator. Beginning in the early 2000s, the term gang stalking became popularized to describe a different experience of repeated harassment which instead comes from multiple people who organize around a shared purpose, with no one person solely responsible.

I can see the point of the digital harassment but feel less sure about Heydon being followed through the streets by a faceless mass. Even so, when I look up, momentarily paranoid, I'm glad to see that no one's paying any special attention to me. Reading on, I come to a section headed *Persecutory delusions*.

Methods involved are listed as electronic harassment, "psychotronic weapons," directed-energy weapons, cyber-stalking, and hypnotic suggestions transmitted through electronic devices as well as other mind control techniques.

If Heydon believed even half of it, then he'd been easy prey, and it makes me wonder how much I can trust his perceptions. I start working my way through social media sites, doing word searches for Heydon Pierce. There are a few mentions on Twitter but mainly just out-of-date appeals for information, and when I look at the users who've interacted with the tweets in some way, I can't see any familiar names or faces. I repeat the same process across Facebook and Instagram, getting similar results. By this point, I've finished my gin and decide to move next door, into the restaurant.

The old girl at the next table stares at the tattoo, and I give her a wink to go with her tart. I order a steak and half a bottle of red, then continue to search, finally watching the few YouTube videos I can find on the subject of Heydon Pierce. When I click the first one, an automated advert starts playing. It shows a stock image of a smiling, sexually available blond woman winking at the camera.

Meet AVAILABLE Ukrainian girls!!!

I wait until the five seconds are up, then skip it.

The Heydon content's just autogenerated dreck from a couple of online outlets, and I'm not expecting much when I start scrolling through the comments. There aren't any at all on the first three videos. On the fourth, I see that a user called @01001000 posted a comment containing a link. There's no explanatory text, and when I click on the profile, it's completely blank. They never posted anything else, not before or since.

I back out of their profile, then follow the link they'd posted, which takes me to a second account. It's called @Piercingeyez, and it shows four videos, each with a minuscule view count, either in the tens or the very low hundreds. And it looks like this user's gone dark too, because nothing's been uploaded in five years. I scroll to the most recent video, then open it, seeing it was posted on 13 January 2017.

Two days before Heydon went missing.

I look up and see an older woman watching me from across the room. She lowers her head and smiles. I stand and walk to the gents. Once I'm locked inside a cubicle, I go back to my phone. The four videos all look similar, and I scroll through the first one quickly. It's been candidly shot on the underground, the cameraman wearing his phone attached to his chest somehow. Going through barriers, standing on platforms, getting on trains. We see what he sees, but we never see him.

The description underneath claims that these recordings are a self-defense tactic, taken against multiple unnamed and apparently unknown individuals who the cameraman believes to be stalking or watching him. In the first, he focuses his attention on people in his immediate surroundings. Although he doesn't react or speak to them, he holds the camera on his subjects for uncomfortably long periods of time, and it's clear that some of them notice the attention. When the people on platforms and trains glance back at the cameraman or flash annoyed looks in his direction, he notes it in time stamps in the video description as proof of the harassment he's being subjected to. I cycle through the three other recordings, finding near-identical viewing experiences.

Girl in hat glares @ 0:29.

F*ckboy with Thor cap follows @ 2:20.

So was this Heydon's secret YouTube account?

And was this the kind of unhinged recording he'd been sending to CTRL? Because if so, CTRL had clearly been taking advantage of him. As hard as I look, there's just nothing here. I scroll back and watch the most recent video right through, paying close attention to the highlighted time stamps. But I can't see *girl in hat glaring* at 0:29 or *couple following close behind* at 1:14. I just see normal people going about their business. Commuters, glancing up at a man who just so happens to be secretly filming them. The only thing the video proves to me is how paranoid Heydon was. But when I scroll to the comment section this time, I find something. Posted five years ago, the same week the video was. The same week that Heydon went missing. It just says: *siCk*.

The user's called @vncntcntrl.

Someone rattles the door handle.

"Excuse me," says a refined voice.

"Busy," I call back.

"What are you doing in there?"

I stare at the door for a few seconds.

"A fucking shit, mate," I say, enunciating clearly.

"*Well*," the man says, his voice going farther away. "I suppose I asked."

I click on @vncntcntrl's profile, seeing it contains a link to his Twitter account. His username's @CTRLR. He's got 4,111 followers and a blue tick by his name, but I don't know what that really means. His full name's listed as Vincent *Control*. It seems like he works in cryptocurrency or at least in that realm, in the online space somewhere. His bio claims he was briefly the richest teen in the country in 2001.

When I scroll to the pinned tweet at the top of his page, it's an ad for a digital networking conference he's appearing at here in the city this weekend called Cryptocon. The promo shot for Control's talk shows him dressed stylishly, somewhere between a goth and a teddy boy, standing on the tarmac in front of a private jet, with a dazed look on his face. Like he made his success happen so easily that he can't see what all the fuss is about. The talk's called *"Taking CTRL of Your Narrative."*

I check the details, then the time.

I exit the cubicle and go back to my table. I tear open the envelope that Reagan had given me, memorize the PIN, then throw it away. I pay with the card, tipping huge, feeling like it's free money. Then I call the QEII conference center, asking if I can book a last-minute ticket for Control's talk this evening. Lucy from the front desk says I can't buy a single ticket this late in the day, but she'll be pleased to sell me a full weekend pass for £159.99, covering the rest of the conference's program. I say, *"Whatever,"* and she agrees to leave it under my name at the counter. I swallow the wine, then climb the stairs back up to street level and start walking. I might not have long here, and there's too much I don't know.

15.

When you're stalking someone, what you really want is to know your target. Understanding their habits gives you a certain amount of stuff that you can rely on. Knowing their favorite coffee place or lunch spot, etc., can make all the difference for those split-second, sudden turns. Without that kind of understanding of Vincent Control, without much of anything, I need to know my surroundings. Exits, side doors, void spaces.

In a perfect world, I'd have visited the center last week, presenting myself as a prospective client. I'd have asked for a guided tour of the building, then if I could take a look around on my own. From there, I'd have moved slowly through the corridors, paying close attention to unexpected quirks. I'd have a firm handle on the size and location of each of the thirty-two event spaces—the Churchill on ground, the Fleming on third, the Mountbatten up on sixth—and once I left, I'd have studied the schematics for the fastest routes on and off each of the seven floors.

I'd have arrived at the event itself yesterday, seeing how it altered the landscape, updating the map in my head with stalls, salespeople, and photographers, probing for focal points of the increased staff and security presence. I'd have taken the temperature of the crowd, corrected my posture, accent, and attitude, and made myself fit in.

Without time for all that, I take a virtual tour of the building while I make my way over. I don't know what to expect from Vincent Control. I don't know what to plan for. I might walk right up and introduce myself. I might hang back and follow him home. His talk starts at eight p.m., so I kill a few hours, moving between different modes of public transport until I'm sure that no one's following. The virtual tour allows me to walk through the building like I'm actually there. I memorize the fire exits on the ground, then switch to the interactive floor plan, cycling between levels, making note of cafés, shops, cloakrooms, and elevator banks. And special note of the first aid center.

—

I get less success looking into Vincent Control, and something about that makes me uneasy. Where Heydon's online footprint seemed to have been erased, there's an abundance of Control. He's got two different dates of birth, a string of vanished companies to his name—a haze of dead links and ghost sites. Even the thing about him being the richest kid in England has a note beside it on Wikipedia, saying *citation needed*. His Instagram account just shows him looking dazed in a succession of penthouses with a succession of women.

#KINGSHIT, #HUSTLE, #SUCCESS.

The comments have been deactivated.

I search Control's friends list for Bobbie, wondering if they know each other, but she's not there. When I scroll to her page, I see she hasn't posted since leaving for rehab. I guess, most likely, she hasn't got her phone. Things have been moving fast, and although it's occurred to me to send her a message, I haven't had the chance. Anyway, I haven't needed her until now. But Bobbie's my best bet of talking to someone who might actually have met Vincent Control. When I check the time on the West Coast, it's three p.m.

Hey, I try.

I'm sitting on a red double-decker, on the front seat at the top level, like a tourist. When we bang past St. James's Park, I squint, but it just keeps on going. I'm about to ring the bell when my phone vibrates.

It's Bobbie.

Hey...

                    I wasn't sure you'd have your phone.

Bleh. Set times. At least we're
done sharing for the day...

                              How's it going?

She sends me a selfie. She's wearing a large pair of sunglasses, a bright white T-shirt, and an unamused look, sitting in the shade of a palm tree.

I've broken the world record for cigarettes
smoked in a 48hr period. Otherwise fine.

A few seconds go by.

What about you?

I don't know what the family's been telling Bobbie, if anything, and I'm not sure this is the time for the unvarnished truth. Besides, we both know there's only so much we can say on-screen.

> **Yeah OK. Miranda set me up in a hotel. Says she'll pay to get the tattoo removed...**

Is that what you want?

> **I don't know yet. Can I ask you something?**

There's three dots for a second, then they go away. A minute passes.

I need to get back.

> **Wait. Does the name Vincent Control mean anything?**

???

> **Old friend of your brother's...**

I don't think so?

I forward the flyer for Control's event, not wanting to go in there with nothing.

I've never seen him before. Who is he?

Ugh. They're shouting, i've gtg x

Fuck.

16.

The QEII conference center's a multilevel block of concrete in Westminster—57,855 square feet of event space, right by the Houses of Parliament. There's a utilitarian vibe about the place—gray, functional, no flash—and the website informs me that it's government-owned, operated by the Department for Levelling Up. That makes sense, because my understanding is that large-scale events like this are being canceled up and down the country out of sensitivity for the queen. But the QEII must have friends in high places. The only sign that anything's wrong here are the flags out front, flying at half-mast.

I put my green lenses in, then walk by the girls in tube tops, handing out flyers. Past the neon-pink vending machines selling dubious-looking cryptocurrencies and NFTs, through into the main entrance. I'm standing in a shoebox-shaped reception area with soothing white walls. There's a large digital screen at the far end, displaying the event's logo, as well as a few stalls where enthusiastic salespeople are pitching their services.

I approach the front desk, pay for my pass, and put on the

lanyard. Then I turn left, walking toward lift bank B. From the virtual floor plan, I know I'll disembark closer to the Burns room, on the east side of the building, where Control's due to give his talk. Burns is the smallest room in the facility, with a capacity of just twenty-one people, versus the thousands that some of the larger event spaces can hold. When I'd scrolled through Control's Twitter account, he hadn't seemed particularly active on there, with just a handful of tweets from earlier this year, none of which had generated much interest. He's got mine though. The texts Miss Lao found suggested that Control was the last person to see Heydon before he went missing. I can't help but wonder what kind of crowd he'll draw. The lift takes forever, stopping at every level. By the time I depart on fourth, I realize that Control's talk must have already started.

It's only scheduled to last for ten minutes, so I hurry, turning right out of lift bank B, then left, into the small anteroom outside Burns. I show my pass, and the kid on the door puts a finger to his lips, then lets me in.

——

"*Anyway*," Control says, his eyes darting to the door. "Fox Searchlight bought the rights to the *GQ* article, but I don't know. That industry's all bullshit, basically. I got tired of all these, like, fake people? So now I'm just writing the screenplay myself. And it got me thinking how, like, more people should write the story of their own life."

He's wearing a microphone headset that looks like it's been specially made, matched to the pale color palette of his skin, and his voice booms through the center's PA.

Control's dressed in Doc Martens, skinny black jeans, a tight black shirt, and a waistcoat. The clothes must have been tight when he bought them, but he's bigger than that now. His calves look like they might explode out of the trousers, and I wonder if the waistcoat's there to cover the straining buttons on his shirt. With his teddy-boy quiff and black fingerless gloves—with the bags underneath his eyes and the gin blossoms blooming on his face—he looks like a street magician who's run out of tricks. There's a spotlight on him, so when he turns to look at the door, he can't see me, and I take a seat in the third row.

Of the twenty-one padded red chairs that have been set out, just five of them are occupied. There's three loners, spread across the room, then two guys sitting next to each other at the back. Hawaiian shirts, handlebar mustaches, backward baseball caps, etc.

"Thank you for joining us," Control says, not looking at me. "We welcome all comers. Right now, you're a part of one of the most exclusive clubs in the world."

The line's supposed to be self-deprecating, a knowing wink to the small crowd, but Control's bitterness comes through loud and clear. When I glance down at my phone and consult the picture of him, standing in front of that private jet, I can't help but wonder if it's been staged or photoshopped.

"We're discussing a once-in-a-lifetime opportunity to own a little piece of the future…"

The future he's talking about involves something called Control Tokens, a currency of his own invention, with exclusive benefits, like VIP access to clubs, hotel discounts, and various exclusive events. For just ten K, we can become Control *Freaks*, gaining access to all this and more. We'll earn bonuses for putting more cash in and especially for bringing in new members. The currency hasn't been floated to the exchange yet, so we won't be able to withdraw our funds—*yet*—but when it does go live, in twelve to eighteen months, we could be sitting on as much as ten times what we'd put in.

"And if all that sounds too good to be true," Control says, stepping to one side so we can see the projector screen behind him, "then take a look at this."

A series of enthusiastic testimonials starts to play from stiff, fake, or confused-looking people, all talking about how much Control Tokens have helped them in their lives. The social and community aspect of the CTRL App gets stressed heavily, and it's clear that the whole thing's set up to appeal to young, socially awkward men. We're even told that today's new sign-ups are eligible to attend the CTRL after-party. There's some feel-good music for the big finish, but it more or less washes over me, and soon the lights go up. There's a smattering of polite applause, then Control collects some business cards and leaflets, moving toward us, working the room. The lone man at the front takes a card, and they start talking. The rest of them get up and leave.

Control doesn't notice me until I'm the last person sitting there, but when he does, he seems to freeze. His eyes go wide; he can't look away. He tries to go through the motions, still talking to the man in the front row, but his answers become distracted, and a minute later, when he's lost the sale, the man gets up to leave.

Then it's just the two of us.

Control smiles uncomfortably, looking to the door like it's some kind of prank. "Can I help you?" he asks.

"Where do I sign up?"

Control stares at me for a moment. "I'm afraid we require a nonrefundable deposit of three and a half thousand pounds," he says, sounding like he's trying to talk me out of it.

I get up and walk toward him, holding out the card that Reagan had given to me. She'd said it was one of the household accounts; I assume it's usually used for domestic purchases. My fee's been paid in full though, if it actually comes to that. And most importantly, it's got the family name printed right there on the front.

I hold the card out, even though Control doesn't seem eager to take it. When he looks down, he lets out an involuntary gasp, immediately hands the card back, then looks over my shoulder at the door, like he doesn't want to be seen with me.

"I'll tell you what," he says, his voice catching. "We can deal with the formalities later. I'm so sorry, I don't think I got your name, Mr...."

"Pierce," I say, holding out a hand. "Heydon Pierce."

17.

Control's quiet in the cab, and we move away from the conference center in silence. I've made sure to take the fold-down seat, facing him, for maximum discomfort. It's dark, but I can see that he's going through something. He digs a vape pen out of his backpack, glancing past me at the driver, crouching down to take a furtive hit. He blows a dank-smelling cloud out the window and gives me a direct look. He's still wearing his microphone headset.

"Something wrong?" I ask.

"I was just wondering if we'd ever met," he ventures.

"Not as far as I remember," I tell him.

Tonight, my Heydon Pierce is suffering from memory loss. He has to be, because I can't refer to their previous conversations or easily explain what I'm doing here. With Badwan, it had seemed like an easier tightrope to walk just because it had been a business transaction, first and foremost. He'd had good reason not to ask me a lot of questions. But with Control, I'm getting up close and personal, and I know at some point I'll have to sell him my far-fetched cover story. Amnesia feels like the weakest part of my disguise, much less effective than the lenses, the suit, and the tattoo. The pure shock of my appearance. So it's a conversation I'd like to put off for as long as possible. At least until we get to the after-party.

Luckily for me, it seems like Control's having some memory problems of his own. "*Hm*," he says. His eyes linger, but he doesn't push it.

When we'd exited the lift, Control had gone ahead, trying to keep his distance. He was still grimly focused on getting out of there when he hailed the black cab, but by the time it stopped, some kind of survival instinct must have kicked in. He'd been trying to avoid even looking at me until then, but he'd straightened up, steeled himself, and made an effort to stare into my face. His eyes snagged on the tattoo, and he'd taken a step back, looking genuinely appalled. Then he'd climbed into the car and barked an address at the driver. I'd climbed in after him.

Control glares for a few seconds, then his eyes come back to the tattoo, seeming to compute what he's seeing or who. He looks quickly away, playing distractedly with his phone. There's just the low hum of the motor, the city, gliding by. When Control grips and regrips his phone, I see that he's trying to keep his hands from shaking.

"H-how did you find me?" he asks. His eyes are glassy from whatever's in that vape. I don't say anything, and he corrects himself. "Us," Control says, smiling belatedly. "I mean, how did you find us today?"

"Online," I say vaguely, still not wanting to talk about what I'm really doing here.

"And your interests are, like, crypto, social, the market?"

"Control," I say. "That's what caught my eye."

When I smile at him, Control sees something that he doesn't like, and he seems to shrink back into his seat. His eyes go to the window and stay there for the rest of the journey. He doesn't ask any more questions.

———

It's the tallest structure on what looks like a brand-new waterfront development, south of the river, right by the decommissioned Battersea Power Station. The chalk-white sidewalks have never been walked on, and the neat strips of grass are a glowing, man-made green. Control leads us past the main entrance, around the corner to what looks like a nonpublic part of the complex, an external corridor created by the meeting of three separate buildings, with a neat bank of industrial-size wheelie bins running down the center.

We go to a side door, and he spends a few seconds sorting through keys on a bunch before opening it, looking left and right. I'm not sure why we're taking the back way, but it suits me, and we ride the freight lift up to the tenth floor.

The penthouse is six bedrooms and six bathrooms. Exactly what I'd hoped for, exactly what I'd do. Completely anonymous, looking like a showroom. Blandly decorated and brand-new. Nothing you couldn't just walk out on. We're standing in a huge open-plan kitchen space with a north-facing wall almost entirely made from glass, giving a mega view of the Thames. It's dark out, but you can see other waterfront properties, twinkling in the distance, on the far side of the river. As Control walks into the room, motion sensors activate the lights above him.

"Make yourself at home," he says unenthusiastically.

I guess that this is the Control after-party.

He yanks open the wine fridge and takes out a two-liter bottle of Coke Zero and an oversize bottle of Jack Daniel's. Then he takes down a tumbler and pours himself a large one, splashing Coke all over the hardwood floor. He glances back at me in question, and I nod.

When he hands me mine, he says, "What are you really doing here?"

It's the first time he's looked directly at me since we walked in, and I hold eye contact for a few seconds, making him more uncomfortable.

"You know what I'm doing here," I say.

"In fact, I don't." Control breaks eye contact, turns away, and walks toward the wall of glass. He pulls his microphone headset off and hurls it across the room. "I don't know the first thing about you."

"You don't know the first thing about Heydon Pierce," I say. "That's funny."

Control almost looks over his shoulder at me before turning the other way. "I know that you're not him," he says.

"What makes you so sure?"

"Oh, maybe the fact that Heydon's dead?"

"Yeah? And who told you that?"

"What do you mean, who told me?" He glances back. "Listen, *man*. I don't know what someone's been telling you, but I met the guy, like, three or four times, max. We weren't close. How did I know he was dead? Like, they've got these things called newspapers?"

"Which newspaper do you read, Vincent?"

"I don't know," he says, visibly bristling at my repeated use of his name. "Whatever's around."

"You don't remember?"

"What difference does it make?"

"Not one newspaper reported me dead. Try again."

"They said that you—" He stops short. "They said that *he* parked his car on a bridge in the middle of the night. He left the doors wide open."

"But we both know that's bullshit," I tell him.

Control risks another look in my direction.

"I don't know anything," he says.

"Well, when it comes to motivational speeches, I'm inclined to agree. But when it comes to me and you—"

"Stop saying you're him," he demands.

Control feels dangerously close to telling me that he knows for a fact I can't be Heydon Pierce, but I don't want him to notice that line until he's crossed it.

"What kind of car do you drive, Vincent?"

"*Ha*," he says. "Oh, dude. If you're here to collect some kind of debt, then you've fucked it. I'm bust. I'm in here for the night, on grace, because I used to bang the agent. I drive a GT86. It's leased, and guess what? I'm three months behind." He glares at me, looking like he's regained some confidence. "If you jacked it, you'd be doing me a favor."

"I was really just curious if you could drive. My point is anyone could have parked his car on that bridge. Even someone like you, who doesn't know anything."

"You think I parked it there?"

"Why not?"

"Whoever's giving you this stuff's sick, mate."

"You've given yourself away tonight, Vincent. Right here, in this room."

"Ha…like…"

"How come the family have never heard of you?"

Control scowls at me for a second.

"Why should the family have heard of me?"

"Because you read about his disappearance in the newspaper."

"The newspaper again," he says, flashing an annoyed look. "What's the newspaper got to do with anything?"

"Well, the articles I read asked for anyone with information about his disappearance to come forward."

"And, like, why—"

"You were the last person to see him alive," I say.

Control stares at me but doesn't speak.

"I wonder why you don't want anyone to know."

"What are you saying?" he whispers.

"Vincent, I'm looking at a guy who tells lies for a living. Someone with a fake name and a fake job who's pretending to live in a penthouse. And whatever, more power to you. But five years ago, you took fifty thousand pounds from a mentally ill man—"

"No," Control says, rubbing his head.

"—and you promised to take him to a fake place that could solve all his problems for him. Congratulations," I say. "I'm not Heydon Pierce. No one's seen him since he left home to meet up with you five years ago. I think you fucked with his head, you ripped him off, and then you killed him."

"What the fuck?" Control says.

"Vincent, if it wasn't you, then someone really wants it to look that way."

"I want you to leave," he says.

"Do you know what a dead man's switch is?"

"A dead man's switch?" Control remains completely still. He frowns at me for a few seconds, then nods.

"Well, spoiler alert, you get a shout-out in Heydon's. He left a recording."

"So?" he says after a moment. "I admit that we met."

"He went to a lot of trouble to hide that phone, Vincent. He says he's worried about the people he's wrapped up with. Yours is the only name he mentions."

Control starts patting down his pockets. "I'm calling a lawyer."

"No, you're not."

"Just watch me."

"This won't happen out in the open, Vincent," I say. "After what went down with Heydon, you should know that better than anyone."

Control looks at me for a long moment. "You said someone wanted it to look like I killed Heydon."

"I said it's either that, or you killed him."

He swallows. "And what makes you say that?"

"The texts you sent to each other, for one thing."

"Texts?" Control says unconvincingly. "What texts?"

"The texts where Heydon names a figure of fifty thousand pounds and you promise to give him a location. You called him back a few minutes later. Next thing we know, his car's on that bridge." Control just stands there, turning whiter. "Look. If you don't feel like talking, I'll just clone the phone and take it to the cops."

He watches me, trying to gauge if I'm serious. Once he realizes that I am, I see the relief flooding into his face.

"The cops?" he says, starting to smirk. "The cops? Do you know what, mate? Why don't you just go ahead and do that. Maybe I'll take my *chances* with the cops."

"I'd think carefully about that," I say. Control squints. "Well, if

you were in it on your own, then you're right; you've only got the
Met to outsmart."

"What do you mean, if I was in it on my own?"

"I'm just saying, if there was anyone else involved in Heydon's
murder, then you should factor them into your thinking. Once
your name starts getting dropped in the same breath as his, you
never know…"

"You never know what?" Control says.

"Well, from the outside, you might not look so solid. Someone
might see the fake name and the failing business, the loan sharks
circling, and think you look like a loose end they can live without.
Then there's that fifty."

Control eyes me. "What about it?"

"Well, they could have taken Heydon Pierce for millions if that
was what it was about. But they didn't."

Control watches me closely.

"The burner," I say. "The last-minute meeting, the secret location. That fifty K wasn't part of this," I decide. "That fifty's a
middleman, taking everything he can get." From the way Control
just stands there, it's clear he can't deny it. "Whoever put this
together was slick. They knew how to wipe their prints off it. But
they messed up, because they used you, and you got greedy."

Control just stands there.

"*So.* Keep it under wraps, and you might be OK. They might
not know you've blown it. But let me walk out of here, and we both
know the next person through that door won't be asking you any
questions, Vincent."

Control just stares into space for a moment.

He mumbles something to himself.

"I'm sorry?"

"This is the most fucked thing I've ever heard."

"Yeah," I say. "I'm giving you the chance to keep it between us."

"Heydon's phone," he says darkly. And I feel like we're back on solid ground. It's just another transaction to Vincent Control after all.

"If I like what I hear, I'll wipe it," I tell him.

Control glowers, but he hasn't got a choice.

"Fine," he says. "What do you want to know?"

"Everything there is to know, right now."

"You're not asking for very much," he says bitterly.

"Vincent, I'm not asking at all."

18.

"Start at the beginning. Where did you meet?"

Control goes to the counter and mixes himself another drink. "Cryptocon Sixteen," he says.

"Like the one we were just at?" I ask. Control nods. "Same time of year? September?" Control nods again. "So you knew him for roughly four months."

"Exactly," he says. "Four months. Nothing."

"Except that they were the last four months of his life, Vincent. How did you meet?"

"I just told you—"

"You told me where," I say.

"Right," he says, shrugging, like that's all there is to know. "We were both at the conference."

"Doing what?"

He sighs, making a face to indicate that he's casting his mind back. "2016? I would have still been trying to get Control Tokens off the ground," he says. "I suppose Heydon must have come to the show? We must have gotten talking or something."

"That must be the benefit of drawing such a small crowd," I say. "Your talks feel like one-on-ones."

"Right," Control says sarcastically.

"So then what?"

"Then nothing," he says.

"OK." I drain my Jack and Coke, then throw my tumbler up in the air, watching it fall and shatter on the hardwood floor. Control looks at me in shock, then takes a step back. "Let me explain something, Vincent. I don't care about you, and it feels like you're fucking me around. We've got two options here. You can tell me what you know, or I can go public."

"Go public," he spits. "See where that gets you."

"Vincent, all I need to see is who they send around with the black bin bags."

Control glares at me for a few seconds, then wavers.

"Heydon and I were introduced," he says finally.

"Introduced by who?"

"I only ever knew him as Sebastien."

"Knew him, past tense?"

"We haven't spoken in five years," he says.

"Sebastien what?"

"I don't know," he says.

"What does Sebastien do for a living?"

"I don't know that either," Control says.

"But you've got some kind of an idea."

"If he finds out I spoke to you—"

"He won't," I say firmly.

"He said he was like a talent scout."

"A talent scout for what?"

"For new kinds of thinkers," Control says. "To me, he was just an angel investor. Someone looking to get in on the ground floor with deregulated banking."

"How does Sebastien first come onto the scene?"

"I don't know," he says. "We met at a conference in Dubai. Maybe six months before Heydon?" Control shrugs. "He was the one person who came to my talk that trip. Afterward, we went out into the desert and partied. That's still the drunkest I ever drove…" He catches himself. "At the time, I was dealing with some evil tax shit from the year before. Truth be told, I was in a pretty dark place."

When Control looks at me, his eyes are wide open for the first time since we've met.

"Sebastien was like a hand, reaching down from the heavens, right when I was about to go under. He saw something in me. Or so he said. I think his main interest was always the business."

"What part of it specifically?"

"He liked the idea of moving money untraceably. He offered to come in as a silent partner."

"So Sebastien was some kind of lender?"

"A loan shark?" Control snorts. "Try great white."

I wait for it.

"Well, at first, it crossed my mind that he might be intelligence," he says, sounding like he's flattering himself. I don't say anything, and he goes on, justifying his theory. "I was working in an emerging financial market, traveling internationally, meeting influential people…"

He speaks like he's never said any of this out loud before, like he's afraid of the words leaving his mouth.

"Don't forget, *in trouble with the taxman*," I say.

"No." Control forces a smile. "How could I?"

From the sketch he'd drawn of his life, for all I knew, he might have looked like a good asset to someone at the time. He'd been moving in new and moneyed circles, in a largely unregulated area, and with financial problems that made him easy to manipulate. But somehow, Sebastien sounds too good to be true, a faceless investor that Control can put all the blame on.

"So what did this Sebastien want in return?" I ask.

"Well, just emails at first. Minutes from meetings, contact details, things of that nature. It seemed like such a small price," he says, still trying to rationalize whatever he did to Heydon. "They were things he might believably have been entitled to anyway."

"You said at the time you thought Sebastien might have been intelligence, so now…"

"Now I know that the kind of cash involved counts the state out entirely."

"How much did he give you?"

"Personally?" He doesn't hesitate. "Upward of three hundred."

"Thousand?" I ask. Control nods. "And more for the business?" He shuts his eyes, then nods again. "And you didn't get his surname when he paid you," I say.

"I told you, I don't know it. He paid me through his company."

"Which was called?"

Control takes a breath to speak but lets it out. He swallows with some difficulty, then tries again.

"The Black Door," he says slowly. "Out of Panama."

"Like a shell corporation?" I ask.

Control nods. "There's not a single thing to know about them except that they exist. Or they did back then."

"And that didn't raise any alarm bells with you?"

Control looks at me but doesn't say anything.

"OK, you're saying it's not the state, so…"

I'm setting Control up, expecting him to dive right off the deep end, into the same troubled waters as Heydon. To start talking to me about electronic harassment from unknown forces, being a targeted individual, getting gang stalked, but he surprises me.

"I came to believe that Sebastien was ex-SAS."

"Ex-SAS?" I say. "What made you think that?"

"We played a game of squash," he says. "Once, before a meeting. Fucker thrashed me, of course. He had a tattoo. The knife with wings, on his upper left bicep."

"I'm not sure I'm with you here, Vincent."

"He reminded me of men I've met in finance, in the City, the ones behind the scenes who do the due diligence."

"Like some kind of security consultant?" I ask.

"Sure," he says. He pauses for a moment. "Or, I guess, more like private intelligence?" He glances up at me. "All those firms are packed out with ex-military, ex-spooks. They operate just like the real thing, except they're registered companies with offices in Mayfair."

I stare at him for a few seconds.

"Let's say Sebastien was working for one of these firms. Why would they want you and Heydon together?"

"Simple," Control says. "Because I told Heydon I was going through the same kind of harassment he was. They used me to keep him in line."

"Who used you? Why?"

"Well, isn't that always the question?" he snaps. "The whole point of these organizations is to give the elites access to the same quality of tradecraft the state gets." Control gives me a bleak smile. "Just without the budgetary constraints or any kind of oversight."

"Or, in this case, any kind of motive." I look at him. "Like, I'm sorry, Vincent, but why would the elites be interested in you?"

"They're not," Control says. "They weren't. I was just someone they knew that they could use. But if Sebastien's the kind of guy I think he is, then you can bet that his clients all share a certain socioeconomic background."

"Tell me about him."

"After Dubai, Sebastien and I started meeting every few weeks," he says. "These long, boozy lunches in the basements of empty restaurants in town. Bottomless brandy and wine. He always picked up the check. He'd ask me where I'd been, who I'd met, what was going on in the market, that sort of thing. It was during one of those lunches that he mentioned this friend of his, Heydon."

"This was in the run-up to Cryptocon?"

Control nods. "Naturally, Sebastien knew I'd be there. He'd made arrangements to attend my talk. And he said that by strange coincidence, his new friend might be attending too. He suggested we grab a coffee."

"All three of you, or just you and Heydon?"

"All three of us," Control says. "Although Heydon really wasn't there for long. We barely spoke."

"You didn't hit it off?"

"Public spaces were difficult for him. People too." Now that Control's convinced himself I'm not Heydon, he feels brave enough to give me a direct look. "He certainly never put a question quite like you," he says with disdain.

"If you hadn't killed him, I wouldn't be here."

Control's eyes go wide. "I was trying to help him," he says. "Sebastien said that Heydon only trusted other TIs. People who saw things the same way he did."

"And you went along with that," I say.

"If I was to befriend him, I had to gain his trust."

"Wow," I say. "Well, I guess the best ones always believe their own stuff."

"I'm telling you the truth."

"You're telling me your arse. You expect me to believe that if Sebastien just bought you a coffee and nothing else, you'd still have gone along with this shit?"

Control doesn't say anything.

"Why did you need to befriend him, Vincent? What had he done to deserve a friend like you?"

Control rubs his face. "He had an idea for an app. Needed help on the tech side. Sebastien put us together."

"What was the app?"

"Well, in the end, we never got up and running, but it was a way of connecting other targeted individuals. They'd live stream their harassment, discuss it with other users, be able to see hotspots of activity."

"Sebastien was paying for all this?"

Control nods.

"And that's what you were doing those last four months?"

Control nods again.

"Where?"

"Sebastien hired a workspace in Soho House. Heydon and I met there once a fortnight."

"And as far as you knew, you were just working on this project."

"Right," Control says with a sigh.

I draw out a long silence, waiting until he looks up.

"Vincent, why did you call him *bro* in those texts?"

Control closes his eyes.

"Jesus Christ," I say. "So you were letting him imagine a touch more than just the harassment."

Control opens his eyes again, staring at the floor.

"I swear I didn't realize it was such a big deal at first. There were just certain biographical details that Sebastien asked me to emphasize in our conversations. He'd planted other talking points online so that when Heydon googled me, he'd be taken down the rabbit hole."

"Talking points like…"

"Well, that I was a targeted individual myself, of course. That was out there. Then that I was rich. I think they even changed my birth year on Wikipedia."

"So it matched Theo's?" I ask. Control nods. "That's pretty fucked up, Vincent."

"Don't you think I know that?"

I'm not sure how far I can trust his story, but I can hardly call it self-serving. It's hard to think of a reason why he'd make himself sound so bad unless he was telling some version of the truth.

"So Sebastien puts the two of you together…"

"The three of us," Control says. "Although we'd had several sessions before Mr. Peck joined the party."

"Describe him to me."

"Somewhere in his midforties, gray-faced, intense. He had those acne scars on his cheeks."

"And he was there all the time?"

Control shakes his head.

"He'd show up unexpectedly. His job was to nail down Heydon's philosophy, or so they said. Sebastien told us that Peck represented the hedge fund. It was nonnegotiable. They'd have these super-intense five-hour breakout sessions, record everything…"

"What were they talking about?"

Control just stands there.

"Vincent, what were they talking about?"

Control glances up, then away again. "Peck's focus was Heydon's kid brother. The day of Theo's death."

I stop for a second, trying to think it all through.

"And in the meantime, you're dropping hints that you might actually be Theo?" Control nods. "From the tape I saw, you had him convinced."

"I was only involved in the first of those breakout sessions," Control says. "The idea was that Peck would relax us into a kind of trance so we could answer his questions as our most honest selves." He sees the way I'm looking at him and glances away. "At the end, I told a story that Sebastien had prepared for me about a recurring dream. We'd been in there for hours by this point. Peck wanted to know where the dream came from, and I told him it was from when I was small, before I was adopted—"

"Were you adopted?"

Control shakes his head.

"In the dream, I was a small child inside a large house. There was a storm raging outside. There'd been some kind of argument inside, but I was too small to know what. Then I was on my own, walking into this huge kitchen space, hearing something strange, like a chirping sound. I followed it to the waste bin and looked inside. There was a bird in there. Stunned but still alive. I took it to the door and stepped out. The bird flew away."

Sebastien had provided a happy ending to the magpie story. And he'd planted the suggestion that Control might be Theo in one fell swoop.

I close my eyes for a second.

"So what did Heydon think?"

"We never discussed it directly. But I'm certain he suspected I was Theo." Control rubs his face. "He always liked to be around me after that."

"Was Sebastien around for all this?"

Control shakes his head. "I only ever saw them together twice. The first time and the last."

"What was his relationship with Heydon?" I ask. "How did they meet?"

"I don't know," he says. "In that first meeting, he referred to himself as Heydon's patron."

"And what did Heydon say about him?"

"Heydon called Sebastien the all-seeing eye."

"The all-seeing eye," I repeat. I think for a second. "Where did Sebastien get the magpie story from?"

"Ugh," Control says. "Well, he showed me a psychiatric report, doctor's notes…"

For some reason, my ears start ringing. "You were using things Heydon had said to his doctor?" Control looks up at me and nods. "Do you remember the doctor's name?" I ask.

He shakes his head. "I don't think I ever saw it."

"OK," I say. "So let me get this straight. You've got this mystery friend—this Sebastien guy—bailing you out from all your tax woes as well as propping up your failing business. He introduces you to a disturbed man called Heydon, and you guys start this company. But in reality, you're leading him to believe that you're his dead brother, Theo, while a third man interrogates him about the day Theo drowned."

"I suppose you could put it that way," Control says.

"And you don't know why."

He throws his hands up in the air and lets them fall.

"So what happened in 2017?"

"In January, something changed."

"Changed how?"

"I don't know. Suddenly there was this pressure, this urgency, coming from above. Sebastien called and told me there'd been a change of plan. He said that Heydon was losing it. He needed an immediate breakthrough."

"Meaning?"

"Sebastien said that Heydon needed to relive the trauma of that day. It was the only way to move past it."

"You faked a medical emergency," I say.

"After this weird pressure started to come down from above—I guess a couple of days before Heydon went missing—Sebastien instructed me to start complaining about chest pains, hinting I'd been ill for some time."

I turn slightly so I don't have to look at him.

"That's what you told him the fifty was for."

Control closes his eyes for a second before going on.

"When I met Heydon that night, I said it was getting worse. I needed to see my specialist. Sebastien found that the Pierce kids had all been screened for some genetic illness in their teens, which of course, Theo hadn't. He had an anonymous room made up to look like a medical center, a team of nurses to stick tubes inside me. They took me away and kept him waiting. They made the situation sound dire. When they let Heydon in to see me, he was with Sebastien and Peck, completely out of his mind. He started telling the doctor I had to be tested for this or that." Control stops, looking older than when we first met just a few hours ago. "When they asked Heydon how he could know that, he told them I was his brother. He said he couldn't lose me again."

The ringing in my ears gets louder. "Then what?"

"Well, of course, I was supposed to be out of it, so I just stayed put. Sebastien and Peck took Heydon into a side room. It sounded like they were grilling him. By this point, I'd had enough. There was no one in the room with me, and I felt hideous, just lying there. So I pulled out all my tubes and left. It seemed clear that they weren't trying to help him."

"I wonder how much sooner you'd have cracked it without that three hundred thousand."

Control glares.

"I hoped he'd see that I was gone, that the whole thing was a charade. It felt like the one decent thing I could do in that moment. But then, the next day, I read that his car had been found on Albert Bridge."

A minute goes by while I try to picture it.

"Do you know what?" I say finally. "This is too crazy. I think that Sebastien, Peck, the phony doctor, this whole thing, is just another one of Vincent Control's doomed business ventures."

"Jesus Christ," he says.

"You've been fooling the world for so long, you've started to fool yourself, pal."

"Fuck you," he says.

"Get in line. You took fifty grand from Heydon, then he went missing. Time to get real, Vincent."

"He actually *insisted*—"

"You were exploiting a paranoid guy who'd cracked up and started seeing things," I say. Control shakes his head. "Come on, man. You hacked his shit and had him chasing shadows."

"You're wrong," Control says stubbornly. "And besides, Heydon wasn't paranoid."

"In the texts I saw, he sent you some kind of file. A photograph or video. You said, *Jesus fuck, is that now?* Do you remember?" Control nods. "Was it really such a shock to see him filming couples on the underground? Or do you think that might have been one of his paranoid days?"

A wild, confrontational look comes into his eyes.

"Why don't you tell me?" he says.

———

It takes him a minute to find his laptop, because he can't remember which of the six bedrooms he left his stuff in. He pauses for a few seconds, looking confused, then walks abruptly to the balcony.

I follow close behind.

The balcony's got a glass floor and a glass wall, a partition that comes up to the waist. Control slides open the door, and we step out, glancing at the black river below.

"Who actually lives here?" I ask.

Control shrugs. "Some Russian sausage magnate who's never seen the place. Soph said it went for twelve point three. I just thought it'd look sick on social if I had any VIPs to bring back tonight. I can't believe I'm wasting it on you."

As we move along the balcony, I see that several of the bedrooms open out onto it, granting any occupants a river view. Control looks through the glass doors, trying to find his stuff. When he opens the last one, I follow him inside. There's a black bag on top of the bed.

"Slowly," I say.

Control slides out a laptop and opens it.

When he does, I see that the computer's synced up with the wall-mounted flat-screen. Control selects a file, and the still image of an underground station appears on the TV. He hits play, then stands to one side, watching me, watching the tape.

———

The recording is in the same style as the ones I saw online. We're watching from the cameraman's perspective as he walks into an underground station, glancing back at the people standing behind him on the escalator.

"This is Heydon?" I ask.

"This is Heydon," Control says. "Watch."

There's a young couple, touching noses, completely oblivious to him. He leaves the camera on them for an uncomfortably long period of time, but they don't seem to notice. Then he turns so the camera's facing the escalator to his right, watching the people on their way up. Five or six faces glide by, all preoccupied with phones or nodding their heads to music coming from their earbuds. Then a woman stares directly into the camera. From the way Heydon holds on to her, he clearly finds it significant. He moves the camera with the woman, watching her go up, but once she passes him, she turns away. It's easy to see why he might have interpreted the look as hostile, but most likely, he'd stared at her first. She'd had every right to stare back at him, especially if she'd seen the camera.

When Heydon reaches the bottom of the escalator, he follows the corridor onto a platform. It's early evening, past rush hour, before the night traffic. The commuters are sightseers, heading back to hotels; they're office drones who've worked late or gone for drinks in town. Heydon walks to the far end of the platform, passing fifteen or twenty people. When he can't go any farther, he stares into the black tunnel, and for so long, it feels like he's drawing our attention to it. At length, he turns, looking left, back along the platform. The same fifteen or twenty people he'd just passed are all standing around, waiting for the next train. Then, as if responding to some invisible signal, four of the faces turn and stare directly at him for a fraction of a second. They all give him the same hostile look, the same chilling flash of the eyes, then go immediately back to what they'd been doing, just like it never happened.

———

When the tape ends, I look to Control, starting to form questions. There's a knock at the door, and we both stop.

"Who's that?" I ask.

"Fuck," Control says, producing his phone. The lock screen shows three missed calls. "The agency must have given her the wrong time."

I stare at him. "Get rid of her."

Control walks through into the main space, eager to get the door open. I take a second to scan the room, then go immediately for his bag, rifling through, finding some crumpled-up letters. I force them into a back pocket, then see something else at the bottom. It's a glossy photograph, folded down the middle. I open it and see myself, sitting on a Soho street corner with Reagan yesterday. I'd seen the black SUV with the smashed wing mirror there. The same one I'd seen Bobbie get into at Heathrow.

What the fuck?

I turn it over, see a phone number scrawled on the back, then follow Control through into the main space, just in time to see him getting the door open.

"*Hey*—" he starts.

There's a loud pop, his head jerks back, and blood splats into the wall. Every muscle in my body contracts. Somehow, Control just stands there for a second with a black hole in the center of his forehead.

Then he hits the ground like an inanimate object. The door starts to open farther. It's moving toward me, so I can't see who's behind it, and I break left, skidding behind the kitchen counter, ducking down.

I press my back into the cupboards and listen. The shot had been silenced, and I don't hear any commotion or concerned neighbors. Just footsteps as someone enters the penthouse and closes the door behind them. I can hear a man, breathing heavily through his mouth, bending to Control, checking he's dead. If he goes forward, into the main space, toward the balcony, then I've got to try and surprise him. Pop out and hope there's a knife on the counter, go for the throat, all or nothing. If he goes left, toward the bedrooms, then I make a break for the door. The man stands there for a few seconds, still getting his breath back. Then I hear footsteps. Heavy boots on creaking rubber soles. He goes left, toward the bedrooms. I wait until the footsteps are almost inaudible, then go immediately for the door.

Control's lying in front of it with his eyes wide open. He'd had his phone in his hand, but it's gone now. His keys are on the floor beside him, and I grab them on instinct. I get the door open, wipe off my prints, and glance back for a second. Then I'm retracing my steps to the freight lift, bursting through the fire door, and flying down the stairs. I exit, standing in the refuse alley at the rear of the building, breathless, then start for the underground, keeping my head low.

When I got the door open, I'd glanced back and seen Control's killer, just for a second. He'd been twenty feet away, at the far end of the hall. He was wearing black boots, black trousers, and a black bomber jacket. As well as a black balaclava, with holes cut for the eyes and mouth. I'd scanned past him so fast that all I can see in my memory's a blur, but the farther I get from the building, the more certain I feel. When I left that penthouse, he'd been staring right at me.

19.

I don't stop until I'm safely underground. Until I've changed trains a few times, then found a rancid-looking public toilet to sit in. I'm grateful for the one space in this city that's not being watched by CCTV, and I lock myself inside a cubicle, then breathe.

My heart's going like a speed bag, and I ball up some handfuls of toilet paper to wipe the cold sweat from my brow, underarms, and back. Someone had approached Control with my picture. Whether they'd told him I was a fake or the real thing, clearly he'd contacted them and sold me out. After that, they'd had no more use for him. I hadn't wanted his story to be true, but Control's violent death gives everything the ring of authenticity. I just wish it gave me something I could prove. I unfold the crumpled letters I'd taken from his bag, watching my hands tremble. They're unopened late notices, and tearing the envelopes, I see that Control was telling the truth about one thing at least. His car was a GT86, and he'd been behind on the payments.

My eyes go to his mailing address.

Cumberland Street, in Pimlico.

Off the top of my head, that's not far from Chelsea. Not far from where I am now. I feel Control's keys in my pocket. In a few hours, there'll be cops crawling all over the place. But if I can get there first, if I can find some link between Control and Sebastien, some indication of who Sebastien is, then it might be a lifesaver. Control's killer saw me leaving the penthouse; I feel sure about that now. The fact that he didn't give chase means he'd been more interested in securing Control's personal effects than any eyewitnesses. I'm at least a few minutes ahead of him, and it feels like an advantage I've got to push.

———

After the dark warren of the underground, the wide-open, hangar-size main space at Victoria feels like too much. It's so exposed from all sides, so garishly lit, that I might as well be center stage in a play. I take the escalator, then walk through the arcade, following Google Maps to Control's place. I cross the road outside the station, walk through a bus depot, and find myself moving through Pimlico's backstreets, the houses that line the train tracks. They've been built in the same style as the ones in Chelsea. Three-tiered wedding cakes. Except here, they're mostly off-white and run-down, looking like they've gone stale.

Looking left on the main street, I see shuttered, boarded-up shops. Homeless guys sitting outside Tesco and tragically ravaged, prune-skinned heroin addicts, panhandling for change. Control's address is just a ten-minute walk away, and in that time, the area goes from rough to well-off to rough again, seeming to alternate with every street. When I turn left onto Cumberland, I can see why Control might have felt like he was better than it. There's a council block at the top of the road, social housing on the street itself. The buildings are beautiful but in differing states of repair. Some are gleaming with fresh white paint and hand-stenciled numbers on the door. Some are draped in weather-damaged scaffolding that looks like it's been up a while.

Control's place is somewhere in between. Well-maintained but a few decades out from its last paint job. Even in the dark, it's closer to rain-colored than white. I make a slow pass of number 10, walking on the opposite side of the street. His address on the late notice said Flat 2, which I guess means either the ground or first floor. There are no lights on, but I don't turn my head to look. I make a slow circuit of the block instead, hearing the whole night coming to life around me. Latchkey kids out past their bedtime, past eleven, screaming with laughter nearby. Drunken conversations drifting up from a pub a little farther out. Then the sirens, wailing endlessly on, somewhere off in the distance.

On my second pass, I'm walking on Control's side. There's no one in front of me and no one behind. There's no one on the other side of the street. Glancing right, I see that there aren't any lights on in the building opposite Control's. I'm two doors down, reaching inside my pocket for the key, when I hear tires screech. I tense up. A nondescript van parks bluntly outside the house, and the side door slides open. I grip the key in my pocket, ready to fight, but the two guys who jump out are all business.

They go to Control's door, open it, and walk in.

I don't stop, and I don't look back until I'm standing at the end of the street. The lights come on in a ground-floor flat. I catch a glimpse of one of the men, throwing things into a bag, then the other guy comes to the window and pulls down the blind. I take a very deep breath, then walk back to the hotel.

I lean into the double-locked door for a few minutes, my eyes closed, detaching myself from my surroundings. Then I do it the old-fashioned way, standing on my own two feet and breaking open the minibar, tearing the heads off two miniatures of Stolichnaya and pouring them into a glass. I hang the *Do Not Disturb* sign on the door and drag the heaviest pieces of furniture in front of it. Then I take a long, scalding-hot shower, trying to burn off some kind of stain. I stand there for ten minutes, then twenty, my head directly under the nozzle, nothing but the roar of water in my ears.

The man on the front desk had stared into the side of my face when I got back, but I didn't bother looking at him, and I didn't see any Rayner guys in the lobby this time either. Although Ronnie knows where to find me, I'm not especially worried about him right now. Our earlier chat proved he wasn't quite as serious about all this as he thought, and anyway, as far as the family knows, I'm out of it. That doesn't put me in the clear with him, of course. Most likely, Ronnie's licking his wounds somewhere, plotting something worse. I insulted his masculinity, and I get the sense it means a lot to him. He'll want to handle me on his own terms, and personally.

I'm more worried about what I've seen and heard tonight. Control's story was intense. And the tape suggested that Heydon really was being followed. Maybe even gang stalked, as he'd understood it.

But like with the magpie story, my guess is that Sebastien, whoever he is, had just zoned in on Heydon's preexisting fixations, then exploited them. With the close knowledge they'd gained from hacking his accounts and with insights apparently gleaned from medical professionals—with Control's deception and Mr. Peck's grill sessions—they'd had a direct line to Heydon's deepest fears.

They'd just found the ones that furthered their agenda, then made them come true. I can still see those four strangers, glaring at him on the underground, that hostile flash of their eyes.

To hear Control tell it, the plot had to involve hundreds of thousands of pounds as well as the bribing of doctors and the use of plainclothes surveillance operatives, hacking, and public harassment. And that's before you even get to murder. It explains Heydon's erratic behavior and maybe his disappearance too, but it leaves me with a few questions.

I don't know who Sebastien is or what entity he works for beyond this shell corporation, the Black Door. I don't know why he was so interested in Heydon five years ago or what his focus on the day of Theo's death means. Most of all, I don't know why he'd go to all that trouble just to mess with some dropout's head.

Control had been a loose thread with the potential to unravel what sounded like a dark conspiracy.

Then someone cut him off.

I climb out of the shower and dry myself, then I unplug the room phone. I switch off every electronic device I can find, turn off all the plugs, and turn out the lights.

I can still hear that ringing in my ears.

——

I've been lying awake for a few minutes when I get up, paranoid, groping around in the dark, looking for the source of that ringing sound. When I find a light switch, I go to the chair I'd slung the suit on, feeling through the pockets, the lining, for some kind of tracking or listening device. By the end of it, I've gotten a handful of loose change and the picture of me I'd found in Control's backpack. And the ringing in my ears just gets louder.

Unfolding the picture and looking closely, I realize it *wasn't* taken from the SUV I'd seen Bobbie get into. I'm fairly sure I'd seen it that day; the photographer had to have been standing on the same street at roughly the same time. Most likely, it's the same person. I just can't say for sure. I stare at the picture another second, then throw it pointlessly at the wall.

20.

I order breakfast in bed this time, taking things as slowly as possible. When I call down, I consider asking for the newspapers, then decide I don't want to know what's in them. A nation in mourning, two nations at war, a world on the brink, blah blah.

I move the furniture from in front of the door to let the cart in, but I haven't buttered my toast before the last few days start to catch up with me. The smell of the eggs turns my stomach, and I grab a plain roll from the cart before wheeling it back outside. I'd been spared my usual restless night. From my head hitting the pillow to now just felt like a black shroud, falling down around me. A smash cut from one scene to the next. When I opened my eyes again, I couldn't believe any time had gone by at all, let alone the nine hours I'd been out for.

Over coffee, I search for news about Control's death, not expecting to see much yet. It's already been picked up by the Associated Press though, with the story filtering through to various online publications.

London: Man dies after gunshot wound

A man in Battersea has died as a result of a gunshot wound, the Metropolitan Police have confirmed.

The incident occurred on Saturday 10 September.

According to MyLondon, apartments in the Patmore Estate were put on lockdown as emergency services rushed to the scene following the incident late in the evening.

A spokesperson for the Metropolitan Police confirmed that an unnamed man was found with a single gunshot wound to the head. Paramedics were unable to revive him. His next of kin have been informed and are being supported by officers.

The death is not being treated as suspicious.

The story's interesting for a couple of reasons. First that they'd chosen not to identify Control, despite saying his family had been informed. That might be some kind of formality, but searching through similar stories from the same publication, most deaths got names once they'd been identified. For some reason, the detail makes my ears start ringing again. It gives me the feeling of information being suppressed or at least parceled out slowly. I can see the faint outline of a hand, somewhere behind the scenes, tipping the scales ever so slightly.

Especially because of the second detail that sticks out. Control's death isn't being treated as suspicious. The Met aren't looking for anyone. Could they really see it as suicide? It's the best-case scenario for me, just completely unlikely. Not something you'd even expect to see reported for a week or so. A few days at least. I check the time.

Control's been dead for less than fifteen hours.

By the sounds of it, his financial status had been dire, and although he'd struggled on for a few years after Sebastien stepped in to keep him afloat, his career had clearly been winding down. He'd seemed burned out and deeply bitter, even without the Heydon situation. Factor in his own paranoia, the drugs, the cost-of-living crisis, the world, and it wasn't so crazy to conclude that Vincent Control had committed suicide.

But first, you'd want to know who was at that talk. You'd want to trace and speak to all six attendees. Most of all, you'd want to know who he left that conference center with and if he was alone when he walked into the tower. You'd be especially interested in any messages he'd sent or received in the minutes leading up to his death, and you might even wonder why he'd decided to blow his brains out in the doorway.

I don't need a newspaper to tell me what's up with the Met. I'm not surprised by their disinterest or by them doing a sloppy job either. If anything, it's the speed and efficiency of their reaction that sets off alarm bells.

I think of that nondescript van, screeching to a halt outside Control's building last night. The two guys who jumped out had clearly been containing the scene. I'd seen one of them throwing things into a bag before the other one pulled down the blind. They'd been there within an hour of Control's death. No doubt they'd grabbed any electronic equipment as well as any files, file sticks, or hard drives. But my guess is they left something behind as well.

From the way that Control's murder seems to have gone unnoticed, my guess is that they must have planted some kind of suicide note at the scene, maybe scattered some bottles and drug paraphernalia for good measure.

It doesn't bode well for my prospects of turning up a link between Control and Sebastien, but I've still got his keys, and I feel like I've got to go back there and try.

Before leaving, I consider putting the Pierce family in the picture, but I know that means tying myself to Control's death. That's not something I feel comfortable doing until I know more about what's going on.

I shower, dress smartly, and do my best Heydon Pierce for the mirror. I'm visiting Control's flat in broad daylight this time, and I can't afford to stand out. I lock my passport in the room safe and cover the tattoo with a bandage. Then I smooth down my hair and leave the room, rehanging the *Do Not Disturb* sign on the door.

21.

The estate agent unlocks number 21, and we walk into a narrow hallway with two doors leading off to the left, numbered 2 and 2b. We take the stairs straight ahead, passing another flat on the first floor, taking the next flight of stairs, up to the second.

"It's two beds," the agent says, letting us in. "Both en suite, with one family bathroom as well."

He shows me the smaller bedroom on the right, then the master straight ahead. Then we climb the stairs up to the main living space, above the two bedrooms. It's a large kitchen-lounge with a balcony at the far side. I'd booked the viewing as an alibi, a believable reason for me to be walking around the area, just in case anyone asked. I'd turned up as a formality, but when I go to the balcony, I realize it's closer to Control's flat than I'd thought.

"Could we take a look outside?" I ask.

"Of course."

The agent crosses the room and unlocks the door. Outside, I hear the familiar sounds from last night. Kids screaming, drinkers talking, sirens wailing off in the distance. I'd arrived early so

I could stand on the street for a minute, watching and waiting with no questions asked. There'd been a cop car outside Control's place, and craning my neck out on the balcony, I see it's still there. I hadn't passed close enough to see if there was actually an officer inside, but it stands to reason.

"So what do you think?" the agent asks.

I look down to the street, then back at him.

"I think I'll take a look around," I say.

——

When I stroll past Control's flat, the blinds are back up, and I see an officer, sitting, bored, at the kitchen table, scrolling through his phone. He doesn't look up as I walk by, and I make a slow circuit of the block, trying to come up with a plan. There's a couple having a screaming row a few doors down. I could call 999 and report a domestic disturbance. It's so close to where the cop's stationed that he might leave his post for it. Then I'd have five to ten minutes to quickly search Control's flat and hope I got lucky.

But if there's anything left to find, which feels unlikely, then it has to be well hidden. The place has already been searched by the two guys from the van, and I know they must have taken things away. Most likely, the police have conducted their own search as well. I'm still trying to decide what to do when I realize there's something I've missed.

Control's GT86.

I've covered a lot of ground in this neighborhood across the last couple of days, and I don't think I've seen it. Control had been behind on the payments, which means he might not have wanted to park right outside his house. And he might well have driven it to the QEII. I make another slow circuit of the block, moving down

Cumberland, looping onto Winchester Street, really looking this time, but I still don't see it. I move out onto Alderney Street, then get to St. George's Drive and stop.

There's a burned-out wreck sitting in front of one of the great white houses. A fastback coupe with a low chassis. Control's GT86. The windows are shattered, and the tires have burned to nothing. The interior's a charred, empty shell. Killing Vincent Control clearly wasn't enough. Someone was wiping him off the face of the earth.

———

When I walk into the underground, I'm still trying to get everything straight. Some dickhead in a hoodie bangs into my shoulder, but when I turn and look after him, he's already on his way out.

Reagan said that Heydon had been out of control ever since Theo's death, a tailspin of drink and drugs. Then, for some reason, Sebastien had arrived on the scene. Control claimed to know nothing about him except that he'd fronted a nonexistent company called the Black Door. But Sebastien had introduced Control to Heydon; he even funded a co-venture between them. He'd already poured hundreds of thousands of pounds into Control. He'd spent a few months messing with Heydon's head. Hacking his accounts, flooding his inbox with concerned messages, taunting him with dead birds, isolating him.

Then he'd moved in for the kill.

Seeing Control five years after the fact, he hadn't struck me as much of a Theo. But when I think of the lean, green-eyed neo-goth from the flyer, it makes more sense. Control said the shadowy Mr. Peck had started to appear at their workspace, unannounced. He'd presented as some kind of ideas guru, dispatched by the moneymen to nail down Heydon's philosophy. But really, he'd been rooting for details about the day of Theo's death, trying to lure Heydon into revealing some dark secret.

But what?

The Wi-Fi on the underground cuts in and out as we move through stations, but I search for news reports about Theo's drowning. Because it happened in 1997, before the internet was everything, it's hard to find a definitive news story online, and I piece it together from oblique mentions in a few different sources.

Miranda was alone in the house with the two boys on her day off. She was working on a troubled production, *Wilderness Years*, four months into what was supposed to be a two-month shoot. There'd been an urgent call from the set, and when the signal failed, Miranda had asked Heydon to keep an eye on his brother, then gone upstairs for what she thought would be a two-minute call. It had taken slightly longer, and when she got back to the pool, she'd found Heydon pulling Theo out. That's where Heydon's tape diverged from the public record. At the time, Heydon told his mother it had just happened, but he'd actually pulled Theo out minutes before, then frozen up. Miranda had accepted full responsibility for the drowning in public. There'd been no way to protect Heydon from the emotional fallout, but he barely featured in the written record at all.

They'd called an ambulance and tried to revive him, but whatever Heydon had been led to believe in the years since, Theo was dead. And it had completely derailed his life. What more could anyone want to know?

I'm sitting in the carriage, lost in thought, when two girls take the seats opposite. Big long hair and skateboards. The kind of best friends who look like twins. They're buzzing off something, slightly drunk or stoned. But deep in conversation and laughing. The one with the nose ring glances at me.

"Who did you kill?" she asks.

"*Rosa*," her friend says.

"That's what it means."

I put a hand to my face, realizing the bandage's fallen off. Probably when the hoodie shoulder-barged me.

"Ha," I say, smiling. "I haven't killed anyone."

It's the wrong thing to say, and they just stare at me.

"I mean, I think it's a teardrop that means you've killed someone."

"Right." Rosa squints at the tattoo. "So what does a cracked heart mean?"

"Y'know…" I think for a second, then shrug. "I've got absolutely no idea."

Rosa frowns, looking concerned for my well-being.

She leans forward.

"But shouldn't you have?"

22.

When the barmaid looks over, I realize I'm tapping hard on the table.

"Sorry," I say.

I'm staring down at the picture I'd found in Control's backpack. Me and Reagan, sitting outside a coffee shop in Soho. It would have been simple enough to get a picture of me alone or to crop Reagan out of this one. But the moment looks intimate—she's staring into my face—and the clear implication is that Heydon's come back. That this is some kind of heart-to-heart with his sister after being out of touch for five years.

I turn it over and look at the phone number. Control had kept me talking. He'd known that backup was on the way. But from who? I withhold my number and call it, but the line goes dead.

The phone's already been disconnected.

There's no one else around. The bar's empty, and I hadn't seen anyone weird on my way over. I could still grab my passport from the hotel, head to Heathrow, and go. I might even feel safer for a minute. But Control's death says that these people have got long memories. And they don't mind redecorating the walls with some-one when they step out of line. Anyway, if I leave now, I'll have to see Heydon's face in the mirror every day for the weeks or months it takes to remove a tattoo. I'll have to rub him out, like they did.

I rub my face instead.

Control had summed it up best. The most fucked thing he'd ever heard. But he also feels like an object lesson in where running away from these things gets you. Him getting his nose wiped on the doorstep wasn't a surprise. Not really. That bad energy you put out there's always coming back around. When you know what you've done to other people, you know what to expect. Looked at like that, Control was a mercy killing. He'd backed himself into an impossible corner, completely out of charm, leapfrogging from one lie, one loan, one long shot to the next. If I take that cab to Heathrow, then I'm him in five years. If I even make it that far.

I lift my head from my hands, trying to think, seeing the picture on the table, my face. I think back to my conversation with Rosa on the train. I'd assumed that Heydon's tattoo was some delayed reaction to the trauma of Theo's death, a tribute of some kind. As well as something to distract himself from the idea that he was being watched. But I don't know that for sure. Bobbie said she'd drawn it, and I find myself scrolling her Instagram page again. There's a new post. Bobbie's hand, holding a cigarette up to an endless LA sky. The picture of me and Reagan hadn't been taken from the black SUV with the smashed wing mirror. But I'm fairly sure I'd seen it in the same place at around the same time.

I want to know who's driving.

Can I ask you a question?

I swipe Instagram away, go back to the bar, and order another, thinking of possible ways forward. I snag on what Control had said about Sebastien using doctor's notes to zone in on Heydon's neuroses. In the tape, Heydon had mentioned a Dr. Carr, from when he was younger, and a Dr. Matten, who'd sounded more recent. When I google Carr, it's a bust. No therapist under that name operating in the area, and the name's too common to search any wider. I'm searching for Dr. Matten when my phone vibrates. It's Bobbie.

What's up??

I try to think of everything that's happened since we last spoke. The plot against Heydon. Control's murder. The guys I'd seen ransacking his flat.

TBH getting quite into the idea of this tattoo...

A few seconds go by.

...ur joking?

I was wondering where it came from?

You mean the design?

Right.

I hadn't spent much time thinking about it until now, but I take a selfie. The tattoo's just the outline of a heart, but it's got a

IMPOSTER SYNDROME **183**

particular shape. An angular nib, with a voluptuous back end, like
the spade in a deck of cards.

> You'd have to talk to Heydon. He gave me the
> stencil. I assumed he came up with it himself.

> **Huh.**

> Anything else?

I look down at the phone. There's all kinds of things I'd like
to ask her, especially about the family dynamic. And especially
about her meeting with Badwan. Especially about the night
we met.

> **Well. This is weird. That car you got into at the airport...**

Bobbie doesn't say anything.

> **I feel like I've seen it around a few times...**

> Shit.

> **???**

> I'm going to sort this out.

> **Sort what out?**

> It's nate. It's my ex

Your ex is your dealer?

Look. I've gtg., But you can forget about this, I swear.

I send another message, but she's gone.

Well, that's put my mind at rest. If Bobbie's telling the truth, which feels remote, then her dealer ex could be the same person who's been showing my picture around town. But because the photo hadn't been taken from the SUV, I can't say for sure.

As ever with Bobbie, something's missing.

Scrolling back through her grid on Instagram, I can't find any pictures of her and Nate. I guess she took them down when they split. But looking at the pictures she's been tagged in, I find a Polaroid snap of the two of them from a wedding a couple of years back.

In an echo of Bobbie's last picture with Heydon, she's sitting on Nate's lap. Except where Bobbie looks beautiful, wearing a long, silk bridesmaid dress, smiling at the camera, Nate's completely wasted. He's around my size, but his whole head looks swollen with drink. And he's got his mouth wide open, roaring back with laughter. His and Bobbie's eyes have both turned red from the flash.

When I swipe away, I see the results of my search. A Dr. Kate Matten, in the Westminster area. Her office is located in a modern tower block on the sixteenth floor. I'm surprised to see she's got office hours. Google lists them as open until 6:30 p.m. If someone got there at 6:15, they might catch her after the last patient of the day. They might catch her completely off guard.

23.

The mezzanine reception for Millbank Tower has fresh cut flowers in black vases, and it caters to business and residential properties across thirty-three floors. It's 6:11 p.m., but when I approach the front desk, the woman on duty greets me like it's first thing.

"Good evening, sir. How can I help?"

"Hi," I say. "I'm here for Dr. Matten."

There's a flicker of something in the woman's face as she takes in my appearance. I'm wearing the green lenses, but her eyes linger on the tattoo.

"Do you have an appointment?" she asks.

Sounds like Dr. Matten doesn't usually get callers this late in the day.

"Heydon Pierce," I say. "She's expecting me."

"Just one moment, sir."

I step away from the counter while she makes the call, admiring some of the bloodless artwork on the walls, making sure she can describe me in case anyone asks. I can't hear what she's saying, but I get the gist. Dr. Matten's receptionist isn't expecting me either.

They talk back and forth for a minute, the woman cradling the phone in her hand, speaking low, then she hangs up.

"Someone should be right down," she says.

I thank her and take a seat.

Five minutes later, I hear scalding heels echoing across the otherwise quiet lobby. She's a British Asian woman in her early twenties, smartly dressed, with short black hair. She uses a pass to get through the security barrier and goes to the front desk, talking quietly, not looking at me.

Then she turns.

"Good evening, Mr.…Pierce?"

"That's right," I say with a smile.

"Mr. Pierce," she says. "I'm Jaya, from Dr. Matten's office. I'm terribly sorry, but we've got no record of your appointment."

"Well, that's OK. I just need a word with Dr. Matten. You told her I was here."

Matten's receptionist smiles nervously.

"Of course. I'm afraid she's seeing a patient at the moment, but—"

"That's OK. I don't mind waiting."

Jaya looks at me, and I see her swallow. "Very well," she says. "If you'd like to follow me?"

———

When we reach the sixteenth floor, Jaya leads us through to a small reception space. There's another door beyond this point, and I take it to be Matten's office.

Jaya's phone's plugged in on the desk, and the screen's still lit up from her last search. She'd been looking for *Heydon Pierce*. Either the name had rung a bell, or Matten's reaction had put her on edge about something. I scan away from it to the walls, and Jaya sits at her desk, turning the phone face down. She starts to type, but when I glance back, I see her eyes darting to Matten's door. At length, there's voices behind it, the door opens, and a man leaves the office. He talks briefly to Jaya, confirming the date of his next appointment, and leaves.

Then Dr. Matten appears.

From the way she holds on to the doorframe and just stands there, it's clear that she recognizes me. Or at least the effect that I'm going for. Matten's a mixed-race woman in her midforties and conforms to my uninformed idea of what a psychotherapist might look like. Well-educated, well-dressed, and physically healthy. Slender, with no serious worry lines creasing her face. There's deep, dark shadows underneath her eyes though.

Something's been keeping Dr. Matten awake.

"Good evening," she says stiffly. "Mr....?"

"Pierce," I say.

"Yes." Matten looks to her receptionist. "Thanks, Jaya, I'll see you in the morning," she says.

Jaya looks between us, sensing trouble. "I've got a few things to finish up," she says, sorting through some loose papers on her desk.

"No, no," Matten says with false cheer. "I insist."

Jaya stops what she's doing and gives a tight smile. "OK," she says, grabbing her bag. "I'll see you tomorrow then, Kate." She glares on her way out. Jaya's got a bad feeling about me. The door closes, and we listen to her moving farther down the corridor.

When I look back at Matten, she's holding up her phone. "One push gets building security. Even if you take it from me, they'll trace it."

"Be my guest."

Matten just stands there.

"Maybe you can explain to them why you let me in. Why you sent your girl away." She doesn't move. "I think you've got a guilty conscience, Doctor."

"If this is what I think it is, then you can fucking go to hell," she says, her eyes glistening.

I glance over my shoulder. "Is this the wrong floor?"

She lets out a brief, bitter laugh.

"You're not Heydon Pierce."

She'd thought it as soon as she saw me, but I can see that she needs to say it out loud, to tell herself it's true.

"What gave me away?"

"You're a dick," she says simply.

I pat a hand on my chest. "Ya got me. You said, 'If this is what I think it is, you can go to hell.' What do you think it is, Doctor?"

Matten watches me closely, recalculating. She'd assumed I was here representing someone in particular. Now she's not so sure. When she answers, her voice is steady.

"You've clearly come here in character," she says. "My guess is to try and extract personal details about a former patient of mine."

"I'm told that's a service you provide."

Matten's jaw tightens.

"Then I'm afraid you've been misinformed. As a practicing psychologist, I'm bound by the rules of doctor-patient confidentiality. As a professional—"

"I'd say it's a little late for all that, wouldn't you?" Matten doesn't move, and I take a step closer. "So Heydon *was* a client of yours?"

"If there's something you want to say, then you should come out and say it."

We just stand there for a moment.

"Last night, I met a man who said he'd been paid a large sum of money to work as part of a scheme against Heydon."

"A scheme of what kind?"

"First, they followed him around. Hacked his accounts, impersonated him. Prodded him with childhood memories. They wanted him paranoid, on edge, isolated."

When Matten frowns, it looks sincere.

"For what possible reason?" she asks.

"Well, from what I can tell, they were trying to convince him that his dead brother was still alive," I say.

Matten lets go of the doorframe and staggers back into her office. When I follow, she's gulping water from a bottle.

"And they were smart," I say. "But they couldn't have done it on their own. To screw around with someone like that, I think they'd need help. Maybe even a professional."

Matten's standing with her back to me, one hand on her desk.

"They paid the guy who pretended to be his brother three hundred thousand. I was just wondering what you got."

Matten turns slowly. "Excuse me?"

"That big promotion," I say, leaning into the doorframe, taking in Matten's office. "Maybe the lease on these rooms."

She frowns and takes a step toward me.

"You're saying my salary, my place of work, my life, has been handed to me? Is that correct?"

"I'm just wondering if Sebastien's an equal opportunities employer. Three hundred thousand—over or under?"

Matten swipes a paperweight off the desk and throws it at my head. I get my hands up in time, and it bounces off.

"So you're saying it's less."

She starts walking toward me, and I back out.

"How *dare* you?" she says, shaking with anger. "You can get out and you can—"

"*Listen*," I say. "I can't get out. I know too much." We stare at each other for a few seconds. "Or at least I know one thing for sure. If I don't find them, they'll find me." I take a step back and give her some space. "And that's bad news for you."

Matten's trembling from the adrenaline.

"Why?" she says. "What's it got to do with me?"

"Because whoever did this is cleaning up after themselves. And I don't see anyone else trying to stop it."

She shakes her head. "What are you talking about?"

We're both breathing hard, and I try to lower my voice. "Does the name Vincent Control mean anything to you?" Matten thinks for a second, then shakes her head. "When did you stop treating Heydon?" I ask.

She's about to argue, then relents, on this point at least. "May 2016," she says. Four months before Sebastien introduced him to Control at Cryptocon.

"How did it end?"

Matten glances away. "Heydon no-showed, stopped attending his sessions." She thinks for a moment, then looks at me cautiously. "Who is this Control person? What do you mean, they're cleaning up after themselves?"

I nod over her shoulder, at the computer on the desk. "Google 'apartments locked down on the Patmore Estate,' in Battersea last night."

Stiffly, Matten goes to her desk, sits, and types.

She scans the results, then stops.

"It says an unnamed man died of a gunshot wound...not being treated as suspicious."

"Meet Vincent Control," I say. "He's the man who passed himself off as Heydon's brother. And I wouldn't believe everything you read. When he shot himself in the face, he was holding his phone with one hand and opening a door with the other."

Matten closes her eyes.

"Less than an hour later, two guys turned his flat over. When I went back there this morning, it had been locked down by the cops. My guess is those two guys rigged the scene."

Matten shakes her head. "Rigged the scene?"

"Suicide note, hard drive full of smut, half-snorted lines on the counter. Whatever."

Matten grips the edge of the table and stares down, taking slow, measured breaths. At length, she seems to come to some kind of resolution.

"A man came to see me," she says hoarsely.

"What man?" I ask. "Here?"

"He came to the office. Threatening me." She looks up pointedly. "Making demands."

I glance away. "This is 2016?"

Matten nods. "He handed me an envelope. When I opened it, there were pictures of my children." She looks at me. "School drop-offs. With friends. Asleep in bed."

I don't say anything.

"Then he explained that he represented a group who'd taken a special interest in one of my clients. He wanted to talk to me about him."

"Did this man introduce himself?"

"No," Matten says. "But the name given for the appointment was Alan Peck."

I try not to react. "Can you describe him for me?"

Matten closes her eyes for a second. "Compact, muscular. Black hair with streaks of gray. Pitted cheeks." She breaks off and looks up. "He was frightening."

"What did you tell him?"

"I tried to hold my nerve," she says. "The whole thing seemed so unreal. I knew he couldn't be serious. I said no matter the circumstances, it wouldn't be possible."

"Then what?"

"Then he made a call. Mumbled something into the phone and hung up. He asked if I knew where my daughter was. I told him I did." Matten takes another drink of water. "It was early afternoon, my daughter's nap time. She was at home with my mother-in-law. He told me to check her baby monitor. It was an app on my phone. When I looked, I could see a man standing over the cot with a knife. My blood just fucking froze."

My ears pop and start ringing painfully. "So what did you tell him?" I ask.

Matten's eyes come suddenly to me.

"Who are you? What's your angle in this?"

I'm so used to misleading people, pretending to be someone else, that for a second, I have to think.

"Three days ago, I ran into Bobbie, Heydon's sister, at the airport. Long story short, she tattooed my face, then left the country. When I went to the family to get it removed, Miranda had other ideas. They'd received word that Heydon left a locked suitcase with some loan shark in town. Miranda wanted me to meet the guy in character, as Heydon, to see how he reacted, trying to gauge if he was involved in the disappearance."

Matten frowns, trying to follow the thread. "That's—" she starts. She shakes her head. "And?"

"Strikeout. But we did find a tape. Heydon recorded it the night before he went missing. That's where he first claimed his brother was still alive."

"This is Theo?" she says, reaching for the name.

"Right. Heydon thought he could bring him home, save his family, save himself." I cough. "Do you mind if I grab some water?" There's a fresh bottle on the table.

"Help yourself," Matten says, watching me.

I rip the lid off, take a long drink, then continue.

"Heydon said if we were seeing the recording, then it meant he was, well…" I trail off.

Matten watches me for a moment.

"What happened to you?" she asks. "You look completely exhausted."

"It's been a long week."

"I mean before that." I don't say anything. "What could you be running away from that's worse than this?"

For a second, I see Clare.

I lose my thread, and an airless moment passes between us. I make a kind of scoffing sound, then take another drink to buy myself a few seconds.

"I'm not running away from anything," I say finally.

"This doppelgänger business, pretending to be Heydon. You didn't actually go through with it?" I shrug. "Who are you to try and do something like that?"

"I don't know," I say. "A gifted liar."

"I'm sure. But for work?"

I sigh, making it clear that we haven't got time for this. "Well, the last few years, I've been sort of drifting."

"Doing?"

"This and that."

"Mr...."

"Lynch."

"Mr. Lynch—"

"I'm a con artist," I say. I'd danced around it with everyone else. I'd danced around it with myself. In some ways, it's a relief to say it out loud. But it misfires. I'd wanted to sound flippant and offhand, but it comes off defensive, like a rebuttal. Daring her to have a problem with it. "I'm a thief," I say, sounding more honest.

"So while you were drifting..."

"I was ripping people off," I say. "And no. I wasn't Robin Hood either." I see something change in Matten's face. "It's not like that," I say. "Look, I'm trying to do things differently. They paid me to go to this loan shark. Then when I saw Heydon's tape..." I trail off. "Well, I agree with Miranda. I think I'm in a unique position to get some answers here."

Matten shakes her head. "Armed with a tough-guy tattoo? Do you have any idea what you're up against?"

"Not exactly."

"Because this is—"

"I saw them kill a man," I say. Matten stops. "It's life or death, us or them, right now. I get it."

"If you want to live, you'll forget the whole thing."

"I want to understand," I say.

"And I suppose you've examined your reasons for throwing your own life away."

I look at her for a moment. "Is that what I'm doing?"

"Perhaps you feel guilty about—"

I close my eyes for a second and hold up a hand. "Let's just stick to Heydon," I say finally. "If we get on to me, we'll be here all night." I take a breath, resetting myself. "Like I said, someone was stringing him along. The tape pointed to Vincent Control. Except that when I found him, he told me he'd been put together with Heydon by a third party." I'm watching carefully when I say his name. "*Sebastien*." Matten doesn't react. "Is that a name you recognize?"

She frowns. "Sebastien what?"

"That's all I've got."

"That's all you've got?" Matten looks suddenly fearful, but it sounds like she's answering honestly. "No," she says. "It's not a name I recognize in this context. I only ever dealt with Peck, that one time."

"Do you know how he made the appointment?"

"I'm sorry?"

"Phone, email, secretary. Anything that might help me find him."

Matten blinks. "You're not listening to me. This isn't someone you want to find."

"Peck cropped up in Control's story too," I say.

She doesn't want to ask. "Cropped up how?"

"They needed Heydon where they could watch him, so they built a front. A fake web development firm where they pretended to work on an idea he'd had for an app. Sebastien paid for the offices, the equipment, the staff. At the same time, they'd hacked Heydon's personal accounts, started sending weird messages to half his contact list."

"What kind of weird messages?"

"They sent DMs, claiming to be Heydon, pleading with people to respond, then telling the magpie story."

I see a flicker of recognition in Matten's face.

"Always in the early hours of the morning. Then he'd get all these calls and texts about it the next day."

"Reopening the wound of Theo's death." Matten looks at me. "But why?"

"Well, when they connected him with Control, they started dropping hints that Control was Theo. That he'd been separated from the family somehow. They even put on a show of having him finish the magpie story."

Matten waits.

"Control said he had this recurring dream. Walking into the kitchen of what he guessed must be his birth parents' place, finding a live bird in the dustbin..."

Matten makes a kind of choking sound. "As though Heydon really had brought it back to life."

"They needed him to think he was special. It was the only way they could convince him about Theo."

"But why would they want to do that?"

"Well, that's what I was hoping you could tell me."

Matten shakes her head. "I'm not making the same mistake twice. I've told you everything I can and more."

"What happened that day, with Heydon and Theo?"

"No," she says. "Absolutely not."

"Someone went around the houses to pull this thing off. They threatened your family, paid three hundred thousand pounds to Control, built this fake business, got what they needed, then covered it up and vanished."

"I've got as much antipathy for them as you. If not a good deal more. But I've spent the last five years turning myself inside out for what I did. Frankly, the results are worse than anything I could have imagined."

"So help me to fix it." Matten doesn't say anything. "Last night, they killed a man to keep him quiet. That tells me they killed Heydon too. And they'll kill anyone else who gets in their way."

"Then don't engage them."

"Two men are dead, and every trace is going up in smoke. I think they're engaged."

With a look of self-reproach and the set jaw of someone trying to get through it, she talks down to the desk. "Heydon never spoke about that day," she says.

"He never spoke about his brother's death?"

"On some level, it just wasn't possible for him. We hadn't made the breakthrough. The magpie was his way of talking about it without talking about it."

"And what did Peck think about that?"

"He was furious. And of course, he didn't believe me. He demanded to see my notes." Matten shudders. "And after seeing the baby monitor, I showed him."

"It sounds like he didn't give you a choice," I say.

But Matten doesn't look convinced.

"So once Peck realized that Theo was a bust, he started looking for other stuff."

"Heydon was working through a particular paranoid delusion. In his case from a combination of childhood trauma, mental illness, and drug abuse."

"He thought he was being followed," I say. "Yeah, they made the most of that. From what I can tell, it sounds like the hacking, Peck's visit to you—this whole scheme with Heydon's brother, his disappearance, everything—was all about them getting closer to the day of Theo's drowning, finding something out. There's got to be a reason. And why nineteen years after the fact?"

Matten's just staring straight ahead, not looking at anything. "Perhaps it wasn't their first attempt."

"Go on."

"Heydon once told me a story about a strange encounter with a young woman, a one-night stand. A lingerie model who'd connected with him online. Heydon threw her out because she kept poking around for details about that day."

"Did he have any idea why?"

Matten's still not comfortable disclosing this, and she goes on, not looking at me. "I think the invasiveness, the single-minded approach, all put him in mind of something like a tabloid fishing expedition."

"You're saying the girl was like a honey trap?"

Matten nods, and I try to think it through. If the girl had been an earlier approach, then I could understand why Heydon might have seen the press in it. The Pierce family had a profile after all, and Theo's death had been a sensational tragedy. If someone really had wanted the lowdown from him about that day, then a pretty girl might be the first thing they'd try. Wire the room, get him drunk, get him off, and get him talking. But that's where they must have run into their first snag. Not only did Heydon never speak about Theo's death, it sounded like the mere mention could provoke a meltdown. So they'd tracked down his therapist and extorted her. Peck can't have been thrilled to discover that Heydon didn't discuss his brother in this setting either. But he kept on pecking until he got what he wanted. Heydon stopped attending his sessions shortly after, launching his project with Control.

A total mind-fuck.

I'm just not sure the story scans as tabloid fodder. First, I hadn't gotten the sense that Heydon was harboring any further dark secrets about that day. His account in the tape had felt truthful, like a moment of intense shame that he finally felt able to release himself from. If only because he hoped that no one would ever see the tape. Nothing I'd seen and heard about Theo's death suggested foul play or some darker story. Just two kids, a tragedy, and no obvious villain for the headlines. Except for Miranda, of course, if you really wanted to go there. But why would you? Her account of that day was public record, and it's not as though it paints her in the best light.

So what were they trying to find?

"Could you stop doing that?" Matten says.

I've finished the water and realize I'm crushing the plastic bottle in my hand.

I take a step forward and drop it in the bin.

"Peck's appointment..." I say.

Matten watches me levelly for a moment, then types at her computer. "It was made through the web portal, by an assistant."

"Could I get the details?"

Mechanically, Matten takes a pen and starts writing the details on a slip of paper. Then she stops and looks up.

"What are you going to do?" she asks.

"Find them."

"And then what?"

I don't say anything.

"They'll come at you through your loved ones."

"Probably not," I say after a moment.

"Then they'll just come for you."

"Then maybe I'll get a straight answer from someone in all this."

Matten snorts. "That's what this is about after all." I just stand there, and she goes on. "In Heydon's recording," she says, "when he unspooled this nonsense scheme about fixing everything, beating death, you could see that he was fooling himself. Correct?"

I still don't say anything.

"He'd invested too much into the story he was telling himself to back down. And now you're charging in the same direction, right off the same bridge."

I just stand there, and at length, Matten looks back to the screen, completing the note that she'd been writing. When she holds it out to me, I can see it's a test, but I cross the room and take it anyway.

Matten avoids my eyes.

"You'll get your answer all right," she says darkly.

I glance down at the slip of paper, then hold it up in thanks. "I'm grateful for your help, Doctor. If I were you, I'd take that trip you've been promising yourself."

I leave the office and cross the small reception area.

"You know, it's not just your life you're risking," Matten calls after me.

I stop at the door to say something in response, but after a second, it doesn't come. I can hear Matten, listening for me, but I don't turn around. I just get the door open and go.

Jaya's waiting pensively in the corridor. She watches me for a second, then walks right by, back into the office, to check on Matten. A decent person, a good friend. The way she avoids my eye and walks stiffly past makes me feel like the exact opposite.

24.

I haven't eaten since that bread roll this morning, and I find myself drifting automatically into the first burger place I pass. I get a chicken breast with blue cheese on a brioche bun, with an order of rosemary salted fries, washing it down with an IPA and a shot of Jameson's. You'd get a family meal down the street for what it costs, but when I leave, it feels like the blood's flowing again.

I consider the underground but flash back to Heydon's video—those watchful eyes—and decide to take a cab back to the hotel instead. The streets are dark, and I lean right back into the seat, luxuriating in a few minutes where I don't need to make a decision or try and push things forward. At the Mandarin, I walk straight through the lobby, making a point of staring straight ahead when I call the lift. The doors open, and I step inside and go.

I reach the room, put my key card to the door, see it flash green, and step inside. Then I bolt it behind me, grab a fistful of miniatures from the minibar, and crash down onto the sofa. When I'd stopped into a corner shop for some supplies, a gorily packaged carton of Marlboro Reds had found its way into the bag. I haven't bought a pack of cigarettes since I first met Clare in Naples three years ago.

I'd landed in a street corner café one morning, still winding down from the night before. I'd ordered a beer and found a seat outside. I was working my way through the pack, burning a hole in the ozone layer, reaching for my third or fourth, when I glanced up and saw her at the next table.

Clare had washed-out blond hair. A strong jaw and slim neck. She was wearing sunglasses and reading a book. She'd chosen the seat with the best light. I was just trying to stay out of it. I hadn't seen her sit down, and when I glanced up, she noticed. I'd smiled and held the cigarette in the air for a second, asking if she minded.

"I'll move," she'd said easily. An Irish accent.

"No," I'd said, sliding it back into the carton. "I'm always looking for a reason to give up."

She'd looked at me.

My pale cheeks and bloodshot eyes. The cloud of smoke hanging over my head.

She'd smiled. "I'd say you've got that covered."

We'd spent the next few days walking around town, talking. She was from the old country. Not quite a Galway girl but getting on that way. And so real that it just seemed to pour out of her. Unlike me, pigging it out with phrase books and hand gestures, Clare spoke Italian. And Irish and German and French. She'd managed this by working her way around places over the years. There was a hands-on farm girl in there somewhere. She could take things apart and put them back together again. Her main interest in Naples was the archaeological museum; she liked to see that stuff close-up. I think that's what called her out into the world, but she never said as much. Clare preferred ancient history to her own.

She had two tattoos, both of which she said she regretted. But for me, they were mysterious clues about her past. The one on the back of her neck was a compass that she could make disappear by letting her hair down. The other was a small, weird-shaped A on her inner left wrist, which I came to understand was the Aphex Twin logo.

I'd finished the cigarettes over the next few days, but after that, I hadn't wanted more. They just made her go farther away. Now, lying back, alone, watching the smoke curl, I see I've solved that problem once and for all.

I'm sighing, sitting up for another, still brooding on Clare, when I see the wardrobe door's slightly ajar. I'd left the *Do Not Disturb* sign up, and I'm fairly sure I'd shut the wardrobe on my way out.

I drop the cigarette, get up, and go to it, feeling heavy. I input the code for the room safe, and it pops open. First, I look, then I rifle around inside for a few seconds, but it's completely empty. Someone had let themselves into the room, opened the safe, and taken my passport. I walk out and slam the door behind me.

———

When I get to the front desk, there's two members of staff. The manager from the first night, who'd tried to hand me off to one of the Rayner goons, and his colleague, a smiling blond woman. There are a few people in line ahead of me, and by the time I get to the front, the woman's free. I stand to one side, letting other people go first, waiting for the manager. He's avoiding my eye, taking as long as possible with the elderly man he's checking out.

When the man finally leaves, the manager gives me a look like he's seeing me for the first time, like there's no history between us. Like he can just smile it out.

"Busy night?" I say, approaching the counter.

His name badge says *Chip*.

He glances at his colleague, seeing that she's distracted, checking in a large group, then back to me.

"What seems to be the problem, sir?"

I take a breath, lower my voice, and speak calmly.

"The fucking problem, arsehole, is that I've got a roomful of witnesses."

I watch it land, and his expression hardens.

"Are you *threatening* me?" he says, raising his voice.

I feel the glare of the large group checking in. The blond woman doesn't look at me but catches someone's eye across the lobby, and a security guard drifts over.

"We all good here?" he asks.

The manager stares at me.

"We're delighted," I say, smiling at the guy.

He backs off to a polite distance, out of earshot.

I turn back to the manager. "Where is it?"

"Sir, I have absolutely no idea what—"

"My passport," I say. "It was in the safe in my room. Now it's gone. Where is it?"

"Truly. I can't believe what I'm hearing. Of course you're upset." Chip lifts the receiver from his phone. "I'll notify the authorities immediately," he says, starting to dial, acting the whole thing out.

I stare at him flatly. "That won't be necessary."

He keeps his mouth under control, but I can see the smile in his eyes. "Very well," he says, frowning slightly, like he's perplexed by my decision. "You will permit me to make some inquiries though?" he asks. "Find out who cleaned your room this morning and so forth?"

"The *Do Not Disturb* sign was up," I tell him. "Anyway, what would the maid want with my passport?"

Chip makes a face.

"You'd be surprised. We've had to let no end of girls go after items went missing from VIP rooms."

"I'll bet," I say with a tight smile.

"Strictly between us, of course, but…" He trails off.

But Chip's got a cushy number here. I can push it and bring the law down on my head while getting some poor woman fired, or I can take it with good grace.

"Yeah, yeah," I say. "I get the picture. Well, let's just leave it there for now then."

Now the smile goes all the way to his mouth.

"Of course," he says. "Whatever you think best." He leaves a polite silence. "Was there anything else I could help you with this evening?"

"No," I say after a moment. "You nailed that one though. Thanks."

25.

When I get back to the room, I lock the door and try to wrap my head around the message it feels like I'm being sent. Taking my passport does two things at once. It stops me from blowing town, and it leaves me in no doubt that I've been fucked.

Chip's my number one suspect for the theft itself, of course. I've already found him online. I've already mapped out his commute to and from work using social media. It's enough to follow him home and find out where he lives if it comes to that. I could catch him off guard, go in at three a.m., and play the hits. But since I've already seen him with the Rayner guys, and since those guys had been working for Ronnie Pierce, it feels safe to assume that the missing passport's Ronnie finally getting back at me for not handing over the case.

I can guess what reaction he's looking for. My scene with Chip, only more so. Hitting Tregunter Road in the middle of the night and bringing the house down. Blowing Reagan's phone up, going berserk. It feels a bit late in the day though, and I decide to do nothing for the moment. I'll pay Ronnie a visit first thing.

That leaves me with Mr. Peck to find, then I'm angry about the passport all over again. It had featured heavily in my plans for tonight. I'd wanted to pace up and down with it, weighing my decision. Follow Heydon into the dark, or take the money and run?

Now, I haven't got a choice.

For a second, I linger on the possibility that Ronnie didn't take it. There are other forces at work here after all. Control's killer had looked right at me when I left the penthouse. And someone had been circulating my picture before that. In fact, if I hadn't gone through Control's bag, the cops would have found my picture at the scene.

I'm pacing up and down, chain-smoking, laughing dirtily about the mess I'm in. At this rate, I'll get through the whole pack before the cardboard hinges on the carton have had a chance to go weak. I cross the room to stub out my cigarette, catching my crazed reflection in the mirror. I've still got the green lenses in from my chat with Matten.

I see Heydon's face and stop.

He'd been about to solve his own mystery, or so he thought. In reality, someone had been manipulating his every move, lighting the path toward his disappearance in such a way that it was irresistible to him. So does that make Matten right? Am I walking into the same thing?

———

I force myself to sit down and search for Peck. But either he's kept a low profile, or his name's been suppressed from the search results. Heydon all over again. There's various Alan Pecks, but none of them look like my guy. And there's nothing when I try his name against other search terms like *Heydon*, *Control*, *Sebastien*, *military*, *special forces*, *SAS*, *security*, etc.

But when I put his name into an unfiltered search engine, I get a hit. *Alan Peck + security* brings up a site called XTech Holdings. I click through, but the site's dead.

I go back to Google and try XTech Holdings, just as an experiment. No results. But when I try again on the unfiltered site, boom. A listing on Companies House.

The overview says that XTech was a security firm and lists Peck as a director. According to the paperwork, the firm was rolled up in 2018. I start working my way through their filing history, looking for names I can latch on to. The director before Peck was a Mikhail Nazarov. I search for him, seeing he's gone on to bigger things. He's the director of a much shinier company now, in property development. All giant checks and hard hats. When I try and find out where the money's coming from, it's not clear. But searching between names that keep cropping up, following their trajectories on into the business world, I find myself repeatedly being led back to something called Hartson Holdings.

I back out of Companies House and search for it.

I click the first link I see, then sit back.

Hartson Holdings is an international conglomerate with links to energy, health care, property development, and security. The greeting screen just shows the company logo. Minus the cracks, it's exactly the same design as the heart tattoo on Heydon's face. Exactly the same as mine.

26.

I'm lying on top of the bedsheets, staring up at the ceiling, several drinks deep, when there's a light knock at the door. I'm not exactly hard to find and not exactly popular, so when I get up, I don't know what to expect. I edge to the peephole, then stare through. When I unlatch the door and open it, she's just leaving.

"Reagan," I say.

She turns slowly.

"Are you OK?" I ask.

She doesn't say anything.

"Would you like to come in?"

She nods, and I stand to one side.

I close the door, then follow her through to the lounge. Reagan just stands there, like she can't remember why she came.

"Take a seat," I say. "Can I get you a drink?"

She looks at the empty miniatures scattered across the desk. "If you think you can spare one," she says dryly.

It feels like the first smile I've had in a minute.

"Let's see," I say, going to the minibar. "OK, we've got tequila?"

I glance over my shoulder at her. "That's a no. Alcohol-free beer, no. Oh, some rosé?"

"Sure," she says.

I pour her a glass, then open the tequila miniature to say cheers with. We both take a drink.

"I wanted to apologize about yesterday," she says.

"Nothing to apologize for."

She watches me. "Perhaps I overreacted."

"I don't think so," I say. "After what you had to see, it seemed fair."

She doesn't say anything.

"Has there been some kind of breakthrough?" I ask.

Reagan looks at me for a moment. With effort, she dredges up details that, I see now, she was trying to forget.

"Well," she says at length, "Miss Lao thinks that this CTRL person from Heydon's phone is likely the same man he mentioned in the video."

"Sounds possible," I say carefully.

They hadn't connected Control with the man who'd been shot, because he hadn't been named.

"Not that it makes any difference," Reagan goes on. "Whether this person helped to facilitate things or not, it seems clear that Heydon knew what he was doing."

I don't say anything.

"Anyway," she says. "I suppose this is none of your business anymore."

"I'm always happy to talk," I say.

Reagan nods, then smiles uncomfortably.

"You're wrong about me, you know," she says.

"I'm wrong about you? How so?"

"When you were telling me about the different ways that people reacted to you," she says. "Your performance as my brother. You said I wanted to get as far away from you as possible."

"I didn't mean anything."

"No, you were right about that. You've just got the wrong idea about why."

"We don't have to—"

"Yes," she says. "We do. When we met for the first time, it was overwhelming. I had an intense emotional reaction. You think it's because your impersonation of my brother was so flawless, you even fooled me. It wasn't," she says. "You didn't." Reagan looks at me for a long moment. "To tell you the truth, I must be the one person who can't see the resemblance."

"So what made you so upset?" I ask.

"I could see and hear the effect that you were going for," she says. "And I could tell at a glance that you weren't him. Somehow, the entire performance struck me like a tasteless joke," she says. "A bad Halloween costume."

I look at her for a few seconds, then nod.

"And I was wondering…" she says.

"Wondering what?"

"How can you do something like that?" she asks.

"Oh," I say, surprised. "Yeah, I should probably talk to a shrink or something."

"No." Reagan shakes her head. She's not asking hypothetically. She wants to know. "*How?*"

"You mean, like—"

"This shape-shifting thing," she says. "Your accent, your posture, even your height. It all changes depending on how you want to be seen in any given moment."

When I glance up, she's looking right at me.

"I'm not always who I need to be," I say.

Reagan smiles. "Is it really that simple?"

"Why not?"

"You just choose another personality from the fancy dress box?"

"You're the actor," I say.

"The failed actor."

"Only if you quit. For me, it feels more like I'm tuning myself into the room."

"Aren't you afraid?"

"Afraid of what?"

"Of everything," she says. "Getting caught, the consequences, being found out…"

"People find me out all the time. You did."

"So what's the trick?"

"I don't know. I think the trick is to just keep going."

"But you must know what I mean."

"The fear," I say.

Reagan looks at me for a moment, then nods.

"Well, if you're lucky, that never goes away."

She considers this for a moment.

"And what about when it's all over?" she asks.

"When what's all over? How do you mean?"

"I mean like now," she says. "When your contortions are finished for the day, when you need to return to your original form. When there's no one left to fool."

"There's always someone," I say.

Reagan gives me a questioning look.

"Is that why you think I came here?"

"I was talking about myself," I say.

"I see." She smiles. "I think, in a roundabout way, that might be what I'm asking. How do you remember who you really are?"

"I think, in a roundabout way, that's what I'm telling you," I say. "I try not to." Reagan waits. "For me, it's better to just stay in the moment, a blank. That way—"

"You can be the person you need to be," she says. "I can't decide if that's highly evolved or the saddest thing I've ever heard."

"I'm aiming for somewhere in between."

Reagan smiles but doesn't laugh.

She puts her wineglass down.

"So who do you think you need to be right now?"

Before I can say anything, there's a knock at the door. Neither one of us moves, then they knock again.

"Just a second," I say.

I go to the peephole, then open it.

"Excuse me, sir," Chip says. "I tried to call."

I stare at him for a few seconds.

"I unplugged the phone," I say.

"Ah. We actually prefer guests not to—"

"What do you want?"

"I've got an urgent message," he says. "For Ms. Reagan Pierce."

He tries to look past me into the room, and I see that he's carrying a folded note.

"I can give it to her," I say, holding out a hand.

"I'm under strict instructions to pass the message to Ms. Pierce personally," he says. "You understand?"

I sigh at him, then open the door farther.

Reagan appears, and I walk back into the room, giving her a moment. When she thanks Chip and closes the door, I turn back to her.

She stands there, staring at the note.

Numbly, she says, "I have to leave."

"Something wrong?" I ask.

She shakes her head, but she can't speak.

"Reagan," I say, taking a step toward her.

She backs into the closed door, looking like a trapped animal. "I'm sorry," she says, shaking her head, not meeting my eye. "This was a mistake."

She gets the door open and goes.

—

I watch the door for a few seconds, then pull on my jacket and walk out. The elevators are left from my room, but I go right, for the stairs, taking them down to reception, then out. I go to the taxi rank outside the main entrance, walking to the last cab in line.

"First car, pal," the driver says, waving me on to the front of the rank.

"I'm playing a prank," I say. "It's an extra hundred plus the meter if you're game?"

The driver eyes me for a second, then nods, and I climb into the back, sliding to the right, as far from the curb as possible. A few seconds later, Reagan emerges from the building. She's with a muscular man in a fitted gray suit. He's gripping her tightly by the arm, like he's escorting her out. It looks like they're having an argument of some kind, and they go quickly down the white stone steps. The man marches Reagan to the first car in the rank, then they climb in.

"Now follow them," I say.

The driver eyes me in the mirror. "This is a prank then, yeah?"

"Just some harmless fun," I tell him.

27.

We move slowly down Brompton Road, past Harrods on the left as well as a few other fancy department stores and five-star hotels.

I hadn't been shocked to see the other man. In fact, I'd been wondering why Reagan's message had come to my door at all. I could imagine her leaving word that she could be reached at the Mandarin Oriental. I just couldn't see her giving out my room number. The message had to have been sent up from the lobby, from the bodybuilder in the gray suit. He could have easily knocked on the door himself as well. He was certainly big enough. But for some reason, he hadn't wanted me to see him.

When they turn onto Tregunter Road and pull up, I tell the driver to keep going. As we pass by the big house, I see that every single light in the place is blazing.

"Here," I say once we're five or six doors down.

The driver pulls in, and I turn to look back. Reagan climbs out of the car, then hurries toward the house, realizing she's left the door open, coming back to close it. She leans in, listening to something she's being told by the man, still sitting inside the car.

Then a hand emerges, caressing her face. She stands stiffly, then winces a smile and closes the door, going straight up to the house.

"Now what?" the driver says.

I don't speak until the cab behind us has started up again. I let them pass us and get to the end of the street.

"Now follow him," I say.

The driver watches me in the rearview mirror for a few seconds, then pulls out, following at a distance.

——

The drive from the Mandarin to Tregunter hadn't taken long. Maybe twenty minutes through fairly heavy traffic. But as we work our way out of Chelsea's grand residential estates onto the busy main road, keeping the Thames on our right, I settle in for the sightseeing tour.

We pass Albert Bridge, where Heydon's car had been found five years ago. It's interesting to see how close it is to the Pierce house, considering how busy he'd been that night, and it makes me feel even more sure that he didn't park the car there himself.

We drive for thirty or forty minutes, skirting Pimlico, then crossing the river, somewhere around Lambeth. I've got no idea where we're going, and all of a sudden, the rain's coming down so hard that I can't keep track of where we are. Gleaning what I can from street signs and Google Maps, my guess is we're heading farther south. Then the car in front changes direction, taking us through Southwark and unexpectedly back across the river on Waterloo Bridge. We loop left, heading into the city center, having taken the really long way around.

The driver glances back in the rearview mirror.

"Dodging this queen shit," he says.

The car in front leads us to a dark square off Pall Mall, behind

Jermyn Street. There's a large, gated, and locked-down leafy green at the center, surrounded on all four sides by three- and four-story town houses. Most of them look like high-end businesses or private members' clubs, and we drive by large, darkened lobbies with meaningless pieces of corporate art displayed prominently in the windows. Six-foot pink flamingos and life-size plastic trees. Transnational oil conglomerates with stock photos of perfect, smiling white kids playing in unspoiled, natural beauty spots, with phrases like *Our Pledge* written across their faces.

The car in front pulls up just around the next corner, outside a building where the lobby's still fully lit.

"Stop here," I say.

The car in front just sits there.

"Now what?" the driver says uncomfortably.

I don't say anything.

A woman exits the lobby, holding an enormous umbrella, walking to the cab, and opening the door. The man in the tight suit emerges, standing beneath the umbrella for a few moments, speaking to the woman. Then he runs on into the building, and she turns, walking through the rain, right toward us.

She reaches the car and opens my door.

She looks like a secretary, a good one, with a robust clothing allowance and literally the healthiest-looking skin I've ever seen. When she smiles, her teeth are so perfect that I close my mouth instinctively.

"Good evening," she says over the sound of the rain.

"Good evening."

"I'm not sure how good it is," she says, laughing at the weather. "I'm Miss Brandt, Sebastien's PA. I'm afraid he's still tied up, but if you'd rather wait inside."

I stare at her for a few seconds. *Sebastien's* PA.

Looks like the tasteless jokes are on me.

———

The umbrella's so roomy that we can walk side by side, and when I catch Miss Brandt's scent, it's the next echelon up from Chanel, way out of my range. She takes us toward the glowing, double-height lobby. There's a big guy on the door, probably getting on for three hundred pounds. He's ex-military, a killer of some kind, with a face that looks like it's been chewed on. From the way his eyes pass smoothly over mine, he senses some kind of trouble. But he smiles and stands to one side in a way that says he's used to seeing all sorts come and go from this building.

A golden plate on the door says *The Agency*.

Miss Brandt uses her passkey to open it.

The lobby's comfortably the size of a family home. An almost entirely pristine, empty space, with a discreet front desk set off to the side and a row of gleaming white marble torsos—headless women with their tits out—leading the way to a stainless-steel security barrier, with a staircase and lift bank beyond. The chandelier's so stupidly oversize, so vicious and sharp-edged, that it hangs over us like a threat. The lights are humming so hard you can hear the money burning. Miss Brandt closes the umbrella, drops it in a stand, then smiles.

"Shall we?"

Her heels echo off the tiles as she leads us to the security barrier. She uses her passkey to open it, then takes us to the lift and presses for the fourth floor. The walls are reflective on all sides and polished to such a brilliant sheen that when I glance at them, they feel like a cold dose of the truth. I'd left the hotel in a hurry and unexpectedly, throwing a crumpled suit jacket on top of a crumpled shirt—on top of a crumpled man—and my hair's going in six different directions at once.

Exiting the lift, Miss Brandt leads us through another secure door to a reception with a comfortable waiting area. There are six leather seats, more "art" on the walls, and just one door beyond this point. Even though it's after hours, I can faintly make out the murmured voices of two men coming from behind it.

"Do take a seat," Miss Brandt says. "He'll be with you as soon as possible." I stay standing. "Is there anything I can get you?" she asks. "Tea, coffee…"

"Well," I say. "I was wondering if you could tell me a little about the agency itself."

"Of course," she says. "What would you like to know?"

"What does Sebastien do here exactly?"

Miss Brandt smiles.

"The Agency was founded four years ago with the goal of bringing all client requirements under one umbrella." She smiles again. "So to speak. Sebastien's our innovation director. Or that's his job title." She goes on confidentially, "I happen to know that he thinks of himself more like a kind of human rights activist."

"Right," I say. Then after a moment, "That's not what I'd call him if he had me working late on a Sunday."

"There's nowhere I'd rather be," Miss Brandt says.

I smile like it's a joke, but her face doesn't change.

It sounds like the murmured voices coming through the door might be reaching some kind of conclusion. One man relaying what sound like detailed instructions and another man agreeing, giving one-word answers.

We turn to the opening door.

The man who walks through it looks like he's come directly from the front desk of a luxury hotel and after a long shift too. I don't recognize him from the Mandarin, so it must be somewhere else. He looks just as out of place here as I do, and from the way he glances nervously about himself, he clearly feels it. When he sees me, he blushes and looks quickly away, not needing another human face right now. Not wanting to see anything that he shouldn't. He flashes a brief, service industry smile, then gratefully follows Miss Brandt out.

I don't move until I hear the lift.

The door to Sebastien's office is slightly ajar, and I can hear him talking quietly on the phone. I edge closer, pretending to take in the walls. Between all the art—the little girls holding heart-shaped balloons and the men with mushroom clouds for heads—there's some framed pictures of Sebastien, smiling and shaking hands with people who I don't recognize but understand to be celebrities. I look for Heydon or any member of the Pierce clan, but as far as I can see, they're not here.

Then I get the very edge of Sebastien's conversation.

"I think when you look at it from that angle, the simplest thing for everyone is to avoid letting this thing leak out into the public consciousness," he's saying.

A clean English accent.

I hear the lift again, the tick of Miss Brandt's heels. I lower myself into a seat before she sees me. When she reenters the room, she smiles, walking to Sebastien's door, closing it firmly. She looks like she's about to resume the PR spiel she'd been giving me about Sebastien and the Agency, but the door opens again.

Sebastien emerges, still talking on the phone but sounding like he's concluding his conversation, making perfunctory small talk.

"Of course," he says. "We'll do something special. Get the whole gang involved—"

He sees me for the first time and stops.

"Right," he says, responding to the person on the other end. "It's a date then. Love to Mary-Alice." Sebastien hangs up, staring at me like I'm a glitch in the Matrix. At length, he looks to Miss Brandt, holding the mobile phone out to her. "Get rid of that," he says.

Miss Brandt takes the phone, then melts away, leaving the reception area.

Sebastien's six two, well-built, and wearing a tailored suit that shows off his overdeveloped biceps and chest. Although his head's mostly shaved, he's got a small, credit card–size patch of hair, front and center, styled, and set in a side parting. His mustache looks like something you'd see on a bomber pilot in World War II. With his mini-Hitler hairstyle and with the muscles, it looks like a disguise. Or some kind of a distraction.

"Well, I never," he says.

Sebastien struts back into the office, taking the leather seat behind his desk, inviting me to sit opposite. He looks like he's about to say something when the phone rings. He picks up, listens for a few seconds, then puts it down again, pushing a button to put it on silent.

"Well," he says. "I'm sorry to keep you waiting. Especially since you've come so far out of your way."

"No problem. Miss Brandt looked after me."

"Yes," he says. "And she offered you a drink?"

"It seemed a little late for coffee."

Sebastien smiles. "I was thinking the same thing."

He opens a chilled drawer in his desk and removes a solid block of ice with a bottle frozen into it. I'm guessing it's vodka but can't make out the brand. Sebastien pours two long glasses, then pushes one of them across the desk. We raise our drinks to each other, then try them. I'm no connoisseur, but the vodka's good, so cold and so pure that it goes down like mineral water.

"So, Mr...."

"Lynch," I say.

"Lynch?" Sebastien sounds dimly surprised. "So you're not going to try and tell me that you're Heydon Pierce or something."

"I've got a feeling that you wouldn't believe me."

"Right," he says after a moment. "And what makes you think that?"

"I saw you talking to Reagan back at the Mandarin."

"Of course," Sebastien says. "Yes, she put me in the picture. Wild story though, I must say. To be honest, I wouldn't mind hearing it from you."

He wants to compare my version with whatever Reagan had just told him, forcing me to make a snap decision about how much I can really trust her. If there's something between them, then she's probably told him everything. He knows I'm here looking for Heydon.

"Well, I met Bobbie, Reagan's sister, at Heathrow a couple of days back. She thought I looked a lot like her brother. I don't know if you know them, but he went missing five years ago."

Sebastien just waits for me to go on.

"Anyway, we had a few drinks, blah blah, I woke up with this tattoo on my face."

Sebastien sits back, smiling, shaking his head.

"*Blah blah,*" he says. "Is that what the kids are calling it these days?" When I don't respond, the smile fades slowly from his face. "And what did Bobbie say about all this?"

"Bobbie left to make an early flight. When I woke up, she was already in the air. I sent her a message, making my displeasure known, and she tried to make it up to me. She suggested I go to her mum and dad's place to see if they'd pay for the removal. Miranda agreed, and they stuck me in the Mandarin until it's sorted."

Sebastien takes a long drink, letting the silence stretch out, encouraging me to keep filling it, but I stop.

"*Mm.*" He swallows a mouthful of vodka. "OK," he says. "So how come you're following me?"

"I wanted to ask you the same question. Like I say, I saw you talking to Reagan at the Mandarin."

He looks at me for a moment, then opens a drawer, takes out a photo, and throws it to my side of the desk. I lean forward. It's the same picture I'd found in Control's bag. Me, outside a coffee shop in Soho, with Reagan.

Sebastien puts his glass down, giving me his undivided attention.

"Two thugs pushed their way in here today," he says seriously. "One big, wearing a leather jacket, one long and thin, wearing an anorak. They wanted to know where they could find Heydon Pierce."

I just sit there.

I'm grateful for a description of the people who've been showing my picture around, but I've got to wonder—are they looking for Heydon or looking for me?

"Why would they come to you about that?" I ask.

"Heydon engaged me for a project," he says easily. "We worked together for a short time. By the sounds of it, they'd been showing this picture all over town, trying to get a lead on where they might find him. Eventually, that brought them to me."

"So what did you tell them?"

Sebastien watches me for a moment.

"I told them Heydon went missing five years ago. Then I threw them out on their arses. What's the story there? You owe them something?"

"Apparently."

Sebastien smiles.

"Once they were gone, I couldn't quite shake what I'd heard, so I asked Miss Brandt to place a call to Miranda's lawyer at Andrews and Ziff. When she asked them if Heydon was back in town, if the family had seen or heard anything, they completely denied it."

"Then they told you the truth."

"I suppose so," Sebastien says, not willing to relinquish control of the conversation. "I'm still not quite clear on why you followed me though."

"I'll be honest," I say. "I know these guys are looking for Heydon, and I know I look like him. So when I see a strange man dragging a woman out of my hotel after getting her to leave my room, it makes me curious."

I'm right back on the tightrope here.

Sebastien's playing innocent, and so far, he's doing a reasonable job. But if he's telling the truth about the two guys turning up, then it's deeper than them just planting a picture on Control.

They're out there, right now, looking for me.

However much I might want to get up and walk, I can't afford to show weakness in front of Sebastien. And whatever Control might have said to the contrary, I've got to at least act like he's not involved.

The phone on Sebastien's desk starts flashing.

"That's it," I say with a shrug. "There's no mystery. Reagan left with you, so I followed her to Tregunter Road. When she got out of the car, I followed you. The end. You still haven't told me what you were doing at the Mandarin, by the way."

"Well, that picture caught my imagination," he says. "I didn't think it was likely, but it looked as though there was a chance. After Andrews and Ziff turned us down flat, I wondered if Heydon could have come back, incognito, without telling anyone. *Maybe he owes these men cash. Maybe I can help.* So I decided to make some inquiries of my own."

The phone's still flashing on his desk.

"Sure," I say. "But what brought you to the Mandarin?"

"Oh, I've got eyes at most of the bigger places in town. I just asked if anyone had seen a guy with a heart tattoo."

"Huh," I say, wrong-footed for a second. "Speaking of the Mandarin, what was your note to Reagan about?"

Sebastien nods calmly.

"When I arrived, I thought I saw Ms. Pierce on her way inside. We're old acquaintances and—"

"Through her brother?" I ask.

"Right," Sebastien says. "I smiled and tried to say hello, but she looked away, almost as though she didn't want to be seen. Once I'd put two and two together about where she might be going, I simply wanted to warn her that you might not be the real thing."

Now we've both presented our cover stories, there's not much more to say, so I ask, "What is that you do here?"

"I'm in client care," he tells me.

"What does that mean?"

"Well," he says, throwing out his left arm, revealing the Patek Philippe on his wrist and checking the time. "I'm still here at gone eleven on a Sunday evening." He shrugs. "So I suppose it means whatever it has to."

"What did it mean with Heydon?"

Sebastien smiles self-effacingly. "We founded the Agency post-Heydon," he says.

"But your relationship was…"

"*Business*," he says, like that's the only kind there is.

"What business?"

"Client care, just a more rudimentary version."

"What kind of stuff does 'client care' cover?"

Sebastien eyes me carefully.

"I'm just wondering if anything you said or did could have contributed to Heydon's disappearance," I say.

Sebastien snorts. "Absolutely not."

"You sound fairly sure."

"I simply trust in my heart that I only ever tried to help him. If you really want to know, then it was Heydon who terminated our relationship."

"Can I ask why?"

"We had what you might call creative differences. I'm sorry to say I came to find that he was a truly broken person. That's why we drifted apart."

"You weren't in his life when he walked out?"

"We hadn't seen each other in months."

That tallied with what Control had told me at least.

"In what way did you find Heydon to be broken?"

"You'd have to talk to the family about that," he says, eyeing me. "I just can't say I was surprised when they found his car on that bridge."

"You weren't surprised when he killed himself?"

Sebastien stares at me. "What are you driving at?"

"I don't know," I say. "Nothing. It's just that when I googled him, I didn't find anything about the two of you working together.

To be honest, I couldn't find much about him at all. And no trace of his online life from before his disappearance either."

"Perhaps Heydon was a lurker?"

"Yeah," I say. "I don't know. It almost feels like stuff's been taken down or deleted."

"Taken down or deleted," he repeats.

"Either that, or he never existed at all."

I say it like a joke, but Sebastien just stares at me.

The phone's still flashing on his desk.

There's a knock at the door.

Sebastien looks past me. "Yes?"

Miss Brandt opens it a crack.

"It looks like they've found him," she says.

I'm confused for a moment, wondering if she's referring to Heydon. I don't move or say anything. Sebastien thanks her, then picks up the flashing phone.

"Yes?" he says. "You're joking." He checks the Patek again. "Yep," he says. "Don't let him leave."

He hangs up, then looks at me.

"I'll tell you what," he says. "It's been that kind of a day. If you really want to know what I do for a living, I'll show you."

28.

When we climb into the back of the black Mercedes, I see that
the driver's the same monster who'd been standing on the door.
Sebastien doesn't speak to him or me, instead spending the entire
journey looking between three different screens. Texting from one,
scrolling through social media on a second, checking in with news
feeds on a third. He doesn't look up from his work or seem in any
way self-conscious about it. And a minute or so before we reach
our destination, he puts everything to one side, staring straight
forward, getting in the zone, preparing himself.

Then we're walking past the convertibles parked outside the
building into the after-hours lobby of another luxury hotel. It's
not nicer than the Mandarin, but it's bigger and with gold set into
almost every surface.

The man I'd seen leaving Sebastien's office is standing at the
front desk. He doesn't move for a moment when we walk in, then
he leaves his post stiffly, walking toward the lift bank without
acknowledging us. We follow at a distance, then join him in the
lift. The man presses for the sixth floor, and the doors close. He's

careful not to look at Sebastien, but he steals a glance at me. My sense is he's unsettled about whatever he's gotten himself mixed up with here, but he can't help wondering what my role is.

I'm thinking roughly the same thing.

Sebastien hadn't indicated what we were doing other than watching him work. From what I've seen so far, that might mean anything, but my guess is that one of his clients has gotten themselves into some trouble. They went dark for a while, and now they've resurfaced. Control had described Sebastien as everything from a shady talent agent to an angel investor. From a silent partner to a shadowy intelligence guy. Right now, everything's still on the table. On the sixth floor, the guy from the hotel leads us to a door, glances pointedly at it, then walks away.

We're the only people standing in the corridor.

Sebastien stops, listening for a few seconds.

There's the soft sound of a TV on low volume. Two murmured voices. Zips being closed on bags.

Sebastien glances back. "Not a word."

Then he turns and bangs hard on the door.

The murmured voices stop. The TV too.

Sebastien bangs again, harder this time.

Then there's footsteps coming to the door.

Someone looks through the peephole.

"Who is it?" a girl says. She's got a croaky, screamed-out-sounding voice. An upper-crust London accent.

"It's Sebastien."

There's total silence for a few seconds.

Then heavy footsteps coming to the door.

A second person looks through the peephole.

"Jesus fucking Christ," a guy says quietly.

The door opens, on the chain.

"Sebastien?" the guy says, sounding even more hoarse than the girl. "What are you doing here?"

"You know what I'm doing here," Sebastien says. "And the longer I stand outside, the more chance there is of my being seen."

"Just a sec," the guy croaks, closing the door.

There's intense whispering from the other side, some kind of terse disagreement.

"*Cool*," the guy says with fake enthusiasm, either winning the argument or just ignoring the girl entirely.

The chain's drawn back, and the door opens, revealing a big guy—bigger than Sebastien—with *GYM* tattooed across his neck. He stinks of vomit and looks like he's had his stomach pumped or maybe just spent a few hours throwing up. We walk past him into the room, and he closes the door behind us. The girl's wearing a wrinkled little black dress. Her mascara's smudged, and it looks like the lipstick's been kissed off her face.

She glances at me as this thought crosses my mind, and I walk on into the room. It's a decent-size suite, with a lounge space that all four of us can stand in. The door to the bedroom's slightly ajar, and I see two cases with clothes thrown in them. The girl walks to the door and shuts it. I take out my phone and look at the screen. 11:54 p.m. on a Sunday night. Checkout time...

There's a dog-eared magazine on the coffee table, and when I glance down at it, I recognize the cover star. It's the guy who just let us in. In the picture, he's topless, showing his pecs and eight-pack, wearing a white bath towel around his waist and a cool frown.

The shoutline says *Who's the REAL Gym Morrison?*

"Who's this psycho?" he says, glaring at me.

"My assistant," Sebastien says. "Don't worry about him. I'm more interested in your new friend."

"Look," the girl says. "Who the fuck are you?"

"I'm an old friend of Gym's," Sebastien tells her.

"We're not going into all that," Gym says quickly.

"No," Sebastien says. "Because that all went away." The girl frowns at Gym, but he doesn't say anything. "So," Sebastien says, clapping his hands. "I think you'd better tell me what happened this time."

"I don't know what happened," Gym says.

Sebastien stares at him for a moment.

"I'm telling you the truth."

Sebastien sighs, strides over to the window, and draws the curtains closed. Then he turns back to us, talking low. "She arrested on her way to University College Hospital," he says. "So if I were you, I'd start thinking."

Gym shakes his head. "Shut *up*."

"What do you think I'm doing here?" Sebastien says. "You're lucky I've got someone on the staff."

Gym swallows. "Is she...like...gonna be..."

"Calm down, Mr. Morrison," Sebastien says soothingly. "She's still alive, if that's what you're asking."

Gym puts his head in his hands in genuine distress. He starts unconsciously styling his hair before catching himself and looking up. "OK," he says, trying to think. "So there was this awards show tonight, and—"

"Tonight?" Sebastien says.

"It was *last* night," the girl puts in. "Gym's just too trashed to remember."

"Oh, I'm trashed," he shouts. "You're the one who said she'd wake up when they found her."

"Because I was trying to avoid this," she shouts. "She's probably writing her statement as we speak, Gym."

"Bullshit," he says. He looks at Sebastien. "I know her family. She'd never…" He trails off, looking between us, then catches himself. "Anyway, I mean, like, the important thing is that she's going to be OK."

There's a knock at the door, and everyone stops.

"*Mulverhill*," says a man's monotone voice.

Sebastien catches my eye and nods. I stare back at him for a second, then go to the door, looking through the peephole. A big guy in a bad suit with a broad, bland tie.

When I open the door, I think he's going for a gun, but he just scratches his armpit. I stand to one side, and he walks straight past me to Sebastien, wafting stale sweat. He whispers something in his ear. I've just got the door closed and turned back to the room when Sebastien nods and Mulverhill turns on his heel, on his way out again, still rooting around inside that pit.

"Oh, allow me," I say, letting him out.

I see a sardonic smile, then he's gone.

"Well," Sebastien says. "The good news is there's no statement. Bad news is they can't bring her around."

Gym stands almost comically frozen to the spot.

The girl sits abruptly on the floor.

"So," Gym starts. "Like, what do we…"

Sebastien pats him on the shoulder, and Gym winces. "Now you tell me everything," he says.

━━━

In faltering, stop-start speech, Gym Morrison tries to piece together the bender they've just been on. He'd taken Steph, the girl currently crying in the bathroom, to some awards show, and they'd hit the town afterward, deciding to make a night of it. They'd met this other girl at a club and brought her back to the hotel to keep on partying.

"He thought he was on for a threesome," Steph calls through from the bathroom.

Gym closes his eyes.

"Go on," Sebastien says.

They'd been the only customers in the hotel bar at three this morning, and although the staff could see that they were plastered, they'd been only too happy to pour drinks and pose for selfies with a real-life influencer. And if Gym, Steph, and this other girl had kept on disappearing into the toilet, then so what?

Then, at a certain point, someone noticed that the other girl hadn't come back. Steph went to check on her, then quietly took Gym to one side and spirited him out. The staff found the girl a few minutes later. She'd been unresponsive, and they'd called an ambulance. That was when Sebastien caught wind of things. He'd moved fast to secure any incriminating pictures as well as security footage from the hotel. Then he'd arranged terms with the staff, finding the right price to help them forget who'd been there. It was a ruthless business. Gym got the bill, and Sebastien, no doubt, got copies of all the incriminating evidence he'd gathered, owning a little piece of his *client* forever. Fuck knows what happens to the girl.

It's enough to make me wonder what Sebastien's got on Heydon though. Watching him nipple-twist the truth out of Morrison feels like seeing a master at work. When Gym hesitates about what went down, Sebastien's fast to remind him that he doesn't have to be here, to underline how bad Gym's prospects might be without him. That terrace in the West End won't pay for itself, and he can kiss his

CK One contract goodbye. Sitting there in front of him, all bloated and tearful, Gym looks like a lost little boy, wearing XXXL.

Once Sebastien's extracted everything of value and once he confirms with the manager that he can get Gym's name taken off the register, he calls a car and sends them both home. The demonstration's complete. Steph walks out without looking back, glad to go, but Gym turns, sharing a binding, confidential look with Sebastien.

"Thanks again, yeah?" he says.

He walks out and closes the door.

After that, it's just the two of us.

The room smells of vomit, sex, and drink.

"So you're telling me Heydon got himself into some kind of trouble," I say.

"I'm not telling anybody anything," Sebastien says. "Loose lips and all that." He looks at me for a moment. "I can't work you out, your interest in him." I don't say anything, and he rocks back and forth on his heels, fingering the mustache, deciding to take a chance. "Reagan tells me you're a con artist."

"Yeah?"

"Nothing more to say on that?"

"I don't know where she gets it from."

Sebastien looks disappointed with the evasion.

"You know, it's a terrible thing when a confidence man loses his nerve," he says, not unkindly.

"Did Reagan say that as well?"

Sebastien smiles. "Just joining the dots, old boy. You blow into town broke, prey on a mixed-up girl, then turn up at her grieving family's home, expecting a fat check. It's pretty desperate stuff."

"Pretty desperate times."

"Well, that's just what I'm getting at. The most casual observer can see that conditions are fine. Public trust at an all-time low, personal debt at an all-time high." He goes to the window, staring through the split in the curtain, down at the street. "Look at the situation in the right light, and everything's rosy. The pigs are swallowing down their slop, and the lambs are lining up for the slaughter." He turns to me with a smile. "Desperation hours. So when I see a con artist who can't make ends meet in this climate, I know one of two things about him."

"Yeah?" I say.

"Either he's no good or he's lost his nerve."

"I don't know what you're talking about."

He hears the edge in my voice and smiles again.

"Lying to someone else is really just a way of lying to yourself," he says, sounding like he's given it some serious thought. "If you're living off your wits and then lose them, I'm afraid that reality comes crashing back like a bitch. See the lie in yourself, and you see the lie in everything."

"Sounds like experience talking," I say.

"You don't spend your professional life working with the Gym Morrisons of the world without learning a thing or two about grifters."

I smile tightly and wait.

"Well," he continues, "everything about you guys is fabricated. Made up. When you lose your nerve, there's nothing underneath it. You go into free fall. I've seen it happen. It takes you down every time."

"So what makes you any different?" I ask.

"Well, that should be obvious."

When I don't respond, Sebastien gives me another disappointed look. He strides past me and opens the door. When he looks back, his eyes lock on to mine.

"I've never lost my fucking nerve," he says.

He stares at me for a moment, putting an exclamation mark on whatever point he's making, putting me in my place. The only sound's the buzzing light out in the hallway, and it feels like my last chance to make something happen.

"What's Hartson Holdings?" I ask.

He just stands there for a moment, still smiling.

"Can't help you with that one," he says carefully. "But if you're still curious about Heydon tomorrow, then why don't you drop by the office? Perhaps Miss Brandt can dig out some of the content we took down on his behalf." He smiles. "Make sure we're all on the same page."

It sounds like confirmation that Heydon's past life got wiped off the web. And even though the invitation feels like at least as much of a threat as it does a genuine offer, I know I can't turn it down.

"I'd appreciate that."

"Shall we say four thirty?"

"Sound."

Sebastien smiles. "Perhaps then we'll lay this whole business to rest." I smile back but don't say anything. "Can we drop you somewhere?" he asks. "The Mandarin?"

He'd been ready to get rid of me until I'd mentioned Hartson Holdings. After that, Sebastien's energy shifted, getting darker, more intense. It doesn't feel like a good idea to get back in that car.

"Do you know what?" I say, stepping past him into the corridor. "I've got a feeling that the walk might do me some good."

———

I hit the room and start reading up on Hartson. There's so much, it's overwhelming. Listed on the London Stock Exchange. A constituent of the FTSE 250 Index, etc. Founded in 2001 as a gas exploration concern, operating in Senegal. They'd acquired $500 million of drilling rights in Africa in 2006, then discovered a massive oil field there in 2007. Major new discoveries in Owo and Ghana that same year.

When I open the *Controversies* tab, it goes on forever. Pollution, strong-armed tactics to quash local unrest, propping up warlords for improved contract terms, destroying elected leaders who tried to regulate them. They'd even gotten the foreign secretary into trouble for calling the Ugandan president on Hartson's behalf, asking him to wave a $200 million tax bill.

So pretty much what you'd expect.

After Matten earlier and after Reagan's visit—and especially after my wild night with Sebastien—my brain's creaking under the weight of what I do and don't know, and I swipe away, looking for something lighter to drift off with. I find a *Telegraph* article, a puff piece, *At home with the Hartsons*. In the picture, Matthew Hartson's flanked by two long, gangly boys in their midtwenties—named in the caption as Maximilian and Alexander. Where he's glowing with health, the boys look pale and drawn. Reading on, I see that Hartson's a fitness obsessive, that he gets regular plasma transfusions from his sons. He's fifty-five but looks like he's in his early forties, with an unlined face and luscious, shining black hair.

For some reason, Alan Peck had intimidated Dr. Matten on his behalf. For some reason, Sebastien had put Heydon together with Control. It seemed like they'd been trying to coax him into saying or doing something. And for some reason, Heydon had tattooed Hartson's corporate logo onto his face a few weeks before walking out.

Staring into Hartson's gleaming white smile, I can't help but think of the movie poster from Heydon's room.

Irma Vep.

Vampire.

29.

That night, I roll around, fighting the bedsheets for a few hours, until I sense daylight seeping through the curtains and finally admit defeat. When I get up on Monday morning, my body feels stiff and heavy, and my head's not doing much better. I do a double take at the mirror, thinking I see Heydon's face instead of mine, realizing I've left the green lenses in. When I lean in to get a closer look at the tattoo, I see it's almost entirely healed, and somehow that feels wrong, like there's some kind of transformation taking place, like it's almost complete, and I hurry through my morning routine, racing the voices in my head.

I can't help but hear Sebastien, telling me I've lost my nerve, and I can't help but see Reagan, standing in the lounge, looking quietly concerned, asking me how I remember who I really am.

I pace up and down, trying to get myself straight. Heydon had walked out of his family home five years ago, highly agitated, and his car had been found parked on a bridge overlooking the Thames. When I'd seen the video recovered from his flight case, I'd filed it alongside that haunted final photograph, his troubled smile. My sense that Heydon couldn't see a future for himself. I'd been dubious about Control's story at first, but then everything started to get a little too real. Not only had Control been able to back up Heydon's claims of harassment and gang stalking with video evidence—his murder made it clear that Heydon's killers were still out there, still a threat.

I'd seen the cover-up in motion, and after my meeting with Sebastien, I could imagine him pulling something like this off. He had the resources as well as the nerve. I just can't work out what he had to gain.

———

Once I've dressed, I drag the furniture from in front of the door and unplug my phone. I see I've gotten a missed call from Reagan, but when I try her, it goes straight to voicemail.

"It's Lynch," I say. "Sorry I missed you."

I unfold the crumpled photograph on the bedside table. Me and Reagan, sitting in Soho. There's two men out there, showing this picture around town, apparently to people from Heydon's life. So at some point, I know I'm going to open a door and see them on the other side of it. I've got to get out of this room though, and I can't face another scene in the breakfast lounge, so I head outside for some fresh air. The Mandarin's right by Hyde Park—you're in the city one second, then 350 acres of green fields and trees the next. I cross the busy road, buy a roll from a kiosk, and get lost. The rowboats on the lake, the weird, well-manicured mazelike structures, the fancy bridges and statues. The massive, wind-rocked trees, acting like a buffer against the city.

I scroll Miranda's Wikipedia page while I walk, trying to see what was going on in her life when Theo drowned. Of course, she was making her troubled passion project, *Wilderness Years.*

I don't recognize the name of her costar, Christopher Jacobs. When I click his profile, I see he died soon after the film was made, in 1999. Handsome guy in a rough sort of way. And I guess that hint of sadness in his eyes made him the full package. But there's not much there. When I open the *Personal Life* tab, it says he got divorced in 1998. Right after they finished shooting.

I google *Christopher Jacobs + Miranda Pierce Rumors* and get a hit. Kind of. I'm led to a celebrity gossip forum, a thread on Miranda and some of her iconic roles. On page twelve, someone mentions *Wilderness Years,* and a few posts down, a comment catches my eye.

> Word is it got hot and heavy on set...

When other users respond, asking for the full story, the original poster links to a blind item site. Anonymous posts trafficking in rumors, gossip, and innuendo. Each entry's just a paragraph long, usually phrased as some kind of question, probably as a legal defense. I'm looking at an anniversary post for Jacobs:

> RIP to award-winning talent Christopher Jacobs, 20 years gone, but not forgotten. But was there ever any truth to rumors that he and Miranda Pierce found each other in the wilderness?

I stare at it, wondering why they'd care.

On my way out of the park, I try to breathe in the peace and take it with me. But when I cross the road, I see the Rayner goon with the cauliflower ears. The same one who'd wanted to take my case that first night. I haven't seen him again since he was glowering over Ronnie's shoulder in the dining room. But he's standing there now, watching me. I take the steps at a clip, flash a smile, and walk past him, on into the building.

—

When I get to my room, I put my key card to the door, but the panel flashes red. I try again, but the door won't unlock. When I go down to the front desk, naturally Chip, the guy I hate, is the only one standing there. I can see at a glance that he knows what's going on because of the way he tries to make his face go blank.

"Hi," I say.

He checks his watch.

"Good afternoon, sir."

"Yeah, yeah, my room key doesn't work."

"Ah," he says, taking it. "Yes."

"Do you think you could do me a new one?"

He makes another effort to force his face blank.

"Checkout's at twelve p.m., sir. It's seven minutes past now."

"I'm not checking out," I tell him.

"Hm," he says, pretending to read something from his screen. "Ah yes. I'm afraid that your reservation was canceled this morning." He smiles. "I spoke to Mr. Pierce personally."

"And I was supposed to just guess this?"

"We would have called, sir," he says, careful to underline my transgression before going on. "But we know how you prefer not to use the telephone."

So Ronnie had thought long and hard and then had me evicted. In one way, it scans like a good thing. It means he's still operating along class lines. Not sending the bone breakers in just yet. A shitty thing to do, but it could have been worse. And at least it's an easily solved problem, probably what Reagan had been calling about this morning. It starts me wondering about something else though.

"How much for your cheapest room?" I ask.

Chip looks momentarily surprised, then checks.

When he looks up from the screen, he's smiling.

"Our junior suite's available for eight hundred and fifty-nine. Plus VAT."

"For a night?" I ask.

He just stands there, smiling.

I take out the card to try and book it. "OK, cool."

He takes the card with a frown, running it through the reader, handing it to me for the PIN. When I input the code, it doesn't work, and I see the warmth flooding back into his face. He tries it a second time, smiling strongly now, then a third, just for his own enjoyment.

"I'm so sorry," he says. "Your card's been rejected."

"So I see," I say, taking it back.

When you subtract that £35,000 from my net worth, it comes down to the cigarettes in my pocket and whatever's left on the Oyster card.

Chip looks over my shoulder. "We took the liberty of having your things brought down."

I turn to see the porter with the cauliflower ears, the Rayner goon, carrying my bag, which no doubt he's already searched. With the passport gone and the photograph in my pocket, it's just the new clothes that Reagan bought me, my Heydon costumes. The Rayner goon drops the bag at my feet, then just stands there, staring.

"Well," I say, picking it up. "At least this wasn't a total waste of your time."

———

With the clothes, I'm technically still up, but they don't mean much to me. And anyway, as far as I'm concerned, I earned that money.

Time for a word in Ronnie's ear.

We need to talk about my passport anyway.

More importantly, while I'm over there, I've got to get Miranda talking about the day of Theo's drowning somehow. And maybe what all that trouble was on the set of *Wilderness Years*.

30.

It's midafternoon by the time I get to Tregunter Road. Every single light in the place is still blazing, like last night. I bang on the door, face the camera, then wait. Nothing happens for a few minutes, so I knock again. There's still no answer, but when I go to knock a third time, I hear someone opening the door. It's the maid, Anya. She's been crying.

"What happened?" I ask.

She opens her mouth, then Ronnie appears. He's wearing loose, salmon-colored cords and a rakishly open shirt. And he's got a beaker of what looks like brandy in his hand, the glow of the morning drinker in his cheeks.

"Mr. Lynch," he says. "How can we help you?"

Anya vanishes back into the house.

"What's going on, Ronnie?"

"Well, let's see," he says, thinking for a moment. "Her Majesty's coffin arrived in Edinburgh this morning. She's due back in town tomorrow. They're queueing round the block in Westminster."

I just stand there.

"OK," he says, taking a mouthful of his drink. "Let's see. Russian forces knocked out the power across eastern Ukraine last night." He smiles. "That's a good one. Like every story there is, all coming together at once. One last hurrah before the big finish."

I just stand there.

"The one I've really got my eye on's the PM sacking two treasury officials, scant days before announcing her new budget. I stand to make—"

"What's going on with Miranda? Where's Reagan?"

"Ah," he says. "Perhaps you'd better come inside?"

He turns and walks back into the house, climbing the stairs, drink in hand. When we reach the first floor, Ronnie leads us through a series of doors into what looks like a decent-size apartment. There are other doors leading out from this main space as well, I guess to bedrooms and bathrooms. Ronnie and Miranda have got separate living quarters. That's how they manage not to speak to each other while occupying the same house.

"Drink?" Ronnie says over his shoulder.

"Where's Miranda?"

"Yes," he says, topping up his glass, then turning to me. "Of course. Well, I'm afraid that my wife has fallen ill."

There's a curdled smile on his face.

"Shit, Ronnie. Is she OK?"

"Touch and go," he says, the smile fading. "She's fighting for her life over at the Chelsea and Westminster."

"When did it happen?"

He looks at me for another moment, then sighs.

"I found her last night."

"I guess Reagan's already there?" Ronnie nods. "What say we grab a coffee and head over?"

"Something wrong with my beverage of choice?"

"No, and I get it. I'm just saying hospitals are the worst place to be hungover." Ronnie frowns. "I know you've had your differences, but you still want to be there."

Ronnie licks his parched lips.

"Miranda didn't want me at her best," he says in a controlled voice. "So why should I want her at her worst?"

"You know, man," I mumble. "Just a suggestion."

Ronnie looks at me seriously.

"May I ask you a question, man to man?"

I shrug. "Of course."

"What is it with all this *man* and *dude* stuff?" he asks. "Why don't you pronounce Ts at the end of words?"

I laugh in surprise. "What?"

"It's wha*t*," he says, hitting the *T* sound like a whip. "I've heard you do a reasonable impersonation of my son. You know how the words are supposed to sound. So why do you choose to speak like a barnyard animal?"

I stare at him for a few seconds.

"Where's my passport, Ronnie?"

"Excuse me?"

"Come on, I've just been through this with that jizz stain at the Mandarin."

But the glimmer in his eye looks real.

"Someone took your passport?" Ronnie says warmly. He plainly hadn't known about it. His eyes are glowing with some other secret knowledge about me though, and I don't want to know what it is. With Miranda out of action, it's not safe for me here. It might not be safe for me anywhere. There's only one more response I want.

"Ronnie, I spoke to an old friend of Heydon's. Someone who was in his life before he went missing."

Ronnie swallows. "And?"

"And he mentioned an associate of your son's," I say. "Sebastien. I was just wondering if that name means anything to you?"

There's a cautious look in his eyes, but Ronnie seems to think about it. At length, he shakes his head.

I'm watching closely, but it doesn't tell me anything.

"I think he was working for a man called Hartson."

Ronnie frowns. "Matthew Hartson? Doing what?"

"That's not entirely clear. They were developing an app together at some point."

"Yes," he says. "I recall something like that. And…"

"And I was wondering if Hartson was someone the family knew."

"Of course, we know *of* them. But as far as I'm aware, we've never met. Any of us." He's looking right at me, either telling the truth or relaxed lying about it.

"So there's no bad blood?" I ask.

Ronnie scratches an ear. "Nothing I can think of."

I stare at him for a few seconds. I'd come here to shout it out, but the situation's changed.

"Look," I say, turning to the door. "I'm going to go and see what's up at the Chelsea and Westminster. You're welcome to split a cab, but I think I'll sit up front."

I turn the handle and open it.

Mike's standing there with two other guys.

He starts to smile, and I close the door in his face.

"I was rather hoping I might borrow you for another moment," Ronnie says when I turn back to him.

I clap my hands together.

"Yeah, man, I'd be delighted."

———

Ronnie leads us to a door, holding his signet ring up to the keypad. I hear a mechanized click, and the door slides open, revealing a lift. We get in, and Ronnie pushes a button. The doors close slowly, and we start to move with a sudden jerk. My guess is we're on our way up to the loft. The door opens onto pitch-black darkness. Ronnie stands to one side, motioning me out. The only light's coming from the lift, and I can sense a large space in front of us. I take a step forward and see the walls sparkle. Glass cabinets and framed pictures, catching the light.

"After you," Ronnie intones.

I don't want to go first, but Ronnie just stands there until finally, I smile and walk past him. He follows me out, and the doors close behind us. The sparkling walls go black. There's no windows, no light.

"I'm afraid I've had to take certain steps to protect Miranda from herself," Ronnie starts. I can't see him, but he's standing so close I can smell the brandy. "Since there was no contract signed, and since I wasn't consulted on the particulars of your agreement, it seemed right and proper to cease all unexplained outgoings."

"Of course it did," I say.

"I'm so glad that you agree."

I hear the click of a switch, and soft lights glow to life around us.

"I want you to know it's nothing personal," Ronnie says, careful to preserve his honor. "These are just the times that we live in. We've all got to tighten our belts. I myself have been forced to accept certain cutbacks."

He looks past me, and I turn.

Famous faces line the walls. Framed black-and-white photos of actors, musicians, politicians, public figures. Each has a lot of space on either side, making them look like shrines. And every single one of them's a woman. Marilyn Monroe, Judy Garland, Natalie Wood, Carrie Fisher, Amy Winehouse, as well as dozens more I don't even recognize. In pride of place, at the far end of the room, there's a black jacket in a display case. At first, I think it's got to be something to do with Heydon, that this is some kind of confession or power play, but I see it's a woman's jacket. There's a framed picture of Princess Diana beside it. And for the first time, I realize that all these women are dead. For a second, their faces crowd around me. I try to focus on Diana, her soothing smile, and take a step toward it.

"She was wearing that jacket the night she died," Ronnie says to my back.

"You're not kidding," I say, not looking at him.

"Cost a pretty penny, but it's the apple of my eye. Although with that said, I'm not sure which one of them I could really live without." When I turn to look at him, he's breathing deeply, staring at the walls with admiration, drawing strength from them. "Since Heydon, this room's been a kind of sanctuary to me."

"What is all this, Ronnie?"

"This is my collection," he says. "All these items were either on or around them when they died." He points out an example. "One of the barbiturates from the bottle that killed Marilyn Monroe." He moves on to the next. "Whitney Houston's belly-button piercing."

"I don't know what to say, Ronnie."

"People never do," he says with a satisfied smile.

"Where do you even get all this stuff?"

"Now, it's not so bad," he says. "Now, we're a thriving

community. Back when I was first getting into this kind of thing, I'm afraid that sometimes you had to get your hands dirty." He glances at me and laughs. "This is small fry. Between you and me, some guys start getting into this stuff and really go off the deep end."

Finally seeing the scope and obsession of Ronnie's collection brings something together in my mind.

"Heydon broke in, the night he went missing," I say.

Ronnie looks at me.

"The CCTV went down an hour before he left. He could have taken anything outside without being seen."

When he turns to look at me, it's like there's a part of Ronnie I've never seen before, staring out from inside his head. I feel my skin turning cold.

"That was something a little different," Ronnie says, going to a filing cabinet in the corner of the room. He turns a key, feels around inside, and removes a red file, some kind of paperwork. It's floppy, just a page or two. Ronnie holds it up like a prize. "Now, happily, restored to my collection."

Badwan insisted that Bobbie got her stuff back from him safely. Yet somehow, she'd still gone home that night with a black eye.

"How did you get hold of it?" I ask.

"It was taken from me," he says. "So I took it back."

"This is after Bobbie went to meet Mr. Badwan?"

"And you'd just love to know what's in there, wouldn't you? I think you've got a soft spot for her."

I don't say anything.

"Come on," Ronnie says. "Don't be squeamish now. You've finally snuffed out my daughter's dark secret. Must be quite a thrill."

"Show me or don't, Ronnie. Just get on with it."

Ronnie thinks for a moment, then shares a look of amusement with himself, holding the file open, forcing me to walk toward him. I'm looking at two plastic envelopes, each with a single sheet of paper inside. They're marked Exhibits A and B. Exhibit A, on the left-hand side, looks like an itemized phone bill. It's old, the type on the page has faded, and I squint, trying to work out what I'm seeing. My eyes go to the dates. *September 1997.*

The same month that Theo drowned.

The bill shows outgoing calls in one column and incoming calls in another. I look to the twelfth. Nothing listed, in or out, until a 999 call at 10:27. After that, there'd been a growing avalanche of incoming calls.

I look at Exhibit B, on the right.

It looks like call data too, but for a mobile number, covering the same period. Although it presents a similar log to the landline, it doesn't look like a customer-facing document. It looks more like data you'd have to get out of the phone company somehow. Officially or not. And it shows the same thing as the house phone. Nothing on the morning of the twelfth until a spate of emergency calls.

I frown at Ronnie, and he turns Exhibit B over.

The final sheet in the file's something different.

A letter from the Rayner Group, from 2016.

The year everything went crazy for Heydon.

The letter says Exhibits A and B have both provided positive matches for Bobbie's fingerprints. In 2016. I'm still reading when Ronnie closes the file in my face.

He smiles and goes back to the cabinet.

"They say that information's power," he starts. "And of course, there's some truth to that. But I'm afraid that without the requisite *smarts* to interpret that information, you're just a monkey with some clothes on."

It's clear there's no explanation coming, and I try to cover my confusion by taking the moral high ground.

"Look, whatever it means, I think that file's really hanging over her. I'm sure rehab goes a lot more smoothly if you give it back."

"Give it back?" Ronnie looks at me pitiably. He drops the file back inside the drawer and slams it shut. "Well, that rather gets to the heart of what I brought you here to illustrate." He raises himself up. "You said something offensive to me at breakfast."

"I'm sorry?" I say, looking from the cabinet back to Ronnie. "Look, if this is about the knife—"

"Don't be so ridiculous," he says, taking a step toward me. "But I offered you a large sum of money, and you threw it back in my face."

"Right," I say, not following.

"Now you'll leave with absolutely nothing." He takes another step toward me.

"So?"

"So the next time you're told to do something by one of your betters, you do it." Ronnie leans in close, and I feel his hot brandy breath in my eyes. "Because believe you me," he says. "*Everything's* for sale."

—

We ride the lift down in silence. Ronnie's done with me. When I open the door to walk out again, Mike and his two backup singers are still waiting, blocking the way.

Ronnie slams the door on us.

"So you've decided to stick around after all," Mike says with a smile. He's keeping a careful distance from me. There's some new understanding in his eyes too.

Mike's been looking into Paris.

"There were some questions I wanted to ask you."

"Kind of busy at the moment."

"Oh, something tells me there's a lot of free time in your future," Mike says. "*Le temps est un grand maître*." He smiles. "I've been brushing up on my French."

I don't say anything.

"We picked up your trail in Paris. Found you in a café last week, acting very strangely. Beautiful girl though."

I don't say anything.

"I'm just wondering if it's her blood we found in the room." He watches me closely. "I've got a team out there, taking samples, as we speak."

When I still don't respond, he snorts, nodding at one of the two goons. He grabs me roughly by the arm, and they jostle me to the stairs, leading us down. Mike's walking ahead, conjugating verbs about how fucked I am in French. They don't see the stairs as dangerous. They don't understand how far I'll go not to talk about Clare. We're at the bottom of the first flight, turning, with ten or so steps to go.

I feel the moment passing by, then commit myself to it, sinking low on my right leg. I launch myself forward at Mike, dragging the goon who's got hold of my arm along too. We crash down the stairs, Mike and me rolling clear of the others, landing in a painful heap at the bottom.

Mike's groaning, holding his head, looking hurt.

I crawl toward him, ripping the steak knife out of my waistband.

There's a rumble of footsteps on the stairs behind me, but before the two guys can get close, I'm pressing the blade, hard, into Mike's face, into the skin underneath his right eye.

I look up, and the two men stop in their tracks.

Their shirts are untucked, and their hair looks crazy.

The only sound's all four of us, breathing.

I nod at the nearest one to me.

"*Open the fucking door.*"

31.

I can't hang around at the Chelsea and Westminster, so I ask for Miranda, telling them I'm her son. I'm directed to lift D, the Chelsea Wing, for private patients. I'm watching for Rayner guys, so it takes me a minute to get onto the ward. When the coast seems clear, I follow a nurse who uses her passkey, catching the door at the last second. I walk the halls for a few minutes until I find Reagan, sitting outside one of the rooms, staring into space with red-rimmed eyes.

"Hey," I say.

It takes her a moment to disengage from her thoughts and look up. "Oh, hi," she says.

"Mind if I sit?"

She shakes her head, and I take a seat beside her.

"She's in there?" I ask.

Reagan nods, still staring at the door.

"And what do they think—"

"What are you doing here?" she asks.

I stop. "Well, your dad said—"

"I mean, where were you?" she asks.

"I'm sorry?"

"Where were you?" she repeats, turning to look at me. "I called."

"There was a mix-up at the hotel this morning. I must have missed it."

"Not this morning," she says. "Last night. I didn't have my mobile until Anya came, so I called your room."

"Ah," I say. I'd been following her, then following Sebastien. "I think I must have left the phone unplugged."

"Yes," Reagan says. "I remember. That's why I asked the night manager to go up to your room and knock. I said it was an emergency. You weren't there."

Naturally, the fucker never mentioned it.

"Right," I say, trying to recover. "Yeah. I think at some point, I took a walk to clear my head." I see Reagan's jaw tense with something undisclosed. "What?" I ask.

"I sent them up there three times. Once at eleven, once at twelve, and once at one a.m. In the end, I just gave up on you."

There's a long silence.

"Yeah, you know, I ended up getting a few drinks."

"They're not sure if she'll regain consciousness."

"I'm sorry," I say. "So that's what the note was?"

"Note?" she says, looking momentarily confused. Then she shakes her head. "Oh, yes, of course."

It had already occurred to me that I'd been played the previous night. Clearly, Sebastien had known about Miranda's condition. Whether he'd planned on my following him or not, he'd drawn me away from them. First with our long, meandering drive through London, south of the river, then north again. Then chewing the fat at his office, and finally with his surprise offer to watch him work.

I'd thought I was getting a glimpse behind the magician's curtain, but I'd been falling for a slick piece of misdirection instead. It had been getting on for two a.m. when I got back to the room, when Sebastien could be fairly sure I was done finding things out for the day. But why?

"Who was the man I saw you leaving with?" I ask.

"Excuse me?"

"Last night," I say. "When you got that note. I was worried, so I followed you out to make sure you were OK. I saw you leaving with someone."

Reagan turns so she's facing forward again.

"No one," she says, but something catches in her voice, and she goes on, trying to smooth it over. "Just an old friend of my brother's. Sebastien Keeler."

"How did Heydon know him?" I ask.

Reagan looks at me.

"They were working on some project together. Before Heydon went missing," she clarifies. "Long before."

"Did Sebastien come with you to the hotel?"

"What?" She frowns like she can't work out why we're talking about this. "Of course not," she says. "We saw each other when I walked in, by chance, down in the lobby." She shrugs. "Then he happened to hear of my mother's fall and wanted to make sure I knew. He asked the front desk which room I'd gone to."

"Right," I say.

"What?"

"It just looked like he was being a bit rough."

Reagan stiffens. "I think you're imagining things."

"Yeah, probably," I say. "So hang on a second. Miranda fell?"

Reagan looks at me like I'm stupid.

"What do you think we're doing here?"

"I thought her illness…"

"My mother fell down the stairs last night. My father found her."

"Huh," I say.

Ronnie told me that Miranda had *fallen* ill. The truth was technically in there, just cleverly concealed and in a way he could pass off as an honest mistake or as a simple mishearing on my part. There's a chance it really was a slip of the tongue. He'd been drinking after all, and even taking into account his and Miranda's strained relationship, it had to be an emotional moment. But it feels more like another evasion, some sleight of hand.

"How did Sebastien know about your mother's fall?"

Reagan looks at me steadily. "I suppose my father…"

I frown. "Wait, Sebastien knows your dad?"

"Of course," Reagan says airily.

Ronnie had just denied it.

"Was Miranda conscious at all after she fell?" I ask. "Did she say anything?"

"No," Reagan says. "Of course not."

"And Anya wasn't around."

"She'd already left. Why? What are you implying?"

She knows what I'm implying, and the speed she'd reached the same conclusion tells me she'd been having similar thoughts or actively trying not to.

"I mean," I go on, trying to choose my words carefully, "you said yourself, things between them—"

"I want you to leave," she says.

For a moment, I consider trying to put her in the picture. Control, Dr. Matten, Sebastien. Why her father's friendship with him feels like a red flag. I'm just not sure where to start or what conclusions I can really draw. And even if I could put it all together, even if she could follow, this is hardly the time or place.

"OK," I say. "Fair enough. Is there anything I can—"

"Just go, Mr. Lynch."

——

I find a coffee shop across the road, then a quiet corner where I can gather my thoughts. One by one, I can feel the doors closing. My conversation with Ronnie couldn't have gone worse. And Miranda's closed off to me because of her fall. If that's what we're calling it. My eyes are still adjusting to the post-Miranda landscape, and I start seeing predators everywhere. Snakes like Chip from the front desk and lizards like Mike. Smiling, fat crocodiles like Ronnie Pierce as well as the untouchable great whites like Sebastien Keeler, like Matthew Hartson...

But I'm more worried about what Reagan just confirmed. Ronnie and Sebastien were acquaintances of some kind. The fact that Ronnie denied it just makes me more certain.

It felt like Reagan had been getting ready to open up about something when Sebastien's note arrived last night, but I'd missed my chance. I think again of how pale she'd been at the hospital, how tightly controlled. Of course, there was the shock, but it felt like there'd been something else at play too. She'd known exactly what I was getting at when I'd started to ask questions about her dad. She'd shut them down and sent me away.

Well, no matter. Ronnie was connected to the man who'd been harassing his son. And he'd been acting off-the-charts weird when I went over there this morning. And however subtly, he'd lied to me about Miranda's fall.

I can only think of one reason why.

Seeing that Sebastien's is the last door open, I can't help but feel like he's designed it this way. Heydon had called him the all-seeing eye. Reagan had called him Sebastien *Keeler*. When I google his name and find that the only solid result takes me to a LinkedIn profile, I break my last remaining rule and create an account.

———

According to LinkedIn, Sebastien Keeler had spent four years and three months in the SAS, and although I can't find a rank, his role's listed as systems engineer. It means about as much to me as innovation director, his role at the Agency, but a series of bullet points underneath outline, in the vaguest possible terms, what he'd been responsible for.

- Led multidisciplinary and cross-functional technical teams and military personnel in theaters of war
- Scoped, planned, and delivered critical mission presentations for senior military leadership using business products
- Demonstrated the business case for use of classified networks (Confidential)

I stare at the screen for a moment, then google *classified networks*.

A classified (computer) network is one that stores information that is sensitive and should not be made available to the general public.

So his role in the military hadn't been a million miles away from what he'd ended up doing on the outside. Gathering, storing, and exploiting sensitive information. Reading back through the bullet points, I try to work out what they're really saying. Sebastien must have been an officer if he'd led men in the field, but it looks like he'd specialized. The second point hinted that he'd been responsible for data collection of some kind as well as presenting it to leadership.

Making the "business case" for classified networks was the point that really caught my eye. Google said that *classified networks* were exactly what they sounded like—electronic systems that stored or transmitted confidential information. To me, that reads as highly specialized, certainly not the work of any normal grunt, even one who'd clearly had his eye on the business sector from early on in his career.

According to LinkedIn, Sebastien's role at the Agency includes helping clients and firms integrate cryptocurrencies and NFTs into their business models. The kind of work that could have brought him into Control's sphere. But if he'd presented himself as a novice there, then he'd fooled Control just as slickly as he'd fooled me. Sebastien had been working in crypto for years before they even met.

I think back to what Control had told me about private intelligence companies, offering the superrich the same level of espionage as the state. There's a lot of firms listed in Sebastien's employment history after the military, all of them sounding security-adjacent, and I wonder if every one was a different operation of some kind.

I scan through, looking for the Black Door, the company that Control said Sebastien used to pay him, but it's not there. Too toxic. There are dozens of more shady-sounding entities though. Tech Co, Sec Corp, Systems Design Pro, LifeTech, etc. Some of these stints lasted for just a few months; others had started almost immediately after the SAS, with some of them running concurrently, right up until the present day.

A selection of bullet points from across these private sector companies:

- Managed a multidisciplinary and cross-functional team tasked with creating war-game tools for military and intelligence leadership to understand terrorist flows
- Elicited customer requirements for terrorism and antiterrorism modeling tools and translated those requirements into war-gaming solutions
- Developed proof of concepts for using social media and sentiment analysis to model terrorist propaganda
- Modeled and simulated movement of internally displaced individuals during failed and fragile state conditions

War-gaming tools for intelligence leadership, using social media to "model" terrorist propaganda, something called sentiment analysis...

Control said that Sebastien was the mastermind of a conspiracy. With Heydon's disappearance, his car on that bridge, Control's murder, and now this murky black ops angle—I get the nasty feeling that he might have been right. Those shady intelligence links go deeper than just an SAS tattoo.

When I check the time, it's 2:55 p.m.

Everything I've heard so far suggests that Sebastien was behind the harassment. And most likely he's responsible for Heydon's disappearance too.

So what's left to prove by going over there?

It's not like I'm about to reason with him or make a citizen's arrest.

And although my mention of Hartson seemed to catch Sebastien's attention last night, I haven't had the time to read any deeper on it. Sebastien won't say anything he doesn't want me to know anyway. Sebastien just needs to work out what I've put together.

Matten said I was following Heydon into the dark as a way of running from my own problems. I'd scoffed at her, but here I am, wearing his clothes, his eyes, his life. Completely isolated, with an unbelievable story to tell. Blood on my hands, a head full of conspiracies.

I can't even pat myself on the back for still being here. Somehow, it's less terrifying than facing up to things with Clare. Besides, if I had my passport right now, there's a chance I'd be sitting in the first-class lounge at Heathrow, relapsing, looking for easy marks, telling myself I'd tried my best.

I want Bobbie to be OK. I'd wanted to come through for Miranda. And for whatever reason, I'd felt like I owed something to Heydon. Maybe to the universe. A goodwill gesture after the last few years. Something big enough to wipe out the bad karma.

But with Miranda in the hospital, Mike closing in, Ronnie's warning, and my passport still missing, with someone out there looking for me and a killer I'd stood twenty feet away from, everything seems so much darker than before. I stare into my cup for a few seconds, deciding if there's anything left to gain by seeing Sebastien. I picture a long, empty day stretching out in front of me instead. All the time in the world for reflection. Then I drain my coffee, get up, and go. I was never going to solve myself anyway.

32.

Miss Brandt greets me warmly at the door, then leads us past the marble statues of headless women in the lobby, through the security barrier, and up to Sebastien's office. If he's told her anything about me or what I'm doing here, then she doesn't show it. She conducts me across the corridor to the waiting room with a smile.

"I'm afraid we're having one of our crazy days," she says, showing me through. I'd been expecting to hear something like this. No doubt we're about to find Sebastien's door firmly shut, a waiting room full of more important people, people with assistants, appointments, a clue. But when we step through, I see that the waiting room's empty. The door to Sebastien's office is open. He's standing behind his desk, pumping weights, listening to someone talk through the speakerphone.

Sebastien looks at me for a moment, then lowers his arms and puts the weights down. He's taken his shirt off to save it from getting sweaty, and he wears a brilliant-white vest, tight across his overdeveloped body and chest. I see the SAS tattoo that Control had mentioned on his upper left bicep, the knife with wings.

A woman's voice drones from the speakerphone. "*When we begin to chart the potential reach of this project, the returns, both financial and—*"

"Elsa," Sebastien says. "Just a second."

The woman on the other end stops speaking.

From the look he gives me, I can see he wasn't sure I'd come. But because of the sweat on his skin, because of his flushed cheeks and the straining vein in his forehead, I can't tell if he's impressed or just pissed off.

"Listen," he says, talking to me, still slightly out of breath, "I'm completely slammed." He collects the Patek from his desk, sliding it onto his wrist. "To be completely honest with you, I wonder if we might be better trying this another time."

I shrug. "I wasn't expecting you to hold my hand. I just wanted to set my mind to rest on this stuff you took down for Heydon."

Sebastien doesn't say anything.

"Make sure we're all on the same page," I add.

He looks at me for a moment more, smiling at length, then he nods at Miss Brandt.

"Make sure Mr. Lynch gets everything he needs."

——

Miss Brandt sets me up with a laptop in a windowless meeting room, explaining that Sebastien had authorized her to unlock the Pierce file. I see it contains several videos that I guess Sebastien pulled down on Heydon's behalf.

"I'm afraid I'll have to ask for your phone," she says. I look at her. "Of course you're welcome to keep it. I'll just need to sit in with you. I'm sure it goes without saying that we can't permit copies to leave the premises."

I don't feel great about handing my phone over, but on balance,

I feel worse about Miss Brandt hovering at my shoulder, so I take it out, switch it off, and pass it to her. She smiles and takes the phone away with her. When she closes the door, I half expect to hear the click of a lock, wondering how stupid one man can be, but I just hear the tick of her heels walking away.

Turning to the laptop, I see there's six numbered videos in the finder in a folder marked *Pierce*. They're named and numbered *YouTube One*, *YouTube Two*, *YouTube Three*, etc. I swipe away from the screen, trying to open a web browser, but the laptop's not connected to the internet, and when I try to join one of the nearby networks, all of them are password protected. I go back to the finder and try to examine the files themselves, but my know-how only goes so far as right-clicking and selecting *Get Info* from the dropbox. I'd been hoping to see the times and dates that the files were originally saved, but they were all created today, a few minutes ago, when Miss Brandt transferred them to the machine.

I can see that the videos have been numbered in order of upload though, because each has a still image of Heydon as its icon. His physical deterioration's so marked that it looks like a public service announcement, a warning of some kind. In the first four, he hasn't gotten the tattoo yet. He's still got that boyish sheen to his skin. In the last, he looks like a completely broken man. I select the first.

"Hey," he says, trying to sound casual but clearly self-conscious about talking to the camera. "If you've found this thing, then it's probably because someone's watching you." I sit back in my chair, and he goes on. "Don't worry," he says. "You're not alone."

———

Across the six videos, Heydon presents as what I'd guess is a fairly typical targeted individual. That is to say, he outlines his harassment at the hands of shadowy figures, who he claims are trying to disrupt, monitor, and control his life. Although we don't see any of his candid camera work this time, he describes his initial experiences of being followed through the underground as well as out on the street. It's not an easy watch. I'd been hoping for some further hint about the day of Theo's death. Some idea why it mattered to someone so much.

But all I can really say for sure is that Heydon had been deeply troubled in the months leading up to his disappearance. There's a decorated tree up in the background of one of the videos, telling me he'd gotten the tattoo sometime before Christmas. In fact, it tells me two things. The tattoo seems fully healed in the video, and because Heydon doesn't explain or refer to it in any way, it suggests I'm not getting the full picture here, like there's uploads missing.

It feels like a sly nod from Sebastien.

A suggestion that Heydon might well have linked the tattoo to Hartson. He might even have explained his reasons, pointed the finger. But if he did, I'll never know about it. I'd walked in afraid for my safety, but I see now that was stupid. Anything that might explain what was really going on got wiped a long time ago.

I walk numbly into the corridor, gripped by a kind of second-hand shame at having watched the tapes at all. On the one hand, I hadn't seen anything unexpected. I knew where Heydon was coming from by now.

Someone had been distorting his reality.

"Find everything you were looking for?" Miss Brandt asks, coming around her desk. She's holding a small black box, a Faraday cage. She unlocks it, removing my phone.

"Well," I say, accepting it. "I was wondering if I could get a minute with Sebastien to talk it all over?"

"I'm so sorry," she says, sounding sincere. "He's chockablock for the rest of the day."

She sees me glance at the closed door.

"I just need—"

Miss Brandt steps in my way.

"That won't be possible," she says firmly.

I walk past her and open the door anyway.

Sebastien looks up from a phone call.

Then I see the three-hundred-pound killer standing to one side, watching me like an attack dog, just waiting for the word.

Sebastien stares.

"Wrong door," I say.

"This way, Mr. Lynch," Miss Brandt says firmly.

Sebastien watches me from behind his mustache.

"Carl, I need to run out for a bite," he says to the phone. "Back here in twenty-five?" Carl agrees, and Sebastien pushes a button, terminating the call. Then he looks up at me, speaking gently, like he's calming down an escaped mental patient. "That's quite all right, Miss Brandt. I was just about to head out." He smiles. "Perhaps Mr. Lynch would care to join me?"

———

Out on the street, it's dark already. Smartly dressed men and women are leaving their buildings, exiting through bright lobbies, heading to the underground and home. A black SUV creeps slowly down the street behind us. When we turn left, the car follows. Sebastien leads us through a pedestrian walkway between two department store buildings, and we lose it. We cross a busy street, gridlocked with black cabs and red double-decker buses, and my phone vibrates in my pocket. When I pull it out and glance at the screen, it's spam from LinkedIn.

"So what do you want to talk about?" Sebastien says, letting me know from his tone that I haven't got long.

"I'm not sure where to start," I say.

"You can see why he wanted them taken down."

"So Heydon asked you to do it, not the family?"

"Why should the family?"

"I don't know, social awkwardness? I assumed you took them down after he went missing." I'm still groping for Sebastien's full relationship with the Pierces.

"As I said, Heydon and I had drifted apart by then. I hadn't seen him in months when he went missing. His takedown requests came remotely."

"But the family…"

"We're really not acquainted," he says lightly. "In fact, so far as I can recall, I only ever met Heydon's sisters. Once, by chance."

Reagan told me he knew Ronnie.

"So Heydon approached you himself?"

A man in a hoodie walks past and shoulder-checks me, hard. I turn and look after him, but he's already crossing the road, walking away.

"That's right," Sebastien says smoothly. He turns to me like nothing happened.

"To take down some videos?" I say, trying to refocus. Sebastien doesn't move. "For some reason, I thought Ronnie put you in touch."

"Can't say I've had the pleasure," Sebastien says.

We're standing on a busy sidewalk, but he seems oblivious to the pissed-off people walking past.

Sebastien steps closer, getting real.

"At the Agency, we offer a pioneering service called *Clear History*. A kind of clean slate for people who prefer to move through this world without baggage. Now, that might mean a super-injunction to keep an unexpected bastard out of the press or a few thousand pounds to buy back some selfies that should never have been taken in the first place. We offer people a second chance."

"Just as long as they can afford it," I say.

Sebastien smiles and starts walking again.

I fall in step beside him. "So Heydon asked you to 'clear' his history?"

"That's right," he says briskly.

I think back to Miss Brandt's spiel.

"Heydon went missing five years ago," I say. "The Agency wasn't even a thing then."

"My previous outfit provided a more rudimentary version of the world-class service we're offering today."

"Your previous outfit, the Black Door?" Sebastien doesn't react. "Interesting that you wiped his whole life for him, right before he went missing."

"You think this was all a part of his plan to go dark?"

"Or a part of someone else's," I say. He doesn't respond. "I mean, you didn't just get overexcited and accidentally delete him along with all his data?"

Sebastien's pace increases slightly.

"When I first met Heydon Pierce, he'd recently suffered the latest in a series of devastating mental breaks. He'd whittled his friends down to single figures, and the family couldn't take it anymore. If a little anonymity helped take the pressure off, then who are we to judge?"

"What pressure are we talking about here?"

"You saw the recordings yourself. Heydon thought he was being followed, monitored, shadowed…"

"You don't think anyone encouraged that?"

Sebastien squints. "Well, now that you mention it, there was one friend. Vincent *Carnage*?"

"Control," I say. Sebastien glances at me, and I explain. "Heydon mentioned him in a recording he made just before he disappeared."

"Yes," Sebastien says, like I've just jogged his memory. "That's right, Vincent Control. I can't say I knew him, but I seem to remember Heydon introducing us at some conference or other."

A slick inversion of what Control had told me.

"So you didn't like him?"

"Always seemed like a bad influence," he says dismissively. "Always with his hand out, always in need. Always telling Heydon what he wanted to hear." Sebastien glances over. "Now, that said, my bugbears aside, *he's* who you should be talking to about Heydon Pierce. I'm sure he'd give you chapter and verse. If you like, I could try and work my magic. Get the two of you in the same room."

Given that Vincent Control's currently on a slab somewhere, it lands like a threat.

"That's OK," I say. "Thanks though."

"Can't say I've heard of him in years," Sebastien goes on. "Makes you wonder what becomes of them all."

"Who's that?"

"Life's bit players," he says. "Those small parts and background roles. People who only get one or two lines."

He glances over, including me in the group.

We walk in silence for a moment. It feels like watching someone rewrite history in real time, and it seems obvious that this was always meant to be Control's role, on some level. To provide a plausible buffer between Sebastien and Heydon, something to muddy the water if the project ever went south.

"I searched out this Hartson firm you mentioned." He says it casually, not looking over. "I couldn't see what they could possibly have to do with all this."

"I don't know," I say. "Probably nothing."

"So what brought them to your attention?"

"Well, it's funny you should ask," I say. "I've got their logo tattooed on my face." Sebastien pointedly doesn't look over. "Which means Heydon got it tattooed on his for some reason. And just a few weeks before he walked out."

"I don't understand," Sebastien says, glancing at the tattoo for less than a second. "It's just a run-of-the-mill heart." He corrects himself. "No, of course, the crack."

I smile. "The crack isn't on the logo."

"Well," he says. "There you are. Was there anything else binding them to Heydon?"

"Not so far as I know. Like you say, it's probably a coincidence."

"So what made you mention them to me?"

"I'd just seen the logo for the first time when I followed you from the Mandarin. I guess it was on my mind." I shrug. "You seemed like a connected guy. I thought you might have heard of them."

I'm not mentioning Mr. Peck. Not yet.

There'd been a faint thread linking Peck to a firm associated with Hartson. I don't want Sebastien clearing his history until I've had a chance to make copies. Sebastien walks into a small deli and queues, giving me a minute to think. It doesn't feel like enough, and I'm still churning when he emerges with a brown paper bag.

"Listen," he says, flashing his watch and taking a look at the time. "That's it, that's all I can tell you. I barely knew the guy, and certainly not the fam—"

"How did you hear about Miranda's fall?" I ask.

Sebastien stops, caught momentarily off guard.

This time, he flashes an annoyed look at the people streaming past us on the pavement.

"As I said, Miss Brandt had been making some inquiries."

"What's that got to do with Miranda's fall?"

He smiles patiently.

"After Miranda's guy at Andrews and Ziff gave Miss Brandt the bum rush, she put a call in to the house, hoping to speak to a member of the family. She could only get the maid. I suppose the maid was upset."

Reagan said that Anya had gone home.

"So you didn't speak to Ronnie?"

Sebastien eyes me.

"No," he says. "As I believe I've mentioned, we're not acquainted. In fact, we've never met."

Now they've both denied knowing each other.

Almost like they've got something to hide.

Sebastien smiles and starts to walk away.

"I read your LinkedIn," I say to his back.

He turns. "And what did you think?"

"I noticed you didn't put the Black Door on there."

Sebastien glares at me.

"You've got absolutely nothing, Mr. Lynch," he says. He steps back, looking me up and down with a smile. "Quite literally. I'm sure you'll understand when I tell you that I expect this to be our final conversation."

33.

When Sebastien pats my arm and walks away, I'm momentarily disoriented, and I wander, dazed, to Piccadilly Circus, standing at the entrance to the underground. It feels like the passing faces are taking special notice, looking at me strangely, and I try to get out of the way while I work out what I've just heard.

After gearing myself up to follow in Heydon's footsteps, I'm almost deflated by how my encounter with Sebastien had fizzled away to nothing. I hadn't wanted to ask about the passport. The uncontained joy I'd seen on Ronnie's face this afternoon had been hard to swallow, and I don't want to make Sebastien's day as well. He wouldn't tell me anything anyway. If he's the one holding my passport, then I'm not going anywhere. Sebastien's got me right where he wants me.

My phone goes off, and I pick up, distracted.

"Yeah?" I say.

"Mr. Lynch?"

"Hello?"

"It's Reagan. Am I calling you at a bad time?"

"No," I say. "I'm sorry. What's up?"

"My father finally made it to the Chelsea Wing a few hours ago," she says. "He told me about your conversation." I dread to think which part, so I don't say anything. "Hello?" she says.

"I'm here. You spoke to Ronnie?"

"Just a flying visit, but he told me he'd canceled your reservation," she says. "He said he'd stopped the card. I apologize. I wanted to let you know that I mean to honor the terms of our agreement."

"That's good of you," I say. "But look, you don't need to think about this right now."

"Honestly, a change of scene might do me some good," she says. "In fact, I was just about to head home."

There's something in Reagan's voice, and I wonder if she's ready to pick up where we left off last night. It had felt like she was working her way up to saying something.

Ronnie had made it clear I wasn't welcome there. And of course, things had been ugly with Mike. The mood I'm in, that makes two good reasons to go back. I'm not buying Sebastien's explanation for his relationship with Heydon. And not the way he'd tried to distort Control's version of events either. Most of all, I'm not buying the way that Sebastien had casually shrugged off the suggestion of his friendship with Ronnie Pierce.

In my mind, they'd been in it together. Whatever it was. Getting Reagan in the same room as her dad might be my last chance to prove that he's lying.

"Mr. Lynch?" Reagan says.

I take one last look around me.

The hostile faces, pushing past.

"On my way," I tell her.

—

When I walk through the barrier, I get this feeling like I'm being followed. I look back but just see normal people, going about their business. A gay couple, a hoodie, some Japanese students. Out on the platform, I go right to the end, finding myself staring into the dark portal of the tunnel for so long, it feels like it's drawing me in. Then I turn and look back along the platform, just like Heydon had, at the fifteen or so people I'd passed. I glare at them for five seconds, then ten, then twenty, but no one looks back.

I turn to the light at the end of the tunnel, the arriving train. It comes to a stop, the doors open, and I climb aboard. A few people crowd on around me, and the doors close. Once we start moving, I become aware of a man watching me from the other side of the carriage. He's still wearing the hoodie he'd used to disguise himself on the street. He's the same man who shoulder-checked me when I was walking with Sebastien. He must have followed me from the office.

Neither one of us moves for the first two stops. Then he throws back the hood, revealing close-cropped ginger hair. The man plunges both hands into his pockets and crosses the carriage until we're standing eye to eye.

We're approaching the next station, Waterloo, and he leans tight into my ear as the screech of the tracks reaches a crescendo. I brace for the knife, hearing the last thing that Sebastien had said to me.

I expect this to be our final conversation.

"Don't *ever* come back," the gingernut says flatly.

Then he gets off the train and disappears.

34.

I'm turning onto Tregunter when my phone vibrates, and I see I've gotten a message from Reagan. She's still tied up at the hospital but says she won't be long. I step through the wrought iron gate onto the driveway, looking at the unlit house. When I glance over my shoulder, the street seems quiet. No goons or idling cars. And without even thinking about it, I find myself trying the dropbox, feeling a spark of something when it pops open, revealing the key inside. I take a step back and look at the house again, still not sure why Bobbie first sent me here.

Then I put the key in the door and unlock it.

I don't get that same golden hush this time. For some reason, I can feel static crackling in the air. I listen close but don't hear anything. Slowly, I retrace my footsteps from the first time, walking into the lounge.

I glance through the floor-to-ceiling windows, but there's no black SUVs cruising the block. Backing out, I pass the study and take the stairs down to the lower ground level. I pass through the second lounge, where Heydon had filmed his dead man's switch tape five years ago, through to the stainless-steel kitchen. I walk into the dining room with the gigantic round table, still set for eight, then down the next flight of stairs into the basement, passing the wine cellar on the left, the private cinema on the right.

I hesitate when I pass through the mirror-lined gym. It feels like I'm surrounded by reflections of Heydon on all sides, and I move quickly past the two exercise bikes, the two weight benches, the two treadmills, etc.

Then I step through into the subterranean swimming pool, hearing myself breathing hard.

The pool's something like twenty meters from end to end and softly lit by hidden floor lights. I almost slip, seeing that there's water all over the floor. When I reach the poolside, I see why. It looks like there's been some kind of a struggle, and there's a dead body floating, face down, in the pool. My guess is it must have just happened, because there's still blood melting from a head wound in the top of the man's skull, turning the water red.

I'm making too much noise, and I hold my breath for a few seconds, listening, turning in a circle. When I don't see anyone, I exhale and edge closer to the pool, seeing that it's Ronnie.

Instinctively, I start for the door, then stop, thinking about his collection. The file on Bobbie, locked inside. Ronnie had used his signet ring to open the door to the lift. I stare at the water for a second, then leave my phone on the side, lowering myself in and wading out to the body. When I reach him, I try not to notice the back of his head, the chunk of missing skull where something had hit him, hard. I feel for his left hand instead. When I lift it above the water, I let go, recoiling.

The ring finger's been cut clean off.

I climb out of the pool, grab my phone, and retrace my steps into the gym, through the hall of mirrors, past the screening room and wine cellar, shaking off water, just wanting to get out. On the lower ground level, I fly through the dining room into the kitchen, then through the second lounge, up the stairs, past the study, into the hallway. The front door's right in front of me. I'm gasping for breath, soaking wet and stained with Ronnie's blood, but I stop, looking back at the grand staircase.

I think for a second, then go quickly up.

On the first floor, I take the door through to Ronnie and Miranda's living quarters, passing through two further doors, reaching the room that Ronnie had taken me to on my last visit. The door to the lift's standing open, and there's something on the floor beside it. Ronnie's signet ring, still attached to his finger. I look away, enter the lift, and hit the button. The doors close so slowly it feels like torture. A second passes, then the lift jerks abruptly and starts moving up. When it reaches the top floor, I don't know what I'm walking into, and I try to stand to one side as the doors slide open. There's glass all over the floor. Smashed display cases, shredded memorabilia.

Ronnie's collection's been trashed.

Stepping cautiously out of the lift, I turn to the cabinet he'd locked Bobbie's file inside, but the whole thing's been turned over. Completely gutted.

━━

I exit the lift in Ronnie's quarters, take the stairs down, slam into the front door, then back away from it. I move through the lounge to the french window, unlocking it and walking out into the dark back garden. I'm moving toward the wall when I hear a footstep, turning just in time to see a shadow tearing out of the darkness toward me. The man tackles me, and I hit the ground winded, choking up at the night sky. Then his face is looming over me. He's wearing all black as well as a black balaclava with holes cut for the eyes. I can hear him breathing heavily through his mouth. He's on top of me, pinning me to the lawn, gripping my neck with one hand and a house brick with the other. The garden's dark, but the sky's clear, and I can see his eyes in the moonlight.

They're green and staring straight through me.

The man raises the brick, ready to bring it down.

Then he turns his head to the sound of approaching sirens. He glares at me another moment, then drops the brick, gets up, and goes. I climb to my feet and stagger after Ronnie's killer, after Control's. But by the time I reach the wall and lift myself up, I can already see the black figure climbing over the next one. He disappears and I go after him, collapsing on the other side, crossing the next garden, forgetting the motion sensor lights I'd edged past the last time. They go off, and I hold my hands up to the glare, seeing they're stained pink with blood. There are lights on inside the house, figures in the windows, and I go to the fence, then hurl myself over. Out on the street, a cop car goes right, sirens blaring. I turn left but hear tires screech like they've seen me.

I need to get to Earl's Court, the underground, but I'm running blind, and when I look back, the ultraviolet cop car's starting to turn. I limp to the end of the street, looking left and right. The cars on the busy main road leave light trails, and it feels like everything's moving too fast. Then a black SUV stops in front of me. I look back at the cop car, still turning. A flatbed truck pulls into the road, blocking their way, buying me a few seconds. I turn to the SUV, open the passenger-side door, and throw myself in.

35.

Bobbie makes an illegal left, overtakes two cars, then makes the first right. She speeds to the end of the road, taking a few wing mirrors with her, then takes another left. Then she glances into the rearview and starts to slow down. She's still covering what's left of the black eye but with a smaller pair of tinted glasses now.

When I turn to try and look back at where we've just come from, I'm half expecting to see myself still standing in the street with a stupid look on my face. It takes me a few seconds to twig that the ravey dance beat with a woman sing-talking on top of it is coming from the speaker, not from my head, and when I look at the display, it says "Used to Know Me" by Charli XCX. I mash my hand on the panel to stop it, to think. Then there's just the sound of my breathing.

I look at the streets blurring by for a few seconds, then realize I'm rubbing my soaking-wet sleeve between forefinger and thumb, as if to prove to myself that this is real. I turn to look at Bobbie in the driver's seat. She doesn't look at me.

It feels like I'm going insane.

"Long time, no see," I say, still out of breath.

"Surprise," Bobbie says, sounding flustered.

"What are you doing here?" I ask.

"I was on my way home. I—"

"In London. What are you doing in London?"

Bobbie just drives. "I never left," she says.

"Reagan told me you'd checked into MBR," I say as steadily as I can.

Bobbie keeps her eyes on the road.

"There's a girl with a fake ID doing it for me." I just look at her. "She's getting paid," she says, like that's the real issue here.

I twist around again, still expecting blue lights. I'm not sure if they saw me jump into the car, but it won't take them long to put it together.

"Well, either way," I say. "I'm glad to see you."

Bobbie drives. I can see that she's afraid to look at me, afraid to ask, and I keep my bloodstained hands closed.

"So what happened back there?" she says finally.

I just watch her.

"You're telling me you don't know."

She flashes me a confused look.

"Bobbie, you might want to pull over."

"Not yet," she says, her eyes on the road.

I see a sign for something called *World's End*.

"Listen, Bobbie," I say. "Ronnie's dead."

She doesn't say anything.

"Bobbie..."

"I heard you," she snaps.

I'm relieved to see that Ronnie's death looks like news to her, and at length, a tear rolls out of her shades.

"We need to go back," she says, indicating and pulling into a brutalist housing estate right on the river.

"Bad idea," I say, but she's already turning.

"We have to," she says.

"You can't help him—"

"I know that," she says, stopping. When she does, she looks at the wheel, then at her surroundings, like she can't understand how she got here. "It's not my father." She takes a breath. "He has something of mine. I have to make sure that—"

"The file," I say.

Bobbie freezes, both hands gripping the wheel.

"How do you know?" she asks, not looking at me.

"Ronnie showed me his collection earlier today."

"Then…" She trails off. She swallows. "You've *seen*…"

"He didn't show me what was inside," I say evenly.

Bobbie relaxes a little, wiping the tear from her face.

Then I hit her with it. "But when I went back there after finding him, it was gone."

She regrips the wheel. The fact that the file's missing seems to hit her just as hard as Ronnie's death, maybe harder. But I want to hear how she explains it before I admit to seeing anything.

"Look," I say. "I think we need to lose this car."

——

We leave the car with the smashed wing mirror at the World's End housing estate, then walk along the Thames until we reach a commercial pier. I'd washed my hands with a bottle of mineral water, and the suit's stopped dripping. The darker-than-navy-blue material just seems to absorb the blood.

We don't talk until we've paid and boarded the clipper, then

Bobbie leads us outside, to the rear. When she puts her hands on the railing and stares back upriver, I realize we're looking at Albert Bridge, where Heydon's car was found parked with the doors wide open five years ago. The bridge is brightly lit, like a solid beam of light blasting across the Thames.

Bobbie takes out her scuffed pack of designer cigarettes and sparks up. She doesn't offer me one but turns and holds out hers for a drag. Somehow, it feels like an affectation this time, and I can't help but notice that the tabs are too short for the dog-eared packaging they're inside, that she's been restocking the Yves Saint Laurent box with a cheaper brand. I don't like what that seems to say about Bobbie, and I'm glad to find the gorily packaged carton of Marlboro Reds in my pocket instead.

"They call it the trembling lady," she says, blowing smoke at the bridge as we start to pull away. "Bad vibrations."

For some reason, the image brings Reagan to mind.

"You should try and get hold of your sister," I say.

Numbly, Bobbie turns to me, the river at her back.

"I'm not sure how much you know," I go on. "But Miranda took a serious fall yesterday."

"I heard," she says vaguely.

I take a drag. "I think she was pushed," I tell her.

The wind tussles Bobbie's hair, and she blinks hard. "Pushed?" she says. "Pushed by who?"

"Well, my number one suspect was Ronnie, but…"

She sees something in the way I'm looking at her.

"Are you fucking accusing me?" she says.

I shake my head. "I didn't say that."

But the thought had crossed my mind.

Bobbie was the one who'd brought me into all this, and her

motives still aren't clear. Now as far as I can tell, she's been moving in the background this entire time. The woman she'd hired to do her ninety days in the hole might even look like a paid alibi to some. And I can't look past the fact that she'd appeared out of nowhere moments after I'd discovered Ronnie's body. Clearly, she wasn't the man in the black balaclava, but that didn't mean she wasn't involved. I'm about to say something when some guy from the boat starts shouting at us for smoking. We each take one last drag, then put them out.

"Look, you guys are in danger. I was supposed to meet Reagan tonight at the house. The cops pulling up like that probably kept her safe for now. But someone's already hurt Miranda, someone's already killed Ronnie…"

Bobbie stands there for a few seconds, then takes out her phone and calls her sister.

"Ray," she says. She closes her eyes. "I know," she says. "I *know*," she repeats. "Listen, where are you?" She looks at me. "The Chelsea and Westminster?"

"Tell her to stay put," I say quietly.

"You should stay there," Bobbie tells her.

"Is there anyone with her?" I ask.

"Ray, are you with anyone?"

Bobbie listens for a moment. "Anya," she says.

"Security," I say quietly. "Has she got security?"

"Ray, is there security? Are you safe?" She listens. "Rayner," she says. "OK, right."

"Tell her you're on your way."

Bobbie glares at me.

"Ray, I'm in town." She listens wearily. "Look, I know. Just don't ask. Yes, fine, you can send someone. I'll give you an address. I'm coming to you, OK?" She listens for another second. "Yeah," she says. "*Love.*"

Bobbie hangs up, then turns to the railing, watching the ship's wake, the bridge of light disappearing.

The suit's starting to dry by now, but without the cigarette, I can feel the chill. My brain's telling me to get off at the next stop or maybe to throw myself overboard and swim. Away from Bobbie and the murder I'd just walked in on. Away from the Pierce family altogether. But I know I'd be taking my biggest problem with me. And whether I made it to dry land or not, at some point, somewhere, I'd still sink like a stone.

"Bobbie, we need to talk," I say to her back.

"What's there to talk about?"

"What's going on here?"

"I don't know."

"As you understand it…"

"I don't understand it."

I stare into the ship's wake for a moment.

"Why did you first approach me?" I ask.

Bobbie half turns. She frowns.

"It was an accident," she starts. "I just thought—"

"Cut the shit, Bobbie. Three people are dead."

"Three?" she says, properly turning to me.

"Your brother, your dad, and a guy who got caught up in it all. Vincent Control." I say the name to see how she reacts, but she squints and shakes her head. "He was a friend of your brother's, or pretending to be."

She looks down at the deck.

"I think they killed him so he couldn't answer any more questions about Heydon."

Bobbie turns uncertainly, taking it all in. The black sky above, the black river below. The glowing high-rises either side, creating a kind of corridor of light. She holds the railing tightly, looking like she might be sick. At length, it passes, and she loosens her grip.

"Look," I say. "I think I've got some idea who's doing this, but I need to know everything."

She doesn't move.

"I've told you, I don't—"

"We're past all that." She still doesn't move, and I try to change gears. "Look. You saved my life back there. I'm grateful." *But I don't trust you*, I think. "But we're not out of this yet," I say. "I can't get us out until I know what I'm in."

She starts speaking slowly, not looking at me.

"It's true that I thought you were Heydon," she says. "Just for a second, on the underground. You looked so out of it, like you were running away from something."

"This was before we met in the terminal?"

Bobbie nods. "Your head was moving with the motion of the train, but your arms stayed wrapped around yourself. You stayed alert."

Not alert enough.

I'd come to on the train with the sense of being watched. I just hadn't clocked who was doing it.

"Anyway, I forgot all about you," Bobbie says. "I went on to Heathrow." She shrugs. "I didn't give you a second thought until I saw you again at the hotel."

I still feel like I'm not getting the full story.

"So bumping into you, our big scene…"

"I just wanted to speak with you," she says.

"And what about the car? The coke?"

"What about them?" she asks.

"Who was driving?"

"I've already told you," she says.

I just look at her.

Bobbie's shoulders rise and fall with a sigh.

"His name's Nate. He's my ex. It's his car."

"Right," I say, thinking back to the car for any clue she's telling the truth. Nothing comes to mind, but the whole scene feels like those streets I'd watched flying by. Moving too fast to really focus on, a blur.

"And I asked him if he'd been following you," she says. "He's got form. And he didn't like the idea of us going off together."

"Sounds like something you could have mentioned, Bobbie. So what did you tell him at Heathrow?"

Something about the look on my face makes her hesitate. "I told him I thought that you were my brother."

I rub my face with both hands.

"So come on then. What's he saying?"

"He admitted to watching you. He was sitting outside my parents' place the next morning when you left with Ray. He followed you to Soho."

"But now you've called him off?"

"I swear, I explained everything."

I take an unconscious step closer.

"This is important. There's two guys out there, showing a picture of me around town. It was taken at the same time and place I saw Nate's car, in Soho."

"Wait, showing your picture around, like—"

"I found one on Control when they killed him."

Bobbie shakes her head.

"Who were the two guys?" she asks.

I try and remember Sebastien's description.

"One big, wearing a leather jacket, one long and thin, wearing an anorak." Now I think of it, they sound more gangland than anyone else I've seen around here.

Bobbie thinks. "Look. That doesn't sound like him. At all. But I hear you. If they *were* looking for Heydon on his behalf, then I assure you, they're not now."

"*If?*"

"What can I tell you? I don't know."

"So what about the drugs?" I ask.

"What about them? I told you, I asked him—I asked Nate—to bring me something since I was stuck at Heathrow."

"You asked him to bring you a bag of sugar?"

Bobbie's shoulders go rigid.

"He gave me a line in the car so I wouldn't go crazy, then sent me to the hotel with the sugar so I wouldn't realize until I got back."

"Why sugar?"

"I suppose he didn't want me to use," she says.

Then he's not like any dealer I've ever known.

"And what about the drug you spiked me with?"

"I don't know what you're talking about," she says.

Yes, she does, and it seems clear that's what our meeting with the black SUV had really been about. But I can see that the more I prod, the further away from me she gets. And there seems no point in stating the obvious—that she'd tipped off Mike about a possible break-in at the house, that she'd set all this in motion.

"So you're saying you had no idea what you were sending me into when you tattooed my face?"

"I needed help," she says bleakly.

It sounds something like the truth.

"So why didn't you just ask?"

"You wouldn't have done it," she says, turning to me, her back against the railing, the wind catching her hair. I want to tell her she's wrong, but I'm not sure.

"Why did you need help?"

"A few days ago, a strange man approached me."

"Mr. Badwan?" I ask.

"He told me that my brother had left something of mine in his care before he went missing."

"You used Miranda's jewelry to get it back."

Bobbie doesn't dispute it but looks at me with sudden anger, like I've breached some kind of firewall. "I knew that if I went to my parents, they'd just use the Rayner Group to make the payment," she says. "To me, that felt like the same thing as handing it over to my father. Which I suppose is what I ended up doing anyway."

"Ronnie followed you?"

"His men in black," she says bitterly. "After Badwan gave me the file back, two Rayner guys insisted I get in a car. My father was inside. We fought. He took it from me."

"That's how you got the black eye?" I ask.

Bobbie nods. "He suggested I go to Miranda and tell her I'd relapsed. That I'd pawned her things. He thought I should get away for a while until it all calmed down."

Ronnie had been working overtime to try and contain something, and it just makes me more certain he'd been covering some deeper, darker connection with Sebastien and Heydon's disappearance.

"And what about Heydon's stuff?" I ask. "Why didn't you get the case he'd left with Badwan."

"Badwan didn't even tell me about it until I'd handed over Miranda's stones," she says. "I'd given him everything I had just to get that file."

When I look at her now, the windswept black hair, the skinny frame, her tinted glasses, I can't help but think of the smiling blond Bobbie I'd seen in the picture. Her transformation reminds me of Heydon. His ever-more-haunted photographs. Like there's just some madness, reaching out of the past, slowly eating them all alive.

Time to have it out about the phone bills.

"What's in the file, Bobbie?"

"The worst mistake I ever—"

"For real this time," I say.

Bobbie looks back at me fearfully.

It looks like she feels sick again.

"When we were small, my father was obsessed with the idea of Miranda being unfaithful," she starts. "They fought constantly. He'd interrogate her about where she'd been, who she was with. He'd follow her and go through her things. When Theo drowned, Miranda was working on a film called *Wilderness Years* with—"

"Christopher Jacobs," I say. Bobbie looks at me. "I read that his wife left him right after the shoot."

"He was an alcoholic. Miranda was his sponsor."

"Huh," I say. "So that call from the set was…"

"A personal crisis. Miranda was trying to talk him down from the ledge. Literally. The signal was terrible down by the pool, so she went upstairs."

I think back to the documents Ronnie had been brandishing. There'd been no calls in or out from the landline on the morning of Theo's accident. And none from what I now assume to be Miranda's mobile either.

"OK," I say. "So the worst thing you've ever done…"

Bobbie looks at me like I'm being impatient.

"I'm just explaining that my father was paranoid, hoarding all this poisonous stuff."

I just wait.

"When Heydon went missing, I was still in school."

"This is 2017?"

"Well, actually, this is earlier, the year before. I was sober when I started, but Goldsmiths turned out to be super druggy." She looks at me. "That's where I met Nate."

"He was a student?"

She shakes her head.

"But we were partying pretty hard, and I was broke. I went home while the house was empty."

"To Ronnie's collection?"

"I was basically looking for anything of value he might not miss. Then he came home unexpectedly. I had to hide."

"What happened?"

"He was taking a call on speakerphone. He was brusque with the man, told him to make it quick."

"Did this man introduce himself?"

"No," she says. I let out a long, involuntary sigh. "But he mentioned a company called the Black Door."

"The Black Door?" I say. "You're sure about that?"

"Unfortunately, yes. He said he was grateful to Mr. Rayner for putting him in touch with my father. Said he represented certain parties who thought it was time for Miranda to retire quietly."

"They wanted her to retire? What did Ronnie say?"

"He said that my mother was hardheaded."

"So…"

"The man agreed. He said that was why she needed to be encouraged somehow."

I don't say anything.

"The man said he'd heard a rumor from the set of *Wilderness Years* that Miranda and Jacobs had grown close to each other. It was getting on for twenty years ago by that point, but he wondered if my father could substantiate it. He wondered if Miranda might even have *been* with Jacobs when Theo drowned."

"What did Ronnie say?"

"He was outraged. Dressed them down for asking, told them not to call again and hung up. Then he left."

I still don't say anything.

"And I'd just been trawling through all this insane stuff he'd gathered on my mother." She sounds out of breath. "I went to the 1997 file and found itemized phone bills from the day that Theo drowned."

The bills showed no calls in or out on that morning. Until the emergency call, after Theo's drowning.

"So what did they prove?"

"Well, that was the best part," Bobbie says. "They proved nothing. Miranda was so tired of my father checking up on her that she bought a separate phone just for Jacobs. That's why there was no record."

"So what did you do, Bobbie?"

"Look," she says. "First of all, I could see how insane it was. Whoever these Black Door people were, they were struggling, digging around in a day that was getting on for two decades ago. Second, I knew that Miranda wasn't being unfaithful. I was only six when they were making *Wilderness*, but I'd been on set. I'd seen enough to know what was going on. Jacobs was sick. So I knew that these Black Door people were looking for something that wasn't there. And anyway, there *weren't* any calls that morning. So I knew if I approached them with the phone bills, they'd pay. And they'd see there was nothing to it."

"If Miranda was just helping a friend that day, how come she never went public with the real story?"

"At the time, I think she wanted to protect Jacobs. He was in a terrible place, especially after the accident. If the press had found out that Miranda was talking to him while Theo drowned, then they'd have eaten him alive. There were already rumors on set because they spent so much time together. His relapse would have gone public. He didn't last much longer after that anyway. Then there was my father's wrath." Bobbie sighs. "I'm not sure why she never cleared things up after Jacobs died. Once there was nothing left to protect. I can only think that she wanted to punish herself. She allowed everyone to think she was this heartless bitch who put her career ahead of her kids. I suppose that's how she felt. At times, it felt more like a punishment for the rest of us, but I could see her reasoning. My father nursing those phone records like a private wound was what made me sick."

"So you wanted to out him?"

"I knew that if those bills ever leaked to the press, if anyone ever asked, she'd know exactly where they came from. His madness would be exposed. He'd deserve it."

"How did Ronnie find you out?"

"I copied the bills so I could send them to my email." She closes her eyes. "I left them on the scanner in his office."

That explained the fingerprints, the weird hold that Ronnie had over her. "So what did he do?" I ask.

She looks at me. "Weirdly, nothing. He called me into his office and showed me a letter, saying he'd had the bills fingerprinted. Then he sent me away. It was less than a year after that when Heydon went missing."

"How did Heydon get hold of them?"

"He broke into my father's collection, the same night he left. He took the file. Cruelly, my father never said a word about it. I found out for the first time last week when Mr. Badwan approached me."

Heydon might not have known what the phone bills meant, but the letter confirming that Bobbie's prints were all over them must have set off alarm bells. With Ronnie hoarding them as part of his collection and unable to find Miranda's notorious phone call—and already paranoid about the events of Theo's death—it must have felt like some kind of betrayal. He'd left that night with one last hope. That he could bring Theo home and reunite the family. It just hadn't worked out that way.

"When you sent them to this company…"

"Nate sent them," she says. "So it couldn't come back on me. They never asked where they came from anyway. Then, after Heydon went missing, I looked them up again, these Black Door people, but they were gone. The site had been scrubbed, the emails bounced back, everything."

Sebastien, clearing his own history.

"Do you know a company called Hartson?" I ask. Bobbie just stares at me, and I touch the tattoo. "Because this is their corporate logo." She doesn't say anything. "A man from the same company threatened Heydon's doctor."

"You mean *Matthew* Hartson?" I nod, and Bobbie thinks for a second. "He's an oil guy, kind of a joke."

"A joke how?"

She looks at me uncertainly.

"Like, obsessed with staying young. He's had every kind of surgery, takes every kind of supplement…"

"Has he got any connection to your family?"

Bobbie frowns. Ronnie had denied it, but Sebastien's reaction made me sure something was there.

"Bobbie, does he—"

"Yes," she says. "He and Miranda had some war of words in the press, back in the day."

"Back in the day, when?"

"I don't know, like five or six years ago…" She trails off, then looks up at me. "Hartson was the head of UKPA."

"UKPA?"

"UK Petroleum…something, an oil lobbying firm. Of course, Miranda's Nazi green. They'd been sniping at each other in the press, then she said some cutting thing in some big speech, with him in the front row. Hartson tried to have her removed from the charity she was working with at the time."

"Successfully?"

She thinks for a moment.

"Well, Miranda sort of retired when Heydon went missing anyway."

"I couldn't find much between them online."

Bobbie digs out her phone and starts searching.

"Hartson bought out the media firm who filmed the ceremony," she says. "He owns the footage. He must have a team of people working round the clock to try and keep it down." She searches for a minute. "You can usually find it on Reddit." But nothing comes up, and Bobbie sighs. "I can send it to you later."

"But Miranda insulted him?" I say. Bobbie nods. "And then right before Heydon went missing, he got Hartson's logo tattooed on his face." Bobbie frowns, and I dig out my phone, showing her the Hartson website. "Have you got any idea why?"

She thinks for a second, then shakes her head.

We're both wiped out, and we go quiet for a minute.

"I could see that you were struggling," she says.

"I'm sorry?"

"Why I sent you. I knew that if you went there, they'd have to cut you some kind of check, find you somewhere to stay. I wanted to help."

"Right," I say, still uneasy with her watching me on the underground. Even less comfortable with the pity. I look at her. "Did you take my passport, Bobbie?"

"What?"

"It went missing from my room last night."

"Of course not," she says with a flash of anger.

At the very least, she'd sent me into that house to try and provoke the situation somehow. She couldn't have anticipated Miranda's suggestion that I impersonate Heydon or that my meeting with Badwan would lead me to Control, then Matten, then Sebastien. Her explanation for her fingerprints on those phone bills sounded authentic too. It hadn't exactly made her sound good. And in the end, I've got to give her credit for getting me off Tregunter, away from the Met.

"Please," she says. "Tell me what you've learned."

But at the same time, I don't like the sound of *Nate*, and I still feel like I'm not getting the full story.

"Later," I say. "We need to get back on dry land."

"Why? Where are we going?"

"You're going to the Chelsea and Westminster. I need to talk to an old friend of your father's."

"What old friend?" she asks. "Who?"

"Sebastien Keeler," I say, watching closely.

Bobbie looks back at me, brushing the hair out of her face. "I've never heard of him," she says.

36.

I take the Bakerloo line from Embankment to Piccadilly. There's
no one weird on the way down, no glaring women or menacing
hoodies, but the journey still feels intense. I'd been warned to
stay away from Sebastien. First by the man himself, then by the
gingernut on the train. It sounded like good advice as well. Except
that someone's taken my passport, so I can't leave. Except that
someone's trying to hang two murders on me.

It's time to have it out with Sebastien about his connection
to Ronnie Pierce, his connection to Hartson. About Hartson's
involvement in Heydon's disappearance. When he'd patted me
on the arm and walked away, I'd thought it was another demonstration of how untouchable Sebastien was, how little I knew. I'd
thought the guy on the underground was my final warning.

Now it feels like another distraction. Sebastien could have sent
Ronnie to the Chelsea and Westminster, provoking Reagan's call
to me, her invitation to the house. After that, I'd walked through
the door and framed myself for murder. Sebastien had put the
bow on it.

When my phone connects to the Wi-Fi, I get a message from Bobbie. She's managed to find the clip of Miranda at the awards ceremony on a dubious-looking Russian streaming site. I have to wait until I'm aboveground again to listen, but when I do, it's worth it. Miranda's wearing an elegant black dress, holding a trophy, addressing the crowd. She picks out Matthew Hartson.

"And our good friend, Mr. Hartson," she says.

The camera cuts to him, sitting front row.

He's staring at the stage, expressionless.

"Not content with sucking the lifeblood from our planet, he's moved on to his own children."

Big laughter, big applause.

When the camera cuts back to Hartson, he's just scowling at the stage.

———

When I arrive on the square, I keep my distance from Sebastien's building. It's after nine, and his is one of the few lobbies still fully lit. There's two guys on the door. The oversize ex-military one I'd seen last time and one closer to my size, both wearing all black.

There's a light on in the fourth floor.

Watching from the street, I see a figure walking back and forth, looking like he's alternately listening, then talking to someone, not looking back into the room, most likely having a conversation on the speakerphone, like I'd seen Sebastien do before.

I know I'm not getting back inside, not past the guys on the door, and even if I did, I'd still need to bypass Miss Brandt before facing Sebastien on his home turf, at his most untouchable. I think for a second, then google the phone number for the agency.

———

"Evening," I say heavily, thickening my voice and putting a few more miles on the clock. "This is Detective Inspector Smith with the Metropolitan Police," I drawl. "I'm trying to get in touch with a Sebastien Keeler."

"Good evening," Miss Brandt says after a micropause. "I'm afraid that Mr. Keeler's currently in transit, traveling on urgent business. May I ask what this is in relation to?"

"Just a formality," I say. "I'm afraid a close acquaintance of Mr. Keeler's was assaulted and killed in his own home this afternoon."

"That's terrible," Miss Brandt says. "May I ask who?"

"Ronnie Pierce," I say, still watching Sebastien walk back and forth in front of the window. There's just silence for a few seconds, then hold music—dueling, synthesized pianos. A moment later, Sebastien turns from the window as if to someone walking into the room. He disappears, and a minute or so later, Miss Brandt comes back on the line.

"I'm so sorry to keep you holding," she says. "I'm afraid Sebastien's uncontactable at the moment. Is there a number where we can reach you to schedule a meeting?"

"I'm actually in the area," I say. "Ten or so minutes out. Might be easier if I just drop by."

"That…would be fine," Miss Brandt says. "My shift finished a few minutes ago, so I might not be here. But I'll make sure that the front desk has access to Sebastien's schedule. Thank you for calling, Detective Inspector."

———

A minute later, I see the monster on the door put a finger to his earpiece. He listens for a moment, says something in return, then nods at the smaller guy, who walks a few bays down and unlocks the black Mercedes. The lights flash, and he opens the rear door, waiting. When Sebastien walks through the lobby, he's still pulling his coat on, and I see that Miss Brandt's trailing him with a leather satchel and a hard-shell flight case. I start walking toward the building as they exit.

Sebastien sees me first.

"Stay the fuck away from me," he says seriously, pointing over the roof of the car. The monster starts walking around it toward me, and the smaller guy in black steps away from the building, closer to Sebastien.

"Going somewhere?" I ask.

"On to better things," Sebastien tells me. "You should try it sometime."

"It's always a sad sight to see a confidence man losing his nerve."

"Oh, come on then."

"I know what you did," I say.

"You know what I did?" Sebastien stares at me. "Lynch, so far as I can tell, you just killed a man."

"Fuck you, Sebastien. The same guy who did Ronnie did Vincent Control."

The amusement on Sebastien's face falls away.

"Yes," he says, leaning on the roof of the car, glaring at me so hard that it feels like the rest of them aren't there. "And in my view, they should take a closer look at the circumstances of Mr. Control's demise."

"A few hours ago, you couldn't tell me his name."

"You jogged my memory," he says. "How strange that you should show up so soon after his violent death, asking me questions about him."

I can feel the rest of them staring at me.

"You were the one who brought him up," I say.

Sebastien makes a face. "That's not how I remember it at all. In fact, I mentioned our conversation to Miss Brandt when I got back to the office."

Miss Brandt's staring at me like I'm a madman. "Sebastien said you mentioned an old acquaintance of his," she says, her face drawn. "He asked me to look him up, since he hadn't thought of the gentleman in years."

"There you are," Sebastien says. "Nothing between us. Can you say the same?"

I don't say anything.

"As for Ronnie Pierce, what can I tell you? My right hand to God, I don't know the man. But I certainly wouldn't want to be a penniless drifter impersonating his missing son right about now. You've got a lot of questions to answer, Lynch."

"Me?"

He shakes his head. "Who else?"

Maybe it's just Sebastien hitting all the right notes, but he's starting to get under my skin. From the way he's talking to me and from the way his eyes are popping out of his head, I'm starting to get the feeling that he really is shocked about Ronnie's death, and he's shocked to see me here too.

"If that's all..." he says.

"You're not going anywhere."

I start walking toward them, feeling the weight of the knife in my pocket. The monster shifts, moving his jacket, showing me the holster underneath, and I stop. He nods at me to back off, and after a moment, I do.

I try to think.

"Listen, Sebastien, if you're saying it wasn't you, and I'm saying it wasn't me…"

"Some other interested party," he says flippantly. "Big-fish shit. You're out of your league."

"Sure," I say, still trying to think. "But what about you?" He frowns. "I mean, I thought you were the one doing all this. I thought you were the mastermind."

"Honestly?" he says. "So did I. The world changes, Mr. Lynch. Sometimes at a moment's notice. One reality ceases to exist, and a new one emerges. It's the slow movers like you who can't adapt that always go extinct." He smiles. "Best of luck, living in the past."

I can't think of the right thing to say or do, and when Sebastien sees it on my face, he gives an amused look before climbing into the car, followed by Miss Brandt. The smaller guy gets in on the passenger side, and finally the monster, giving me a menacing stare.

"Good luck predicting the future," I say under my breath to no one. Then I turn and start to walk, finally sick of them. The past that they'll keep on editing, like a Wikipedia page, the unwinnable, infinite, stupid fucking argument of the present. All the future that's got to go up in smoke to make sure everything always goes their way.

When they pull past me, Sebastien doesn't even glance over. He's deep in conversation with Miss Brandt, already on to the next thing. The car gets to the end of the street and indicates. Then there's the strangest moment of silence, and it feels like everything stops. There's just the girls on the corner, saying good night, the lit windows in the buildings around us. There's a loud, metallic crunch, followed by a low boom, and the black Mercedes explodes, roaring up into a thirty-foot fireball.

37.

I'm looking up at the blurred night sky, wiping dirt out of my eyes. My brain feels like it's fresh out of a paint shaker, and I roll over to see I'm lying in the street, covered in grit. I put my hands on the pavement and feel shards of glass pressing into my palms. When I stand, the ground's like a trampoline, and the street sways in front of me. I can see car alarms going off—the lights flashing—but for some reason, they don't make a sound. When an injured woman crosses my field of vision, walking confused from the scene of the explosion, wiping blood out of her eyes, I can see that she's screaming; I just can't hear what. It's easy to walk, because I can't feel my legs, and I glide fifteen feet to the corner, floating around it into a wall of flame. The car's going like a bonfire, thick black smoke billowing out, burning my eyes and skin. I wipe the sweat out of my face and try to get closer.

The front of the car looks roughly intact. I think I can see the outline of the monster, burning in the driver's seat, as well as what might be the shape of his partner on the passenger side. The rear of the car must have taken most of the blast, because it's just not there anymore. Backing off, I see what looks like one of Miss Brandt's heels, lying singed in the street. Then I look ahead of the car and see Sebastien, face down, twenty feet away. The explosion must have thrown him clear. Either that or he'd crawled out of the wreckage somehow. I drift cautiously toward him, feeling like it's fifty-fifty, and I have to wonder what it takes to put someone like Keeler down.

But when I reach his body, it looks like he's died twice. His neck's broken, and his face is smeared across the pavement like jam. I pat out the fire from his coat, watching him smolder for a few seconds, becoming slowly aware of the sounds around me. The roar of the flames, the screaming hysteria, the sirens drawing in. Then, on instinct, just one bullshit artist to another, I crouch down and start feeling along Sebastien's wrist for the Patek. It's burning hot, but I unlock it, slide it off, and put it on. Then I try to get off the street.

———

On my way to the underground, I can feel it. One reality just ceased to exist, and a new one's already emerging. People are talking on their phones or in small groups, seeming scared. When I turn to look back, I can see the plume rising up above the buildings, connecting with the black sky. Even so, official word hasn't reached the underground yet, and I descend quickly, hoping I can slip away before they shut it down.

When I push through the barriers, I sense some kind of presence, something taking an interest in me, but I don't look back. There's a multistory car park's worth of alarms and lights going off in my head. Everything's flashing red or running on empty. Displaying some kind of warning sign. I've just got to hold it together long enough to get out of here.

Most people are on their way out, looking at phones, or talking to strangers, and I can see that news is traveling fast. When I reach the train level, I turn left onto the first platform, then go all the way along it, following the signs through to the next, crossing from the north- to the southbound line, passing fewer and fewer people, onto the first platform I see with no one. As I step out, there's three chimes, then the crackle of a microphone.

A thick London accent.

"*This station's closed,*" a breathless man says, sounding like he's leaving in a hurry. "*Repeat. This station—*"

He's cut off by an automated message.

The soothing voice of a trained actor.

"*Attention, please. Due to a reported emergency, would all passengers leave the station immediately.*"

I keep walking onto the platform, seeing a train explode past and scream through the station. There's a flash of red, white, and blue-colored carriages, the frozen faces in the windows, then it's gone.

The automated message keeps playing on a loop.

"*Attention, please. Due to a reported emergency, would all passengers leave the station immediately.*"

When I look back at the passageway I just walked through, I see a figure standing at the end.

I recognize his silhouette. The long, thin man I'd seen on the underground before. The gingernut who'd told me to never come back. As he draws closer, I see he's wearing an anorak. Like the man who Sebastien said had been going around town, showing my picture.

I back off, looking down the platform, and see his partner, the big guy in the leather jacket, lumbering toward us.

"Sebastien's dead," I say to Mr. Anorak as the two of them start to close in on me. But really, I've got no idea what they want or who they work for. He takes a knife from his pocket, baring his teeth.

I glance back, seeing that the guy in the leather jacket's moving in, much closer than I'd thought. There's a distant rumble, a light at the end of the tunnel.

The sign over the platform starts flashing.

STAND BACK TRAIN APPROACHING

They're trying to force me onto the tracks.

I look at Mr. Anorak for another second, then start abruptly toward the big guy in the leather jacket, taking the knife from my pocket.

He gives me an amused look.

"Yer can stop pretending to—"

I slash, backhanded, across his face, and a curtain of blood falls in front of his eyes. The man falls to his knees, howling, his head in his hands, his hands overflowing with blood. I step around him, still backing off from Mr. Anorak, whose beaded black eyes never seem to leave mine.

"Did you hear me, *psycho*? Sebastien's in bits."

He's still baring his teeth, and after a moment, I realize he's smiling.

"Who said anything about Sebastien?"

I stare at him for a moment.

There's just the sound of us both breathing hard, the big guy sobbing blood. The train approaching.

Mr. Anorak's eyes flick over my shoulder, and I glance back, following his sight line, thinking I see a third figure standing at the end of the platform, watching.

"Attention, please. Due to a reported emergency, would all passengers leave the station immediately."

Anorak takes a step toward me, and I slash at him.

I can feel the lights bearing down on us. I can hear the train screaming into the station. We both stand there, a second away from just going for it, holding knives on each other, until it's blown past. Then we're just breathing hard. Anorak's eyes go to his partner, still on the ground, bleeding out of his face. Carefully, we walk around each other. He bends to the guy, still keeping his knife on me.

I back away and walk.

I'm at the exit before I remember the figure I'd seen. The third person, watching from the shadows. Dazed, I turn and look to the end of the platform, but whoever it was is long gone. If they were ever really there.

———

I walk, retracing my steps, first onto the northbound line, then all the way along it, through to the first platform, still hearing the scream of that train.

"Attention, please. Due to a reported emergency—"

When I step out for the escalators, I'm glad to see that there's still people leaving the station. I breathe deeply, catching my reflection in a filthy mirror. The suit's a disgrace, covered in dust and frayed at the edges. My expression's locked into a humorless death stare. But I'd been lucky to only pick up cuts and bruises from the debris. The escalators have been deactivated, and I trudge endlessly up, turning from the two scowling transport police officers on their way down.

"Attention, please. Due to a reported emergency—"

The barriers are open in the ticket hall, and I walk through, taking the stairs up to street level. The night air hits me like a slap in the face, and there's cops on every corner, everywhere you look. Guys in black, guys in high-vis, guys in riot gear. Guys on motorbikes, guys on horses, guys in choppers overhead. There's guys with dogs and guys with Tasers and guys with nightsticks and guys with guns. I freeze for a second, not knowing which way to turn, when someone touches my arm.

It's Mike, and when I look at him, his eyes stay carefully neutral. I glance back at the cops for a second, doing the math, then I follow. I don't trust him, and I don't like seeing him here like this, but right now, he's better than the alternative. We join the other few hundred people still being evacuated from the block, obeying police instructions to clear the area, filing down the street, away from Piccadilly, toward St. James's Park. As we go, I see that the entire block's been cordoned off, with police vans—brightly colored tactical aid units—pulled dramatically across the roads. Mike leads us off the main drag, left, into a waiting SUV. It feels like I'm holding my breath the whole way.

38.

We've been driving for a minute before I can loosen my grip and let go of the handrest. At first, there's this heavy pressure sitting on my chest, and I just sit there for a few blocks, trying to breathe it out. As the pressure lifts, I feel my heart beating furiously underneath it all, refusing to accept the situation and move on. The tips of my fingers start to tingle, and my legs turn cold.

Once my ears have stopped ringing, I become aware of the sound of my breathing—shallow, rasping breaths—and I try to even it out. Finally, the sound of the engine comes into focus, and I lean back into the seat, closing my eyes, feeling grateful, like I need every mile I can get between me and what just happened.

When I turn to Mike, sitting beside me in the back of the truck, he looks away, seeming uncomfortable.

"Gis a kiss," I say, aiming for something light and hearing it land with a thud. When Mike turns to me, he swallows, avoids my eye, then looks quickly away.

He's blinking like crazy.

That's when I become conscious of the woman sitting opposite.

She's wearing a long black raincoat, skirt suit, and heels, and she's got short blond hair with light streaks of gray in it. Her face is neutral, expressionless, and she watches me for a moment, her legs crossed, exuding total authority.

"Good evening, Mr. Lynch."

"All right?" I say after a moment.

"I'm fine," she says. "Thank you for asking. How are you this evening?"

When I glance at Mike, he's facing the window.

"Yeah," I say at length. "Y'know, it feels like the end of a long day."

"I can imagine," she says, already moving on from the pleasantries. "My name's Elsa Carhart. I'm a senior partner with the same firm as Mr. Arnold—"

"Old man Rayner?" I say, holding out a filthy hand.

She flashes another smile, and I slowly retract it.

"It's interesting you should bring him up," she says. "Mr. Arnold and I were just discussing Mr. Rayner's current business interests in North America."

"Right," I say, not following.

"Yes," Elsa goes on. "As I'm sure you know, the Rayner Group is a private consultation firm with offices in sixty cities around the world."

"Right," I say, still not following.

"I simply remarked how unfortunate for all parties that Mr. Rayner's unforgiving schedule didn't allow him to take the lead in this case or any involvement at all."

I stare at her for a moment, then glance at Mike, who'd told me Rayner was involved personally. He doesn't meet my eye, and Elsa goes on.

"One feels sure that his cool head could have prevented some measure of this senseless tragedy."

"I'm sorry," I say. "I zoned out for a second there. My takeaway from all this is that Mr. Rayner had no involvement?" Elsa just looks at me. "I mean, except for the fact that he pays your mortgage and owns this car."

She allows a brief real smile.

"Well, of course, we accept that the family enlisted Mr. Arnold's expertise in the first instance, but when they decided to go in a different direction, that's where we got off. Our involvement ended right there and then," she says. "Following your meeting with Mrs. Pierce and her daughter on Friday afternoon—following his dismissal—Mr. Arnold was reassigned. I had him consulting on other business that same evening. The family rehired us this afternoon."

No doubt that's what the paperwork would say.

"So Mike was off the case too." I glance at him, but he's still looking away. "All right, understood."

"There's nothing to understand," Elsa says lightly.

I just stare at her for a moment.

"So you're Mike's boss?" I say. Another tight smile. "Well, I want you to know, he's been doing a bang-up job—"

"Shut the fuck up, Lynch," Mike hisses.

When I look at him, he's still facing the window.

"I'm sorry," I say. "We've been having a lot of fun with each other. Please, go on."

"According to Mr. Arnold, the family secured your"—Elsa pauses—"services in making a onetime payment to an underworld figure in furtherance of retrieving certain personal items belonging to Heydon Pierce."

I stare at Elsa for a few seconds.

"I went and got his case back, yeah."

"Excellent," she says. "And you returned said case to the family on Saturday, September tenth?"

"I guess."

"Mr. Lynch, could you outline the terms of your agreement as you understand them?"

I stare at her for a few seconds more.

"Get the case and take it to Miranda. She wanted to know how Badwan might react when he saw my face."

"Your physical similarity to Mr. Heydon Pierce," she says quickly. "Yes, of course. And you communicated these impressions to Mrs. Pierce during your meeting?"

"Yeah." I shrug. "My sense was that Badwan—"

"Excellent," she says, moving swiftly on, not wanting to know what I've learned, not wanting to hear it. "May I ask for the family's side of this agreement?"

I realize that my eyes are still streaming.

"Thirty-five thousand pounds," I tell her, wiping them.

"I understand that there was some trouble with the payment."

"Well," I say. "Ronnie stopped the card. Nothing personal though. Just the times we live in."

"Yes, I see," Elsa says. "Well, Mr. Lynch, I'm pleased to inform you that we've been authorized to release those funds immediately."

I become aware of a case sitting at her feet.

I turn, looking through the rear window, trying to get my bearings, not totally sure that this isn't some kind of dream sequence or nightmare. But when I turn back to Elsa, she's waiting patiently for some kind of response.

"You're telling me there's thirty-five grand in that case?"

Elsa smiles, but this time it lingers, and she holds my eye, giving the transaction a kind of charge.

"The payment's for *fifty*," she says. "The family wanted to take into account your living expenses as well as something to settle the original dispute."

I realize she's talking about the tattoo, and for some reason, my hand goes to my face.

"That's a lot of money," I say.

"It sounds like you've earned it."

When I look at her, I wonder if that's true.

I squint for a second, then turn to Mike.

"What the fuck happened back there?"

Mike's still staring out the window, and I realize that his hands are trembling. He closes his eyes.

"An incendiary device was detonated at 9:26 p.m. on King Street, resulting in the deaths of all four passengers of a Mercedes S-class." Mike swallows. "Most likely attached to the underside of the carriage. Most likely detonated by remote control. We're hearing there was some commotion in the street earlier today. Road crew asked the doorman if he could move the vehicle for a few hours while they worked. City's got no record of sending anyone…"

He trails off, then lets out a breath.

"So what do you think—"

"It had no connection whatsoever to you or your now-concluded work for the Pierce family."

It sounds less like a statement of fact than an order.

"And more importantly," Elsa says lightly, leaning forward to emphasize the point. "It had no connection to the Pierce family whatsoever."

"Is the fire even out yet?" I ask, looking at her.

"Well, that's what we're trying to do here."

"OK," I say after a moment. "Sound." I turn back to Mike. "The underground," I say. "What the fuck just happened on the underground?"

"What are you talking about?"

I just stare at him.

"Where the fuck did you appear from?"

He snorts. "We followed you to St. James's," he says. "We were with you when the bomb went off."

For a moment, there's just the hum of the engine. They'd seen me losing my shit with Sebastien.

"OK," I say, shaking my head. "And then what?"

Mike frowns. "Well, Christ, Lynch, you were there."

"I'm saying, you didn't pick me up on the square."

"We lost sight of you in the immediate aftermath," Mike says. "We picked you up again on your way out."

"And?"

"And we traced you to the underground," he says slowly. "You might remember the armed response units."

"You're saying you didn't follow me down?"

"I'm saying I lost you but knew the station was being evacuated anyway, so I hung around." His eyes dart to Elsa. "At considerable personal risk, I might add."

"Personal risk?" I say.

"I wasn't expecting roses, but…"

All I can see's that figure standing at the end of the platform, watching the two guys close in on me, trying to push me onto the tracks.

"You were gonna let them do it," I say.

"Lynch, look, I think you're in shock—"

"I'm not shocked at all," I say, turning to face forward. I catch a questioning look from Elsa to Mike, but he shakes his head like I'm crazy. If he had followed me down there, if he had seen something, then clearly he'd kept it to himself.

"So," I say, "you're telling me I did one job for the family a few days ago, and now it's finished."

"That's correct," Elsa says, glad to be back on track.

"All parties held up their end of the bargain," I say.

"Precisely."

"No one tried to kill Miranda, Ronnie didn't get his brains bashed in, and a car bomb didn't go off. No one died."

Elsa smiles.

"You're allowing yourself to be cynical," she says.

"Really?"

"You're not thinking about the protection that the family can afford you. That we can."

"What protection's that?"

Elsa shrugs. "Well, you were witnessed leaving the scene of a serious accident on Saturday night at Battersea Power Station."

"Was I?" I say.

"And you were seen in a taxi outside the family home last night, shortly before Miranda's fall."

I open my mouth, but nothing comes.

"And that's not to mention—"

"No, go back. I was in a taxi outside Tregunter."

Elsa's eyes move coolly to Mike, and he takes a small pocket-book from his jacket, finding the right page.

"License plate, Lima-Sierra—"

"The time," I say.

"You pulled onto Tregunter at almost exactly nine thirty," he says. I just sit there. "Ronnie found her at gone ten."

"You're telling me Miranda fell after I was there?"

Mike nods. That's not how I'd understood it.

"Right," I say, hearing how shredded my voice sounds. "But I left straight away."

"Your cab turned off the road," he says. "But that's where we lost you."

"Crazy how that keeps happening."

Elsa goes on. "And of course, the CCTV footage from neighboring houses on Tregunter Road in the immediate aftermath of Mr. Pierce's tragic demise could make for interesting viewing too."

I snort out a laugh.

"Then there's this business in Paris."

I look up, and Elsa smiles, acknowledging the flash of pain on my face with interest.

"We found you on camera at a café on, oh, I hope I'm pronouncing it right, *Rue Bobillot.*"

I don't say anything, and she watches me, savoring it for some reason.

"Seemed intense."

I close my eyes. I'd met Clare in a café there last week. It feels like a lifetime ago now. We should have been watching our target, but I'd looked up and seen that she was lost in thought. Again. Clare wasn't happy. I knew that. She wanted to be doing something better with her life, and it was clearly the end of our hot streak. I'd overreached in Barcelona; we left Spain with nothing. I'd been lucky to get away with cuts and bruises, and Clare looked at me differently after. Like she was waiting for me to admit how bad things had got. To snap out of it and be myself again. We got to

Paris with a feeling of desperation hanging over us, like something was at stake. The train wreck of a job I got us into there was the final nail. Sitting across the table from Clare, I could see that she wanted to be somewhere else. When our man paid his bill and started to leave, I was glad to follow him. I'd only be a few minutes. I could try and think of something to say.

By the time I got back, she was gone.

Mike shares a look with Elsa. "Cold of her to do it in public so you couldn't make a scene."

I turn and look at him.

"Still," he says, holding my eye. "Might have taken a few days, but you got there in the end."

I don't say anything.

"So she dumps you in this café, and you stalk off alone to this apartment block under yet another name. Then, just after midnight on the eighth of September, she comes to see you." He catches the look on my face and smiles. "Old girl on fourth saw three different people walk in."

The car's moving, but I try the door anyway. It's locked, and Mike snorts.

"First, she saw the tired man, who'd been living there for a few days," he goes on. "Then the nice girl, who arrived in the early hours of the morning. And then the big angry man, who got there an hour or so later. So come on," Mike says. "Whose blood was it on the walls? The guy or the girl?"

A moment passes, and I turn to Elsa.

"You're right," I say. "I'm being cynical."

"I'm so glad you see it that way. Your suite at the Mandarin has been reinstated until the end of the month. We can drop you there right now with the case."

"Sounds almost too good to be true."

"Of course, we'll need your signature for the nondisclosure agreement."

"Of course," I say. "Two questions though. I know we're pretending that none of this happened, but who just killed those people?"

Elsa eyes me for a few seconds, then leans in again.

"Mr. Keeler was a complex man," she says. "He came from a military-intelligence background, and he wasn't shy about deploying his specialist knowledge in the business sector." She shrugs. "He gathered sensitive information on some very powerful people. For some very powerful people. He made a lot of enemies."

There's an almost luxurious warmth to Elsa's voice as she says this, and I realize it's because of how hard a job the authorities have got, working out who killed Sebastien. There's no end of ways to spin, bury, or deflect if need be.

"What's important to remember," she goes on, "is that his death had absolutely no link to you—"

"Or any member of the Pierce family," I say. "Right. Well, that was actually my second question. From what I can tell, two-fifths of the Pierce family's dead, and Miranda's fighting for her life."

Elsa inclines her head ever so slightly.

"Right, so what family are we talking about here?" Elsa just stares at me. "Like, who sent you here with a case full of cash fifteen minutes after a bomb went off?"

"Mr. Lynch, our meeting in these circumstances is entirely coincidental. I was already on my way to—"

"Fine. Who are you working for?"

"Ms. Reagan Pierce, acting on behalf of—"

"I want to talk to her," I say.

"I'm afraid that won't—"

"OK, then you can let me out."

"As I said, we won't be able to release—"

"Were you standing too close to the blast, Elsa? I just told you I'm not signing shit until I've spoken to Reagan. You've just explained to me that our business here's done, so let me out of the fucking car."

Elsa sits back, her expression shifting subtly.

She touches the intercom button on her handrest.

"Chelsea and Westminster," she says neutrally.

39.

At the Chelsea and Westminster, Mike takes us to the lift, and we ride up to the Chelsea Wing in silence. We'd arrived twenty minutes earlier but waited in the car until Mike received some kind of communication to his Bluetooth earpiece from someone inside. He'd listened for a moment, then nodded at Elsa.

The cops had just left the building.

As we approach the ward entrance, I see a man on the door. The Rayner goon from back at the Mandarin, with the flat nose and cauliflower ears. Mike goes over to him, and they speak quietly for a moment, both staring disinterestedly at me. Then the guy uses a key card to unlock the door, giving Mike directions.

"You should pay him more," I say as Mike leads us through the corridors. "You've got him working two jobs."

Mike gives absolutely no response.

When we arrive at a small private room at the end of a short corridor, I see Reagan, waiting, through the wire-mesh window. She's sitting with her hands clasped in her lap, bound tight with tension by the mother of all bad days. Or make that the mother and the father. When we'd first met, she'd been a struggling actor, straining to leave some kind of mark on the stage. Now, with her brother's body still unaccounted for, her dad dead, and Miranda fighting for her life, she'd been shoved under a crueler kind of spotlight.

She couldn't even go home.

Reagan looks drawn and tired when we walk in, running on empty, stripped of everything nonessential, but in a way that seems to reveal something of her inner core. A baseline of strength that brings Miranda to mind. She doesn't say anything when we walk in, and it's clear that she's waiting for Mike to leave.

"I'll be right outside," he tells her.

"The end of the hall," Reagan says, not looking back at him.

I sit opposite her. Mike walks out and closes the door. We listen to his footsteps moving farther away.

"How can I help you, Mr. Lynch?" she asks flatly, staring into nowhere. From her red eyes and raw, wounded face, it looks like she's cried a lifetime of tears since we last spoke.

"Are you OK?" I ask. Reagan frowns. "Stupid question," I say. "But here's another. How's Miranda?"

Reagan unexpectedly lightens for a moment. Her eyes find mine, and at length, she finds the words.

"I'm pleased to report that my mother regained consciousness this afternoon. Just for a few hours, and she's still confused, not out of the woods yet, but…"

"That's great," I say. "And what about you?"

"What about me?" she says.

I can't tell if Reagan's selflessness comes from something inside her or if it's just an act. My sense is that the right combination of words could unlock it, but as she evades yet another personal question, I have to accept I don't know the combination, and anyway, I'm out of time.

"Look, I didn't come here to be another problem. But these people want me to sign something that—"

"It's a nondisclosure agreement," she says. "Perfectly standard."

"Right," I say. "But they're trying to shut everything down." She gives me a look of exasperation. "I thought you might want to know what I've learned first."

"What you've learned?"

"About Heydon, about Ronnie, about—"

"Mr. Lynch," she says, rubbing her eyes. "My brother was a troubled young man. He took his own life five years ago. My father, it seems, was the victim of an armed robbery gone wrong. There were some valuable, one-of-a-kind items in his collection. The authorities suspect that they were stolen to order."

"And what?" I say. "They think that Ronnie disturbed the intruders from three floors down?"

When Reagan doesn't look at me, it becomes clear she'll only discuss the agreed-upon version of events. The world's changing for her too, and she's not prepared to fight against the narrative that's solidifying around us. It doesn't look like she's got the strength.

"Most likely, my father was marched down there," she says uncomfortably. "I suppose he resisted."

"You suppose?" I say. "Where's the CCTV?"

"The system was deactivated," she says.

"Deactivated?"

I hadn't thought much of Elsa's threat that I could swing for Ronnie's murder, because I'd felt sure it was impossible to get in or out of Tregunter Road without being seen. But if the only footage is of me, staggering through the neighbor's yard with blood on my hands, then I'm in bad shape. So it's the worst possible time to push, but I know it's now or never.

"You don't find that strange?" I ask after a moment.

"I don't like it any more than you," she says tersely. "But that doesn't change the fact."

"And you don't think that Sebastien—"

"Sebastien Keeler?" she says, looking at me. Her jaw hardens. "I have to say, Mr. Lynch, I think you're obsessed."

There's a knock at the door.

"For Christ's sake," I say, turning and seeing Mike through the window, standing there with a doctor.

"Excuse me for a moment," Reagan says.

She gets up stiffly, through sheer force of will, then steps outside, speaking quietly.

She opens the door.

"I'll be just a minute, Mr. Lynch."

I wait a few seconds, then open the door, seeing Reagan and Mike at the end of the hall. I walk slowly after them, around the next corner, realizing I'm retracing my footsteps from earlier, back to Miranda's room.

The door's open, and when Reagan goes in, still talking to the doctor, Mike waits outside, looking on into the room. When I reach his shoulder, I see that Miranda's conscious but confused, stripped of some grace by the hospital gown. There's still something definitive about her. She's the very first and last of her kind. She looks over, seeing me, causing Mike to turn.

"Get out of here," he says, grabbing my arm.

"Heydon?" Miranda says.

Everyone stops.

Mike closes his eyes and loosens his grip. Reagan scowls from inside the room. But Miranda's watching me with what looks like burgeoning hope. I don't want to lie to her, and I don't want to disappoint her with the truth. So in the end, I just smile awkwardly, and for a second, it looks like the light catches her eye. Then the moment passes, and she blinks it away.

"If you'll excuse me," Reagan says, walking out, shutting the door behind her, taking me by the arm and leading me down the corridor, letting me know in no uncertain terms that I've outstayed my welcome. "Mr. Lynch," she says quickly. "I apologize for not making the time to speak with you personally, but as you can see, there's rather a lot happening here. You said you didn't want to be another problem."

She leads us to the ward entrance, where I see Elsa arriving, carrying the black case. I look to Reagan, then to Mike, standing down the hall with a hand to his earpiece, talking to the guy on the other side of the door. And I'm trying to do the math on how many people have died. How many questions they need to go unanswered to keep the family name out of print. First, there was Heydon, chasing his hopeless dream. Then Control, who'd made it come true. There was Ronnie, who'd assured me that everything was for sale, right before someone lowballed him for his collection. And then there was Sebastien, the all-seeing eye who'd been taken completely by surprise. For a man who'd always clung to the shadows, he'd gone out like Bonfire Night, taking Miss Brandt and his security detail down with him.

When Control died right in front of me, I'd decided it had to be part of a cover-up. But Ronnie's murder seems like something more personal. And Sebastien's flameout scans as an act of revenge, if not outright war. When you step back and look at the bigger picture, the killings feel like a statement. I just don't know who's making it or why.

And finally, it's all too much.

"Just tell me where to sign," I say wearily.

———

We return to the private room to go through the forms. Reagan sits in the corner, her arms wrapped round herself, while Elsa outlines what they consider to be "confidential material." It's more or less my every waking move from the day I first met Bobbie until now.

The substance of the document covers Bobbie tattooing my face, Miranda asking me to impersonate Heydon, my meeting with Badwan, and the contents of Heydon's flight case. There's stern language about any situation arising from these events too, and although she doesn't come right out and say it, Elsa's implication is that this language covers any illegal activity I might have undertaken on the family's behalf as well as my run-ins with Sebastien and Control.

There's a long spiel about penalties, the legal action I'll face in breach of contract, the charges, but I check out, since I don't even have an address where they can send the letters. From the way Rayner had arrived on the scene of Sebastien's murder, the way I'd been spirited out, no questions asked—and from the way they're throwing free money in my face, keeping the cops at arm's length, pressuring me into signing an NDA without legal representation—I know that this is all about damage control. Crisis management. When Elsa reaches the end of the document, she sits back, smiling, but I can hear her foot tapping under the table, hurrying me along.

"Do you think I could have a minute?" I ask.

"Take all the time that you need," she says. "I have some calls to make." She flashes a smile, checking it's OK with Reagan, who nods. When Elsa leaves, it's just the two of us.

I catch Reagan looking at me, still holding herself tight, just wanting me gone. I take up the forms, then sign and date in the six places Elsa had indicated. Once I'm done, I push the papers to the center of the desk, seeing Reagan visibly relax.

"You said that note was about Miranda."

When she looks at me, it's like there's a part of her I've never seen before, staring out from inside her head.

"You must have knocked on my door just before nine," I say slowly. "I followed you and Sebastien back to Tregunter Road."

She starts to say something, but I go on.

"We got there at 9:30," I say. "Ronnie found Miranda at ten." Reagan's eyes meet mine. "So what was that note really about?"

She stares at me for a moment, hyperalert.

"He didn't want me seeing you," she says.

"Sebastien?" I ask.

"He said you were dangerous."

I've got to laugh at that.

"And your relationship was…"

"Strictly professional," she says. It's not exactly what I'd been asking, and my nonreaction encourages her to go on. "Miranda always point-blank refused to vouch for me with filmmakers in town. She refused to open a single door. Sebastien was like a skeleton key."

"So the note?" I ask.

Reagan eyes me for a moment, then reaches inside her jacket pocket, removing the folded slip of paper. She gets up and hands it to me carefully, like a keepsake, then walks to the door, standing with her back to it, watching closely, a kind of defiance visible in the hard set of her jaw. She's not riding some kind of thrill or getting off on it. Just showing me who she really is. Daring me, of all people, to find fault. When I unfold the note and open it, it says:

DOWNSTAIRS. NOW.

I frown for a few seconds, then stand.

"I didn't tell him I was coming to see you," she says. "To tell you the truth, I didn't know it myself."

"Well, what's wrong with that?" I ask.

"Sebastien didn't like me talking to other men."

"Sounds professional."

"It *was.*"

"Why did you come and see me, Reagan?"

"It's strange," she says. "But as loud as he could be—as twisted sometimes—I always knew the way around my father." She looks at me. "Men are simple."

"But things were tougher with Miranda?"

"Things were impossible with Miranda."

"She's always seemed OK to me."

"She's always seemed OK to you because you're a symptom of her sickness," Reagan says. "Do you have any idea how long my life's been on pause, waiting for this fixation with my brother to burn itself out? Do you have any idea how many stupid men with tattoos on their faces I've had to talk to? How many cheap men have tried to sell my brother's belongings back to me? Do you have any idea how many psychics and shut-eyes and empaths I have to deal with on a day-to-day basis?"

When she breaks off, she looks lighter for having said it. Like the walls have come crashing down, and some terrible pressure's been released.

"I didn't realize things were so bad."

"Neither did I at first," she says, still getting her breath back. "Sebastien was helping me to see things more clearly. These last months, he's set me free."

The idea of Sebastien setting anyone free almost makes me choke. "Reagan, an hour after you got that note, Ronnie found Miranda at the bottom of the stairs."

Reagan turns to the door, where we can hear Elsa outside, walking up and down, talking on the phone. When she turns back to me, there's a look of self-possession I've never seen in her before.

"Did Sebastien ask you to do something?"

"Sebastien never asked me to do anything I didn't want to do myself," she says. "Truly. He simply asked me to try and reason with Miranda."

"That's what you went there to do?"

"I tried to tell her that Heydon was gone," Reagan says with no shortage of feeling. "I wanted her to see that this obsession was keeping us all frozen in the past, unable to move forward."

She's not exactly wrong, but it comes out like spin, sounding like something Sebastien might say.

"After you and I spoke, I went there as a blank," she says.

It's the same way I'd described myself, and I can't tell if she's taking the piss or being sincere.

"I just let the situation come. Tuned myself into it and decided who I wanted to be. Of course, Miranda became upset."

"Upset?"

"We were in her rooms, talking, when she stormed out for some fresh air. I heard a crash and followed her. She was lying on the stairs."

When Reagan's tearful eyes meet mine, it feels too perfect. But that doesn't necessarily mean she's lying.

"So…" I start, "you didn't…"

"My mother *fell*," she says firmly.

For a minute, there's just the sound of Elsa, talking at the end of the corridor. We stand there like strangers.

"So what's next?" I ask finally. Reagan looks up. "As far as I can see, Miranda's still casting that shadow."

"Oh," she says. "But now I feel like it's the best of both worlds. Now, she's the one who needs me."

I smile. "Your dad covered. He told me he found Miranda sick, not in a heap at the bottom of the stairs."

She looks genuinely moved.

"Yes," she says. "I think he suspected."

"Is that why he had to go?"

Reagan draws back. "I loved my father," she says, almost like she can't imagine why I'd accuse her. "I can assure you that aside from the fight with Miranda, aside from lobbying to remove you from the investigation, I've had nothing to do with the rest." She waves a tired hand. "After today, I told them to shut the whole thing down. I don't even want to know."

"And you don't think there's a chance that Sebastien was using you?" Reagan frowns. "Look," I go on quickly. "I think there's more to his relationship with—"

"You know," she says, interrupting me, "you couldn't be any more different from him." She looks at me for another moment, then her face hardens. "Sebastien never had to pretend to be someone he's not."

I don't say anything, and Reagan steps back, smoothing down her skirt. She goes to the door and knocks in signal to Elsa, who opens it and sticks her head in, smiling, still holding the phone to her ear.

"We're finished," Reagan says.

Elsa ends her call and checks the paperwork. Then she smiles and hands me the case.

Reagan's watching closely as I walk to the door. Then she makes an instinctive decision, crossing the room, holding her hand out.

"Thank you," she says. "For everything."

I look at her for a second, then turn to leave.

"That's right," she says quickly. "I think that's best. You never belonged here, Mr. Lynch."

I get the door open and look back, frowning.

"Reagan, who the fuck would want to?"

I take the case and walk out, retracing my footsteps back to the ward entrance, hitting the green button to exit. The Rayner goon from the Mandarin's still standing on the door, but I don't look back. I just press for the lift and go.

The doors slide shut, and I lean into the wall until they open again on ground. When they do, I see Mike, looking only too pleased to escort me to the door and finally out of his life forever.

"So when she met you in that café in Paris…" he says casually picking up the thread of my breakup with Clare.

I sigh. "I'll answer one of yours if you'll answer one of mine." Mike considers this for a moment, then nods. "Clare was my partner," I say. "She wanted out of the life." I shrug. "I told her I couldn't do anything else."

"So the room…"

"Yeah, there was something she wanted to tell me. I guess the big, angry man was following her."

"And he was…"

Vogel, the crooked art thief who Clare and I had been planning a job with for a few weeks. He hadn't believed us when we told him we were separating, that we were out, that it was off. When he'd followed Clare to the room I was using, he'd thought we were cutting him out of the deal. He'd flashed a knife and threatened Clare. He'd overreacted. I'd just overreacted more.

Then he was staggering out with a knife wound, and there was nothing left to say. Vogel was a disaster from the start, a job taken out of desperation. But watching him exit the building, stumble to his car, and go, I didn't feel like I'd fixed anything. If he went straight to a hospital, he'd be OK, in a sense. The way that Vogel ate and drank, he'd be dead in six months anyway, and good riddance. I'd said as much to Clare, trying to keep the tremble out of my voice, still staring out the window, not wanting to face her. She didn't answer, and when I finally turned, I couldn't stand the way that she was looking at me. The way she seemed to be really seeing me for the first time. Forcing me to see myself. I walked her to the door and opened it.

The last thing she said to me was, "*Wait—*"

"That's three questions," I say, remembering Mike.

We're at the main entrance now.

There's a heavily pregnant woman walking in. A group of burned-out nurses, drinking coffee on their break. A digital display overhead, flashing the names of rooms and personnel.

Dr. Garek, Neonatal.

I sigh and follow Mike out.

"Your turn," I say as we walk. "Was it you on that platform or not?"

Mike glances at me with a frown, then snorts and shakes his head. "You should check yourself into one of these places, Lynch."

I nod and start to walk.

He calls after me. "What did she want to tell you?"

I turn and look at him for a moment.

"She's pregnant," I say, hearing the strain in my voice. "I'm going to be a dad. I mean, technically."

It's the first time I've said it out loud.

"Huh," Mike says at length. "Well, at least you won't be in their lives. Or mine. See ya never, Lynch."

40.

I walk out of the Chelsea and Westminster, get across the road, and look back. When I do, I see the Rayner goon from the Mandarin taking up position on the front door. The building feels like an impenetrable wall of money that I'm finally permanently outside of. I consider flagging down one of the passing black cabs, but right now, I just can't face it. The creak of the pleather, the locking doors, my faint reflection in the glass. I wouldn't even know where to go. So I stare at the hospital a few seconds more, then pick a direction and walk.

I look at the Patek to check the time, but somehow, it catches the light wrong. I find myself looking away. The watch feels heavy, like it's weighing me down, like I'm cuffed to Sebastien, dragging him around with me, and I pull it off like a shackle.

I hand the Patek to the first bag lady I see, telling her she should keep it safe and sell it, that it's probably worth a house in any city but London. Then I stop into a corner shop, grabbing a bottle of water, a bag of peanuts, and a king-size Twix. Some days you just feel like you've earned it. When I point at the large bottle of vodka behind the counter, the kid takes in my disheveled appearance and kindly pretends I'm pointing at the half size. With the lack of food and sleep and with the destroyed suit and the dying phone, it almost feels like I'm back to normal. All except for the tattoo. The cuts and bruises.

All except for the briefcase full of cash.

Elsa told me I'd earned it, and by the terms of my original agreement, that's true. Miranda had asked me to impersonate her son and return his case to her. But once we'd opened it, there'd been no going back, and my search for Heydon had become all-consuming. The same thing as this break I was trying for in life, my last chance to prove that Clare wasn't wrong about me, that I could change.

And not just another personality from the fancy dress box, as Reagan had said. I'd wanted to try and do things differently, for better reasons. I just hadn't known how. Somehow, I'd thought if I found Heydon or worked out what happened to him, I might catch a glimpse of myself, slipping around one of those corners.

The man Clare thought I could be.

But I'd found a house of games instead. Somewhere it didn't really matter what you said or did, because tomorrow you'd just remember it differently, to suit whichever new reality was starting to emerge by then.

I'd found a cynical plot to exploit someone's lowest moments. Then the cover-up of a cover-up, with so many lives taken, so many versions of the same events, so many bad angles to see myself from, that it feels like I've been walking through a hall of mirrors.

In the end, I'm just glad to be out of it.

Back at the Chelsea and Westminster, I'd briefly considered turning it up to ten. Throwing the money back in their faces and making a scene. Asking Elsa if she was the same person I'd heard Sebastien talking to the last time I'd visited his office. That was what he'd called her, the woman on the phone. She'd had the same high-class accent, and they'd sounded close. But what was the point in hitting her with it? She wouldn't tell me the truth. She didn't have it in her. All I'd ever find out from Elsa was how she was going to lie to me about it.

So I'd taken the money and agreed to keep my mouth shut, like everyone else. All those differing versions of events had finally been boiled down to one. Heydon was gone. Ronnie too. Miranda was out of it. And Reagan was something else entirely. Control had died badly, at the end of his rope. And Sebastien had checked out from on top of the world, taking Miss Brandt with him as well as his security team.

That just leaves Bobbie. And I'm still not sure what her game was. I think back to the first time we met. The "chance" encounter, the black eye, the sob story. The cigarettes, the withheld number. The opening notes of "Bad Guy." I think back to the black SUV in the multistory car park. The man who'd been sitting inside, watching me. And then, for some reason, I find myself lingering on Bobbie's hotel room at Heathrow. If that was what it had really been. I think of the weird reaction when I'd told the woman at the front desk that my friend had checked out.

I see myself switching off the TV.

Goodbye, Doc. Renee Yiph.

She'd never turned up. Heydon had mentioned a Dr. Carr, who seemed to have either moved out of the area or retired, and a Dr. Matten, whom I'd tracked down.

But no Doc. Renee Yiph…

I stop dead in the street, half turning, looking back in the vague direction of the hospital. I squint, trying to work out what had caught my eye on the way out.

That digital announcement screen.

Dr. Garek, Neonatal.

The written prefix for doctor isn't "Doc," it's "Dr."

Oh, please don't let me be this stupid. I fumble my phone out of my pocket, watching the battery drop to 3 percent. I go to my message thread with Bobbie and hit call.

"Hello," she says quietly.

"Bobbie, where are you?"

"I don't want to talk with you," she says. "It's done."

An automated, robotic-sounding voice from somewhere in the background says, "*Ground Floor.*"

"Bobbie—" I start, but my phone dies, disconnecting us. I try to think about where I've heard that robotic voice before, then I turn to the street, looking for a taxi, still kicking myself for not seeing it sooner. Heydon's favorite film was *Irma Vep*. Irma Vep was an anagram of vampire. I'm about to step off the curb to cross for a cab when a big black SUV pulls up in front of me. I'm backing off from it when the window comes down.

"Listen, guys. It's been fun, but I'd rather stick—"

Then I see the gun pointing at me from inside.

I stare into the black hole at the end of it for what feels like a long time, probably just a second or two. And it hits me that I should have called Clare when I still had the chance. I should have swallowed my pride and made sure she was OK.

"*Get in,*" says a young, well-off-sounding guy.

. "Look," I say wearily. "Whatever this is, you're too late. I'm out of it. I'm past the point of caring—"

"Get into the fucking car," the man hisses. "*Now.*"

I stare into the black hole for another second.

"Well, when you put it like that."

41.

When I climb into the SUV, I recognize the two guys sitting on the back seat opposite me. They're identical twins. Both stupidly tall, with weird, lean faces, the look of unethically bred dogs. Like the same six families just kept fucking until they broke the six-foot-five barrier. I'd seen them in the article I'd read on Matthew Hartson. His two boys, the blood donors. Maximilian and Alexander.

They're wearing expensive fitted suits and awkward smiles, and although they're twins, I can tell that they're different. The one on the passenger side, who'd waved the gun out the window, seems like he's got a bit more about him. He's got the nerve to look right at me. His brother's just as excited, but he can't quite meet my eye. He giggles when I first get in, but when I hit him with an unimpressed glare, he can't take it and glances away.

The driver starts up and pulls into traffic.

"Apologies for the hour," says the one on the driver's side. "My brother and I just needed a word."

"Yeah, I can see why you'd need the hardware."

Driver's Side gives me an amused look.

"You've got bodies on you like a bad smell," he says, letting his mouth hang open while he talks, relishing it. He runs a hand across the gleaming silver .45 on his lap. "So I'll just hold on to this if it's all the same to you."

"Can I ask you a question?"

Driver's Side just watches me.

"Do you ever walk up and down with it in front of the mirror?" His smile hardens, and I lean in, speaking confidentially, keeping it between the two of us. "Have you given it a name?"

Passenger Side glances away, not liking to see his brother being challenged.

Driver's Side raises the gun, pointing it directly at my head. "His name's Shut the Fuck Up," he says. But his voice is shaking just as much as his hand. "Would you like me to spell that out for you?"

I stare at him for a few seconds. "Yeah," I say, leaning back. "I think I would." I hold up a finger. "Now, the first letter's an S, but after that, I'm not helping you."

The nervous energy in the car feels palpable, and the fearful look I get from the brother says it all. Driver's Side's a nut, no one talks to him like this, and he's got a hair-trigger temper.

And I'm so tired, so lied to, so far past the last possible exit, that all I can think's *sound*. I close my eyes and try to get comfy. There's not much point in talking to them. They're errand boys.

I hear a snort, then feel the barrel of the gun grazing my head.

"Do you know what?" Driver's Side says. "On second thoughts, maybe I'll just give us all a bit of peace?"

A few seconds pass.

"Yeah," I say, keeping my eyes closed. "Except if you'd ever actually fired that thing, you'd know how loud a forty-five is.

You're talking between one sixty and one ninety decibels in an enclosed space."

"Like I could give two fu—"

"A jet taking off's one fifty," I say. "Pull that trigger, and you're both deaf. You're both blind and ugly from all the bone splinters flying out of my skull. Or just dead from the bullet fragments."

No one says anything.

"I'm sitting with my back to the fucking driver."

I feel the car start to decelerate.

Then I hear Driver's Side's brother whispering urgently. The gun stops grazing my head, but I can feel the look he's giving me through my eyelids.

"Give me a nudge when we get there."

42.

I don't know where we are when we get out except that it's a great big redbrick house somewhere in central London, with a security gate, a driveway, and *land*. It's dark, so I can't see how far it goes. I can't even imagine what it must cost per square foot. It seems quiet, with no cars or voices. The twins jostle me up the steps, through the pillared entranceway and in.

I've seen places like it but never actually been in one. It's like the entire house has been hollowed out, with one enormous, multilevel living space taking up almost everything. There are some doors leading out, and I can see an upper level, private rooms. But mainly it's a wide-open space, with the original brickwork exposed. The interior's just expensive furniture that looks like it's never been sat on.

When I see the man sitting at his desk, in pride of place, I recognize him. Matthew Hartson. As I live and breathe. He's wearing a white linen suit with an open shirt. There's a health smoothie on the desk in front of him, a frank, understanding look on his face.

Then I see the man in black with his back against one of the vast, empty brick walls. He's got black hair with streaks of gray in it. Scarred cheeks.

Like the man Dr. Matten had described, Mr. Peck.

He uncouples himself from the wall like he's part of it, and as he gets closer, I start to sense the power in that compact, muscular frame. He nods at me to hold out my arms, which I do, then he searches me roughly, finding the steak knife in my waistband, the shank in my sock.

"Do you want to try that again?" I say, getting my breath back. "I'm not sure you found it all."

Peck snorts, but not at the joke. He's just openly laughing at me. He backs off a few feet, pocketing my sharps, not breaking eye contact. He's coming from a military background, like Sebastien. He's got the build, posture, and haircut. But from the cool Delta Force duds he's wearing—the black Air Force Ones, the bomber jacket, the ski shades on a chain—it looks like Peck's enjoying a much more lucrative second act as a private mercenary. That means he's probably bounced around the world a few times, protecting Hartson's business interests in "hot" countries. Gold and diamond mines in South Africa. Oilfields in the Middle East. Kidnap. Blackmail. Wet work. Whatever. A hired mercenary. Great.

When I turn back to the desk, I'm surrounded on all sides. Hartson sitting in front of me. The twin with the gun leaning into a pillar on the right. His shit for brains brother lounging on a sofa behind. And Peck five or six feet away on my left, clenching and unclenching a fist.

"You must be Lynch," Hartson says, getting up and coming around the desk. The work he's had done looked convincing from across the room. He's got shining metal hair, the same boyish face as his sons. But his body moves like an older man's, like he's wearing a person suit. Close-up, his skin's pinched back and tight. It reveals too much of the whites of his eyes, making him look permanently awestruck, like he's seeing something we can't.

When I glance at his boys, their pale, concave faces, I can't help but think about what Miranda had said. They look like drained blood bags.

Their dad reaches me and holds out a hand. "Matthew Hartson."

I just stand there, and at length, he retracts it.

"Quite," he says, looking darkly amused. "We've got a lot to talk about." Hartson walks back around his desk and sits down. "I thought we should all get together and settle this over a drink," he says. "Talk it out, us men."

He's waiting for me to say something.

"Well," I start, reaching for anything I can tell him except fuck you. "You've got a beautiful home."

"Oh," he says, looking about the room, surprised to hear it. "This old thing. We picked it up in lockdown so the boys could let off some steam, throw a bash or two without any neighbors around to complain about the noise."

"I see," I say after a moment.

"I just duck in from time to time when it seems prudent to keep certain conversations completely off the record." He takes up a bottle of Scotch from the desk. "I thought we might try and get acquainted with a few—"

"Look, whatever this is, man, just get it over with."

Hartson frowns like I'm fluffing my lines, and I see he's into this. The ceremony, the small talk, the dance.

"I'm too tired," I say, holding up my hands. "None of this is my problem. I don't care."

Hartson's expression shifts, slackening.

"Mr. Lynch, I'm disappointed. I'd been given to expect a man of certain character. A pathological liar, a con artist." He watches me closely, then licks his lips. "Perhaps even a killer."

"Well, take a good look," I say, finding the carton of Reds in my jacket pocket. When I open them, I see there's just one cigarette left. I tap it out, spark up without asking, and blow smoke. "But once I'm done with this, I might need to run out for some more."

I hear snickers from the twins.

Hartson glares at them.

"I think things might have gotten just a touch out of hand," he says. "As you may know, Miranda Pierce and I have some small history."

"Yeah," I say. "She called you a bloodsucker at some award show." I take a sharp drag and exhale. "Anyone in your position would have driven her son insane, then killed him."

Hartson watches me closely.

"You've met *my* son, Maximilian?" he says.

I turn to the brother with the gun, Maximilian, still looming. Since we've come inside, he's kept the .45 hidden. I'm guessing that when Hartson sent them out to try and find me, the gun wasn't part of the conversation. That means there's a chance that neither Hartson nor Peck know about it. And all of a sudden, I like Maximilian a lot more.

Hartson goes on, encouraged by my smile. "So he's ambitious," he says. "So he took on too much. So he overreached. Well, should we prosecute that as some kind of crime?"

But the smile's already hurting my face. "I think, when you drive someone to suicide, yeah."

"*Well*," Hartson chuckles. "Of course, that's not at all what happened here. In fact, that's why I suggested my sons forge a personal connection with you, Mr. Lynch." His eyes move darkly between the two boys. "One feels certain that any reasonable man would be sympathetic to Maximilian's story." I don't move, and Hartson watches me appraisingly. After a moment, he sits back, satisfied, like he knows the right stuff when he sees it. "Now again," he intones, "I hope it goes without saying that all our relationships here are built on trust."

He's watching to see I understand.

"Sure," I say.

"Well then, in fact, it's quite simple," he says. "When Miranda Pierce defamed me in the most shockingly violent terms imaginable, Maximilian and his brother, Alexander, were obliged to see their father, their family, disparaged in the press." He goes on carefully, "Perhaps hotheadedly, they chose to respond in kind."

Hartson looks to his son to continue the story.

Maximilian stares up at the ceiling, sounding like a kid being forced to say sorry.

"*Yeah*," he says. "After the bloodsucker stuff, Al and me thought it only fair we amplify some examples of Miranda Pierce's parental missteps." He nods at Hartson. "Say what you like about my old man, but at least we're still breathing."

"And how did you go about finding stuff like that?" I ask.

"By hiring the best man for the job."

"Sebastien Keeler?" I say. When I drop his name, it's like someone's turned up the gravity, and I feel the glare that Peck's giving me in the side of my head. I absorb it for a second, then turn to Maximilian, smiling. "Well, at least he got rid of the mustache."

I hear a boot step behind me.

"Ah-ah," Hartson says.

When I turn, I see that Peck's taken a big step in my direction.

He'd be right on top of me if not for Hartson. I'm dead anyway. They just need to hear what I've worked out, who I might have told. And it's starting to sink in that no one knows I'm here. If they did, they wouldn't come. And if they came, they couldn't help.

"OK, so Keeler was looking for dirt on Miranda," I say, sounding ragged.

"Right," Maximilian goes on. "And you could sense how much she had to hide, simply because of how hard it was to find."

"Sebastien struggled to come up with stuff?"

Maximilian sees things differently. "She'd just hidden it too well. So when Seb felt like he'd hit a wall, he decided to approach Mr. Rayner, a former employer of his, an old friend."

"Rayner was supposed to be working for Miranda."

Maximilian looks at me like I'm stupid.

"Well," Hartson puts in, sounding like a teacher bringing a slow student up to speed, "strictly speaking, the Rayner organization was working for *Mr.* Pierce. Though I'm certain at different times it's been useful to allow Miranda the *illusion* of control." He throws this in as if to spare my feelings about being wrong. "In actuality, I'm afraid that, just like you and I, Mr. Rayner works very much for himself."

Maximilian yawns into an armpit.

"*Oh*," he says. "Excuse me. If I recall correctly, Rayner did point out the conflict of interest," he says. "I mean, we knew that going in anyway. All we needed was an X on the map. The right place to start digging. So Rayner put Sebastien in touch with Ronnie."

"How'd that go?" I ask.

"Ronnie turned us down cold. Chewed Sebastien out for even asking."

I just stand there.

"Then the next day, Sebastien received an anonymous message, offering two itemized phone bills from Tregunter Road, from the day of Theo's death. We guessed that Ronnie wasn't tipping the maid."

"Offering them for…"

"A steal at thirty thousand."

Bobbie was telling the truth.

About that part at least.

I look around the room. "So…"

"So it's all about this mystery work call Miranda claims to have been on while Theo drowned. Her whole alibi for why she wasn't there." Maximilian lowers his voice like he's blowing my mind. "There *were* no calls in or out that day."

"And Sebastien found rumors of Miranda's affair with her costar, Christopher Jacobs," I say.

"Right," Maximilian says, sounding impressed. "They spent a lot of time in her trailer, if you know what I mean. Brewing up a batch of box office poison."

I shake my head. "But so what?"

"Well, when you're asked to believe that she was taking this call while her son drowned, and when you learn that no calls came to the house or her mobile before the accident, when you learn that no calls were made, and then you learn that she was having an affair…"

"You think she was upstairs with Jacobs?"

"Dream rebuttal," Maximilian says. "Here she is, criticizing my father's parenting, while she's on all fours—"

"I get it," I say, looking about the room. "But by the time she called your dad a bloodsucker, Theo had been dead, like, twenty years." Maximilian doesn't say anything. "Plus, it's not much of a rebuttal if it never actually happened."

"Oh, it happened," Maximilian says.

"Sebastien managed to prove it?"

He starts to say something, then stops and starts again. "Well," he says, "of course, it was tricky. Jacobs died in 1999, so he took it to the grave. And naturally, Miranda wouldn't talk to us. Sebastien took a crack at the girls, to no avail. They weren't even around when Theo died. But Heydon was actually there that day," he says. "His whole crazy world seemed to revolve around it."

"He sounded like a pretty mixed-up guy."

"The simplest nut to crack," Maximilian says.

His brother snorts from the sofa.

"Except from what I heard, it seemed like Sebastien was struggling to get stuff out of him," I say.

"You must be joking?" Maximilian barks. "Sebastien was thrilled with the results. If it was up to him, we'd still be in there, twisting the dials on Heydon."

I glance back at Peck. "Well, let's just hope Sebastien's looking down on us now from that torture chamber in the sky."

Peck doesn't move, and Maximilian goes on.

"He knew exactly where Heydon went online, where he went in real life, who he called, who he texted, what he said, and what he thought. He could drop any kind of hint he liked, tease it out from multiple different angles, make him dance like a meat puppet."

He's trying to give me a taste of my own medicine. To make me feel scared about what I'm up against. I match his greasy smile instead.

"That's actually what first caught my interest," I say. "It's why I wanted to meet you."

I look about the room, then at Hartson.

His shining, lineless face.

"To do what exactly?" Maximilian asks.

It takes me a second. "I wanted to understand."

He frowns like it's a foreign concept. We're having two completely different conversations. He's performing for an audience of one, scoring points with his old man. I'm just trying to work out what the fuck I'm doing here.

"So why the crazy hospital scene with Control at the end there?" I ask. "Making Heydon think that Theo was dying again."

It's so distant for him, he has to stop.

"I think Miranda got that lifetime achievement award in mid-December?" Alexander puts in helpfully.

Maximilian snaps his fingers.

"That's right. She did the bloodsucker routine again, and I'd just had enough." From the way his smile vanishes when he glances at his father, it's clearly still a sore point. Maximilian lowers his voice and goes on. "Sebastien's original pitch to us was that he'd get Heydon talking painlessly, without him even knowing. Super ethical. That's why the whole thing with the fake business. And it worked. Like juice from a lemon. But because Sebastien's methods were, like, super advanced, he was filming everything, documenting it. Heydon was sort of like his sizzle reel. Something he could show off to prospective clients, a taste of what he was capable of."

I clear my throat and make a choking sound.

"So the hospital..."

Maximilian glances at his brother.

"Well," Alexander starts, "we basically thought Seb might have started to get lost in it. The process was going deeper and deeper. Then, with Miranda mouthing off again, we sort of went into Seb and said, like, well..."

"What's the *supercharged* version of this?" Maximilian says.

"Right." Alexander nods. "Quite tense going in. But it was one of those conversations where you sort of walk away thinking, relationships are everything. Like, we went into Seb with this idea of a forty-eight-hour time limit for him to break Heydon. Then he pitched us the hospital thing, and we all went crazy for it. He put it together in, like, a day."

"Looked mega, to be fair," Maximilian puts in. "Like, you walked out of the lift, and suddenly you were on this private hospital ward. Heydon arrived with Control, and they took him away for treatment." He smiles. "But of course, Control was a sick man. He lost consciousness, and the team couldn't bring him around. Sebastien had been pumping Heydon full of all that Theo shit for months by this point. Had him believing he could bring things back from the dead." He shares a look with Alexander and snorts. "Seb was throwing stunned magpies at the windows when Heydon was home alone."

Maximilian's goading me into saying something bad about Sebastien. He wants to see Peck tear my head off.

A moment passes. "So I take it Heydon broke," I say. "He spilled all about Miranda's affair."

Maximilian blows out his cheeks and makes a face, accepting that things could have gone better.

He nods at his brother to go on.

"Well," Alexander says. "In the end, even though we got a lot of really great data, the results themselves were inconclusive." I don't say anything, and he looks to Maximilian. "Y'know, in terms of what we set out to do, I'd say we were, like, ninety-nine percent successful."

"Right," I say, trying to nod along.

"Like, Sebastien *did* get through to Heydon. He *did* get him talking about that day."

I take a deep breath.

"So what did he say?"

"Well, exactly," Alexander says. "There's that one percent. When Heydon finally did start to talk about that day, to be honest, it was a total letdown."

"*Theo, Theo, Theo,*" Maximilian says. "Like a broken fucking record. The guy was so wrapped up in his own shit, he didn't know *what* was going on with Miranda. Then, once they gave up on Heydon, when it was time for him to go, he saw that Control had left his bed. He realized he'd been played."

"And?" I ask. There's a sparkle in Maximilian's eye, but he doesn't go on.

"And Heydon tried to pick a fight with Sebastien."

I turn to see Peck, speaking for the first time. He's got the hoarse, half-powered whisper of a drill sergeant. Someone who's blown their voice out from barking too many orders or just from saying too many hard things. "Wouldn't take fuck off for an answer," he goes on. "Left in a bit of a state."

"And the next thing we know, his car's on that bridge," I say. When I look between them, I feel dizzy. Sick. I look down at the dead cigarette, still gripped between my fingers. I drop it with a sigh. "Well, mystery solved."

But Peck's still staring.

"Not until we know who you are."

I don't like the way he's looking at me.

"My brother and I think Peck's onto something," Maximilian says. "Like, I never believed that Heydon actually went into the water."

I squint between Maximilian, Alexander, and Peck. Their searching faces. If they're entertaining the idea that I might actually be Heydon, then it's worse than I thought.

"I'm no one," I say after a moment.

"Quite," says Hartson. "You certainly keep cropping up though. We were wondering if you could help us with what happened in Battersea on Saturday night."

There's no question mark; that's just what he wants me to say next. I look between them.

"You guys didn't kill Control?"

Nobody moves.

I'd already toyed with the idea that Control's murder wasn't a part of the cover-up. Whatever Reagan said about a break-in, Ronnie's murder looked more like pure rage. And I know for sure that no one in this room killed Sebastien. When I start to ask myself who did, I snag on that weird sensation of being watched I'd felt on the underground before I met Bobbie. Or caught in the headlights of that black SUV in the car park. And I'm trying to keep my face empty but thinking:

Irma Vep. *Vampire.*

Doc Renee Yiph. *Heydon Pierce.*

"That's ridiculous," I hear myself say.

But I'm thinking of Control's killer, staring right at me across a penthouse floor. I'm thinking of his hand around my throat at Tregunter Road.

His green eyes, glowing in the moonlight.

"What's ridiculous about a man faking his own death?" Maximilian asks. "He parks his car on that bridge, takes a cab to Heathrow, and *boom.*"

My ears start ringing painfully.

"So you think Heydon Pierce is back from the dead and picking you off, one by one."

I sound skeptical, but I can hear Reagan telling me how the

CCTV was deactivated on the night that Heydon went missing. How it had been deactivated during Ronnie's murder. I just can't picture Heydon killing Control in cold blood like that. Or bashing Ronnie's brains in. I can't see him tackling me like the man at Tregunter Road, throttling me, getting ready to bring a brick down on my head. Could someone change that much?

When I turn, I see that Peck's almost right behind me. My passport's in his hand.

"Issued nine months ago," he whispers, turning it over. "Just no personality to go with it. Used for the third time on the Eurostar from Paris to London. September eighth."

I don't say anything.

"Dark rumors out of Paris last week."

I look at him, taking in the Hartsons too. The fixed expressions on their faces. Seeing that my mask's been wrenched clean off, feeling like an exhibition. Then there's a winding-down sound, and the lights go out.

Hartson and the twins immediately start talking over each other, and I throw myself right, away from Peck, toward the sound of Maximilian's voice. We collide in the dark, and I try to crush a forearm across his neck, ripping the .45 from his jacket pocket with my dead hand, almost losing my grip and fumbling it. When Peck clicks the flashlight on his belt, I'm pressing the gun into Maximilian's neck.

"Ah-ah," I say.

Nobody moves.

"Hands," I say to Peck. He grins at me, and I flip off the safety, regripping the gun against Maximilian's skull. I feel exposed. The light from Peck's flashlight isn't much, and it's like anything could come out of the shadows.

Maximilian's hyperventilating, and Peck looks grudgingly to Hartson, who's got his mouth hanging open. Finally, Peck holds his hands out in front of his body.

"Turn and face the wall," I tell him.

He stares into nothing for a few seconds, then turns and faces the nearest pillar. The flashlight is on the front of his belt, and the room darkens.

"Where's the other one?" I say, looking for Alexander. He's still frozen to the sofa, a look of awful, dawning fear on his face. "*Hey*," I say, waking him up. I nod at Peck, who's still facing the pillar. "Unclip the gun from his waistband, and hold it by the butt, as far away from yourself as possible," I say. Slowly, looking between the others, Alexander gets to his feet. I press the gun hard against his brother's head. "Fuck one part of this, and you're an only child."

He almost looks back at his brother, who's still squirming in my arms, then he closes his eyes for a moment, goes to Peck, and unclips the gun. Everyone's holding their breath. He gets it free from the holster.

I look out at the enormous room.

"Throw it as far as you can," I say.

He looks between the others, then does.

"Now, get that flashlight and leave it on the desk. Then you and your dad sit on that sofa together. Nice and close."

Alexander takes the flashlight off Peck's belt and bangs it down hard on the desk, the light facing up. Then he goes back to his seat and crashes down. Hartson's jocular demeanor seems to have drained away too. When he stands to walk around his desk this time, he leans on it with one hand while he moves.

He eases himself into the sofa, not looking at me.

I shove Maximilian forward. "You on the other side."

Maximilian takes a few slow steps, thinking about going for the gun. I give him a hard kick up the arse, and he goes to the sofa, sitting on his dad's right side.

Then I become conscious of someone in the far corner of the room, breathing heavily through their mouth. I turn to where I think it's coming from. The Hartsons twist around on the sofa. At length, I hear slow, creaking boot steps coming toward us. When the shape emerges, I see a man in black. He's wearing a bomber jacket, combat trousers, and boots. As well as a black balaclava with holes cut for the eyes and mouth.

Control's killer.

Ronnie's killer.

And from the wires hanging out of his suicide vest, my guess is he cooked Sebastien too. When he stops, just short of the light, looking between us, I feel sure that this is all about revenge.

There's a bunch of wires running from the vest to a button he's holding down with his left thumb. The vest itself is covered with weighty plastic pouches and wires. The man walks toward me, drawing closer, until I see bloodshot green eyes staring out of his black mask. He holds out his free hand.

Still breathing through his mouth.

I look at the vest, the wires, the trigger. I hesitate for a second, then hand over the gun.

The man turns from me, walking toward Peck, who's still facing the pillar. He hears the boot steps coming toward him.

"Now, wait a—"

The man raises the gun and pulls the trigger. Peck's head explodes, then the wreckage of him's just lying there, leaking into the carpet. For a second, there's just the aftershock, the sound of us all breathing. The man in black, Hartson, Maximilian, Alexander, and me. Hartson and his sons are frozen to the sofa. Statues made from fear. The man turns the gun toward them.

And Maximilian's saying, "*No, no, no, no, no, no…*"

"*Listennn,*" Hartson says, trying to sound soothing. His face has turned red, and he's so gripped by fear that he can barely look up. His eyes dart to the carnage that used to be Peck, then back to the man in black, smiling to try and stop himself from being sick. "Money's no object anymore," he says, visibly shaking. "Young man like you—"

The man in black sweeps the gun across us.

He's eight feet away, easily covering me.

Hartson growls, forcing himself to speak. "If I may…" he starts, "listen, ah, Mr. Pierce." His eyes move between the man in black and me. "Whichever one of you that may be. We all accept that mistakes have been made. You can be outraged, or you can be rich beyond your wildest imaginings." Nobody moves, and Hartson goes on, feeling like he's got our attention. "I had no special affection for Mr. Peck. Not for Mr. Keeler either, when you get right down to it. Their abhorrent behavior went far beyond the ideas of natural justice that my sons were pursuing. I'm *glad* that you've balanced the books. Now—"

"*Balance,*" the man says. He's croaking hard, disguising his voice or just completely fried. Hartson winces, and I catch a desperate look between the twins. At length, the man nods. Then he starts sweeping the gun from side to side, between Maximilian and Alexander, like he's playing eeny, meeny, miny, moe. He stops on Hartson, sitting in between them. "*Pick.*"

"Excuse me?" Hartson says.

The man starts sweeping the gun between the two boys again. "*Pick.*"

"Erm…" Alexander says urgently, "like, no?"

Maximilian's staring down at his lap again, chanting. *"No, no, no, no, no, no, no, no, no, no…"*

Hartson's got both hands up.

His hair's standing on end.

Sweat patches leaking through the suit.

"One million," he says. "No questions asked."

"Pick."

"I…" Hartson swallows. "Now, come—"

"Five…"

"Five million?" Hartson asks.

But the man in black's counting down. *"Four…"*

"Have you got any idea the kind of shit that rains down if someone like me dies?" Maximilian's shouting. "Like, there's no way you'll get away with this!"

"Three…"

"Five!" Hartson roars over the room. "Five million pounds. Now, think of the good you'll do. Come on, man."

"Two…"

Hartson gasps, sounding like he's having a heart attack. "Wait," he says breathlessly. "Let's talk—"

"One," the man says, leveling the gun at Alexander.

"Alexander!" Hartson shouts, squeezing his eyes shut. "I want to keep Alexander."

And now everyone's got their eyes closed except me and the man in black. He pulls the trigger, and we all jump out of our skin again. Literally, in Alexander's case. The bullet turns his head inside out. Nought to horror in 0.5 seconds. Hartson's still got his eyes closed, but the blood spatter tells him everything about who's dead.

"I…" he starts. "I…"

Alexander's long body lies sprawled beside his father. The whole left side of his face is hanging off.

"You…" Maximilian starts, turning to his father. "You fucking chose *him*." His throat sounds like a drain, filled with tears and phlegm. "And *you*," he hisses at the man. "*You…*" He stares into those green eyes and trails off as he realizes the same thing I have. Alexander's just getting a head start on the rest of us. I take a dumb step forward as the gun sweeps to Maximilian.

"Oh, God, please—" he starts.

I take another half step.

The man pulls the trigger, hitting Maximilian in the neck. There's enough time for him to shout out in pain, to panic and try to press a hand to the blood spraying from his neck, but it's over in seconds. He slumps forward off the sofa and falls face-first to the ground. There's six feet between us, but I can't make myself take another step.

"Wait…" Hartson says, getting up from the sofa, falling down, crawling backward, away from Alexander and Maximilian, until he reaches Peck and recoils from the blood.

The man walks slowly toward him, raising the gun. When he does, he's sideways on, and I'm finally outside his sweep. The trigger wire's hanging forgotten by his side. Either he needs to press the button rather than release it, or the vest's a prop. I take another step as he raises the gun on Hartson, closing the gap to four feet.

There's an overpowering taste of blood in the air.

When the man opens his mouth to say something, I take my last chance and hurl myself forward, connecting as hard as I can with him, bringing everything down on his right arm, the gun hand. I feel something break when we hit the floor, and the gun slides out of reach. I start to climb on top of the man, but he lets out a full-throated bellow and throws me. Then he's pinning me to the ground, wrapping both hands around my neck, squeezing like his life depends on it.

His green eyes bore right through me, pure meth stare, and I can guess why he's still functioning with that broken arm. He can't even feel it. I get my hands up, pressing my fingers through the eyeholes on his mask, clawing at the man's face. He squeezes harder, and I'm lightheaded, slipping away. Then there's thousands of intersecting lines pouring into the darkness over my head. Like all the unwanted messages and warning signs and bad static that's hammering down on me. All the dark energy that won't leave me alone. The flashlight pointing up at the ceiling makes a spotlight, and as things start to go fuzzy, I see the faint outline of Clare's face in the shadows. I refocus on the man with his hands around my neck and press two fingers into his left eye socket, reaching for the back of his skull, trying to make him feel something. He howls and lets go. I start pushing the mask up past his mouth, but he climbs off me, staggers backward, then crashes through the room to the door. It opens, then slams shut, then he's gone.

I lie there for a few seconds, getting my breath back, then I roll over and climb to my feet. Hartson's standing uncertainly, with the help of the wall. When he turns to me, there's red blood spattered on his face.

Our eyes go to the gun on the floor.

Slowly, I bend to pick it up.

Then I look at him.

"Ten million," he says. "Yours within the hour."

I'd been hoping to reach an arrangement that might let me walk out of here. A million of anything's beyond my wildest dreams. I just can't help but notice how much higher that figure had gotten for his own life. How he let his sons do all the talking, take all the blame. The whole house is vibrating with death; the shock waves are still rolling over us. I don't believe that Hartson wasn't involved, but there's no point trying to get any sense from him now. At the very least, his overreaction to Miranda's comment had set things in motion. Not to mention that the boys had been craving his approval. Most importantly, Miranda's retirement had rid him of a powerful dissenting voice in the oil community.

Mainly, I know he'll say anything to get out of this room.

Once he does, it's a different story.

Hartson watches me, doing the math.

"Name your price," he says, drawing himself up.

I want to say the right thing. Something that captures my reasons and explains where I'm coming from. Something guys like Hartson never get to hear.

I take a step closer and raise the gun.

There's just the sound of my ragged breath.

"Nah," I say.

43.

When I climb out of the cab at Terminal 5, I'm disoriented. I've never walked through the front door before; I'd arrived via the underground. I turn in a circle, looking overhead at the signs, moving as fast as I can without drawing attention to myself. I'd spent an hour in the cab, going quietly mad, leaning forward to try and will the car faster. And not just because of another bloodbath in the rearview mirror. They might have tormented Heydon, but Hartson and his sons hadn't killed Control, Ronnie, or Sebastien. There's something else going on.

The Hartsons set it in motion by hiring Sebastien, ex-SAS, to go black ops on a troubled guy with a dark secret. A sledgehammer to crack a nut. But although Control's death had scanned like part of a cover-up at first, Ronnie and Sebastien had clearly been revenge killings. And committed by a man with green eyes.

I move through the terminal fast, thinking of the poster I'd seen in Heydon's room. The cult film from the nineties, *Irma Vep*. The anagram of vampire. When I get to the Sofitel, the luxury chain attached to the terminal, the hotel where I'd bumped into

Bobbie, I go straight to the counter, trying not to sound as out of breath as I am.

"Hi," I say.

The woman at the counter does a double take.

"I'm running late for a meeting with one of your guests. They said I should call up when I got here."

The woman hesitates.

"Room 229," I say.

She just looks at me.

"The booking's under the name Doc. Renee Yiph."

"I'm afraid they just checked out."

But I'm already backing away, turning and running into the terminal, looking up at the signs for security, sprinting now, not even thinking about how it might look.

Doc. Renee Yiph.

Heydon Pierce.

When I reach the nearest gate, I stop, breathless, unable to go any farther without a boarding pass. It's late, not especially busy, and among the families heading on holiday, the loose kids, the couples walking arm in arm toward romantic getaways, there's a single lone figure carrying a suitcase, walking calmly, unhurried. Just about to round the corner and disappear forever.

"Heydon," I call after him.

A few heads on my side of the barrier turn. But the people on their way out of the country don't look back, don't stop. All except for the lone man carrying that suitcase. People stream past, but he keeps his back to me.

"Heydon Pierce," I call out.

When the guy glances back, it's not him.

For a moment, there's just the ringing in my ears. I'd

exaggerated the decibel report of a .45 to Maximilian, but not by much. It sounds like an ocean of static roaring through my head. I turn into the glare of artificial lights, searching the crowd for hired goons, security guys, earpieces, dirty looks. But for the first time in days, I get the strangest sensation. The feeling of not being watched.

———

It's long after midnight when I walk back into the Sofitel at Heathrow. There's just one person sitting in the bar, at a small circular side table. Two empty martini glasses, a pair of shades, and an iPhone, lying face down. She's staring into space, lost in thought, putting out a strong aura of unapproachability.

"Bobbie."

When Bobbie looks up, she doesn't seem entirely surprised to see me, but as she draws slowly back in her seat, I can see that she's afraid of what I might say next.

I take the seat opposite.

"I hope you don't mind me saying this, but it looks like you're running away from something."

Bobbie watches me cautiously for a moment, then shakes her head. "I'm running away from everything."

"Not quite," I say, staring into the shades. Bobbie's fingering the stem of her empty martini glass. "You can't run away from him."

The stem of the glass snaps in Bobbie's hand, and I see a trickle of blood before she closes her fist on it.

"I don't know where he's going," she says quickly. "I don't even know what name he's using now."

"This is Heydon?" I ask.

Bobbie nods.

I take a breath. "I'm more interested in why he went missing. Why he came back."

"I can't give you chapter and verse. I just know he took that cash, left the country, and started again. Last week, he came back."

Neither one of us moves.

"How long have you known?"

"Not until the night we met," Bobbie says. "Not until I got in that car."

"We were sitting right here when your phone rang. You knew something."

There's just the dark mirror of her shades.

"I suspected," she says. "I didn't know for sure."

"So how did it happen?"

"Last week, two men approached me."

I stare at her for a second, then see that third figure, standing on the platform, watching the two guys close in.

"One in an anorak, one in a leather jacket?"

Bobbie nods. "They were the ones who told me that Heydon had left the phone records with Mr. Badwan."

"Who are they?"

"They said they'd been acquaintances of my brother's before he went missing. If that's true, I can only assume they came out of the drug world."

"Drugs?"

"I suppose Heydon needed unknowns, people from outside the bubble."

"And you went to Badwan yourself because you didn't want the family to find out about the phone records."

Bobbie starts tearing a napkin into strips.

"The phone records looked bad. Of course, my father knew

I'd copied them, but Miranda didn't. I'm not sure she even knew they existed."

"Why would Heydon's *friends* send you for them?"

"That was their whole plan. Heydon wanted us turned against each other. Confused, chasing the wrong things."

"You're saying the case was like a trap?"

"Like a distraction," she says. "Everyone looked the other way while Heydon did what he wanted to." She looks at me. "What he felt he had to."

"Why now?"

"Look," Bobbie says, sounding exhausted, "I don't know everything. That first night was the shock of my life. When we got back to the hotel room, I was just barely holding it together."

"I noticed."

"The only other time I saw him was today."

"You must have asked him some questions."

"I suppose he found out that Badwan was selling. The games could finally begin."

I look at the two glasses on the table.

"He was sitting in this chair?"

She nods. "And you're right. I did have some questions. He even answered them honestly." Bobbie shivers, and I see she's got goose bumps on her skin. "I think that's why I stopped asking."

"Why would you even meet him after what he did?"

"He promised to extract the file from my father's collection, once and for all." Her eyes meet mine. "I had no idea that he'd…" She trails off.

"That's why you stayed in town?"

"After my father took the file, the two men approached me for a second time."

"Mr. Anorak and Leather Jacket again?"

She nods. "They said they'd arrange for someone to stand in for me at MBR. They'd get the file back."

"What did they ask you to do?"

"They told me I should go to the airport, as planned. Heydon was staying here. The man in the anorak came with me. I really did think that you were him for a second." I don't say anything, and she goes on. "When the man saw me noticing you, he took your picture and sent it to Heydon. It was a chance thing. It all came from that."

"And I was just…"

"Another distraction," she says. "Not only a way of turning heads but a good excuse if anyone saw my brother lurking around town. Once you were on Rayner's radar, naturally, they'd just assume any reported sightings were you."

It explains why she'd wanted Mike to find me at Tregunter Road. And it had worked as well. Neither Control, Ronnie, nor Sebastien had seen their killer coming. And not the Hartsons either.

Bobbie averts her eyes. "If I'd had any idea what he was planning…"

"All you did was tattoo my face," I say evenly. "You were right. I was running away too."

But I can see there's more.

"You shouldn't forgive me so easily," she says. "I did spike your drink."

I think back to the message on the TV.

"Whose room was that?"

"My brother booked it under an anagram of his name."

I smile tightly. "I've always been shit at those."

"I wanted to tell you." She pauses for a second. "I just…"

"Had to get that file back. Yeah, I know." I blow out my cheeks. "So did he come through for you?"

The way Bobbie averts her eyes tells me she's not worried about anyone getting their hands on the phone records anymore.

"Right," I say. "Good old Heydon."

We sit in silence for a minute, then her mobile goes off on the table. It's an incoming call from a withheld number. The ringtone's "Bad Guy" by Billie Eilish. Bobbie cancels the call and glances at the departures screen over my shoulder.

"I think that's my flight."

"I'll walk with you."

"You don't have to—"

"I insist."

———

We walk back into the terminal in silence, Bobbie dragging a black flight case behind her.

We stop before security.

"Well," she says. "I suppose this is goodbye."

My eyes lock on to a man standing beside the barrier. He's just lingering there, like he's waiting for someone. He's wearing shades to cover his eyes. There's red marks on his face, and one sleeve of his jacket's hanging loose, hiding the arm in a sling. He seems to do a double take when he sees me, then turns away.

"So, Bobbie, the black SUV that first night. Heydon was driving?"

She frowns momentarily, then glances back, as if for what might have prompted the question. The guy's still facing the other away, a part of the crowd, and she turns to me again, confused.

"Right," she says.

But I'm still staring, and when Bobbie follows my sight line, she turns at the same time he does. They exchange a look, and she's forced to acknowledge him. He takes a step toward us, but she holds up a finger. *One minute.* The man holds on me for a second, then turns away. He's wearing faded jeans and a tracksuit jacket. Nikes instead of black boots.

"Heydon's dead, isn't he, Bobbie?"

She closes her eyes.

"Heydon's dead, *isn't he*, Bobbie?"

She looks at me for a moment, then shrugs.

"He never came back, looking for revenge, did he? Heydon didn't kill those people."

"Name one of them who didn't deserve it," she says.

"Well, Jesus, what about your dad?"

Bobbie remains absolutely still, and I can see that however she might have justified it to herself, Ronnie's murder had taken more out of her than the rest.

"He was guilty as the next," she says from behind the black visor of her shades. "I'd have been a hypocrite if—"

"Wait a minute. You stole those phone bills. You sent them to Keeler. How's what he did any worse?"

Bobbie takes a step back.

"Our situations couldn't be any more different. I thought I was selling some tabloid hack a lemon, a nothing story. But after my father found the originals on the scanner, he had them finger-printed by the Rayner Group."

I don't say anything.

"Well, there's simply no chance he didn't ask Rayner to do deep background on the Black Door, on Sebastien. So he knew exactly what kind of man was out there, working against his family. He said nothing."

I blink for a few seconds, then look past her at the guy still lingering there.

"Nate?" I ask. Bobbie nods. "The guy's a fucking psycho."

Bobbie fronts it out. "Just my type."

"He killed Control."

"I don't know," she says airily. "You did your part."

I stare for a second, then remember the flyer for Control's talk. I'd sent it to her, asking if she knew him.

"You deactivated the CCTV at Tregunter Road."

"Good thing for you that I did."

I shake my head. "How did you get Sebastien?"

When Bobbie straightens her face, I see she's proud.

"Nate and the two guys went there, looking like a road crew. They said there was a sewage problem on the square. They asked the doorman to move the car, and he was nice about it. Parked around the corner, then went back to the building."

I stare at her for a second, then lean in.

"Nate couldn't quite get it done with the Hartsons though, could he?"

Bobbie watches me. "He said he heard a shot."

"I'll bet he did," I say, noncommittal. "Those two guys, then."

She glances back. "Friends of Nate's."

"Who you had going around town, showing people my picture." She doesn't say anything, and I see that third figure, standing in shadow, at the end of the platform. "So was that you on the underground, cheering them on?"

"I'm sorry," Bobbie says. "I'm not sure what you're talking about." I just stand there. "After we spoke on the water, I went straight to the Chelsea and Westminster. Then I came here."

But all I can see's that shadow.

"How well did you know Sebastien?" I ask.

She shakes her head. "I only ever met him once, with Heydon, a few months before he went missing. At the time, I thought I recognized his voice. I just couldn't work out from where."

"The call in your dad's office, the Black Door."

Bobbie nods.

"Well, you weren't missing much. Except for the detail that Sebastien and old man Rayner were friends."

Bobbie doesn't say anything.

"When Hartson told me, I was surprised. As far as I knew, the Rayner Group were working for Miranda. But Hartson said that Rayner worked for himself." She just stands there. "Bobbie, Hartson wasn't just a guy with a grudge. He had hundreds of millions of reasons to try and sideline Miranda."

"And?"

"You said what Ronnie did was worse than you, because Rayner must have told him who Sebastien really was. I'm just saying Rayner might not have given your old man all the facts. Ronnie might not have known."

"You're just trying to make me feel bad," she says.

Looking at her now, I'm not sure that's possible.

Bobbie had been made aware of incriminating evidence that proved she betrayed Heydon, not to mention her old man and Miranda. She'd stolen her mother's jewelry to try and get it back without being found out. But Ronnie followed her and, after a struggle, returned the phone bills to his collection. Him sending her away had turned out to be a gift. Not only had it granted her an alibi for the incoming mayhem, she'd even found me at the airport, the perfect distraction. Someone who looked near enough to the real thing. Most likely, I really was there to confuse

Rayner, to distract Miranda. But the closer I got to the truth, the easier it was for Nate to follow in my footsteps, wiping out Control, Ronnie, Sebastien, and the Hartsons. Or at least most of them.

"So was there a bullet with my name on it back there?"

Bobbie winces. "How could you even think that?"

"How could I not? You've got me at the scene of four murders, impersonating your brother. Staying in a room under an anagram of his name."

"I was the one who got you off Tregunter Road—"

"So I could make a scene with Sebastien. So I could still get picked up by the Hartsons. I'm dying to know how they knew where to find me, by the way."

Bobbie looks momentarily unmoored, but she pushes through it.

"Well," she croaks. "If that's what you think of someone who tries to give you an opportunity…"

I glance over her shoulder at Nate, now twitching badly. And I decide it's time to leave. I start to back away, then stop, conflicted. Bobbie steps closer, removing her shades, searching my face. I take hold of her arms.

"Listen, Bobbie…" I tap my jacket pocket, the outline of my phone. "I got every single word you just said." Her whole body tenses. "Or the cloud's got it, whatever. Anyway, there's a few things I need from you. First, you'd better call Rayner. They might need to work some magic on Hartson if they want to keep the family out of it." She doesn't move. "I'm serious, Bobbie. If anyone comes knocking on my door, your confession's going viral."

She seems to regain herself once she knows I'm willing to make a deal. She nods minimally, holding my eye in a way that makes me feel like I'm meeting her for the first time.

I lean in closer.

"Second, if there comes a time when a sacrifice needs to be made, then lover boy's your man." I nod over her shoulder at Nate. "That must have been your plan before I came along anyway."

Bobbie starts to say something, but I go on.

"I'm sure you've thought about how to put it all on him if you have to. Just make a paper trail. Make it convincing for when the time comes. Text someone that he's acting weird and making you leave the country at short notice, film him threatening you when he's drunk, whatever. Just move heaven and earth to make sure nothing comes back on me, Bobbie."

"You've got me completely wrong—" she starts.

"Look, most importantly, if something happens with Nate, if anything goes wrong, if you need help? Don't call me. Don't come looking. Don't try and find me anywhere." I turn and walk. "Goodbye, Bobbie."

Goodbye, Heydon.

Goodbye, everyone.

44.

I'm in one of the last places on earth where I might still find a pay phone. I drift through the grayer, less glamorous corners of the terminal, not wanting to ask a member of staff. I'm dragging myself around by now, but I've still got the case, and I'm already dreaming of the next hotel room. I just don't know where it is yet. Anyway, there's someone I need to talk to first.

If it's not too late.

My phone's dead, but I walk right past the charge point, not needing it. I'd be stupid to call her from a mobile, and anyway, I know Clare's number by heart. I get tunnel vision, walking toward the pay phone. It's the only thing keeping me conscious. I lean into it for a second, closing my eyes, taking a breath, feeling grateful to be alive. Then I stand up straight and clear my throat. I pick up the receiver and dial.

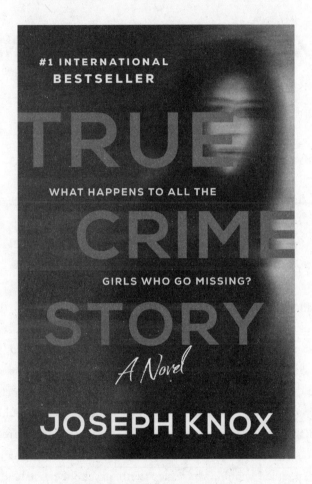

0.
"EXPOSED FOUNDATIONS"

November 8, 2011—forty days before Zoe's disappearance

In late 2018, Kimberly Nolan, Zoe's twin sister, claimed in a rare interview given to the Mail on Sunday *that she had herself once been kidnapped. She claimed that this kidnapping occurred roughly one month prior to Zoe's disappearance, while on a night out with her sister and three other friends.*

KIMBERLY NOLAN, *Zoe's sister*:
I feel like my *Mail* interview covered all this. There are just more interesting things we could talk about. We could go back into Zoe as a little girl, work out if there were any warning signs we all missed. Or we could cut right back to the good stuff, our move out to Manchester. First time in a new city, first time doing a lot of things. We could even rehash the night Zoe went missing, I mean, that's why we're here. I can take you through all that with my eyes closed. Midnight fire alarms, people I shouldn't have slept with, psychotic men standing in the shadows...

I know all of it, all of that, by heart.

But here you are asking me about my weakest subject, Kimberly Nolan. What can I tell you? I hardly know the girl.

FINTAN MURPHY, *Zoe's course mate and friend:*

Right, Kimberly's kidnapping, this sad story. Would you like my opinion? I mean, let's put ourselves in poor Kimberly's position for a moment. Born a girl, an almost identical twin, but with a sister who was simply more attractive than she was, simply more intelligent. A sister who was outgoing and prodigiously gifted musically. Someone who effortlessly charmed everyone she met. I think we all might struggle if we were up against that.

Okay, so, remaining in Kimberly's shoes. You go away to university to get out from under your sister's shadow, but owing to an unfortunate series of events, you end up studying at the same place, living in the same flat even. Your physical resemblance is such that people routinely double take at you around town, seem visibly disappointed when they realize you're Kimberly and not Zoe.

So you lose a load of weight and start wearing black. You cut your hair short and go goth. Your sister is reserved in some senses, so you act out and start sleeping around. She drinks sensibly, so you drink like an open hole in the floor. She goes missing and becomes front-page news, so you generate this harrowing, incredible tale of how *you* were kidnapped once too. I'd say in some senses that's perfectly understandable. It's one of the few things about Kimberly that really is.

JAI MAHMOOD, *Zoe's friend:*

I don't remember much, but I'm fairly sure Fintan wasn't even there that night.

LIU WAI, *Zoe's flatmate and friend:*

I think what probably happened was that Zoe and I decided to go out? I know it was a Tuesday, which is, like, a *big* student night in Manchester. Kim always tried to involve herself in mine and Zoe's plans, so I generally expected her to try and tag along. And she did, in that kind of dour way where it's clear she thinks she's doing you a massive favor. This was before she dyed her hair black and stuff, but she always had that kind of personality. And then, because it was the three of us, the boys ended up coming too. So that made for an eventful evening...

JAI MAHMOOD:

Y'know how some people drink so much of something they can never go near it again? They have to hold their nose while your Jim Beam's being poured because of that night they drank a whole bottle of the stuff and spent six hours blowing it out both ends? *[Laughs]* That's basically how I got sober, bro. One brand at a time, pushing everything so far over the line that I could never touch it again. I think the only thing I haven't had a bad night on by now's hard seltzer, and being honest, that's just so I've got something saved for the deathbed.

ANDREW FLOWERS, *Zoe's boyfriend*:

The Kimnapping? I mean, I know I shouldn't laugh, but we did go to Fifth Avenue. If you don't know it, it's the ten or eleventh circle of hell, this grotesque indie disco warehouse where girls are generally assured of a cheap night out. That's because they order one drink and some pale-faced northern boy called Gaz or Trev or something spikes it with Rohypnol. The girls are legless before they can even request Adele from the DJ. From some angles, that's the only good thing about the place.

JAI MAHMOOD:

Point being, I was fully in that phase of my life back then, yeah? Not just embracing disaster, but taking it home and really giving it one. I'd had my head kicked in a few weeks before, so I thought I had a good excuse for being a fuckup. It was only over the next few years I started running low on excuses. So anyway, I know it's criminal to say, but I don't remember much about that night. It's not one where I can scroll through the viewfinder and see some stills or shaky handheld footage, it's just not there at all. Like, file missing, y'know? But if Fintan's saying he was there, then he's full of it.

KIMBERLY NOLAN:

Looking back, I'm Bruce Springsteen. I wanna change my clothes, my hair, my face. Just please not the dress I was wearing that night. I was starting to experiment, trying to put some of my real self on display. I'd found this cool kind of Wednesday Addams outfit at Affleck's Palace, and it made me feel more like myself than I had before, less like a second-rate Zoe and something more like Kim. It was the only time we ever went out as a group, which is strange when you read the papers from back then. You'd think we were thick as thieves when really we were just thick as kids. And everyone was acting invincible, no idea what was coming around the corner.

Jai had taken something, which he usually had. Andrew was in a bad mood, which he usually was. Him and Zoe were arguing, so the rest of us all had to suffer. Saying that, I'm not sure Zoe even really noticed. She was the most invincible of us all, everything-proof and stunning, wearing this luminescent red jacket, ultrahot red all over. Matching red lipstick and a slightly visible red bra. Zoe was busy *being* noticed.

ANDREW FLOWERS:

After Zoe went missing, the police became oddly fixated on that night, so certain details stuck. Yes, Zoe had on some red thing that they could probably see in outer space. If she'd still been wearing it when she went missing, they'd have picked her up in five seconds flat. And if Kim says we were fighting, then I'm sure that we were, it was more or less our default setting. Once we started in on each other, neither one of us could ever find the off switch.

JAI MAHMOOD:

They told me afterward that I lit up and started blazing on the dance floor. Like I say, that night's a blank slate for me, but it wouldn't be completely out of character. I know the bouncers wouldn't let me in when I went back a week later, so yeah, if they say I got kicked out, I probably got kicked out.

LIU WAI:

It's sad to say, but I think even then Jai was a really troubled soul? I think he always felt like a bit of an outsider. Where I'm one of those people who feels comfortable talking to anyone at any level, quite Virgo, Jai kind of wore his brown-ness? Like, he really *wore* his race. He felt like he had to be kind of street and smoke weed and listen to rap songs, where, I don't know. I've always seemed to fit in much more naturally?

ANDREW FLOWERS:

I thought Jai getting kicked out was the best thing about that night. He was so out of it, he started smoking on the dance floor, offering cigarettes to girls and stuff. Then something painful started playing, "Sex on Fire" or whatever, and suddenly we were surrounded on all sides, just Midlanders, just Waynes and Janes as far as the eye could see. He offered this little blond number a light and she accepted. They were laughing, getting close, then this cinder block–headed prick started pushing him around, speaking fluent fucking caveman. "Hands off my girl," et cetera, et cetera. As I recall, Jai tried to apologize but ended up coughing two lungs full of smoke into the guy's face by accident. He went predictably apeshit.

KIMBERLY NOLAN:
With Jai, people saw his slacker image and stopped looking, but there was more to him than that. He took these pictures, just tuned out the world and found amazing things that we were all looking at but none of us could see. The bouncers didn't know that, though, they just saw trouble. This wasted Asian boy who'd walked in with two black eyes. They were going overboard, pulling him out by the hair and stuff, so I guess there was some racism in it too. I started to follow them so I could explain and check he was okay, but I'd just been *Exorcist*-sick in the toilets. The floor was like jelly under my feet, so I stopped when I got to the stairs. I thought if I was leaving, I'd better find Zoe first and tell her. Something was wrong with me. I felt dizzy and sick, which was weird because I hadn't even really been drinking.

FINTAN MURPHY:
If Kimberly says she hadn't been drinking, then I suppose we have to take her word for it. There's a first time for everything, after all.

LIU WAI:
Kim was plastered.

ANDREW FLOWERS:
No, I wasn't counting Kim's drinks, and no, I wasn't spiking them either, if that's what you're asking me. She'd been gone for some time, so I just assumed she'd left when Jai got kicked out. Zoe and I weren't getting along, and I could never quite stand Liu Wai, so I politely excused myself.

LIU WAI:

I think I was just saying that Jai *had* broken the rules, like, the club *is* nonsmoking. Andrew told me I could wank him off with a pair of chopsticks and stormed out. I mean, aside from being a low-level hate crime, doesn't that imply to you that he's got a small penis?

ANDREW FLOWERS:

I'm sure she remembers better than I do. I'm afraid I didn't necessarily see Liu Wai as a person back then, she was just some strange Chinese tumor attached to my girlfriend.

LIU WAI:

I'm from fucking Essex.

FINTAN MURPHY:

Yes, Andrew and Zoe, the famous loving couple...

LIU WAI:

Andrew and Zoe *were* always challenging to be around. Nowadays, I think we'd call their relationship quite toxic? Just a kind of unsafe chemical spill of a couple. Like, the only possible solution for both parties was extraction. I'm sure Zoe was upset to see him go, she blamed herself when things were bad. It was just that most of the time, Andrew looked visibly uncomfortable around her? You'd see him sort of itching to get away.

But then he'd always be dropping in, always hanging around, always inviting himself out. A lot like Kim when you think about it. Given what happened between them all later, it's one of those things you can't help but torture yourself about afterwards. I mean, let's get it straight. He never loved Zoe.

ANDREW FLOWERS:

Perhaps it might seem circumspect from the vantage point of years passed, but I truly couldn't stand Fifth, and I'm sure that's why I left. In nightclubs, as in life, it's my opinion that too many cocks ruin the broth. And Jai couldn't even remember his own name, couldn't even remember his own PIN—believe me, I tried to get it for the cab fare. So, monstrously, yes, I decided to take him home rather than let him sleep it off in the gutter. If I'd known Kim was struggling that night, I'd have taken her home too. That's just the kind of guy I am.

FINTAN MURPHY:

A selfless act from Andrew Flowers? Another first. After recent events, I'd say we all know for certain what kind of *guy* he is...

LIU WAI:

I want to be fair, but honestly? I don't know what Zoe ever saw in him. I consider Andrew Flowers to be one of the most unpleasant human beings I've ever encountered.

KIMBERLY NOLAN:

Well, Liu lives to judge people. I'm not saying she's wrong on Andrew, but being cynical about everything doesn't make you Nostradamus.

JAI MAHMOOD:

If Andrew really did take me home, it's probably because it suited whatever was happening in Flowers-land.

KIMBERLY NOLAN:

We all scattered, and when I got back to the booth where I'd left them, the only thing I could find of Zoe's was her bright-red jacket. I was feeling so weird, I couldn't tell how long I'd been gone, so I think I assumed they'd all left without me. They were probably just on the dance floor or something. Fifth's this typical Manchester nightclub, a sweatbox that never drops below boiling point.

I was shivering, though.

My teeth were chattering and I was breaking out in goose bumps, so I grabbed Zoe's jacket and put it on. The room's this wide-open mezzanine-type space, like the Roman Colosseum or something—you can see the top floor from the bottom and everything just surrounds you. There was a song playing, "Flux" by Bloc Party, the part where the singer starts screaming "We need to talk" over and over again. And I knew then, from the way I was frozen stiff and the room was looming down on me, from the way everyone had vanished and this song kept insisting, "We need to talk, we need to talk," I knew something bad was happening to us.

FINTAN MURPHY:

Jai's absolutely correct, I wasn't out that night, and I've never claimed otherwise. I don't drink for a start. I'm sure Zoe invited me, but I suppose I was busy or not in the mood. The reason I can discuss those events with some certainty is that I went there the following day looking for Zoe's missing jacket. She'd emailed me mentioning how upset she was to have misplaced it, so I thought I'd see if it was in the lost property to surprise her.

In the event, it was me who ended up being surprised.

The club was closed during the day, but I badgered my way in and pleaded my case. The jacket hadn't been handed over, but Zoe had mentioned where she'd been sitting, so I asked if they'd let me watch the CCTV covering that booth. I came up with some spiel on data protection law, saying people have the right to request footage they've appeared in, and I was doing so on Zoe's behalf. Either I'm a gifted liar or they just got bored of me, because on the twentieth time of asking, the manager marched us back to the office and handed me over to a security guy. He got things running and we watched the booth on fast-forward until Zoe, Kim, Liu, Andrew, and Jai all arrived. We sped through their various comings and goings, then slowed down when we saw the booth had been left vacant. Then Kim staggered back looking absolutely trashed, and I suppose an alarm bell started going off for me then. She checked there was no one around, then put Zoe's jacket on and walked away.

We were able to follow her on camera after that, we saw her leaving the club in her sister's red jacket, as she said in her recent *Mail* interview. Then there were a couple of other things she never quite got around to mentioning. She was certainly confused, certainly disoriented. In fact, in this apparent search for her sister, she stopped in the doorway to check out a guy, even made a grab and shouted something after him. He kept on going. Perhaps her disorientation was also the reason why, when she began persistently calling someone outside, waiting for the phone to be answered, she never once dialed her sister's number, despite telling the *Mail* that's why she left the club in the first place. I have Zoe's phone records from her parents. No incoming calls on that night or the next morning. Of course, I'd be interested to see Kimberly's records...

KIMBERLY NOLAN:
Could *you* find a phone bill from seven fucking years ago?

FINTAN MURPHY:
Look, what I saw on that tape was a young woman undergoing some kind of internal crisis, one exacerbated by drugs or alcohol. She was walking with hunched shoulders, crossed arms, constantly picking at her nails and moving strands of hair, clearly in some kind of emotional

distress, but also clearly on the pull. Whatever Kimberly's problem was, she walked into that building with it.

But once she exited the club and tried to make a couple of calls, it all seemed to fall away. I remember she was looking quite closely at the people gathered in the street outside, she even approached one or two of them. What's interesting is that everyone she looked at or approached was a man. I remember thinking, *Who's she looking for?* The impression I got was that she was searching for someone in particular, and she was confused not to find him out there.

KIMBERLY NOLAN:

There was a hand on my back and I was being pushed into this filthy white rust bucket van. Someone had used their finger to write *clean me* on the door in grime, and I was half laughing at that when everything went black.

FINTAN MURPHY:

Now, because Kimberly never mentioned anything about this assault to anyone, not in the wake of her sister's disappearance, not for seven years afterward, there was no cause for authorities to check cameras in the surrounding area at the time. Conveniently for Kimberly's story, there's no way for us to confirm the existence of this white van now, but I can tell you for damn sure I never saw it on the club's camera. I mean, not to state things too bluntly, but my dealings with Kimberly Nolan have *all* been characterized by tall tales.

KIMBERLY NOLAN:

When I was thirteen years old, I got run down on a pedestrian crossing. They could never find the car, it was just one of those things. I didn't see anything and no one ever came forward. The driver was going too fast, but honestly, I walked out without looking. And the second it hit me, the word *IDIOT* just flashed through my mind in capital letters. It was so clear, I thought, *This must be the last thing people think when they die in an accident*, and I used to tell my friends that when we'd talk about it. How lucky I was to have come so close, to have gotten this glimpse of the other side but still lived to remember it.

The van was the same thing again, like a near-death experience.

There was a hand on me, I was in the back and then the door slammed shut, like it was all happening in one moment. Someone put a bag on my head, this thick fabric with a drawstring tight around my neck, then they ripped off Zoe's jacket and put cable ties around my wrists. I heard the plastic teeth when they pulled them on, so tight I thought my hands might fall off. And my whole brain's flashing *IDIOT, IDIOT, IDIOT* in mile-high capital letters, just like when I got hit by the car, only now I know what I learned from that. That it must be the last conscious thought a lot of people have.

LIU WAI:

I'm not a judgmental person, I say, "Live and let live." You know, a lot of girls have that one drink too many and find themselves in the wrong place at the wrong time. It's just that Kim seems to *frequently* have that one drink too many? She seems to *frequently* find herself in the wrong place at the wrong time.

KIMBERLY NOLAN:

When they started driving, I couldn't speak. I don't think I could even cry. We'd been going a few minutes before it even occurred to me to try and remember the turns or work out where we'd gone. My head was spinning so much, it wouldn't have mattered anyway. I was on my knees, leaning into the wall to stay upright. And I knew there were men in the van, because I could feel their eyes on me. I could smell them through the bag on my head.

ANDREW FLOWERS:

So we're talking gone midnight? Unfortunately, I was in possession of the world's most knackered Rolex back then. I couldn't tell you where I was for sure, even if I remembered. My guess would be that I was pouring Jai into bed.

JAI MAHMOOD:

Yeah, I'd have to go along with that. I was probably in bed or on my way there. I am sure I woke up back at ours the next day. I mean, I'd remember if I hadn't.

LIU WAI:

I think Zoe and me just enjoyed the rest of our night? I was probably quite happy that everyone had left us to it. She was definitely annoyed we couldn't find her jacket, though. I had to wait for Kim's *Mail on Sunday* interview seven years after the fact to get some closure on that.

KIMBERLY NOLAN:

I was told that this bag on my head was the only thing keeping me alive, and if I tried to look at them when they rolled it up to check something, they'd have to hurt me. Only one of them really talked. He sounded northern, but I couldn't be sure. He rolled the bag up to my nose and told me to open my mouth. You can guess what was going through my mind by that point, but I did it. And even though the bag was still over my eyes, I could see the glow from a flashlight. I could tell he was looking into my mouth like a dentist, checking me for something. He grunted and I felt another guy come closer. It felt like they were both leaning in and looking at me. Then they started asking me about my teeth. Seriously, asking me about fillings and stuff while they had me tied up in the back of a van.

ANDREW FLOWERS:
The old cavity search? Right, I think I read about that too. Is there a reason we're going over things I wasn't around for?

KIMBERLY NOLAN:
Well, I didn't have any fillings, which I just about managed to tell them. They said that was good, then started feeling along my arms. I don't think it was sexual, but only because it felt worse than that to me at the time. It was like the way you'd handle meat or something. Turn it over, press it and check it for imperfections. I was so cold I could hardly feel their hands, and the cable ties were making my arms go numb. And at the same time, we were still driving, turning, stopping, starting, and I couldn't see anything. Then they picked me up and started feeling along my legs in the same way, checking for something. They got halfway down my right leg and stopped, still gripping me by the knee.

ROBERT NOLAN, *Kimberly and Zoe's father*:
Well, whatever we might think about Kimberly's gift for invention, the road accident thing's true, I can vouch for that. Music was a big part of our lives at home. I was a professional musician myself for a time, but she always went for different stuff, like, than the rest of us. Punk and whatnot. Some of what she listened to you'd struggle to call music at all. That's partly why we got her the iPod for Christmas, so we wouldn't have to hear it. I don't think she took her headphones off again until she went under that car. She broke her right knee, and she was lucky that's all.

SALLY NOLAN, *Kimberly and Zoe's mother*:

That's when Kim and Zoe drifted a bit. Parents of twins, you know, they do the matching hair and toys and clothes. We never went in for all that, but I suppose you do expect girls to be close. It just didn't happen with ours, they were always their own people. Then around there, thirteen or fourteen, after Kim got knocked down, Zoe started going out more. She was already singing and getting paid and being hired for shows, it just got more. It's probably a chicken-and-egg thing, but the hit-and-run made them more different. After it, Zoe was always going out further and further into the world, and Kim was always going back, further inside herself.

KIMBERLY NOLAN:

Everything stopped. I mean, the van was still going, but everything else stopped. And this man's still gripping me by my knee, not moving, making it clear that something's wrong with my leg. It doesn't reach his fucking leg standards or whatever. So when he asked me about the scar from the accident, my brain went into overdrive trying to work out what to say, how to let him down gently.

I told him there was a flaw in my knee, like a birth defect.

From the way they'd been feeling me, and I know this sounds gross, but I thought they might want to *breed* me or something. It was late 2011, so the Rochdale grooming scandal was going on in the background, this child sex ring that had gone under the radar for years, and there were all these insane stories about sex trafficking round Manchester.

So I was trying to suggest I wasn't the right candidate if that was what they had in mind. I was trying to suggest there was stuff wrong with my body, that I was more trouble than I was worth. They made a big deal about my knee, they asked about it, so I started telling them how useless it was. I said I'd been forced to have surgery, I'd been forced to have steel pins implanted and stuff. I said I had to do an hour's physio a day just so I could walk on it, I said I'd probably lose my leg at some point in the future. I said anything I could think of to make me sound defective, just laying it on as thick as I thought it could go.

FINTAN MURPHY:

I must say, I personally find it difficult to stomach this story of hardened sex traffickers releasing a young woman because she had a bad knee. I think men of that stripe are usually preoccupied with other parts of the anatomy.

KIMBERLY NOLAN:

The whole atmosphere changed. The engine was still going and there were still bumps in the road, but it was like these men, who I knew for a fact were inches away from me, had disappeared.

Like something I said had ruined the party.

One of them banged on the partition to the driver, the van pulled up and they all got out. I wondered if it was stolen. I thought they might leave me there, even torch it with me inside or something, but then I heard them talking, like, arguing. I couldn't make it out because I was too scared to take the bag off my head. I just stood there holding my breath, I didn't move a muscle.

ROBERT NOLAN:

If I've got one regret in my life, and I mean obviously I've got more than that now, but if I could fix one thing, I'd go back and pick Kim up on her lying. I know how that sounds, said of your own daughter, but I really would.

KIMBERLY NOLAN:

When they got back into the van, they were all cheering. Laughing, joking, asking if I was okay. The talker said they were sorry, it had been a university dare or something. I remember thinking he sounded too old to be a student. One of them helped me sit down and said they'd drop me near to where they'd picked me up. I tried to laugh along, like, "Oh, yeah, just drop me anywhere," trying not to be sick through gritted teeth.

LIU WAI:

Well, I heard something supposedly *happened* inside that van...

KIMBERLY NOLAN:

Someone was drawing the bag back down fully over my face, then the driver started up and we jolted forward. The bag got ripped off my head and there was a second, like a split second, where I could see, where I half saw this blur around me, these two shapes, then I screwed my eyes shut. I put my hands up in front of my face, looked at the floor, the wall. Tried to show them that I hadn't seen anything, I was still good for a laugh and they could still let me go.

LIU WAI:

I probably shouldn't say what it was, though. I mean, Kim never came out and said it in her *Mail on Sunday* interview.

KIMBERLY NOLAN:

One of them pushed my face into the wall. He put the bag back on my head, pulled the cord so tight around my neck I could hardly breathe, then everything went quiet. And I knew then the prank stuff was bullshit. I mean, I always did, but even the pretense of it was gone. We were just driving in this dead silence. I could hear them breathing heavier, feel the driver driving differently, more abrupt, speeding up and stopping at the last second, making us fall around in the back. I knew they'd seen me with my eyes open, they thought I'd seen their faces.

When we stopped a few minutes later, someone got out of the back and—it sounded like—opened a gate. We reversed into something—it felt like wet ground, soft under the tires—and when the engine stopped, I couldn't hear any traffic or city or street sounds. One of them picked me up, opened the doors and threw me out on the ground, and I was just saying, "No, please." It was muddy, and I was trying to talk and get up, but my wrists were still tied together, the bag was still on my head, I couldn't see or breathe.

LIU WAI:

No, I shouldn't say. I was, like, *sworn* to secrecy.

KIMBERLY NOLAN:

They started to pour something on me. At first, I thought it was petrol, then I realized it was vodka. One of them held my face up and they just poured the whole bottle over my head. I was coughing and choking, but they kept on going until I was sick inside the bag. They dropped the bottle on to my face, it smashed my fucking front teeth, and I still didn't move. I still didn't dare.

Then I heard the zips on their trousers and definitely two of them, maybe all three, pissed on me. It was so cold that the heat from it was scorching, like, searing to the skin. It went all over my hands and arms, all over my body, and all over the bag and in my face and in my eyes and in my mouth. I was just trying to breathe through my fucking ears or something until they finally stopped and I heard footsteps going away. I heard the driver's door close, then one of them leaned down to cut the cable ties around my wrists.

LIU WAI:

Well, I heard that she actually *did* see something inside that van...

JOSEPH KNOX

KIMBERLY NOLAN:

He leaned into my ear and said, "Tell anyone about this and you'll get it in every hole, sweetheart." He picked me up and turned me facing the breeze. I felt the air sticking the wet bag to my face, all the piss and vodka and sick. He draped Zoe's jacket back over my shoulders and told me to walk two hundred steps straight ahead, said they'd be gone when I got there. If I took the bag off or turned around, they'd have to use me like a village bike and then they'd have to kill me.

So I started walking, shaking, mainly trying not to be sick again. I had my hands out in front of me to stop myself from going into a wall or something. I couldn't have been ten steps in when I heard a loud bang and dropped to the floor, thinking I'd been shot. Then the van started up and I realized it had been the back door slamming shut. They were driving out and away, so I peeled the bag off my head—I couldn't breathe—and saw taillights disappearing over my shoulder. Nothing else because my eyes were streaming and burning, hurting so much.

LIU WAI:

Well, this is all according to Jai, so I suppose you might have to take it with a grain of salt, but apparently she told Andrew what she saw inside the van.

JAI MAHMOOD:

Look, I mean, nah. What would I know? I was out cold.

KIMBERLY NOLAN:

I just held on to the ground and let my eyes stop stinging, adjust to the dark. When I did look up, I saw I was on a building site, the abandoned one off Canal Street in town. It was meant to be luxury apartments like

TRUE CRIME STORY **397**

everything else, but the money had gone wrong, so it was just a hole in the ground with a fence around it. The center was this pit, this twenty-foot drop into exposed foundations, and I was about two steps away from walking into it when I took the bag off my head. They'd wanted me to fall into it blindfolded and drunk, covered in piss and sick.

FINTAN MURPHY:

My questions are just the obvious ones. Why did she take Zoe's jacket from the club? Why does she say she called Zoe when we can prove that she didn't? Who was she actually looking for outside? How come she didn't tell the police about her abduction? I mean, she makes it all sound fairly serious.

KIMBERLY NOLAN:

I'm sure Fintan would have reacted much more rationally. I'm sure Fintan does still have his fucking phone records from seven years ago, but I don't know. I didn't recognize their voices, I didn't think I knew them. And I knew how it looked. It was a running joke between us all at the time when we'd had too much: "Oh, someone must have spiked my drink again last night." But I think I would have said something. I think I would have found the right time or the words, but then Zoe went missing a month later. Nothing made sense to me after that. When I tried to say it, when I even tried to run it through my head, it just sounded pathetic and attention-seeking. Like I was making it up to compete with my glamorous missing sister.

FINTAN MURPHY:

Competing with her glamorous missing sister. I couldn't put it better myself. Funny she was brave enough to tell the story for a five-figure sum, seven years on.

KIMBERLY NOLAN:

I sold it to the *Mail* to defend myself, which I think Fintan knows.

FINTAN MURPHY:

Mainly, I'd ask what happened to the clothes she was wearing that night. They should have been a veritable gold mine of DNA evidence.

KIMBERLY NOLAN:

I walked home, I had a shower, I went to bed. I was frozen, I had to try and unthaw. I slept for about twelve hours, and I don't remember seeing the clothes again. He knows someone was stealing stuff from the tower. Clothes from out of our rooms, Zoe's as well. That's all on record.

FINTAN MURPHY:

Yes, someone was stealing things from the tower, Zoe's too, but what a thief would want with urine-sodden, vomit-encrusted clothes, I don't know. Look, I say none of this to be cruel. Sometimes I think this story we're stuck in has messed with our heads. When people go through this kind of trauma, they don't get closer to each other. Sadly, they just tear apart. The least we can do is try to be decent, and if I'm falling short of that with Kimberly, then I apologize to her here. Of course I do. But Zoe, my best friend in the world, is still missing all these years later, and this is what Kimberly wants to talk about? It's nothing. It's a footnote.

ANDREW FLOWERS:

Liu says that I know what Kim saw inside the van?

KIMBERLY NOLAN:

No, I [*inaudible*]. Look, I closed my eyes like I said.

ANDREW FLOWERS:

She did say something like that as it happens. She told me she saw a face.

KIMBERLY NOLAN:

An illustrated face. Well, a tattoo on the back of one of their hands. This ghoulish laughing clown face, a great big, horrible grin. Look, I never thought I'd say it, but I think I agree with Fintan. I mean, aren't we here to talk about Zoe?

READING GROUP GUIDE

1. If you discovered you had a doppelgänger, what would you do? Would you experiment with switching lives for a bit?

2. How long do you wait before bringing a stranger or new friend into your home? Would you ever send an acquaintance to your home without you?

3. Despite his similar appearance, no one seems to really believe the narrator is Heydon. What makes people's personalities and characters so distinct from one another?

4. We get glimpses of Miranda's mothering style, including her statement to Heydon that he "didn't try hard enough" to bring a bird back to life. What do you make of this style?

5. Heydon begins to see magpies as omens and signs of something, even if they aren't. Have you ever felt that seemingly happenstance events were directed at you personally? How did you deal with the situation?

6. How does living in the shadow of their celebrity mother affect Heydon, Bobbie, and Reagan? Is there a pressure to live up to your parents, whatever their status?

7. Why does Lynch continue with the Pierce family? What makes him want to keep pretending to be Heydon and to figure out what happened to him?

8. If you were Lynch, how long would you have stayed with this family, if you began at all?

9. Why do you think Lynch makes the decisions he does at the end?

A CONVERSATION
WITH THE AUTHOR

What was your inspiration for this book?

Another writer told me that his partner, not knowing me at all, had "hate bought" my first novel because of my author photo. She assumed I was some rich kid who'd been handed everything and only realized I was from the working class when she started to read. That made me laugh and got me to thinking about the judgments we make based on appearances, etc., and where I could go with a character whose face allowed entrance into a different world.

It also fed into the thoughts I was having about grifters, who seem to be the most celebrated artists of our time. We see again and again how ineffective our police/state apparatus is in confronting people who are happy to lie, and I thought a con artist would be better equipped to go up against those people than a police officer. From there, of course, I looked to great con artist books, like *The Talented Mr. Ripley.* At the same time, I didn't want to portray another doomed, dark character, so I wanted him to have some basic goodness/ambivalence about money that marked him out from the bad guys as well as a sliver of hope for a more honest life going forward. I'd recently become a dad and wanted a route to making my writing less cynical.

Did you create Lynch's full backstory ahead of writing this book?

I know a lot more about Lynch's backstory than I can disclose and have some fun ideas about how to play that out in future books. With that said, I want to hew close to the great private eye novels of Chandler/Macdonald/Grafton, where much of the character's backstory is only hinted at by the way they react to real-time events, and we follow a case from the protagonist's entrance into it until the conclusion, often reading super closely for those stray lines that tell us more. Where natural opportunities arise to disclose backstory to the reader, I'll take them. But this is also a first-person narrator who's practiced in not giving anything away. One commitment I did make early on was that despite being a con artist, Lynch should never lie to the reader. He might be an unreliable guy, but he's not an unreliable narrator.

This book has a very complex plot. What was the process for writing it like?

In terms of the plot itself, I was really trying to emulate the feeling of being drawn into the rabbit hole of a conspiracy. I hope the stakes/desperation/characters involved act as metaphors for various plots at play around us. The process of writing the book was the same for me as ever—every day, I rewrite the work I did the day before and try to charge on into new stuff. That means the book gets reworked many times along the way, and then once finished, I'll do full redrafts of the entire thing. I like this process because it almost feels like I'm living in the world of the book, but it can mean that every single thing on every single page takes on heightened significance, leading to a knotty plot. It's something I'd like to become a little looser as the books go on.

What was the most difficult part of the story to write? The easiest?

The most difficult part was the big confrontation with Control in the penthouse he's staying in. I spent so long on (and in) that scene that sometimes, I still wake up thinking I need to get back to work on it! It's toward the middle of the book and required a lot of different things. First, Lynch pretending to be Heydon with someone who doesn't believe him, then dropping his cover, and, of course, introducing the conspiracy element into things. We also get the scariest "gang stalking" video in that scene as well as our first on-page murder!

The easiest parts to write were the back-and-forth dialogue scenes where characters are insulting/being insulted by Lynch. He's fairly unflappable by that stuff, and because he's been a con artist/ is practiced in watching people closely, he usually has easy access to the neuroses/pressure points of other characters. He's happy to look or sound stupid (or even like he's fumbling the case) as long as he learns something/pushes things forward. That recklessness was a lot of fun.

What do you want readers to take away from this book?

More than anything else, I hope readers enjoy the book as a thriller—or a twist on the private eye novel with a con artist taking on the role of detective. I hope they're interested in a flawed character firmly drawing a line in the sand between who he was and who he is and between himself and all the other crooks. I hope they're interested to see where he'll go next without all that baggage.

With that said, the title's no accident. I started/abandoned a lot of different books with a lot of different voices on the way to this one until it started to feel like an identity crisis. Lynch has changed identity so many times he can barely remember who he is, and I felt some sympathy. Ultimately, this was the most difficult book I've written but also the most rewarding because it finally brought me back to my own voice. Much as I might condemn Lynch's actions, I like that he always seems to be himself, even when he's pretending not to be. And I like that when asked for the secret, he says it's to just keep on going. I needed to hear that, so I'm sure that someone else will.

ABOUT THE AUTHOR

Photo © Jay Brooks

Joseph Knox was born and raised in and around Stoke and Manchester, where he worked in bars and book-shops before moving to London. His debut novel, *Sirens*, the first part of the Aidan Waits series, was a best-seller and has been translated into eighteen languages.

For more information on Joseph and his books, see his website at www.josephknox.co.uk.

TRUE CRIME STORY

Just remember: *Everything* you read is fiction.

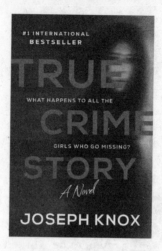

What happens to all the girls who go missing?

In 2011, Zoe Nolan walked out of her dormitory in Manchester and was never seen or heard from again. Her case went cold. Her story was sad, certainly, but hardly sensational, crime writer Joseph Knox thought. He wouldn't have given her any more thought were it not for his friend, Evelyn Mitchell. Another writer struggling to come up with a new idea, Evelyn was wondering just what happens to all the girls who go missing. What happens to the Zoe Nolans of the world?

Evelyn began investigating herself, interviewing Zoe's family and friends, and emailing Joseph with chapters of the book she was writing with her findings. Uneasy with the corkscrew twists and turns, Joseph Knox embedded himself in the case, ultimately discovering a truth more tragic and shocking than he could have possibly imagined…

"This is one of the most engaging cold-case novels I have read."
—*Literary Review* (UK)

For more Joseph Knox, visit:
sourcebooks.com